ADVANCE PRAISE

The Corset Maker is a tale of the twentieth century that celebrates human resilience. It is an enchanting, resonant novel inspired by the life of Dora Libeskind and seen through the eyes of Rifka. Berkovits weaves a story of a quintessential rebel in times of global crisis and war. Threads of Nazism, antisemitism, and sexism make for a compelling, fast-paced narrative that sees a young heroine navigate the world in search of her destiny.

—Daniel Libeskind, architect; Founder Studio Daniel Libeskind; Author of a dozen books including *Breaking Ground* and *Edge of Order*; Berlin and New York

Annette Libeskind Berkovits has made central moments of twentieth century history come alive. An Orthodox Jewish girl rebels against her family and becomes an entrepreneur only to face antisemitism. She travels to Palestine and Spain and France, each time to survive more violence. Love and violence are at the core of this extraordinary novel. Berkovits fills history with romance.

—John J. Clayton, award-winning author of literary fiction and short story collections. His stories have won prizes in *O. Henry Prize Stories*, *Best American Short Stories*, and the *Pushcart Prize anthology*. Clayton's novels include *Kuperman's Fire*, *What Are Friends For*, and *Mitzvah Man*; Leverett, MA

The Corset Maker begins in the fall of 1930. Nationalism is surfacing as Europe teeters. In Warsaw Poland 12-year-old Rifka Berg asks her beloved Ultra-Orthodox father why girls don't have bar mitzvas. His answer brings about an epiphany that changes the course of her life. Thus begins Rifka's life's journey: continents will be crossed, wars will be won, and others lost, there will be love and there will be unspeakable genocide. Even Rifka's name and identity must change for her to survive, but Rifka's search for the truth of experience, for the very meaning of life and her place in it will never wane.

Timely and more relevant to today than is comfortable. This is the journey of the hero in the truest sense of Joseph Campbell.

—Jim Cooper, advertising photographer and author, *Funeral in Montauk*; Mosfellsbær, Iceland

---

The Corset Maker is a compelling story of girlhood, war, survival – and against all odds, a story of finding out who you truly are. It is a beautifully written journey that weaves together the personal and the historical. I was gripped by this unique and courageous protagonist – and found myself alongside her throughout the book. It is without a doubt one of the most fascinating and meaningful books I have read.

—Rachel Arnow, visual and performance artist, author of *Kinder Kalender*, *All the World From A-Z*, and *The Wild West*; Berlin, Germany

With her eloquent and captivating writing Annette Berkovits transports one to the riveting saga of survival, resilience, and ingenuity of a young woman from Warsaw, Poland. Set mainly in the twists and turns of the first half of 20th-century Europe, *The Corset Maker* ignites the reader's imagination of history and brings to life the hard choices and challenges facing young people during that time. The story concludes with an unexpected ending in the last decade of the century. I simply could not put the book down.

—Zvi Jankelowitz, Director of Institutional Advancement, Yiddish Book Center; Massachusetts

This sweep of twentieth century European history seen through the eyes of a young Orthodox Jewish woman is a truly gripping read.

—Joanna Orwin, award-winning author with a strong focus on New Zealand and Maori history. Her latest novel is *Shifting Currents*, Christchurch, New Zealand

In *The Corset Maker*, Annette Libeskind Berkovits gives us a fascinating novel, spanning decades of the history of Europe – from Poland to Spain and France – and Palestine, where the future State of Israel is being born. Through a unique friendship between two women, the author explores profound themes such as feminism and pacifism, while placing those ideas against the stark reality of 20th-century history: the Civil War in Spain or the rise of fascism and antisemitism. The story, set against the ever-present historical and political backdrop, can be read on many levels: the reader is drawn into the rich, powerful, and thoughtful narrative.

—Philip Jolly, journalist; London, United Kingdom

A vivid narrative that poses an urgent and universal question: how to survive as a woman while balancing personal responsibility, solidarity, and pacifist ideals. Readers first meet *The Corset Maker* as she rebels against her Orthodox Jewish upbringing in inter-war Warsaw, striking out for independence with her friend to open a corsetiere's shop. The departure of her elder sister to join Jewish settlers in Palestine and the arrival of Nazism in Poland combine to send her on an odyssey through Israel and Europe during the cataclysms of the mid-20th century. As she encounters danger and suffering and the anguish of an impossible love she is plunged into political and personal conflict. She is constantly forced by circumstances to question and challenge her own deeply held principles, yet her resilience and commitment to the welfare of others continually shine through the darkest moments.

—Maybelle Wallis, MD, author *Heart of Cruelty*; Wexford, Ireland

---

What a life. What a story. What a journey to take the reader on. Page after page, a woman is revealed whom I wish I could have met in real life. She is an inspiration to every woman trying to find her very own path.

—Cilia Ebert, Head of Strategy and Planning, German Federal Ministry for Family, Youth, Women and Senior Citizens; Berlin, Germany

---

Rifka Berg, an intrepid, passionate woman, the protagonist of *The Corset Maker,* must reconcile her pacifism with the violence engulfing the world. To protect loved ones and emerge intact after WWII, she will have to rely on her wits and skill with a needle. Readers will be beguiled by her story.

—Sheila Grinell, author of *Appetite* and *The Contract*; Phoenix, Arizona

How does a woman live three different lives in four different countries without ever forgetting her roots? Discover how in this thrilling, action-packed, emotionally resonant novel, full of intense twists and turns.

The rise of antisemitism in Warsaw before WWII will propel Rifka to Paris, Palestine, Spain during the civil war and to the Argèles-sur-Mer concentration camp in southern France. Caught in the whirlwind of history Rifka will always act courageously, adhering to her convictions, and never denying her Jewishness. A truly exciting read taking place during a dramatic period of history that must not be forgotten.

—Jacques Cousin; Vence, France

In *The Corset Maker* readers meet compelling, realistic characters and follow a courageous protagonist as she matures in a world torn by violence.

—Jo Schaffel, author, *Somewhere Besides Denver*; Tillson, New York

THE CORSET MAKER

A NOVEL

ANNETTE LIBESKIND BERKOVITS

ISBN: 9789493231931 (ebook)

ISBN: 9789493231917 (paperback)

ISBN: 9789493231924 (hardcover)

Publisher: Amsterdam Publishers, The Netherlands

info@amsterdampublishers.com

Cover image designed by Daniel Libeskind, Founder Studio Libeskind

The Corset Maker is a work of fiction. While the historical context is as accurate as possible, all incidents and dialogue, and all characters with the exception of well-known historical figures, are products of the author's imagination. Any resemblance to actual persons, living or dead, events, or locales is entirely coincidental.

The Corset Maker is **Book 4 in the series New Jewish Fiction**

CONTENTS

For my and my brother's children
and our grandchildren
so they may appreciate and learn
about the world and times of
*the indomitable **Dora Blaustein Libeskind**,*
their grandmother and great grandmother

Thou shall not be a victim,
thou shall not be a perpetrator,
but, above all,
thou shalt not be a bystander.

—Professor Yehuda Bauer, Hebrew University

AUTHOR'S NOTE

The book in your hands is my first book of fiction. Before it, I have written three non-fiction books and one poetry book. How does a writer whose work to date had been primarily non-fiction delve into fiction?

The simplest answer is having a particular type of inspiration wherein the idea doesn't leave you. Rather it becomes insistent, knocking on your psyche, pressing you to commit it to paper. There is an adage that non-fiction writers are often accused of incorporating fiction into their narratives, and conversely, that novelists are bound to sprinkle their stories with true, lived experience. I will confess that the latter is quite true for this novel, *The Corset Maker*.

I had, for years, been fascinated by my mother Dora Blaustein Libeskind's remarkable history. She was so unlike my father who spoke of his own history volubly. I learned only a collection of tantalizing tidbits of my mother's story by repeatedly pleading with her for as much information as she was willing to divulge. I suspect my mother's reluctance to share with me the many dark moments of her past, shielded me from pain. She saw the loss of her own mother, four young sisters and countless aunts, uncles and cousins during the Holocaust, the loss of her Warsaw business, internment in a brutal Siberian gulag, privations of a refugee in the former Soviet Union and an unwelcome return to postwar communist Poland.

Dora passed away far too young, in 1980, so it was up to me to try to assemble and reassemble the puzzle of her experiences that took place long before I was born. Amazingly, I also managed to find a few precious scraps of her own writing, most of which she had purposely destroyed before her passing.

Assessing all I had, I surmised it was insufficient to responsibly weave into a memoir, so I took treasured bits and pieces as inspirational nuggets to write a novel whose protagonist is as smart, creative, intrepid, introspective, and brave as was my mother. In my heroine beats my mother Dora's heart. I have also incorporated fragments from my mother's stories about three of her closest friends who I fashioned into composite characters. Though my characters are fictional, the history of the period is entirely true and as accurate to world events as I could make them.

Most historical novels are based on famous real individuals. My novel is also based on a real flesh and blood woman. My mother was unknown, though I suspect that if WWII and its attendant tragedies had not intervened, she might have become a known author. As a teen, she won the top prize in a writing competition sponsored by Henryk Goldszmit who wrote under the penname Janusz Korczak. A renowned Polish Jewish pediatrician, author, and pedagogue in pre-WWII Warsaw, Korczak perished in Treblinka with the 200 Jewish orphans in his care. Though my mother may have remained anonymous, her only son, my brother, the architect Daniel Libeskind, certainly is not. I can easily discern the legacy of my mother's sensibility and ideas in his works.

Though it was my incomparable mother who inspired me to write this book, it would not have happened without the steadfast support of my family and writing colleagues. My husband David lent his sensitive ear and knowledge of history to provide astute reactions to countless drafts. He has the patience of a saint. I am most thankful for his generous heart and keen intelligence and feel lucky to have him in my life. My adult children, Jessica, and Jeremy were enthusiastic cheerleaders, each providing wise input and encouragement when my energies were flagging. Jessica has given keen attention to every aspect of the final draft, from continuity and organization to planning for publicity. She is a treasured and trusted deputy in my writing journey.

My sister-in-law, Nina, and my brother Daniel Libeskind have been more than family. They've been steadfast advocates and fans of my work. I am grateful that I can always count on them. Daniel took time from his projects around the world to design the dreamlike cover. His prodigious creativity is a never-ending source of wonder. I am more thankful to him than words can express.

My beta readers, friends I was fortunate to make in the International Massive Open Online Writing Course (MOOC) offered by the University of Iowa, gave unstinting commentary on select chapters. I am happy to have found such a supportive community of writers. Several advance manuscript readers have chosen to remain anonymous. They know I am thankful to each one of them for joining me on the publishing journey.

I want to express special thanks to my tireless agent Nancy Rosenfeld and to Liesbeth Heenk, Amsterdam Publishers, for seeing this novel as I saw it, a story worth a reader's time.

PROLOGUE

Simone

The noise of the demonstration disturbed Madame Bonheur's nap. She hadn't allowed herself to rest during the day until she approached eighty, an age she thought as undeserved and unwelcome as a curtain call after a failed performance. If her body had cooperated, she mightn't have adopted such a bourgeois habit at all. "I'll sleep when I am dead," was embroidered on one of the throw pillows scattered on the white leather sofas of her elegant Parisian apartment. A gift from someone long ago, a joke at first, that coarse American English, now defiantly displayed. She felt uncomfortable in homes furnished in ornate Louis XV furniture—all those silks, velvets and brocades, tassels, and ruffles, gilding and crystals. She did care about design and fabrics, always had, but favored them sleek and modern, white, and stark—a clean canvas—nothing to remind her of the past. Let the past lie buried. That should be another pillow.

Simone rose from the sofa where she'd allowed herself to fall asleep and stretched, rather easily, she thought, for such a fossil. As she sat still for a moment to gather herself, her gaze fell on the silver-framed photo standing on the mantel, the only object there aside from the candlesticks she used for Sabbath when the melancholy mood struck. The three faces in the black and white image stared back, unsmiling but huddled close, the brooding, jagged peak of Punta Alta at Serra de Pàndols behind them. She shook her head incredulously; it was hard to imagine she had been there. How long ago was it? A crinkled brow and quick subtraction, fifty-eight years! A lifetime. My God, in four years, it'd be a new millennium.

In her white marble kitchen, punctuated by gleaming stainless appliances, Simone put up a pot of tea and waited, thinking how quickly the years had snuck up on her. When she was younger, time dragged on but in more recent years, time seemed to vanish. Today, she was suddenly eighty on the outside, but very much forty on the inside. Steam rose from the teapot, momentarily bringing her back to a certain mountain ridge, a certain dusk, her ears pricked for the crackle of twigs: but nothing, just the distant roar of artillery. She shook herself and poured strong tea—always Black Leopard from Mariage Frères—the color of blood. She drank it down hot.

In her study with its silver linen walls, floor-to-ceiling overstuffed bookcases, white lacquer campaign desk and that outrageously pink upholstered desk chair Jean convinced her to get, she found the thick manila envelope easily, could have found it in the dark. Before she closed it, Simone walked into her bedroom, pulled out a black and white photo of Bronka's family tucked into the mirror frame above her dresser and stuck it into the envelope. She closed the envelope's string closure and cradling it, returned to the kitchen, then dumped it in the trash. She'd kept these secrets too long; time to put an end to them. They'd stay in her brain so long as her head still worked. No one else needed to know them. For a long moment, she stood in front of the cabinet that held the trash, then slammed its door hard.

Back in the living room, unsettled, she raised the Roman shade on the tall middle window. On the street below a mob of casseurs, young people in hoods and black face masks, hurled rocks, paint bombs, rotten fruit, fusillades at the bakery, the tailor's, the sweet little shoe store, the bank on the corner, the café closed up tight. *Merde!* Simone's muscles tightened; adrenaline sped up her heart. A wasted nap.

For at least a year, demonstrators of all stripes had been protesting. Police seemed to be spitting in the wind when it came to Islamic terrorists and every new incident fueled Islamophobia. The summer before, 1995, had been *scandaleux*, bloody. Attacks in July and August at the Saint-Michel train station, at Arc de Triomphe, and then into fall, at the Maison Blanche metro station. Eight dead, hundreds wounded, emergency vehicles, bomb squads, helicopters, police sirens, ambulances, terrified riders. Fear, then anger and police crackdowns in the bloody aftermath. This wasn't likely to end anytime soon, Simone thought then and still believed. Fanatics won't be satisfied till nothing is left but true adherents, and the Seine runs red.

Simone sighed, knowing that once she might have joined a counter-protest, taken up arms if necessary, but now she was tired. One can't change the world, only oneself. It had taken forever, but these days Simone no longer saw the world as black and white. Though now she could discern the grays, she'd die the stubborn mule, always preferring ideas delineated clearly.

Rattled, Simone pulled on her heeled boots—a Parisian woman, she never compromised on style. She put on a flared white cashmere coat with black trim at the lapels and cuffs. Quick check in the mirror above the foyer credenza to adjust the scarf. Out of sheer habit, she reached into the top drawer, tucked her diminutive Beretta into the purse, its heft her security. The black leather of the Hermès bag was worn near the corners, but she liked it. It reminded her of herself back then, a time when the burning desire to swallow the world was still bright.

As she descended in the tiny, mirrored elevator, Simone admonished herself: You never managed to stay away from political turmoil. Oh, to be young again!

On Boulevard Hausmann, a frigid blast of February wind. The protesters had moved on, toward Rue la Fayette, but a handful of rowdy young men had turned back from the demonstration and marched toward Hamdi's spice shop, kicking at frozen piles of snow near the curb.

Hamdi was an old man, stooped but always smiling, always letting her taste a fresh piece of halvah. She'd been a frequent customer back when she cooked, and the old man had always greeted her warmly, a sparkle in his deep-set charcoal eyes: "*Salam Alaikum*, Madame Bonheur."

Simone crossed the street.

The pack approached the store, shouting *sale porc!* and banging with a tire iron on the shop window, shattering it. Shards of glass sprayed over the sidewalk, some landing silently on the snow, almost beautiful. Hamdi ran out of the store. Face tense, hands shaking, he shouted in Arabic.

Simone didn't think; she just hollered for the leader to stop. *"Arrête ça tout de suite!"*

The tallest among them stepped forward. *"Va te faire foutre!* Fuck off!" he shouted, kicking at the glass.

Did he think his crassness would frighten her? Simone slid her hand into her bag, holding his gaze. Her fury in check, she said, "Shame on you. This man has not caused you any harm. That's the French flag in his window! Are you blind?"

The punk sneered, bent down to pick up a shard of glass.

From long practice, she pulled the Beretta from her purse smoothly and pointed it at his chest. "Get out of here now and don't dare come back!"

The leader glared and spat but stepped away. His friends, some guffawing, others mumbling curses and casting dirty looks, followed him slowly. The little fat one spat out, "Look at that old bitch!"

The Beretta in her hand rock-steady, her eyes hard as granite, she said, "You look at me if you dare, you little shit."

He saw she meant business and lost his nerve. The group left the block, turned the corner onto Rue Halevy.

Simone slipped the pistol back into her handbag.

Hamdi stood there silent, still shaking. Then found his voice: "Thank you, Madame, thank you. You've saved my life." He approached Simone and reached for her hand trying to kiss it.

Simone pulled her hand away, said, "Let's not be so dramatic, Monsieur Hamdi. They were stupid youths, not killers. Why don't you go inside and get a broom while I call the police to make a report? And put on a jacket, for God's sake. It's freezing."

Simone heard a loud noise from the direction the youths turned. Maybe another shattered window.

PART 1

POLAND

1 RIFKA, WARSAW, 1928

Twelve-year-old Rifka paced the bedroom pondering her father's morning blessing: *Blessed are you, Lord, our God, Ruler of the Universe, who has not made me a woman.* Why did Poppa rejoice not having been born a woman? It upset Rifka every time she heard it. Worse than upset, it made her plain crazy. She could not figure out why a man as intelligent as Poppa couldn't understand such prayer was hurtful to the women in his family and there were eight of them, including herself, Golda in Palestine, and Momma. Saul was the only boy in the family.

After dinner when Poppa seemed relaxed in his chair with a little glass of schnapps in his hand, Rifka addressed him. She admired his wisdom and wanted him to see her as someone worthy of engaging in a discussion. "Poppa, why are you thankful not to be a woman?"

Instead of taking her seriously he lifted his eyes toward Rifka and looked at her intently, as if he hadn't seen her for a long time. "My, my, you sure have grown since last year. If you were a boy, you'd be ready to study for your bar mitzvah."

The unexpected words hurt. "Why can't girls have a special ceremony to show they've matured?"

"But they do." Poppa smiled broadly. "They have a wedding. Soon you will be a bride."

Rifka felt so offended she stood silent momentarily, but not wanting Poppa to digress from her original question, she refrained from an outburst that sat devilishly at the tip of her tongue. "So about the blessing..." she said.

"Some questions shouldn't be asked," Poppa had said with an annoyed look, and he picked up his paper though Rifka was nowhere near finished.

"But Poppa..."

"You ask too many questions. Why don't you go help Momma?" With that Father disappeared in the pages of Today's News.

Rifka charged out of the room, her cheeks burning with resentment. Why was her father always involved in spirited discussions with his synagogue friends, but when it came to her it was as if she were nothing? Well... He didn't converse much with Momma either, except to say what he wanted for dinner.

In the bathroom, Rifka splashed cool water on her face, her outrage still red hot. Like a dispassionate critic, she stared at the mirror, something she did now and then to understand what men who ogled her on the street saw in her. She certainly didn't consider herself beautiful and was oblivious of the effect her appearance had on the opposite sex: teenage boys at the synagogue casting sidelong glances or their fathers' unchaste smiles. She did not appreciate the red glints or the stubbornness of her abundant chestnut curls, or the small beauty mark on the side of her upper lip. Her almond-shaped green eyes and olive skin stood out among the faces of her peers, and even among her fair complexioned sisters. At barely four- foot-eight, Rifka was short and felt her breasts were too large for her small boned, hourglass frame. She hoped that her full, heart-shaped lips compensated for this anatomical defect. By age twelve and a half, Momma had said, "It's time I make you a starter brassiere," confirming Rifka's self-assessment. But her looks were the least of her interests. She was more engrossed in thinking about her place in the world.

She had to do something to show her father how wrong he was to dismiss her that way.

By morning, Rifka had her solution. So, what if it was outrageous? He needed strong medicine to rouse him from his obtuseness.

When Poppa went out to visit his friend and her mother took the children to shoot the breeze with a neighbor, Rifka found his daily prayer book. She hesitated a moment, then picked up the siddur, stroked the embossed letters on the cover and kissed it. Wetness filled her eyes.

She found the page with the offensive blessing, and she stared at it. Tears ran down her cheeks. It blasphemed against half the humans on earth!

In a flash, she ripped out the page, slammed the book shut and replaced it on the little table. A ring at the front door interrupted her act of rebellion. Her heart beat faster.

Filled with apprehension she tiptoed toward the door and listened. After a moment Bronka's voice brought relief, "Come on, open up. I need to pee."

She let her friend in. "Quick! I am so happy it's you."

Bronka jumped up on one leg, then the other, and eyed Rifka. "What's the matter? You have a wild look in your eyes. What are you clutching in your hand?"

"I'll tell when you come out of the bathroom. Hurry!"

While she waited for Bronka, the enormity of her act begun to register. She'd desecrated the holy book. The crumpled page in her hand stung as if she'd grasped a scorpion. What to do with it?

Bronka appeared in the kitchen where Rifka stood in total consternation. "You have the look of a thief on your face," her friend said.

"I've done something terrible and very stupid. I'd not tell another soul in the world. You are the only person I can trust, but I'm not sure it's right to draw you into my crime."

"Crime? Don't be so melodramatic."

Rifka opened her palm and the crumpled page lay there accusingly. Bronka stepped closer, leaned over to look at the ball. "What is that? I see Hebrew letters on it."

"I tore a page from my father's Talmud."

Bronka inhaled loudly in shock. "Why on earth...?"

Rifka began to explain, but her friend said, "Let's cover your crime, fast, before anyone else shows up." She picked up a small bowl and matches from near the stove and threw the paper in.

"Wait! What are you doing?" Rifka screamed.

The lit match erupted into a mini bonfire as the two girls stood watching with a mixture of horror and guilt.

Rifka pleaded with Bronka. "I beg you, never tell anyone."

"Did you forget our loyalty pledge we swore in the first grade? It was forever and ever."

"Poppa will kill me if he discovers the page missing."

"Don't worry. I have a great idea," Bronka said, but Rifka stood looking dubious. "Let me run home quickly and bring my father's siddur."

"But... I can't... It wouldn't be right," Rifka said.

That prayer book was all Bronka had left of him.

"Just let me get going." Bronka ran out the door.

It didn't take more than twenty minutes and they replaced the desecrated book with a nearly identical copy.

"What would I ever do without you, Bronka? You are my savior."

"Never mind, you'd do the same for me."

Luckily, it turned out Poppa didn't notice the switch and continued to recite the blessing. Rifka concluded Poppa would never change. But what cheered her most was that Bronka would never change either. She could always count on her.

2 FANNY POZNER GYMNASIUM

Rifka's guts churned as she hurried to her classroom. It would be her first day in a new school, made possible only by grandmother Sarah's insistence Rifka get a real education.

Long streaks of light from the tall window at the end of the hallway shimmered on the polished wood floor. A hint of fresh floor wax tickled her nostrils. The hallway echoed with her footsteps. She pushed open the heavy door to Room 202 and froze on the threshold. Two dozen girls stared.

A skinny girl in a maroon and gold sweater called out, "Coming in at the last minute?"

The room tittered, burst into derisive commentary.

A chubby redhead pointed, had to shout, "Hey, newbie, free seat here."

Rifka rushed to the ink-stained desk, no matter, plopped into the seat.

"Just in time," the redhead whispered. "Mademoiselle would kill you!"

More tittering.

Rifka said, all eyes upon her, "I'd have gotten here on time if my little sisters were faster."

Several voices, same message, "Can't your nanny help them?"

Rifka took in the room, hoping to ignore them. Map of France on the wall. Tall windows in need of washing, a girl in Pola Negri bangs, Bata shoes on her seatmate. The girl in front of her, skinny fox face, oversized hair bow, deigned to turn, gave a long gaze that Rifka returned, nearly a standoff. Then in the voice of an empress, Fox Face said, "*She* is the nanny."

Rifka took a long breath. "Indeed," she said. She opened her notebook, that sweet smell of new paper, and wrote her name across the first page, a decorative loop on the "g" in Berg, her family name. Then the date: September 1, 1930.

The door flew open, and a stunning woman waltzed into the room, stack of books weightless under one arm. "*Bonjour Mesdemoiselles! Bonjour, bonjour!*" This was Mlle Janina—windblown hair, parted at the side Garbo-style, stylish skirt that flared past her hips to mid-calf, rich gray wool.

The girls responded in chorus, a couple in the front leaping to help with the books.

The teacher said, "Oh, wasn't summer beautiful?"

"New girl," a chubby student said, pointing to Rifka.

"I know, Rifka Berg. *Bienvenue!* Everyone, let us greet Rifka!"

A chorus of bonjours, then, belied by mocking faces.

"Ladies, ladies, I'm just off the train from Paris. I've postcards!" She rummaged in her Chanel purse. "I want to share!"

"Share your man-friend!" a cheeky girl called out.

Giggles filled the room.

Mlle Janina's cheeks pinkened. "That's a detention, dear Lena! Always your nose in my business! But we'll suspend punishment if you help me pass these cards around."

Lena leaped to help, and distributed the postcards of Paris.

The girls oohed and ahhed and passed the cards around.

Rifka studied the Eiffel Tower, then an ornate train station, the famous Arc de Triomphe, the Champs Élysées.

"I've been there," the chubby girl said. "By the way, I'm Pessy."

"Who hasn't?" Fox Face said.

Mlle Janina produced a folded newspaper from her magic bag, smoothed it with the edge of her hand, held it up, "*Le Figaro,*" she cried passionately. "I picked it up at Gare du Nord. Who wants to try translating the headlines? No, not everyone! Go ahead, Anita."

Anita wiggled her stocky body out of the seat, stood smugly by their teacher. She read, "Unrest in Berlin. Anti-Nazi protesters speak out against Horst Wessel."

"Now Chana."

And Chana rose and read haltingly, "French aviators complete first non-stop flight to New York."

"Now Evgeniya."

Evgeniya was the fox-faced girl! She read the French easily, a difficult headline, nothing Rifka could understand, then translated, "The League of Nations condemns the British for failure to protect Jewish settlers in Palestine."

Rifka let out a yowl, not meaning to.

The class went silent, turned to her.

"My sister," she said. "Golda. She's in Palestine!"

"*Bonté divine!*" said Mlle Janina crinkling her smooth brow. "Let's hope she can speak English and impress the British, or else shoot a gun."

And the girls laughed.

More headlines, a review of vocabulary, the class continuing.

But Rifka was somewhere else.

It was still early in the new school year. After classes, Rifka spotted Bronka crossing Marianska at the corner of Twarda and ran to catch up with her. "Hey, Bronka! Bronka!" she called at the top of her voice.

The two had been inseparable ever since first grade in the Polish public school, but when Rifka transferred to the private gymnasium she worried Bronka would find a new best friend.

Bronka didn't turn around. Rifka adjusted the heavy book bag on her shoulders and sprinted ahead to catch up. Out of breath, she caught up with Bronka and tapped her shoulder. "What? Not speaking to me because I changed schools?"

Bronka turned around abruptly. "Hi, Rifka. I didn't hear you."

Rifka was still peeved at Bronka's seeming indifference to their separation. "I screamed your name. Are you deaf?"

"I just finished reading the final installment of the serial in in the paper. Remember the one I'd been telling you about? My mind is still in the affair between Zina and Noah. I guess that's why I didn't hear you," Bronka said excitedly.

"Still reading that gar... I mean stuff?"

"Are you about to give me another lecture on my choice of reading material, Miss Pozner Genius?"

Rifka laughed. "No, nothing like that. I just couldn't wait to tell you about my new classes. You'd love them."

Bronka looped her arm through Rifka's, and the two walked over to sit on a nearby bench. "Tell me, tell me." Bronka's eyes all agog.

Rifka spoke of her classes, about Mlle Janina's *savoir-faire* and about how fat Mr. Gutkind spoke of things she'd never heard a teacher talk about before.

"Like what?" Bronka asked.

"Like, who are you?"

Bronka turned up her nose. "That sounds ridiculous. Doesn't everybody know?"

"Apparently not. If you ask yourself this question, a natural follow up is: Who do you want to be?"

Bronka's brow crinkled. "Hmm... I admit, *that* is not something I've ever thought about."

"Can you imagine such a thing: women thinking about who they are, and who they want to be?" Rifka imagined her own Momma's perplexed expression if anyone ever asked her such an absurd question.

Bronka sat shaking her head in disbelief. "I bet that is not something they'd be talking about in the Bais Yaakov religious school your father wanted you to attend, and certainly not in my school."

Rifka smiled. "I have my grandmother Sarah to thank for that. You know, she's a very different kind of woman, headstrong and self-sufficient."

"Just like you," Bronka said. "Well... till next time. It was great catching up." Bronka pulled up her slouching knee socks and stood up. "I have to run to take care of the twins."

Rifka remained on the bench regretting they couldn't chat longer. She sat watching until her friend disappeared from view. She'd missed her since she'd moved to the Pozner school. Bronka always managed to make her feel alive. The girls at the gymnasium were stuck up and so entitled. None of them understood the kind of humble lives she and Bronka led. None of them would ever be as close and trustworthy as Bronka.

Rifka didn't feel much like going home. All that hubbub, neighbors arguing, children running down the hallways, sliding on banisters, doors slamming and the ragman intoning his predictable mantra, rags, rags! School was Rifka's blessed refuge. The one negative: she and her best friend could not spend as much time together. Ever since first grade they had grown dependent on one another, like a married couple. Even when they bickered, it was out of complete faith their relationship was unbreakable. Now, between schoolwork and the household chores the two hardly saw one another. Rifka made herself get up and headed home.

As was her habit ever since Golda departed for Palestine after being recruited by the Zionist HeHalutz movement, Rifka rushed directly from school to the mailbox to check for correspondence from Palestine. She missed her sister terribly. Golda, five years her senior, had neither the time, nor the patience for her younger sister. Yet to Rifka, Golda had been the epitome of modernity. She looked toward the future and wasn't mired in tradition as many young women her age in their community. And she was so beautiful. Not that Rifka envied her looks, but just to watch her dress and apply makeup was like watching a goddess. With Hollywood beginning to make talkies, Rifka was sure Golda could have been a star there if she had gone to America instead.

Rifka fumbled in her pocket for the key and turned it in the rusting mailbox door. There was always a moment of hesitation. Would it be empty? The misaligned door didn't give easily.

This day she was in luck. Excitedly, she pulled the thin airmail envelope festooned with exotic stamps and opened it right there. Golda wrote occasionally, but not nearly enough. With Bronka in a different school and her oldest sister gone, Rifka felt lonely. The letters filled her with excitement, longing and fear for Golda's safety. It seemed rash and crazy to Rifka that her sister left home to settle somewhere in a mosquito-ridden swamp. Palestine was so remote, so desolate, so unfamiliar and dangerous, and yet her vain, stunning sister went to resettle it. It was another of life's mysteries.

Rifka stood in the underpass for a few moments reading the letter before taking it upstairs.

Dear Family,

I hope you are all well. This will be brief because we must finish building our shelters before the rains come, though then the mosquito swarms will grow larger. In the kibbutz we all work as one, we have become brothers and sisters, but the work is hard. My fingers are calloused. I don't have to tell you how I hate that! There has been an attack on our settlement from Arabs who don't want us here. Three young men have been killed. We buried them on a nearby hill. It was sad with no family present. Don't worry about me, I will be alright.

Sending my love to all of you, your Golda

Rifka admired her sister's guts, but the mention of the calloused hands made her smile. That was so unlike Golda, who was meticulous about the care of her beautiful body. Rifka couldn't imagine how Golda managed in the primitive conditions, but was sure of one thing, Momma would be very worried after reading the news.

Rifka stuffed the letter in her bag and ran upstairs.

———

The February snow muffled sounds on the streets. Nearly blinded by snow, Rifka stepped around mounds, avoiding getting snow into her worn shoes. She slipped on frozen slush right in front of the school.

A blast of warm air enveloped her in the lobby. It smelled of wet wool and smoke from the chimney. Hurried greetings. Laughter. Coughing. Rifka stamped her feet, peeled off her coat and scarf and threw them on a rack in the coatroom.

In the classroom, Mrs. Mayer, the history teacher, fiddled with her mittens. Bundled up in a thick sweater and scarf, she looked like she was about to leave. "You think I look strange with my mittens still on?" Mrs. Mayer noticed Evgenia's raised eyebrows. "I need time to warm up. Took me forever to get here; frozen tram lines."

Wanting to negate Evgenia's meanness, Rifka said, "We have so little heat at home, sometimes I keep my coat on."

But Fox Face couldn't resist. "Tile stove in your castle broken, princess?"

Rifka threw her a long disapproving look and wiggled into the seat, wishing Bronka was her seat mate.

The teacher rapped on the desk with her now bare knuckles. "Today we'll start on the history of Poland."

"Ooh, boring!" A stage whisper flew from Lena's mouth.

"I heard that, Lena. Do you think combat between handsome young soldiers is boring?"

"No, of course not," Lena sniggered.

"Well, then, I hope none of you are too squeamish."

Mrs. Mayer ignored the gagging sounds and anxious titters. She paced in front of the blackboard. "Believe it or not, the slaughter we'll talk about happened right here," she tapped the map with a pointer. "But when most of you were born around 1916, sovereign Poland didn't even exist!"

"What do you mean 'didn't exist'? How could a country not exist?" Rifka called out.

Mrs. Mayer explained the tumultuous period when Germany and the Soviets contested the Polish territory. "They were like two mad dogs tugging at a carcass," she said. "Can you picture that?"

Finally, the girls were mesmerized.

"If not for the Battle of Warsaw, Poland as you know it, wouldn't exist." The teacher paced the room, her rubber boots squeaking with each step. She regaled the girls with cunning plans to disrupt the enemy, counterattacks, skirmishes, and the sheer confusion of it all.

"But isn't it great we won?" Anita piped up.

"Well, you think about it. Fifteen thousand Russian and over 7,500 of our Polish soldiers lay dead at the end."

"My God, all that blood!" Mousy Mania looked as if she might burst into tears.

Gasps from all corners of the classroom.

"I guess those dead soldiers didn't care who won and who lost," Rifka blurted out. At first, her mind filled with thoughts of the lifeless bodies, the funerals, the sobbing widows. But soon her mind switched tracks. What might have been the reasons these soldiers willingly gave their lives? What had gone through their minds as they faced the enemy? Were they troubled they'd cause another human being to die?

"Wars involve a lot of senseless bloodshed. Your German teacher and I have agreed you'll be reading *All Quiet on the Western Front* by a

German author, Erich Maria Remarque. We shall discuss it in both classes."

"Ugh! Why do we want to read a book written by a German?" Anita's bulgy eyes narrowed in confusion.

"Because he fought in WWI when he was not much older than you and has something important to share."

"Does he want all of us to fight?"

"Not quite. Some of you may become pacifists after reading it."

The class ended.

Rifka sprinted down the stairs; she had to get to the library before it closed. Outside, a cold gust hit her neck. In haste, she'd forgotten her scarf. The heck with the cold. She couldn't wait to read that book.

Later that night she became so engrossed in the story of young German soldiers, keen to show their courage on the frontlines, she could not put the book down. She fell asleep just before sunup and finished the book the very next day after school. Never would she think of war the same way: it was an indiscriminate monster chewing up innocent lives. The reality of it wasn't anywhere as glamorous as Paul, the protagonist had expected.

3 POPPA

The sun already hung low, casting a diffuse light on the tenements, softening their rough appearance. Rifka rushed home to finish her homework, having done some shopping for Momma. In her haste she dropped the grocery bag and scooped it up quickly. Ascending the stairs in her building, she noticed a white trail of flour leaking from the split bag. She balanced it carefully so as not to spill more.

"I'm home," she announced at the door. She could tell from the whirr of the sewing machine, Momma was still finishing her piecework orders—brassieres and corsets—in the back of the apartment.

"Come into the parlor, daughter dear," Father called out.

Why so formal? Poppa never spoke like this.

"Coming," she replied, hung up her jacket, carried the grocery bag to the kitchen, and walked slowly down the narrow hallway toward the parlor.

Poppa sat stiffly in his armchair under the window. Across from him, a gangly young man in a black gabardine coat—elongated face accentuated by long ear locks, eyes downcast—sat at the very edge of the settee. Rifka had overheard the word *shidduch* the other evening when her parents whispered to one another. She never imagined they were talking about an arranged marriage *for her*.

"Say hello to Moshe," Father said, pointing at her skirt. "Tsk, tsk, not lady-like."

Rifka glanced down and brushed off the flour streak. *"A gutn uvnt,"* she greeted the man.

Poppa looked at his watch. "It is almost evening. Where have you been? I was expecting you home sooner. Moshe and I will have to hurry to the synagogue soon for the evening prayers."

"Momma sent me to the grocery," Rifka said, stepping deeper into the parlor.

Moshe's gaze brushed by her nominally and Rifka noticed his watery blue eyes. He mumbled something inaudible and sat cracking his knuckles.

On the low table, two teacups and a silver tea pot sat unused.

"Poppa, would you like me to pour the tea?" Rifka asked.

"Yes, show Moshe what a good *balabusta* you are," Father smiled, a strained smile.

Rifka lifted the glass teacups by their silver handles and poured the tea gracefully, handing the cups to the men.

"See, Moshe, my Rifka, she's a jewel of a girl."

Rifka threw Poppa an exasperated look.

To her surprise Moshe spoke up, but so quietly she could barely hear him. "Do you go the Bais Yaakov school?"

Before she had a chance to reply, Father jumped in with a dismissive wave of his hand. "Ach... school. Girls don't need it! What use is a head full of nonsense when you have to care for babies?"

Moshe blushed.

"Poppa!" Rifka exclaimed, but father's tight-lipped expression signaled disapproval.

This wet noodle a prospect for her husband? Not if she could help it. "Look, it is really dark now," Rifka pointed at the window. "You'll be late."

"Alright, maybe you and Moshe will have more time to get acquainted next Sunday." Father took on a conciliatory tone.

Luckily, a piercing cry came from the bedroom.

"Sorry, I have to take care of Chana," Rifka rushed out in a fury. She found her mother in the bedroom pacing the floor, cradling baby Chana who already quieted and sucked her thumb with gusto.

"How could you, Momma?" Rifka sputtered.

"Calm down. Calm down. If he isn't right, there'll be others." Momma reached out to stroke Rifka's hair with her free arm.

Rifka jumped back. "Poppa wants me to wash this idiot's smelly socks. And you too?"

"But he's a Torah scholar," Momma said, her voice rising an octave. "The rabbi's favorite student."

Rifka stormed out of the room and having nowhere to cool off, ran straight up to the roof. She looked at the rooftops across the street, bathed in moonlight. The quiet and the gentle eastern breeze off the Vistula calmed her. Since she'd begun at the Pozner school, she felt as if someone had opened a lid on her skull and poured in new ideas with a bucket. Now Poppa wanted to shut the lid with a husband. Maybe Golda had the right idea to run away as far as possible.

Bronka already sat on the bench, nibbling on a sandwich when Rifka arrived at their usual meeting spot near the Marble Sundial. "Sorry to be late but... Momma's chores," Rifka waved her hand. "You know all about chores."

"Never mind. Sit and eat." Bronka handed Rifka half a cheese sandwich.

For a while they chomped, and people watched in companionable silence until Bronka whispered, "Rifka, look to the right, but don't stare." She pointed surreptitiously at a young couple necking against a huge oak whose branches formed a leafy canopy above the oblivious pair. Pressed against the trunk, the young woman's thin body appeared flattened by a blond man whose head was buried in her neck. When he came up for a breath, he put his mouth on hers, a long thirsty kiss.

"The Catholics don't have the *shomer negiah* rule (prohibition on touching)," Rifka muttered softly, though the amorous couple was too far to hear. She pulled the gauzy fabric of her blouse away from her chest to conceal her hardened nipples.

Bronka couldn't take her eyes off the couple. "It's not as if we don't have feelings like them," she said.

"We have to keep it all bottled up and saved for some bumbling idiot," Rifka said.

Bronka's eyes grew larger. "A *shidduch*! I knew it, your father is going to make you do it! Am I right?"

Rifka told her all about the encounter with Moshe.

25

Bronka put her arms on Rifka's shoulders. "I feel for you. Your father won't let you marry for love."

"Maybe you should count your blessings you don't have a father," Rifka blurted out.

Immediately, she regretted her comment, but Bronka ignored it. "I will marry for love, I tell you. You can count on it," she said defiantly.

Shortly, a group of young men in their Sunday best passed by their bench. The girls pretended to be engrossed in conversation, but they eyed the men: one, tall in a fedora—a Hollywood detective type—the other, a chubby friend with an incipient mustache. The chubby guy winked.

Bronka's cheeks turned red.

Rifka averted her eyes, then immediately picked up the lunch bag and pushed the discarded napkins into it. "Let's go find a trash can," she said and both girls stood up.

They walked over to another bench, deeper in the park. "Do you know what I learned in my science class, Bronka?"

Bronka looked bored. "I skipped science so I could take home economics," she said.

"I'll tell you anyway. It's something crazy about oak trees. Do you realize that they have both male and female flowers and can self-pollinate?"

"Ha?" Bronka looked at Rifka not comprehending. "So...?"

"Don't you get it? If humans were like oaks, women wouldn't need men to have children!"

"Well, it's a damn good thing we aren't trees." Bronka burst out laughing.

Rifka felt her friend missed her point completely, so she switched the subject and confided how she snuck books forbidden in her home, poetry, philosophy, world history, and then read them on her roof. "You must read *Insatiability* by Witkiewicz. You must!" she said. "It foretells what will happen in the year 2000."

"I see you'll never stop trying to improve me." Bronka curled her lip in annoyance. "The Pozner school is sure changing you. You want to swallow all that was ever written, Rifka. It's impossible. Some of that stuff will pollute your mind."

"I am not trying to improve you at all. You are great just the way you are. I am just suggesting you might like something other than your tabloid romances."

Bronka shrugged her shoulders. "Why don't we go home before we get into a fight. I hate fighting with you. Anyway, I'm sure we are both needed at home. Neither of our mothers can deal with all the little ones too long by themselves."

After they parted Rifka couldn't stop thinking about the oak trees. As far as she was concerned, men were good only at two things: making babies and reciting the Torah.

Walking home, she passed Goscinny Dwor, a market behind the Iron Gate. On a whim, she ambled past dozens of food stalls, mesmerized by the variety, foods she never saw at home: rabbits, pig hooves and heads, shellfish, and sausages of every kind. The smells made her woozy. Suddenly, she dug a few coins out of her pocket and handed them to the vendor who eyed her suspiciously. "I'll have one of those," she said.

And he handed her a kabanos, a thin dry pork sausage with a wry smirk.

She bit into it with gusto. So, what if it's *treyf*. The garlicky taste exploded in her mouth. Heaven!

The first thing Rifka did when she returned home was to sneak into the bathroom—thank goodness it was unoccupied—and brushed her teeth, looking in the mirror. Her face looked oddly greenish, and her stomach lurched. What was happening? A moment later, she threw up violently. *Treyf* guilt.

"Who brushes their teeth before dinner?" Momma never missed anything going on in the home. "Are you alright?" she called.

"I'm fine, really," Rifka replied weakly as another wave of nausea threatened. She doubted she'd eat non-kosher food ever again.

She slipped one of the forbidden books out from its hiding place under her bed and ran up to roof to read and think.

In no time it was dusk. She looked up at the first few stars, realizing she'd missed dinner. No matter, Saul would be happy for the extra helping. She wasn't hungry anyway. Her stomach wasn't her focus, it was something else.

The velvety sky evoked in her such a deep longing. The kissing couple in the park floated before her mind's eye. Her body yearned for touch. She'd never forget how tenderly the young man embraced the girl, how they pressed their lips to one another. Why did Jewish orthodoxy strictly forbid this? Did God really mean to punish her people, forcing them to wither, untouched and unkissed? Maybe even unloved? Her parents... They must have done it. She'd never say the word. How else to account for so many babies? There was never any manifestation of love. None that she could see.

Soon after her sixteenth birthday, the coming summer loomed in Rifka's mind as a huge question mark. What shape would her life take after graduation from the gymnasium? Because she'd successfully navigated around Poppa's efforts at betrothal, now she was at a loss, had no roadmap for life after school. Yet something exciting, daring even—she barely admitted it to herself—had been germinating in her mind for a long time.

Rifka chose the first Sunday after Passover 1932 to take the first step toward her dream. Bronka had an important role in it. She'd agreed to meet Rifka in Łaźienki Park, though she knew nothing of the meeting's purpose.

It was a beautiful April day. The sky hadn't been that shade of blue in ages. Rifka sat waiting for her friend, trying to anticipate her reaction to the proposal. She leaned back and closed her eyes for a moment. Hypnotized by the fragrance of the nearby lilac bush, she inhaled greedily, trying to prepare herself. Today she'd would finally let the radical idea out of her mouth.

Bronka waved from a distance. When she came closer, breathing heavily, she said, "You could have picked Saxon Garden. It's closer." She wilted onto the bench, her plump body settling in for some rest.

"Today we need privacy," Rifka said.

"Why so secretive?"

"What I have to say is for your ears only." Rifka's tone was serious, but her legs swung, kicking up the gravel on the path. Her mind churned, getting ready to spit it out.

After all the weeks of agonizing on how to best approach Bronka,

Rifka blurted out with no prelude, "Are you as unhappy living at home as I am?"

"What? What do you mean?" Bronka's voice rose, alarmed.

"I have a solution. Independence," Rifka said slowly with an enigmatic expression, emphasizing each syllable. "We've got to leave home," she said emphatically, as if it were an edict, or maybe because she didn't want to change her mind. The words hung in the air for a moment, making Rifka both excited and nervous.

Bronka sat up straight and faced Rifka. Her brown eyes nearly crossed, she said, "Are you are crazy? No one does that!"

"Well, then, someone should," Rifka said, and a strange calm came over her.

"But how would we live? We have no money, no apartment, no profession."

Rifka expected this reaction. She could plainly see that Bronka's head was exploding with questions. "We will have to work," Rifka pronounced, running her hand through her tight auburn curls.

"Wait a minute... Why me?" Bronka's eyes crossed fully now.

"You and I, we make a great team, always have."

"What...?"

"Look, let's be brave, Bronka. We both know how to sew. Our mothers have taught us since we were five. It's a valuable skill, not one everyone has. We can open a shop. There aren't any brassiere and corset shops in our neighborhood. Haven't you seen women with their breasts hanging to their knees and bulges on their waists? They need us. We can make money, be independent."

Bronka looked too shocked to laugh. She twirled her braid not knowing what to say. *"Bist meshuge,"* she spat out after a long pause.

This time Rifka wouldn't let Bronka off the hook; the idea was just too good to let it slip away. And she needed Bronka as a partner. Bronka was the most trustworthy person she knew. She was bubbly and much more at ease dealing with people—she'd be great with the customers—and she was a hard worker too. And what's more, she was as trapped in her baby-factory home as was Rifka. Rifka held her breath and waited for Bronka's reaction.

"I... really don't know what to say," was all Bronka could muster.

It was hard for Rifka to tell if her friend was simply astonished by the audacity of the proposal or offended.

"Really, it'll be exciting," Rifka said.

"I better go home now. Mother needs me," Bronka said. She stood, shook her head. "You really are made of a different cloth, Rifka. Where do you come up with such insane ideas?" Still shaking her head, Bronka rolled her eyes one last time and walked away.

"Fine, sleep on it," Rifka called after her, but Bronka disappeared behind a row of trees.

4 A BOND OF FRIENDSHIP

Bronka stood at the sink scrubbing a burnt pot, turning Rifka's proposal over in her mind. When she was done, she dried it with a soggy dishtowel and looked at her chapped hands. Rifka is right; I am the maid here.

She picked up the mop and swabbed the floor perfunctorily then sat down with the *Hayntike Nayes* paper, turning the pages quickly to get straight to her serial romance.

Not five minutes had passed when Hinda, her mother, came into the kitchen, tracking footprints all over the wet floor. "Get your head out of the paper, Bronka!"

"But Momma, I just washed the kitchen floor. I'm waiting for it to dry."

"You never lack for excuses. *Rabeynu shel oylom,* God in heaven, one should have stones, not children." Hinda picked up a basket of laundry from the high kitchen stool and gave Bronka a disgusted look.

"Give me a few minutes, Momma, I'll fold the laundry."

"Well, that's better. I can't be the only one who does everything around this house." Hinda shuffled out of the room.

Bronka set the paper aside. She hated to pause in the middle of a juicy romance. Placing the folded laundry in the basket, Bronka sat to do her homework. She spread her books on the kitchen table, sharpened a pencil, and opened her notebook to do the long columns of sums, but she couldn't concentrate.

Rifka's idea had opened a chasm in her brain that she'd need to jump over. She thought about how different the two of them were and yet, in some undefinable ways, quite alike. Bronka's head was in the here and now. The only thing she liked to project into the future was marriage. In the romances she read, girls married for love, refused to get stuck with some *nebbish*—a matchmaker's foundling, a teenage yeshiva *bocher* so timid at introduction he looked as if he'd faint. And if not him, then a fat widower with a barrel belly and lascivious lips.

These days, Rifka seemed to have forgotten how to have fun. Always so serious with her head in only one of two places: a book, or the clouds. Always thinking up new schemes to gain independence. The one she revealed last Sunday was a shocker. She wanted to flee her home as badly as prisoners in chains wanted to escape the Pawiak prison.

It had never occurred to Bronka to contemplate such a radical move, though she craved to be free of her mother's perennial complaints and the hubbub of their small apartment. Presented with what could be the opportunity of a lifetime, Bronka took time to assess the pros and cons. For one, the most important pro was that she cared deeply for Rifka, looked up to her even, though Rifka was a bit younger.

Bronka's head spun to their early years in grade school. She thought of how they spent time together every day after classes, how they borrowed garments from each other's puny wardrobe, how they invented new hairdos, and how they'd scouted out best spots to collect chestnuts in the fall and made them into necklaces. Their own mothers treated them as if they were sisters. In fact, Rifka has said more than once she felt closer to Bronka than to her own sisters.

A memory floated into Bronka's head. It was something incredible Rifka had done for her. And it wasn't just the deed, it was that Rifka never mentioned it. That was the goodness of it! Irena, a classmate, caught up with Bronka one day as they walked to school. "I probably shouldn't be telling you this," she'd said conspiratorially. "I've heard that Rifka doesn't want you to know about it."

Bronka's ears had pricked up. She and Rifka had no secrets. It was unimaginable she'd kept something from her. Irena's eyes glistened as if she'd bust if she couldn't share it.

As reluctant as Bronka was to listen to rumors, she'd said, "Go ahead, tell me."

"It happened last year, before she transferred to that fancy private gymnasium." Irena began dramatically. "For some reason, you hadn't shown up for a math test and Rifka took your seat. If you recall, her seat was right next to the window, but she took your seat because she didn't want to be distracted by street sounds." Irena paused theatrically, "I'm sure you know why it was a mistake for her to sit at your desk."

"Why?" Bronka remembered being completely stumped.

"Well, just think about your handiwork," Irena had said with glee.

Handiwork? It was then that it began to make sense. At the time, Bronka had been in thrall of Reuven Berenbaum, and she'd carved a large heart with his initials on her desktop. Having been alarmed by the teacher's raised eyebrows—maybe she'd heard her bobby pin scratching—Bronka never managed to add her own initials above the arrow piercing the heart. She felt embarrassed to be reminded of it and had no idea it had been the subject of her classmates' rumor mill.

"What of it?" Bronka snapped at Irena. "What does it have to do with Rifka?"

"Can't you guess who got caught with it? It was Rifka! She must have been trying to cover it with her elbows, because Mr. Duda thought she was hiding a crib sheet. He'd asked, 'What are you hiding?' and she'd said, 'I studied hard, I don't need to cheat.'"

Bronka was mortified. She could feel Rifka's panic. Mr. Duda, a priest, was known as the toughest disciplinarian in school and he was a friend of the school principal. Some upperclassmen swore he had certain students expelled on a whim.

Irena then said, "You should have seen how he shamed her. He said something like, 'You are not only a mathematician, you are an artist,' and the whole class laughed. Then he asked her, 'Aren't those your initials I see? Who is the lucky recipient of your affection?'"

Oh, my God, it had never occurred to Bronka that Reuven and Rifka had the same exact initials.

"And then what happened?" Bronka was horrified Rifka would bear the brunt of her foolhardy obsession with Reuven and that she'd be punished for defacing school property in her stead.

"There must have been no good response Rifka could invent," Irena recounted breathlessly, "So she stammered, 'I am sorry. I don't know

33

what possessed me.'" After a dramatic pause, Irena added, "I swear, everyone could see she was about to burst out crying."

Bronka blanched. Rifka had taken the blame on herself rather than implicate her friend. "So, what happened then?" she asked, unsure she wanted to hear the end of this tragic case of mistaken identity.

"For starters, Mr. Duda got furious with her. As far as he was concerned, she'd sinned. He sent her to the principal's office. Some girls say she'd paid cash restitution and had to kneel on dry beans in the empty classroom for a half hour. When I asked her about it, she warned me not to tell you, but so much time has passed, I thought you'd want to know. Now that she's in another school she won't have a chance to sit at your desk," Irena tittered.

There was no question. Rifka was not only a true friend and a noble soul, she was the most honorable person Bronka knew. She'd be as great a business partner as she was a friend.

It's true that Rifka might be aloof and impudent at times, even bossy, but Bronka felt she could always learn something from Rifka, some mind-boggling discovery about the world beyond. The girl had more intellectual curiosity than anyone. Bronka didn't like to think of herself as a follower, but deep down inside, she knew she could never come up with anything as gutsy as Rifka's latest idea.

Were there any cons to Rifka's proposal? Sure. Bronka almost laughed out loud. Neither of them had any money, or any idea how to run a business.

Four days had passed since Bronka had met Rifka at the park. Since Monday she'd been taking a different route home from school each day to avoid running into Rifka. She still had no definite answer. Sure, she'd like to get away from the endless chores at home. Sure, she was sick and tired of the way she had to do everything, while Mendl didn't. "Your brother is older; soon he will be the man of the house," Momma repeated every time Bronka suggested Mendl share some of the housework. To be able to earn her own money and to show Momma how she, Bronka, could help support the family, that was as exciting and as unlikely as her brother picking up a mop.

Rifka did mention she had some plan to get start-up money, though she'd not say how, kept it a secret, like so many others in that vault-like brain of hers. There was so much to consider in starting a business, not the least of which was the fact that young Jewish girls just didn't do it. Come to think of it, neither did young Polish girls. Striking out on their own before catching a husband? Ridiculous.

Bronka was tempted, but she felt that going into business—business! —with Rifka would be the same as the two of them holding hands and jumping off the Holy Cross bridge into Vistula's icy waters. Still, the idea was like an animal scratching to get out of a trap; it gnawed at her brain. What if...? What if...? To be honest, it excited her.

Bronka looked around the kitchen. There was one more chore, always one more chore, before she could finally read the latest story installment in the paper. She opened the cupboard and rummaged for flour, yeast, sugar, salt and oil, ingredients to make the challah dough. Then she opened the ice box to look for eggs. There weren't any. She walked down the hallway to borrow an egg from a neighbor.

Bronka climbed six flights of stairs. She pushed the heavy metal door open and stepped out onto the roof of Rifka's building. After a moment she caught her breath, then meandered around and between laundry lines, ducking wet long-Johns and sheets, past a rusting drainpipe and around a wooden water tower, almost tripping on some crates. Rifka waited for her in the corner, behind the chimney—her parlor as she called it.

"There you are!" Bronka called out.

"Shh... Let's try to be quiet and businesslike," Rifka said, a finger across her lips.

Bronka pulled over a crate and sat opposite Rifka, whose throne was an upside-down bucket.

"So, are you here to say yes?" Rifka asked.

Bronka was about to respond but stopped when a woman with a basket of laundry passed them. She eyed her friend. The way Rifka fidgeted with her curls made her look uncharacteristically anxious.

"I have a plan," Rifka spoke up after checking the woman had moved to the far end of the roof. "Remember that tiny store on Marshalkowska Street?" she asked.

Bronka bit her lip. "No."

"I showed it to you once when we walked by it."

An image of the bustling main street with fancy buildings, alluring store displays, and sophisticated shoppers came into Bronka's mind.

"Are you nuts, Rifka? That street is for. For. I don't know. Not for people like us."

"What do you mean 'like us'?"

"I mean Jewish and poor."

"Don't ever let me hear you say it. Not everyone is destined to be poor."

Bronka shrugged her shoulders.

Another woman clambered up to the roof with her wash basket and set it down right near them. They stopped speaking for a while, waiting for her to be done. Bronka inhaled the warm air smelling of tar and looked at the wash being hung. So many diapers! So many babies, just like her home.

The woman picked up her basket and looked at the girls. "Don't you two have anything better to do than sit here and shoot the breeze? Go help your mother!"

With that, she left.

Rifka resumed, "Well, that storefront has been shuttered for a couple of years. I bet the landlord hasn't made a penny on it. Maybe he can offer us reduced rent for a while?"

"And what about a sewing machine, and fabrics and eyelets and ribbing and laces for corsets?"

"You worry too much, Bronka. I can borrow the first machine from my aunt. I don't know if you remember my father's sister, the one who lives just off Dluga Street. Her sewing machine days are over since her arthritis got so bad. She had mentioned once that I could have it. And we can buy a second machine once the money starts rolling in. Supplies? We will buy some as soon as we get our first customer."

Bronka did not allow herself to show excessive interest. "But we will need some money for rent, at the very least," she said after a long pause. She couldn't contribute anything else, so she pointed out problems, but her heart beat faster, and her guts churned.

"I promise, I'll think of something," Rifka said.

Bronka could see how her friend's eyes glistened. Who was she to stand in the way of such a grand dream? Maybe Rifka's dream could become hers too? But she was still torn. It wouldn't have surprised Bronka if Rifka tried to borrow seed money from her rich grandmother. But why would a woman of means entrust money to a girl who had no resources and no experience? Bronka was sure her own grandmother would never do such a thing, even if she had money.

The sky turned charcoal gray, and wind began whipping across the roof, making the linens on the lines flap furiously. A few fat raindrops fell; it was time to go.

Rifka stood up and said, "Just one more thing..." Then she stopped.

"What? What are you not telling me?"

"It's nothing, never mind." Rifka picked up her stack of books.

Bronka thought of all the new friends Rifka had made at the Pozner gymnasium, some girl named Pessy who was so rich she'd visited Paris. Or that sharp-tongued Evgeniya.

"So, you think I'm scared? You don't want to put any doubts in my mind." Bronka was surprised at her own assertiveness.

"Well... I could have asked any of my other friends, or even my sister, but I chose you, didn't I?"

Bronka knew instinctively not to argue, certainly not now. She stood, stretched, back sore from sitting so long, didn't say a word.

"So, are you in? I'm not waiting any longer." Rifka's voice rose. She turned away, headed toward the stairs, past women running up to rescue their linens from the rain.

Bronka supposed her answer was yes. She stayed behind, helping the women grab the linens off the lines.

5 GRANDMOTHER SARAH

The grandfather clock chimed; it was already three o'clock. They'd be eating dinner soon, as they did every Sabbath. Still no Grandmother Sarah. But just as if she'd conjured her from the air, Rifka heard a knock at the door, and Sarah entered, calling, "*A gute Shabbos kinderlach!*"

Rifka's heart leaped. Today was the day! She wouldn't miss the chance. Rifka ran to the entry hall, took Grandmother's coat, hung it up and ushered her to the living room.

Poppa set aside his schnapps glass and greeted his mother. "A *gleyzele schnapps?*" He offered her some cherry liquor.

She gratefully accepted, smiling. "Just what the doctor ordered."

"Rifka, please serve your grandmother," Poppa said.

Rifka reached way back into the china closet, looking for a crystal glass that wasn't chipped. She filled it and handed it to Grandmother, saying, "I'm glad you came."

"I do have to look in on my son, every now and then, and the grandchildren, too, before they are all grown." Grandmother threw a wink toward Rifka.

Soon they sat to dinner. Poppa said blessings over the wine and bread and distributed challah to everyone. Momma served the cholent and a fruit compote made of apples that were about to go bad. After dinner, Momma served tea and poppy seed cake. Grandmother made small talk with Rifka's parents and then on to the traditional grandchildren's line-up at which Grandmother distributed plenty of candy. Rifka knew the time had come for her to act.

Grandmother looked out the window. "I see the first stars are out. I can head home now. My coachman must be waiting."

Her parents' expressions made it crystal clear to Rifka what they were thinking. You can't pick and choose which religious rules to observe. That's exactly what Rifka admired about Grandmother; she made her own rules.

Rifka ran to the coat rack in the hall and brought Grandmother's black wool coat with gray karakul trim to the living room. Despite her age, the woman knew how to dress. "Let me help you with it," she said. Grandmother slipped her thin arms into the sleeves.

"Well, I will be going now. A *gute woch*." Sarah wished the family a good week.

Rifka took Grandmother's hand and helped her down the three flights of stairs. Grandmother tottered on every step.

The waiting coachman would get impatient if Rifka dawdled. It was time to make the leap. She stopped at the last landing and blurted out, "Grandmother, I have a business proposition."

Grandmother stopped too, her eyes like two large coat buttons. "Business?"

"I will be very direct. I'd like to open a brassiere and corset shop. I have learned how to make undergarments from Momma for years. I know I can succeed, but I need start-up money for the first month's rent."

Grandmother listened to Rifka's proposal without interrupting and a smile began to form on her upturned thin lips. "Go on, go on, child," she encouraged.

"In no time, I'll be able to help Poppa with extra income," Rifka said breathlessly.

Grandmother took Rifka's hand, held it for a moment before speaking. Rifka's pulse quickened; she held her breath.

"Dear Rifka. I'm old. And your idea pleases me."

There was a sparkle in Grandmother's eyes Rifka had never seen before and the muscles of her wrinkled face looked relaxed.

She continued, "I've been worrying. And you've rested my heart. I won't be around much longer to help your father with money, so maybe if I help you, then you will be able to do it."

Though she'd never done it before, Rifka hugged her, right there on the landing. She could feel her bony frame though her coat. Frail like a bird, she thought, but strong like iron. Grandmother returned the hug, another first!

"I will pay you back every groschen," Rifka said, tears threatening to roll down her cheeks. She hugged tighter, found her composure. No one had ever seen her cry, and no one would now.

"My goodness, my carriage has been waiting. I have to go now," Grandmother pulled away, unused to such an excess of emotion.

"Dear girl, no need to pay me back. But wait a minute!" Grandmother exclaimed suddenly, so unusual for her to raise her voice. She rummaged in her large purse and pulled out a checkbook. Rifka was stunned. Grandmother leaned precariously on the banister and scribbled.

"Here is 5,000 zlotys. It should cover rent for the first few months in a decent small storefront. After that you are on your own."

Rifka gasped. "Grandmother! I... don't know what to say. I know I'll be doing something unconventional, but..."

"Never mind conventions, I wish you luck, child. We women have been doormats long enough."

Grandmother hurried toward the exit gate and waved at the carriage driver. Rifka followed her, too stupefied to speak. The coachman pulled closer and stepped down from his seat. He helped the old woman up the step while Rifka waited. Settled in the carriage, Grandmother addressed her. "You are brave and a bit like me, but I know your parents will be aghast. Never, never be discouraged, the world has a lot to offer those willing to climb over mountains."

The driver pulled on the reins and the carriage rolled away, leaving behind the hollow sound of hooves clip-clopping on cobblestones.

6 MARSHALKOWSKA STREET

It took almost a year of planning, scheming, and cajoling. Rifka and Bronka opened their shop in the spring, just after Passover of 1933. Now that the gray masses of snow on the sidewalks had melted completely, the blue skies and tender green tree buds filled Rifka with hope for their new venture.

Rifka couldn't have spotted a better location. The shop, in the heart of the Polish commercial area, was sure to attract a more affluent clientele. The Jews who frequented the businesses here were assimilated; they were avid users of the nearby Yiddish cinema and the bookstores along Swiętokrzyska—Holy Cross—Street. The proximity of the movie theater, and especially the bookstores, was the icing on the cake for Rifka. In fact, she'd noticed the vacant storefront when she scoured the bookshops for French-Polish dictionaries while still in the Pozner gymnasium.

She'd never forget the day she mustered the courage to knock on the door of the real estate office whose address stood on a "For Rent" card in the dusty display window of the shuttered store. "Excellent location. Only one thousand zlotys a month, electric included" it had advertised. She whistled. Such a sum! She'd done a quick calculation and concluded she'd be able to afford the rent for several months and supplies too.

The agent, a heavy-set Pole, thought she was the new cleaning girl.

"The mop and bucket are in the small closet on the right," he greeted her.

"Uh... You've made a mistake, sir, I'm here about that shop for rent on Marshalkowska street. I plan to set up a corset shop there." She voiced her proposal flatly, sounding as if she were accustomed to property rentals.

The man stood silent for a moment twirling his mustache. He looked totally perplexed. "Tell me again who wants to rent the shop," he said after a very long pause.

"I do," Rifka said loudly, then pulled out a fistful of hundred-zloty notes. "See, I can pay three months' rent in advance."

The man harrumphed, narrowed his eyes, and asked, "You of the Israelite persuasion, aren't you?"

"Yes, I am."

"Hmm, you people are good in business from the cradle." He extended his arm and took the bills into his beefy palm, licked the finger of the other hand flicked it across the edges of the bills counting, then promptly pocketed the money.

"Wait, sir, I need a contract, or some proof you've rented the store to me."

His face reddened. He walked over to his desk, took out a sheet of paper, scribbled a note and handed it to her saying, "Like I said, born to do business; full of chutzpah."

He was still shaking his head when she walked out in a daze. On the street, she bumped into pedestrians and clutched her receipt as if it were a talisman. I am a business owner, she kept repeating to herself.

Things weren't as easy as Rifka had imagined. First, she and Bronka scoured fabric and notion shops all over the city to find the ones that had the most affordable prices for cotton, lace, fasteners, ribbing, thread, and needles for the sewing machine. The most frequent comment they heard was a variant of "Aren't you nice shopping for your mother." After a while, they gave up and didn't bother with a retort.

Even hiring a wagon to haul aunt's sewing machine to their shop was a challenge. The burly young furniture hauler accustomed to dealing with men had a hard time believing she was the proprietor and

42

would pay him his fee. Raised eyebrows followed by, "You?" Rifka flashed a five-zloty silver coin with the image of queen Jadwiga. He relented, albeit with a smirk.

Bronka was waiting at the door of the shop when they pulled up, greeting their arrival enthusiastically. "I have just the spot for the machine!" she exclaimed.

Rifka said, "I hope it's behind the counter, in front of the green privacy curtain. You haven't rearranged everything while I was gone, have you?"

"No, why would I? Didn't we spend hours planning the space?"

Rifka directed the hauler and his teenage assistant deeper into the space.

"And look, Rifka, I brought this little table and my father's old chair from home," Bronka pointed to a corner near the entrance to the shop.

"What in the world for?"

"It'll make a pleasant little waiting area for our customers. I'll bring a vase and we will have fresh flowers. This will be a very special place for women," Bronka bubbled with excitement.

"How did you manage to get the furniture here?" Rifka asked after the men, casting them lascivious glances, left.

"I bribed Mendl. I'll take his turns throwing out the trash into the courtyard bins for a month." Despite the inconvenience of hauling trash bags four flights down, Bronka looked thrilled.

"You know, Rifka, this feels like setting up a home," Bronka chirped, moving around busily, dusting, cleaning the front window, and polishing the old mahogany counter that had been left by the previous shopkeeper.

"I suppose we will spend more time here than at home," Rifka said.

She stood sorting sewing supplies: spools of thread in different colors, straight pins, needles, scissors, thimbles, bobbins, snaps, zippers, and tailor's chalk, and arranging them in boxes on a shelf above the sewing machine.

It was a Sunday, and the shop hadn't yet opened for business, but a woman tapped the still empty display window trying to attract attention. Bronka opened the door.

"Sorry, we are not opened for business yet," Rifka called out. But Bronka invited the woman in and explained what kind of shop this would be. "We will hang up the shingle Monday or Tuesday, when it comes from the sign painter," Bronka said.

The blonde woman in her Sunday best—all white frills and pearls—looked puzzled. "Are you cleaning and setting up for the owner?"

"No, *we* are the owners," Rifka said. "When you see the sign, you'll understand. Fit for Venus, our own brand."

The woman shook her head in disbelief, "But you are so young!"

"Who said young women can't be in business?" Rifka said archly.

"I am Mrs. Kowalska. I hope to be your customer even though I can see you don't respect the day of rest. Have you been to church this morning?"

"Ahem... We are Jewish, and... proud of it," Rifka informed the would-be customer.

"I'll be..." Mrs. Kowalska bit her lip. "I should have known."

She bid them goodbye and hurried out.

"I guess she won't be a customer," Bronka said.

"Don't be so sure. Let us wait and see."

Rifka unfolded tissue paper patterns on the counter and pulled out two. "Tomorrow I'll start with this brassiere and this corset for our display window. They'll be the talk of the neighborhood."

It took only a few days before clients began arriving as the word about Fit for Venus spread in the neighborhood. A heavy-set woman with bosom spilling out her low-cut blouse was one of the first. "Hello, my friend Mrs. Kowalska told me there is a pink-cheeked girl with a crown of honey-colored braids who welcomes customers with a warm smile. Is she here today?"

"She'll be back in a moment. Can I help you?" Rifka looked up from behind the counter.

"And who are you?"

"I am the designer. The girl you are looking for is my assistant."

"Oh, I see. Well, can you really make me look like Venus, as your shingle says?"

"I can certainly try. Come with me to the fitting room behind the privacy curtain."

"You want me to get naked in front of you?" the customer began to lose her nerve.

"Just remove the brassiere you are wearing; it's not doing you any good. And bend forward, please, so I can take proper measurements."

"Can't I just leave it on?"

"You can, but I won't get a correct measurement that way."

Just then Bronka walked into the shop carrying a fresh bouquet of pink carnations. Rifka called out, "Bronka, why don't you come into the fitting room with me and with Mrs....?"

"Lisowska," the customer supplied her name.

"I need you to record the measurements."

Bronka said, "It'll be my pleasure, Mrs. Lisowska. My partner here, Rifka, is a magician. She'll make you a spectacular new brassiere."

Rifka smiled. She'd chosen well. Bronka had a soft touch with clients.

The three women crowded into the small fitting space with a long mirror with Bronka chattering non-stop about anything and everything to make Mrs. Lisowska at ease disrobing.

In just a few months, Rifka had perfected a strategy for best results: three fittings, not only one, like other shops used. The magic happened behind the velvet green privacy curtain, with each fitting getting closer to perfection. Customers could hardly pull themselves away from the long mirror at the final session.

Soon word spread to the actresses performing at the nearby National Theater; now clients had to wait weeks to get an appointment. And it didn't matter if they were Polish or Jewish, actresses or housewives; Rifka had only one pair of hands. Everyone had to wait.

Clients came to know Rifka as the olive-skinned design genius at the back of the shop: the heart of the business. She may not have been as warm and chatty as her partner, but she was the one with an innate understanding of the female anatomy, imagination, and talent.

One evening, with piles of orders still to process, they were still in the shop at eight in the evening. Out of the blue, Bronka said, "You know, Rifka. you are an engineer."

Rifka looked up from the sewing machine. "What are you talking about?"

"You construct brassieres like mechanical hoists and corsets strong enough to hold a barrel together!"

Rifka burst out laughing, then gathered herself to consider Bronka's odd description of her craft. She grew serious.

"I suppose I think of myself more as a sculptor," she said after thinking a while. "I first study the shape of my clients and the way the fabric stretches to determine how to cut my patterns. Don't you think sculptors do that too? Study their blocks of marble?"

Startled by her own declaration, Rifka realized nothing would make her happier than to be considered an artist. She had the highest esteem for artists and writers, people who lived for ideals.

Bronka interrupted her lofty thoughts. "I have watched you tracing patterns on tissue paper and cutting fabric using precision-ground scissors. You seem to think each material has its own personality!"

"But it does!"

"I have learned a lot from you, Rifka. I'd like to start doing more. The second machine you got is going mostly unused. I can do more than measuring and finishing."

"Alright, we can certainly use a second pair of hands. Why don't we start you off with the skinnier clients whose bodies don't require as much..."

"What?" Bronka interrupted her.

"Artistry," Rifka chuckled. "Tomorrow I'll teach you a few new stitches my mother taught me."

———

At first, all the neighborhood gossips clucked about the outrage: seventeen-year-old Rifka and Bronka ran away from home. Who knew where they went and what outrageous things they were doing? Rumors flew that Rifka was with child, that her father had thrown her out, or that she'd converted to Catholicism. But nothing could have been further from the truth. Rifka worked long hours to catch up with piles of orders and came to her parents' home in the dark of night, exhausted. She wasn't as happy as she had expected to be.

· · ·

46

The beginning of fall was unusually wet. Unrelenting rains! In the months since she'd opened the shop, Rifka worked seventy-hour weeks, and that was with Bronka's help. This evening she felt exhausted, couldn't face the usual hubbub at home, but she had no choice. She dragged herself up the stairs, shook out the umbrella in front of the door, still dripping all over the hall runner as she entered. Upon hearing voices in the living room, some unfamiliar, she felt like running out. With her splitting headache, she couldn't deal with whoever was visiting.

Poppa must have heard her coming in. "Come in, come in, daughter," he called in his deep tenor. She could tell he'd been smoking the pipe from the hoarseness of his voice.

"Give me a moment. I'm soaking wet, I have to dry myself," she stalled.

Two men she didn't know sat on the sofa, one much younger than the other. Poppa must have been entertaining them because they laughed when she entered the room, then stopped to greet her. Saul ran through the room chasing sisters Mania and Bayla, claiming they had taken his pen. Poppa tried as politely as possible to get them to leave.

Who were these men and why were they here? Rifka had a sneaking suspicion she knew. Poppa hadn't given up on marrying her off. The older gentleman must be the matchmaker and the younger one a potential husband. Suddenly she wanted to scream. No way!

Having dispatched the *kinder*, Poppa introduced the men. "This is Reb Mayer," he pointed to the one with gray ear locks and beady little eyes. "And this is his son, Aaron. And this here is *mayne tochter*, Rifka." Poppa pointed toward his daughter with something in his eyes resembling pride.

Rifka's mind raced. Why Aaron's father, not a matchmaker? The matchmaker must have gotten sick of offering prospects and given up on her. Aaron had chubby pink cheeks and a twitch in his eye. He looked at Rifka timidly, with a spark of hope. She felt sorry for him.

Just then, Mania and Bayla slipped back into the living room, squatted on the floor in the corner and began playing with their rag dolls. Poppa wasn't happy. He threw them a look they'd have interpreted as dismissal if they were older, but they happily continued dressing and undressing the dolls. He must have decided it would be unseemly to chide them.

47

"So! Let's finally make a *shidduch*," Poppa said, rubbing his palms briskly. He looked directly at Rifka. "I can tell you have figured out why the young man is here. Let's skip the small talk and get to business."

Oh, God, not today, not ever. With her temples pounding, Rifka lost it, abandoned all civility. "Don't you get it, Poppa? I am never getting married! Never! No one is making me into a servant... or a baby factory!" she screamed.

The little sisters' mouths hung wide open.

"Poppa, why is Rifka so angry?" Mania piped up, her chin quivering and tears filling her eyes.

Poppa blanched and sputtered, "This? In front of the *kinder*? In front of my honored guests? You have lost your mind! Get out! Get out now!" he yelled, pointing at the door, jabbing the air. Reb Mayer picked up his black hat and stood up. Aaron glanced at his father, who motioned for him to get up.

Rifka slammed the door and ran outside without a raincoat, without the umbrella. Her only thought: I'll end up married to a loser like Aaron or Moshe if I don't leave home. I've got to get away.

She raced through the deluge until she had no breath left. She found herself in front of Bronka's tenement. Not knowing what to do she climbed the stairs.

<hr />

Bronka looked aghast at the drenched figure in front of the door. "Rifka! What happened?"

Rifka stood silent and dripping, her hair matted, skirt glued to her legs and shoes about to dissolve. She began to shiver.

"Wait, let me get you some towels." Bronka disappeared and soon came bouncing back with a stack. "You are in luck. I pulled the laundry off the lines before it began pouring," she said.

Rifka toweled her hair right in the entryway without saying a word.

"You'll catch a cold," Bronka looked worried.

"I don't care," was all Rifka mustered.

"Come into the bedroom, I'll give you a dry blouse and skirt."

The sweetness of the girl! Rifka followed making a line of drips along the floor.

"What's wrong? It can't be that bad. Cheer up," Bronka said, rummaging in a bureau drawer, then handing Rifka a long navy skirt and a gray linen blouse. She turned away to give Rifka privacy.

Rifka suddenly realized Bronka's house was uncharacteristically quiet. "Where is everyone?" she asked, struggling to erase the unseemly scene at home from her mind. Everything was wrong with it. She'd gotten carried away, but it was Poppa who provoked it.

"Momma took all the children and Mendl to visit her mother. We can talk here without an audience for a change. Tell me what happened," Bronka said.

Rifka dressed awkwardly, piling her wet garments on the floor. Bronka was taller, so the skirt hung almost to the floor. She looked in the cheval mirror and chuckled. "I look like a schoolmarm."

The two settled on Hinda's large bed, where she and four of the youngest children slept.

"I behaved disgracefully in front of my father and a suitor he brought... again. And my two little sisters heard it all. That's what bothers me the most." Rifka began describing the incident in vivid detail.

Bronka listened and nodded. "Well, it doesn't surprise me at all. It was bound to happen," she said. "Like you've been saying, Rifka, you've got to move out. We could move in together."

"Hmm..." Rifka searched for a response.

"I am sorry about the situation, but I am glad you came today. I am so excited about something that happened to me; I've been busting to tell you."

"Alright, tell me. It'll take my mind off my problem," Rifka said, rubbing her temples.

"Do you know Kazio?" Bronka said with an enigmatic expression.

"No, who is that?"

"He is Mrs. Kowalska's son."

"How would I know him? And most importantly, how do you know him?"

"You may have been out of the shop when he came by to pick up an order for his mother."

"The woman is an idiot. Sending a child into an underwear shop!" Rifka had never liked Kowalska since their first encounter.

"He is about twenty. God, he was so embarrassed! We chatted; I did my best to put him at ease. Those blue eyes, the blond hair. He's so tall, a regular movie star, I tell you." Bronka hardly noticed Rifka's irritation. She looked dreamy, eyes closed, cheeks glowing.

"Are you insane, Bronka? He is a *goy*!"

"So what? I think he liked me too. He said he'd come by again." With her lips closed, Bronka's mouth had a determined look as if she were underlining her statement.

"Please, Bronka, come to your senses."

"No, maybe you should, Rifka. Your father isn't giving up. As for me, I will marry for love, and I don't care what others will say about my choice—even you."

Noises at the door. Hinda called out from the entry, "Why is the floor all wet?"

Soon the entire family filed in. Bronka's youngest sisters ran into the bedroom and immediately climbed on the bed, jumping up and down. The youngest one put her arms around Rifka's neck. It was time for Rifka to leave and face her father's wrath.

———————

Despite her initial idea of escaping from home—the shop being the means, not the goal—it still hadn't happened. The shop's earnings were adequate, but after splitting them with Bronka and then giving most of her share to Momma, there wasn't enough left for rent. Rifka walked home along the street slick with rain and contemplated a solution. The cobblestones glistened, and the quiet, empty streets calmed her as if the downpour had washed away her anger, made her think more clearly. It struck her that when the chips were down, she'd run to Bronka, not Pessy, not any of the other friends she'd made at the Pozner gymnasium. They weren't really friends; they were more like acquaintances. Bronka was her oldest friend. She was special.

A cat slunk out of the shadows and brushed by her leg. She leaned down and rubbed its head. It purred. Now she saw it was just a skinny kitten, probably hungry. "There are too many of us already, I can't take you home with me," she said out loud. She'd have to save more so she could get a place of her own.

She thought of Bronka's offer to share a flat. That's not what she wanted. She needed space, her very own space, total privacy. As much as she cared for Bronka, she'd get on her nerves with all that romantic silliness and non-stop chatter. The idea Bronka fell for this Kazio so readily worried Rifka. Bronka will get into trouble if she is unable to resist any male that smiles at her.

The October morning weather was balmy enough for a pleasant stroll. Rifka slowed her pace and walked toward her shop. It was warm so she flung her coat open, enjoying the last rays of sun. Along the way, she counted how many orders had to be finished by the week's end.

Despite Rifka's intense yearning to leave home, she took a great deal of satisfaction from the success of the shop that had been humming for two years. Her father's disdain for the money she brought home, the constant harassment by the taxing authority and the landlord's threats to raise the rent did not diminish the self-esteem she had gained from putting herself on a trajectory to independence.

After the run-in with Poppa, her thoughts of leaving home became more urgent. She was turning over possibilities for financing her getaway: borrow money from the bank? Decrease the sum she gave Momma each week? No. She found these options unacceptable. As she turned the corner onto Marshalkowska, just a few store fronts away from her shop, it hit her! The landlord was coming to collect the rent. She hoped to get there before him as not to leave Bronka to negotiate with him. And here she was strolling, enjoying the weather.

She glanced at her shop's display window before entering and decided to add two new brassieres made of the latest lace from Paris. The shop was quiet when she opened the door. No customers yet.

Stepping inside, she heard some shuffling noises from behind the privacy curtain. "Bronka? Are you here?" Rifka called out.

Bronka responded in a strained, unnatural voice, "Give me a minute, I'll be right out."

"Are you alright?"

Rifka placed her purse in the drawer behind the counter and was about to pull the curtain open when a young man emerged. Bronka trailed behind him smoothing her skirt and introduced the man awkwardly. "This is Kazio. I have mentioned him to you."

The young man smiled sheepishly, swept his blond mop off his forehead, tucked the tail of his shirt into the back of his pants, then extended his hand to Rifka, who stood silent, looking at Bronka with astonishment.

"Well, ladies, I have to go now," Kazio—all six feet of him bathed in embarrassment—put on his cap and slipped out the door so quietly it was as if he hadn't been there at all. Bronka turned away from Rifka and replaited her mussed braid. For a few minutes both women stood silent.

Then Rifka thundered, "What's the matter with you, Bronka? How could you?"

Bronka turned back. With an uncharacteristic dose of attitude, she said, "Kazio saved our behinds."

"What are you talking about?"

"The landlord was here. He demanded an extra hundred zlotys with the new lease beginning next month. Then Kazio stepped in. He asked him not to do it. Turns out he is his grandnephew. 'Leave these hardworking ladies alone, or else...' he threatened to tell his wife about something, but I couldn't tell what it was."

Rifka listened, shaking her head. "Such a pig," she said.

"Don't you insult my Kazio!" Bronka yelled.

"Not him. I meant the landlord, greedy *gelt fresser*."

It was a standoff. Rifka couldn't very well deliver her speech on Bronka's impulsive behavior, at least not at this moment. They sat at the sewing machines, silently focusing on the work. Every now and then Rifka threw Bronka an annoyed look, but her lips were sealed.

By the end of the day, Rifka said, "Let's not have any man come between us."

Bronka smiled broadly, walked over to Rifka, and put her hand on her friend's shoulder. "Never! Such a thing will never happen. We are too close for that. We are bonded since childhood, and we shall die two old, toothless ladies laughing at each other's grandchildren's antics." And as if to illustrate there were no hard feelings. Bronka said, "I've learned new dance steps to the foxtrot. Want to try them out with me at the back of the shop?"

Rifka looked at her as if she'd lost her mind and said, "Dancing is for fools! Moving your legs around in stupid poses? Gyrating? What are you thinking?"

She saw Bronka's fallen face and realized she'd been too harsh.

"I didn't mean to insult you, Bronka. I'm sorry, you know how dear you are to me, but dancing just isn't for me." Genuine regret made Rifka silent. It wasn't the first time her tongue had gotten the better of her.

"Never mind, your loss," Bronka mumbled, disappearing in the back. Soon the rhythmic sounds of jazz filled the shop.

***

Rifka and Bronka had operated Fit for Venus with unheard-of success. Rifka's careful management of finances enabled them to provide financial support for their families to the continued astonishment of their mothers. Both young women worked hard and the working relationship between them had reached an equilibrium.

On this November day, the sky had turned the color of soot, and winds whipped the laundry on the lines trying to sweep it off the roofs. The shop felt so chilly Rifka and Bronka wore heavy sweaters and wrapped thick wool shawls around their shoulders.

The doorbell rang and a customer walked into the shop. A wave of pleasantly strong scent—rose and jasmine—suffused the shop, reminding Rifka of spring. Mrs. Kowalska wore a smart burgundy wool suit whose amply padded shoulders gave her a commanding stature. Over it, a gray fox stole, the unfortunate creature's beady black eyes staring at Rifka. A pink blouse tied in a bow at the neck and high heels made Mrs. Kowalska even more imposing.

She looked around, her eyes flitting from Rifka to Bronka then Rifka again. "It's Friday afternoon; don't you two ladies have to go somewhere?" she asked.

"No, not really. We have a pile of orders to catch up on. We will be here late," Rifka replied.

"Ooh, so your God, what do you call him, Moses? He doesn't care?"

Rifka's chest tightened. She didn't need this aggravation. "What are you getting at, Mrs. Kowalska?"

"I don't want you going to hell with all those bloody matzo makers. I can see you are good girls."

"Don't you mind. We aren't worried at all. We couldn't care less what God thinks. And no one puts blood in the matzo. Only your people put blood in sausage."

Rifka couldn't help herself, but Bronka's face went white, and she puttered at the counter as if she didn't hear the exchange. Mrs. Kowalska plastered her hand over her mouth. Her lips in a sneer, she said, "You people are something... Always have to have the last word."

It looked as if she were about to walk out, but Bronka spoke up. "Never mind, my partner here is just having a bad day. Shall we do the final fitting?"

"I didn't mean to..." Kowalska paused. "I need those brassieres and the corset for the wedding next Sunday. Let's do it." And she walked toward the fitting room, trying to avoid Rifka's gaze.

When Mrs. Kowalska left, Rifka sat at her sewing machine chewing her lip. She felt so aggravated with Kowalska she wished she could dump her order into the garbage.

Bronka approached her instead of getting on with her work. "Don't you ever act so hostile to her! How could you? She's Kazio's mother," Bronka sputtered.

"She's a vile antisemite," Rifka said. "She'd never let Kazio see you... if she knew."

Tears stood in Bronka's eyes. "But would you come to our wedding if we could marry?"

"It'll never happen, but I would... just as I know you'd do anything for me," Rifka said. "But you know what I think about marriage," Rifka rolled her eyes.

"Blah... blah... blah... You've even called it slavery," Bronka chuckled.

By late afternoon, Mrs. Grynberg arrived huffing and puffing. "Goodness me, I rushed to get here before Sabbath," she said breathlessly and began slipping the mink coat off her short squat body. Her large bosom heaved under gulps of air. "Too cold, the wind goes right through you," she said. "I would rather it snowed. But I'm going through the change, always feeling sweaty, even on a day like this."

Mrs. Grynberg had managed to climb out of the Nalewki neighborhood and moved to Próżna street with the Jewish social climbers. She picked up a folded newspaper from the entry table, fanned herself energetically and said, "Well, well, well, I suppose neither of you has found a husband yet." A crooked smile erupted on her fleshy lips.

Had she spoken to Poppa? Did he send her to pile on the pressure? Rifka sported a tight-lipped expression. "You are mistaken, Mrs.

Grynberg, we aren't in the market for men. We are looking to make a fortune and open a much bigger business."

Bronka rolled her eyes, stood up from the sewing machine, and walked toward the back of the shop.

Mrs. Grynberg's breath quickened as she clearly took offense. She puckered her lips and said, "Tsk, tsk, tsk...Let's just get on with my fitting."

After she left, Bronka sat down heavily in front of the sewing machine, picked up a finished brassiere, and began trimming the loose threads. "You shouldn't have answered for me. I do want to find a husband," she said, deadly serious.

"It looks as if you've already found one," Rifka said. "Do you really think you'll like washing his dirty underwear and cooking kapusta or pierogi for him?"

"Kazio?" Bronka chuckled so unexpectedly Rifka stopped her machine and turned to look at her directly. "He is a good kisser and as you've seen for yourself very good-looking, but I probably won't marry him."

Rifka's eyebrows arched in confusion. "Maybe you've come to your senses, but what exactly are you doing with Kazio? Playing with fire? Soon he'll want to steal more than kisses and if you reject him... there'll be trouble."

Bronka didn't answer. She picked at her fingernail, pulling on a hangnail. After a while she said, "I'll figure it out. Just let it go, Rifka."

By seven o'clock they finished the Kowalska and Grynberg orders and several others. Bronka swept loose threads off the floor and dusted the counter while Rifka packed the finished orders.

7 A GATHERING STORM

Mrs. Grynberg entered the shop to pick up her girdle, very agitated. Rifka could see it from the moment she barged in, red-faced, and threw her coat on the chair, a bundle of anxious energy. Bronka wrapped her order in tissue paper and boxed it, then handed her the bill.

"This may be my last order," Grynberg blurted out counting the bills pulled from her purse. "My husband, a lawyer!" she exclaimed wide-eyed. "He says Jews will be thrown out of his law firm soon, discarded like pieces of rotten fruit. No Jews will be allowed to practice. And the same thing will happen to my brother, a doctor. Can you believe it? Professionals unwanted just because they are Jews?" Sheer disbelief was etched on her blotchy face.

"I miss our President Pilsudzki," Rifka said, but seeing the uncomprehending look in Mrs. Grynberg's eyes, she explained. "Haven't we all seen how Hitler's 1935 Nuremberg Laws have inspired intolerance after Pilsudzki's death? It has grown like poisoned mushrooms."

"We should all run away from here," Mrs. Grynberg said. Tears filled her eyes, and Rifka noticed how her hands trembled. Though she'd never liked the woman very much, a wave of sympathy flooded her. She too had begun to think more seriously about getting away, not just from the tense atmosphere at home, but from the violence on the streets that had become commonplace.

"If you need another brassiere or a corset, just come in anytime. Don't worry about the money; we will work something out. This situation can't last long," Rifka said, not sure she believed it given the casual violence—inflicted with impunity—she'd heard about.

The week before, kids no more than twelve or thirteen spat and threw snot balls at Poppa as he walked from the synagogue. He came home, didn't say a word, only asked Momma to clean his gabardine coat. Rifka learned what had happened a few days later. Though she was still on the outs with Poppa, it pained her deeply to see him so resigned, so disrespected. The fifteen-year-old son of a neighbor had been thrown out of his Polish gymnasium because Jews could not go to school past the age of fourteen.

"Mrs. Grynberg, you are not alone," Bronka chimed in. "My mother was turned away from the Holy Spirit Hospital when she went to have a boil lanced. No Jews wanted there either, not as doctors or as patients."

Angry tears stood in Mrs. Grynberg's eyes. Bronka sniffled and dabbed at her nose.

"Now, now..." Rifka stepped in. "We can't lose our heads. No formal antisemitic laws have been passed here as yet. We have to stand up to them."

Bronka blew her nose, said, "Really? How do we do that?"

"I don't know. I have to think about it. Maybe we should emigrate to Palestine."

With that, Rifka walked briskly toward the back of the shop, chastising herself for making an unrealistic suggestion. Even from behind the privacy curtain, Rifka could tell Mrs. Grynberg calmed a bit, because she was speaking to Bronka. "May I hug you, dear girl? I may not be seeing you for a long while."

Rifka felt a stab, deep in her chest.

February 1936 blew in fiercer and colder than any Rifka had remembered. She bundled up, buttoning her coat right up to the neck, then for good measure wound her wool scarf around her neck and trudged all the way up Marshalkowska, turning right just past the Holy Savior church onto Mokotowska.

She'd taken a couple of hours off work, telling Bronka she'd treat herself for her upcoming twentieth birthday with a stack of books from the national library on Koszykowa Street. She had no idea when she'd find the time to read them, but books were always a delicious escape.

To take her mind off the biting cold, she reviewed the list of books she wanted to borrow, with Dabrowska's *Nights & Days* at the top of the list. She'd heard about it. Some papers were scandalized by a wife's recollection of passions amid a time of political turmoil—just the kind of book she'd love.

As she approached the ornate wooden doors to the library, she could see even from some distance a sign hanging on the right door. The wind stung her eyes, making them tear. Perhaps the library was closed due to inclement weather. She approached the door and stared at the hand-scrawled sign: JEWS NOT WELCOME HERE, all in black capitals.

It hit her harder than a slap on the cheek. Until now she had heard about ugly instances of racial hate, but this was directed at her, at her love of literature. Intense pressure squeezed her temples. She felt helpless and indignant.

In a flash, she tore the sign off, balled it up, and was about to hurl it somewhere, then she had a better idea. She'd take it home, smooth it out and show it to everyone she could as *corpus delicti*. Let people see for themselves how low her fellow citizens had sunk. She stuffed the paper ball into her pocket. Before she could turn in the direction of the shop, she felt the scarf tighten around her throat. A half turn and she saw a pimply young thug towering over her, pulling on both ends of the scarf and grinning.

"Didn't like the sign, stinking Jewess? Think you are so learned?"

She struggled to breathe, pulling the scarf at the front of her neck with both hands to loosen its chokehold. He yanked harder, causing her to stumble backward. "Help! Help!" she screamed. A pair of policemen appeared at the far end of the block. The thug let go and ran. Her heart raced; she inhaled the cold air in quick gulps. She wanted to shout out about the unfairness of the assault to the policemen, or anyone who'd listen, but words stuck in her throat like jagged bones. Such harassment had become common; but now it was personal. She struggled against opposing instincts: to run or to walk slower to calm herself down. She ended up walking briskly toward the shop.

On her return to the shop, Rifka showed Bronka the crumpled sign, but Bronka's response astonished her. "That's disgusting, but you know what's worse? We can't marry non-Jews!"

Rifka gulped. "Has Kazio proposed to you?"

"Well… no, but… but the idea we can't marry who we want galls me," Bronka said, then hastened to add, "If I am truly serious about a man, you'll be the very first to know. Who else would I share such good news with if not you?"

Rifka, still deeply distressed about what had happened to her, did not want to pursue the conversation; she had no stomach for it. And it bothered her that Bronka was focused on the prohibition on marriage to Christians, rather than on the immediate physical danger.

They spent a couple of hours working in silence. Noticing Bronka wrapping her gray shawl tighter around her shoulders, Rifka worried about her catching a cold. Bronka was prone to chest infections. "We are running short on coal; maybe we should close early," Rifka suggested.

"Can we afford it?" We have seen fewer Christian customers since the Cardinal encouraged a boycott of Jewish businesses," Bronka said.

"We have nothing on our Fit for Venus sign to suggest we are Jewish, nor do we have 'Jewess' tattooed on our foreheads." Rifka wasn't going to let the sign on the library door affect her decisions.

Bronka shook her head. "Just you wait and see. I've heard that soon Jewish businesses will be forced to add their Jewish surnames to the shingle whether they want to or not."

"That's absurd," Rifka said and noted the growing hoarseness in Bronka's voice.

They fell silent. The machines hummed as if a balance had been restored—albeit temporarily—but it had not. Rifka feared that a more virulent antisemitism would spread across the border from Germany to Poland. She knew that Jews who had the means were leaving Poland if they managed to find a country that would allow them in.

A sudden cascade of Bronka's coughs pulled Rifka out of her thoughts. She glanced up at the clock. It wasn't yet closing time, but she decided. "We are done for the day. Go home, Bronka, drink some hot tea and go to bed."

After the library incident, Rifka worried more about her parents when they walked from the synagogue's evening prayers. She even worried about Saul because he was the kind of kid to respond to insults with his fists and that, surely, would only lead to more trouble.

Though she'd long abandoned her weekly attendance at the synagogue—despite father's objections and insults—Rifka strongly resented anyone who stood in the way of Jews trying to practice their religious rituals. Some days, she couldn't reconcile the genteel Polish poets and writers with angry Poles who accused Jews of all the ills in the world. Why did people hate? Hate was such a useless emotion; it solved nothing. She began to think more about Golda: not only her well-being but, increasingly, about the wisdom of her decision to emigrate to Palestine. She should find a way to go there and look for her, but how? The idea lodged stubbornly in her head, and remained active, just below the mundane tasks of daily life.

The winter had been long and unkind. Now it was late March. This being a Monday, Rifka anticipated some new orders. She was eager for them so her savings would grow faster. As she stepped outside into the pale sunshine, Rifka smiled at the sight of purple and yellow crocuses that began popping out next to gray mounds of snow, but she yearned for the intoxicating citrusy fragrance of linden trees that June would bring. Spring in all its fullness had always made her more cheerful, hopeful for the future. She'd gotten up extra early hoping to take the path through the park on the way to her shop, then remembered Jews were no longer allowed in public parks. The thought sent a shudder through her body. The pleasant moment of anticipating spring evaporated.

Rifka strode to work trying to ignore the unsettled feeling caused by the prohibition. Within a block or two of the shop, she knew something else was wrong: sirens, horse-mounted police meandering among vehicles screeching to a halt, distraught-looking people. She didn't want to believe what she saw, but it was there right in front of her in all its ugliness.

Almost the entire block of shops, including hers, had been vandalized. Broken display windows, swastikas and *Żydzi do Palestyny*— Jews to Palestine—scrawled on walls and doors, fine broken glass sprinkled like sugar and larger chunks, like icicles, all over the sidewalks. Weeping, hollering shop owners. All those shops, Gold's bakery, the shoe store, the haberdasher, the antiquarian book shop and even the magazine stand at the end of the block, lay in ruin.

The police shooed passersby away and mumbled about hoodlums and young men who celebrated too hard on Sunday, but the red and black poster on yellow background Rifka spotted on an intact store window across the street belied the milquetoast promises of 'we will deal with them harshly.' The graphic image on the poster was potent and highly disturbing: a large black broom sweeping out tiny figures of Jews with a heading of *Żydzi do Ghetta*—Jews to the Ghetto.

Bronka arrived only a few minutes after Rifka. Both stood in front of their shop stunned, shaking their heads in disbelief. Two policemen asked them to move; they wanted to cordon off the area for an investigation and told store owners to return later. "But who will watch the merchandise in the store?" Bronka asked.

"We will," a young policeman winked at her.

Rifka stood frozen, staring at the shattered window, her jaw clenched so tight her neck and ear ached. Her finest corset lay in the mud.

"Come with me, I have an idea," Bronka tugged on Rifka's arm. "There's nothing we can do here at this moment."

Rifka followed mechanically, her mind reeling. When they turned the corner, away from the scene of mayhem, she snapped out of her daze. "Where are you dragging me?"

Bronka said, "Trust me for a change. You'll soon see."

They arrived at the Nożyk Synagogue, which Bronka still attended regularly. Rifka hadn't set foot there in forever. Her voice filled with irony, Rifka said, "You want to pray all this away?"

"Pray? No, but we must speak with the rabbi. He is a learned man; he can give us advice about how to deal with all this..."

"You think a man stuck in the Torah all day can shed any light on this violence?"

Ignoring her friend, Bronka pulled Rifka inside, saying, "In any case, we will be safe here. No place safer than a synagogue."

Rifka relented and followed Bronka in.

As it happened, they entered the space between services. It was majestically quiet. "Wait here," Bronka said. "I'll go into the office and find the rabbi." She rushed toward the back of the synagogue.

Rifka stared at the Tablets of the Law on the western facade. All these commandments they broke... Wasn't God watching?

The rabbi walked in slowly behind Bronka with a halting gait that made him look older than his years. Bronka introduced him. The rabbi pushed his glasses up on his nose and looked closely at Rifka as if she were a study specimen. "You are Reb Berg's daughter, aren't you? We haven't been seeing much of you," he said. There was no rancor in his voice.

"Rabbi, something terrible happened to our shop last night. Have you heard about the ransacking of Jewish stores on Marshalkowska?" Bronka took the initiative while Rifka stood silent, still too shaken to engage.

"*Chas v'chalila!* Heaven forbid!" the rabbi exclaimed. "No, no one has told me, but come to think of it, I heard a lot of sirens this morning." Then, "You have a shop?" the rabbi addressed Bronka.

"It's our shop, mine and my friend Rifka's," she clarified.

"Aha, so that's what you've been doing," the rabbi pointed at Rifka. "Good for you. Rumors had it otherwise. How can I help you girls?"

Bronka described the extent of the damage and the ugly slogans scrawled everywhere. "We have to do something, but we don't know what," she said.

The rabbi stroked his beard, his eyebrows moving up and down. "This is not simple but responding in kind is not an option. Violence only breeds more violence." He spoke gesticulating energetically with both his arms as if to strengthen his advice, "First, clean up the damage. We can take up a collection at the synagogue if you need help but leave it alone. Let's keep our heads down. It'll pass. The police will handle it, God willing."

Having made his pronouncement, the rabbi stopped speaking, but his eyes brightened, and an incipient smile brushed his lips. "Instead of tragedies, girls, let's now talk about happier things, like marriage."

"But, rabbi, we have to go back; the police sent us away only for a short while. We can't think about anything else right now," Rifka managed a civil response, but the rabbi was not to be deterred.

"We have some good boys here for you, pious and very smart. You'd make good wives, both of you, and you wouldn't need to worry about any shop," he said.

Rifka shot arrows at Bronka with her eyes. It was a look that said: I could murder you for subjecting me to this.

The rabbi must have seen Rifka's expression. His enthusiasm cooled. He bid them goodbye and walked toward the bimah in the center of the space. Rifka saw him ascend it as if he were about to give a sermon to the empty room. He opened a Torah and stood there shrunken somehow, davening silently.

By Wednesday, they had cleaned up the worst of the damage, only partially succeeding in scrubbing the swastikas off the door. They'd have to repaint it. Kazio showed up with his friend, a glazier, and installed a new front window. Bronka thanked him profusely and asked about the charge, but he said, "It's nothing, never mind," and hurried to leave, throwing her a mournful look. His friend mumbled something of an apology. "I am embarrassed... Such people..."

Whether it was to forget, or because they were too upset to voice their feelings, neither Bronka nor Rifka spoke much about the incident. Yet Rifka's thoughts churned. The only thing the rabbi had said that resonated was that violence only breeds more violence. She agreed wholeheartedly, yet it also troubled her. What could one do to defend oneself? One's family? It bothered her she had no answer. And Kazio's generosity made her realize that you couldn't lump people in one group. After all he was Christian, just like the thugs who tried to destroy the shop.

They focused on the work. Piles of orders were due to be finished before Passover arrived in the first week of April.

It was eight in the morning before opening time. Bronka stood at the sink in the back of the shop, changing the water in the flower vase and rearranging tulip stems. She walked to the front, set the vase on the entry table and admired her handiwork.

Rifka sat behind the counter, perusing the news in the Jewish weekly, her morning ritual.

Bronka came toward her and noticed her face. Her radar, always attuned to Rifka's moods, buzzed. "What's wrong?" she asked.

"More Jews have been killed."

"Oh, God! Where?"

"In the Jaffa riots, in Palestine," Rifka continued reading, her eyes glued to the paper.

"Not good, not good at all," Bronka said. "But it's not next door. Don't worry."

Rifka, her face paler, now looked up. "Have you forgotten? Golda is there."

Bronka could tell Rifka was extremely distressed. Her heart filled with love, she approached Rifka and patted her shoulder gently. "Calm down, Rifka, I'm sure she'll be fine. After all this time she must know how to protect herself. I hate to see you so upset."

"I am calm," Rifka finally put the paper down and looked directly at Bronka. "We have not heard from Golda for months. We don't even know if she's alive. I have to do something about it."

"Like what?"

"I have an idea I'm working on. I'll let you know when I figure it out," Rifka said resolutely.

Bronka looked at her friend. It was just like Rifka. It was impossible to know what brewed in her mind, but flecks of gold danced in her emerald-green eyes.

8 THE NUDELMAN PAPERS

The antisemitic rioting that had damaged their shop and the news about Arab unrest in Palestine were constantly on Rifka's mind. Since the library assault, she'd been trying to figure out how to get to Palestine. Such a trip would serve a dual purpose: finding Golda and assessing the feasibility of *aliyah*. And the icing on the cake would be getting away from the tensions at home, at least for a little while.

In the afternoon, Mrs. Nudelman came by the shop to check if her order was ready. A heavy-set fiftyish woman, with red hair styled in finger waves close to the head, she had been one of their best customers. "Hello, girls," she greeted them cheerfully, as if she were totally unaware of what the shop had been through.

"Your bras won't be ready till next week. We've had a bit of a delay. You might have heard," Rifka said glumly.

"Yes, yes, I have, but let's think good thoughts. It was just a few bad apples," Nudelman said.

Bronka excused herself, said she needed to go pick up a couple of yards of lace and damask at a nearby fabric store.

After she left, Mrs. Nudelman approached the counter where the newest fashion magazines lay and began thumbing through them absent mindedly as if waiting would hasten her order. "You know," she said, "there are some clever people who manage to get far, far away from all this." She swept her arm, motioning toward the shops across the street that still stood shuttered with tape holding the plate glass together.

Rifka's ears pricked up. As the notion of leaving gained momentum, the three ideas: checking on Golda, looking for safe harbor in Palestine and escaping Poppa's pressure to enter an arranged marriage, twisted into a thick cord that pulled her closer and closer toward the ultimate decision. "How? Have you any idea?" she asked.

"Well... I shouldn't..." Mrs. Nudelman immediately regretted her comment.

Rifka took it as a personal challenge to find out. "Please, I really need to know. My sister is in trouble over there." Rifka leaned closer and whispered, "In Palestine."

"As you must know, the British won't let us come in legally," Nudelman said.

"But how did my sister manage to get in?"

"Things seem to be changing over there. They used to admit the Youth Aliyah groups, but now the Arabs are grumbling about too many Jews, so the British have imposed strict quotas."

Rifka frowned. "So, is there another way?"

"Morris, my husband can't bear the idea that we have to sneak into our ancestral land like thieves. He arranges for documents and..." She hesitated, "... the smugglers."

Smugglers. The very word made Rifka cringe.

Mrs. Nudelman picked up her purse and turned to leave the shop.

"Wait, please wait," Rifka pleaded. "You next brassiere is on the house if you tell me more." That was how Rifka learned of Morris Nudelman's operation and how he helped people secure false identity papers and British passports.

"Bless you, Mrs. Nudelman! So how do they get there once they have the proper papers?"

"I have been talking too much. I must go now." Nudelman hurried out. Outside, she hesitated, cracked the shop door open and stuck her head back in. "Get yourself some passport photos, girl," she winked.

When Bronka returned with the new fabrics she saw Rifka's mood had lifted from the funk she'd been in since the attack on the shop. "Why are you grinning so smugly? Did something good happen?"

"Maybe," Rifka said.

Bronka shook her head and sat at the machine.

As they did whenever there were no customers in the shop, Rifka and Bronka chatted as they sewed. Family, the news, the weather—anything and everything—but most of all, books, because it was Rifka's favorite subject. Whenever Bronka wanted to talk about something else, Rifka listened with half an ear, then jumped back to whatever latest novel captured her fancy.

Rifka paused her machine and walked over to the shelves holding the boxes of supplies examining the contents. "Please, Bronka, make a list," she called out.

Bronka obliged and picked up a notepad.

"We are getting low on boning, corset fasteners, padding, elastic, trimming, seam covering tape, snaps and lace," Rifka intoned slowly, stopping occasionally to recount the supply. "But please, Bronka, get only the French Alençon lace, none of the imitation stuff; we can economize on other items."

"I know," Bronka muttered.

Then just like that, all of a sudden Rifka changed the subject. "Have I told you about an extraordinary woman named Gertrude Bell I've just read about?" she asked.

Bronka looked up, put down the list she'd been making. "Who is she?"

"She's an extraordinary British politician who inspired me," Rifka said.

"Inspired you to... do what exactly?"

"Just listen, Bronka. The woman is amazing! She's made an indelible impact, not only on me but on the entire Middle East," Rifka said, her face flushed with excitement.

"Middle East?" Bronka rolled her eyes.

"Yes. She learned Persian and Arabic then traveled to Palestine and Syria and crossed the Iraqi desert on a camel caravan drawing the first ever maps of the area! Who could have ever imagined a woman alone doing this?"

"You aren't planning to follow her example, are you, Rifka?"

Rifka didn't reply, just stood there with a dreamy look in her eyes. She'd already gotten the passport photos suggested by Mrs. Nudelman. Her plan started to take shape. She was anxious to get it done.

The very next day, Rifka met Morris Nudelman in a nearby café. He was a heavy-set man with a florid face adorned by a handlebar mustache. He looked her over suspiciously. "Aha, you are the Rifka my wife has told me so much about? Didn't realize you were so young."

Rifka smiled. He chose a table in the corner, away from the rest, and set his coat on one of the chairs, motioning for Rifka to sit near him. He sat down heavily, making the chair slide and its legs squeak on the tile surface. Then he unfolded the afternoon paper in a way that obscured both their faces. "Are you sure you are up to this? It won't be easy. It's nothing like vacation travel."

Rifka sat up stiffly. "Can't say I've ever traveled for pleasure, but I assure you I'm perfectly capable of dealing with whatever may come up."

"I must say, my wife has described you perfectly." Nudelman smiled. In a whisper, he filled her in on the details and promised to work on British identity papers.

Rifka slipped him the envelope with passport photos. He looked at them and nodded approvingly. She was glad she'd picked out her good wool suit for the photo, the one with padded shoulders and carved wooden buttons. It made her look more worldly than she felt. "Now what?" she asked.

"After you pay me"—he stressed *after*—"I'll contact a representative of the Jewish Agency. He will make arrangements for you to board a clandestine chartered ship in Naples."

"Clandestine?" She paused, considering the implications. "How will I find it?"

"Shh..." Nudelman put his finger to his lips and stood up. "It'll all become clear later."

She handed him the salty fee—a whole month's earnings—whereupon he picked up his raincoat and walked out, leaving Rifka in a state of agitation. False papers? Would she get a new name? Would she need to find another clandestine ship for her return? She'd forgotten to ask Nudelman, and he wasn't in a talkative mood anyway. She hoped, no matter her new identity, it would not change her, that she'd remain the kind of can-do person she'd always been. But the immediate concerns aside, the dangerous escapade ahead excited her.

Three weeks had passed since she'd met with Morris Nudelman, and Rifka still hadn't divulged her plan to Bronka, yet Bronka's agreement was essential. Rifka felt guilty to leave at such a busy time and struggled to find the right words to explain an unanticipated absence. It gnawed at her, made her feel dishonorable. She sat at her sewing machine with a knot the size of an apple in her stomach. This is it; I'm doing it now, she resolved.

"Listen, Bronka, I am going to look for Golda. I fear something terrible may have happened to her."

Bronka looked up from the sewing machine with uncomprehending eyes. "What are you talking about? Palestine is on the other side of the world."

"Don't be obtuse, Bronka. It's far, but people do manage to get there."

"I bet it's that woman you had read about. What's her name? Bell... something? How do you plan to go, Rifka? You don't even know where Golda is living now."

Rifka's eyes darkened; she knew this would not be an easy sell and hated it when Bronka questioned her. "I'll find the right connections. I do have her old address. I'll figure it out, but only if you promise to take care of the shop while I am away."

"The shop? You want me to run this place all by myself and finish all the Passover orders?" There was no mistaking the look of astonishment and horror on Bronka's face.

"Yes, please, I beg you, just for a few weeks. There are plenty of orders you can work on, and I'll send one of my sisters, Leya or Bayla, to help greet the customers."

"Greet? And who will do the real work? Anyway, Leya is too young. She doesn't know anything, and your mother will surely need Bayla to help out when you are gone."

Bronka pouted and sped up the treadle, making the sewing machine's whirr louder.

"Bayla's smart, you can teach her. You are a very good teacher, Bronka. Please do it for me. I'd do it for you."

At that, Bronka looked up. "Alright, but just a couple of weeks and you might as well check out the possibility of our families making *aliyah*."

The tension in Rifka's shoulders melted. She stood up from her machine and walked over to Bronka. "I can always count on you. That's what true friendship is all about," she said, her voice full of emotion. Then she bent down and hugged her friend.

Bronka looked up at Rifka with surprise. "You are not much of a hugger, but you are welcome."

"Given what's been going on here, believe me, Bronka, I have thought about emigrating a lot, but I'm not sure we'd be much safer there. I promise, I'll check, and I'll make sure *you* take a long vacation when I return. I'll even pay for you to go to the spa in Sopot."

"Oy, your imagination will get the better of you one day, Rifka, I swear. Just don't go looking for trouble in Palestine. I wouldn't know what to do if I had to run this place alone..." Bronka's eyes filled with tears.

"What do you take me for, a runaway?"

"I just know how you grab ideas with your teeth and don't let go."

Rifka returned to her machine and picked up the corset she'd been trying to finish. She felt happy to have Bronka's agreement, but as time went on the churn in her brain grew louder. Was her main goal really to find Golda, or was that just a convenient excuse to escape Poppa's attempts to arrange a marriage? Would Golda even appreciate being 'found'?

After work, Rifka went home to bring Momma money and break the news of her plan. When she told her, Momma's first words were, "God forbid! Suddenly, you want to be a hero?" After a few silent moments, she added, "I don't want to lose another daughter." She dabbed her eyes and a flood of tears followed.

Rifka realized there wasn't an argument on earth that would mollify her right now. "Bronka will bring you my share of earnings while I'm away. Trust me, I'll be back soon, you'll hardly notice I've been gone." Rifka left the room. She could not bear the pain she'd inflicted on her Momma. She felt a jolt of shame as the anticipation of a journey to a far-off land bubbled within her; finally, she'd taste real independence!

For two weeks now, Rifka had been stopping in Nudelman's office on her way to the shop. She was impatient to get her documents, buy train tickets, and get going. Each time she poked her head in his office door and asked, "Ready?" Nudelman said, "It's not as simple as you think. Not yet." But finally, he said yes and presented her with an envelope containing the prized papers. She slipped out the dark blue passport book and stroked its cover bearing a British royal crest adorned by a lion and unicorn, then opened it reverently—it was the first one she'd ever had—and right there next to her photo was her new name: Raquela Bluestone, handwritten in sharp sloping letters. She stared at it for a long time. It made her plan real. A shudder tingled her spine. "Why can't I use my own name? Who is this Raquela?" she blurted out.

"This is what I get as a thankyou?" Nudelman's face turned red.

She swallowed hard, "I am sorry, Mr. Nudelman, I didn't mean to be disrespectful."

Rifka felt a knot in her stomach; she should be thankful, but all the unknowns about the voyage that she had managed to squelch suddenly voiced themselves in her brain. How? Where? Who? She didn't even know her exact route. Would she need to travel through Germany? A shudder ran straight from her shoulders to her toes. Would a Jewish woman traveling alone be safe? "Will I have to go through... Germany?" she asked.

"Look, kid, you have a British passport. It should be alright if you don't slip up and forget your new name. Don't be frightened. You'll go to Paris first because we have one of our operatives there to assist people like you. From there, you will board a train to Naples and then the ship bound for Haifa. It may not be the most direct route, but it'll be safer."

"Such a long way..." she said quietly. Her mind swirled. She stood clutching the papers.

"I have work to do," Nudelman said and began shuffling papers on his desk, avoiding her gaze.

She gathered her things, still feeling unsettled despite Nudelman's assurances.

"Just keep one thing in mind; Raquela Bluestone is your real name now. Is that clear? Forget it and you can end up in prison... or worse."

"Yes," she replied, filled with trepidation. She walked out of his office slowly, contemplating his warning. For a few weeks, Rifka would cease to exist; she'd have to get comfortable in Raquela's shoes.

On her way home, Rifka diverted into Bracka Street and stopped by the Jablkowski Brothers department store. She'd never shopped there, but just this time she'd celebrate by allowing herself a bit of luxury. She looked at beautiful sturdy leather suitcases but decided on a small brown canvas and leather rucksack. She'd only be gone a couple of weeks; it would suffice. The purchase made the journey real; her heart and her pace quickened.

Rifka emerged out of the train station clutching tickets for the two legs of her 1,500-mile trip as if they were lottery winnings. She closed her eyes momentarily. This would be more than a journey; it would be her odyssey, make her feel more adult—if that was even possible—than when she started her business. The one hitch in her plan: how to find the contact who'd guide her to the clandestine ship? Sometimes one had to embark on a journey without all the answers neatly in hand. She rushed home to pack.

PART 2

PALESTINE

9 THE COUNT

Rifka arrived at Warsaw's Central station at nine in the morning, her hulking PKP train already on the track. The sweating, massive behemoth of a steam locomotive gave the trip ahead extra momentousness. She found her car, boarded, and found an empty compartment. Good, she could sleep. For now, she felt too bone-tired to think about the unknowns that lay ahead.

She pulled her book out of the rucksack, put it on the seat thinking she'd read for a while, then placed her single piece of luggage—if you could call a small rucksack luggage—on the shelf above the upholstered seat. It was deliciously quiet. She stretched across the four empty seats, moved the book under her head. Lousy pillow, but it would do. The train pulled out of the station with a whistle, and the rhythmic rocking movement put her promptly to sleep.

She awoke with a start, somewhat disoriented and tapped her chest to make sure that the documents tucked into her bra were still there. It was so kind and clever of Bronka to think of sewing special pockets inside the brassiere cups to hold the papers. You'll never lose them this way, she had said. Satisfied the papers were safe—false birth certificate and the British Mandatory passport—Rifka yawned and took in the compartment that she'd barely noticed on entering. She admired the shiny wood finish of the train car, the brass fittings, and the wide window through which the countryside flashed across like a movie.

Absentmindedly, she rubbed her fingers across the window sash, polished like glass, and looked outside, but the trees were just a green blur. The waning light meant soon it would be too dark to see out. A bite of bread might be nice; luckily, she'd packed half a loaf. She stood up to reach for the rucksack. It was gone!

Perhaps it had fallen and rolled under the seats. She bent down to look. Nothing but a stray dust ball! A wave of anxiety washed over her. She tapped her skirt pocket. A small bit of luck: a tight bundle of bills was still there. She'd put some of her money in the pocket for easy access. The rest was at the bottom of the rucksack along with Grandmother's silver locket.

She wasn't concerned about the lost clothes; they could be replaced but losing her grandmother's locket made her feel miserable. She put her face in her hands and issued a stern order: calm yourself, right now, or you'll never make it. She'd think of something.

She felt a rumble in her stomach. She hadn't eaten in hours. What to do? She stared through the window. A thick blackness, mirroring her mood, had descended since her discovery.

Suddenly, a tapping at the compartment door. Before she could respond, the door slid open. A tall man, clean-shaven, with striking eyes that reminded her of the sky on a summer day, asked courteously, "May I join you?" His Polish had an odd accent. Not a native Polish speaker, she decided. She judged him to be in his thirties and well-to-do by the look of his clothes.

"No need to ask if you have a ticket," Rifka said, heart pounding, uncomfortable at sitting alone in a closed compartment with a male stranger.

The man lifted his brown valise, stowed it overhead, and looked around. "Where is your luggage, young lady?" He sat down across from her, but not directly, closer to the door of the compartment.

She glanced down, noticing the sharp crease in his slacks, and matching two-toned brogues. Unwilling to show herself a victim, Rifka made a spur-of-the-moment decision not to mention the robbery. "Umm... I travel light," she said, rearranging her long skirt and sliding closer toward the window, away from where he chose to sit.

"I don't bite," he said.

Rifka was annoyed with herself. Had she given away her nervousness? She twiddled with her fingers, then opened the book that, luckily, had survived the robbery. Her stomach made cat-like noises she hoped were inaudible. The thought of hot soup kept creeping into her mind, making concentration on the book impossible. It was the highly regarded futuristic novel, *Insatiability*, that Bronka hated. The effort she made to avoid the man's gaze stressed her out so much she could barely absorb the words on the page and read the same paragraphs again and again.

Stealthily, she observed his facial features, and found them singularly regular and pleasing. A perfectly straight nose, narrow symmetrical eyebrows, and long eyelashes that gave him a sleepy look. Beneath a head of wavy light brown hair, high forehead, and a strong jaw with a bit of five o'clock shadow. An intelligent face, one that projected self-assurance. The handsomest man she'd ever seen, though in truth she didn't know many.

She wasn't sure how much time had passed since the stranger came into the compartment. Half an hour? An hour?

Now the man stood up and asked, "Would you like to join me for a bite in the dining car?"

Had he heard her stomach rumbling? Rifka was mortified. The offer sounded enticing, but she had never dined with a man before.

Who was he anyway? Maybe the very man who had stolen her rucksack. No, no, it couldn't be. His stylish, high-waisted tweed jacket with fashionably wide lapels suggested someone of means. But she couldn't be sure; crooks could be well dressed. Her hunger won out. Not knowing where the dining car was, or if the zlotys she had stowed in her pocket would suffice, Rifka decided to risk it.

He slid open the door gallantly. "After you," he said with a sweep of his arm.

They entered the dining car, she ahead, he right behind her, holding the door. No wonder the train tickets had almost exhausted her savings! In one glance, she could see this wasn't an ordinary train. The dining car was the most opulent space she'd ever seen. Red velvet settees, brocade-lined walls, crisp white damask tablecloths and oh, the china and crystal goblets!

Her unexpected companion pulled out a velvet upholstered chair and motioned for her to sit down. Rifka blushed, said, "I feel very awkward not knowing your name."

"How rude of me!" He extended his hand. "Count Aleksander

Zabielski," he said. His face broke into a smile that produced crinkles around his eyes.

A count! "Raquela Bluestone," she blurted her new name out loud for the first time, shook his hand quickly and immediately realized the brazenness of her action. One day out of her home and the prohibition on touching completely forgotten. And a new name too!

"Interesting name," he said.

Had she uttered her new name convincingly enough?

The count waved over the waiter, who handed them the menus ceremoniously. In silence, they perused the offerings, all quite unfamiliar to Rifka, though Raquela should have been more sophisticated.

Just the potato soup for me," she said. Soup was the cheapest item.

The count looked at her over the menu, "Good choice." Then he turned to the waiter, "Same for me."

"Yes, sir," the waiter said deferentially and hurried to the galley.

The count smiled broadly and filled Rifka's water glass from the crystal pitcher on the table. "Now tell me to where you are traveling, Mademoiselle Bluestone."

She was startled by his directness, but said, "Palestine, with a stop in Paris."

The count pursed his lips. A sharp train whistle broke the silence of the dining car. Raquela became aware of the other diners, an elderly couple and a well-dressed gentleman wearing a Sherlock-Holmes-style cape. The count looked at Rifka and followed her eyes. "Not too crowded," he said.

"No, sir, it is not. May I ask where you're traveling?"

He didn't reply, only studied her.

"Count Zabielski, sir," she said.

"Please, call me Aleks, no need for such formality," he said, grinning. "I am returning to my studio in Paris. I've been gone too long."

"Studio?"

"I am a sculptor."

Her eyes widened. "What kinds of sculptures do you create?"

"Oh, this and that. Mostly bronzes of female bodies."

She swallowed hard. "Well, we shan't talk about that."

The count, looking surprised by her emphatic response, was about to say something, but a tuxedo-jacketed waiter placed a silver soup tureen on the table, handing them linen napkins and wishing them *bon appetit.*

"What do you think of your recent elections?" she asked, hoping he'd take her seriously.

He raised his eyebrows, apparently surprised by her question. "Well, we elected Leon Blum as our Premier, a socialist and a Jew," he said matter-of-factly.

She couldn't gauge what he thought of it—could he be an antisemite?—but his face did not reveal distaste for the new Premier, somewhat allaying her anxiety.

The door at the far end of the car burst open, and a man entered, running, followed by another, then the portly conductor. Huffing and puffing, they ran straight through the car. Aleksander didn't appear to think about it, but leaped to his feet, pushed the conductor out of the way, and flew down the car in hot pursuit.

It was all so sudden Raquela could barely get her mind around what had happened. She could hear running, shouts, and then, a sudden silence. She looked around, baffled.

The gentleman in the cape spoke. "Dining with Count Aleksander?" He cleared his throat. "You'd better be careful."

An unwelcome shudder shot through her body. She stood up to leave, realized they hadn't paid, sat back down.

And Aleksander strode in, brushing his jacket off. The only sign of his involvement with the men who shattered the quiet of the train was a lock of hair mussed and hanging over his forehead. He smoothed it and sat down. "I am so sorry, Mademoiselle. It was impolite of me to sprint after those... ruffians."

"What did they do? Why were they running?"

"I had seen them loitering in front of your compartment earlier. They were looking for a mark."

"Wait, what did you call me?" Confused, Rifka blushed.

"What I meant was, trusting young ladies who think the best of people."

"So where are they now?"

"Don't worry, you won't be seeing them again."

Aleksander's response sent a chill through Rifka's body. Did he kill them? Throw them off the train? But the refined gentleman before her couldn't have done such a thing. Maybe the train guard dispatched them. Yes, that made more sense.

"Our soup is getting cold," the count said. "May I serve you?"

She nodded.

The count lifted the tureen cover and poured the soup into her bowl with a silver ladle carefully, avoiding leaving drips on the rim of the soup plate. They ate in silence for a while, but Rifka wanted the uncomfortable pause to end.

"How careless of me," the count said. "In all that excitement I forgot to order wine." With that, he motioned for the waiter who stood nearby at the ready. "A bottle of Chenin blanc," he said. "And a bucket of ice, please."

"Certainly, sir. Right away, sir," the waiter obliged.

Wine? Rifka was concerned. Would he expect her to drink with him? She'd only ever had sips of wine at Passover. They ate in silence. Every now and then Aleksander glanced toward the galley, no doubt looking for the waiter and the wine. By the time the waiter returned with the bottle and tray, holding an ice bucket and glasses, they had finished the soup.

Rifka imagined the count was accustomed to speedier service because of the look he gave the waiter.

"Bill, please," the count said, a barely noticeable note of irritation in his voice. He picked up the bottle of wine. Then he turned toward Raquela. "May I suggest, Mademoiselle, that we return to the compartment to relax now."

"I am terribly sorry for the disturbance and the delay, sir. The soup and wine are gratis," the waiter obliged.

The count nodded and took Rifka's hand as she stood up.

The compartment was still empty when they returned. They took seats opposite one another, albeit not as far apart.

"Tell me something about your family," Rifka said, feeling awkward about the silence. "And no need to call me Mademoiselle, you can just call me Raquela." She swallowed hard. She hadn't realized how difficult it would be to use a different name and made a mental note not to slip up.

He smiled, a radiant smile. "Hmm, my family... It's a long story," he began, looking so directly into her eyes she could see nothing dishonorable in them.

"We have plenty of time." She began to relax a little.

"I'll make it short. My grandfather, Count Zabielski, emigrated from Poland to Paris in 1899 with his only son, Jan. Four years later, Jan married my mother, Sophie Bloch, now Mme Zabielska. She was a Parisian beauty... still is," he corrected himself.

"So, wouldn't your mother be Countess Zabielska rather than Madame?"

Aleksander chuckled. "She doesn't like noble titles."

Rifka liked her already. And the name Bloch rang a bell. It was the name of a family in their synagogue.

"And what can you tell me about yourself?" Aleksander inquired.

"I love books. Books are my first love."

Aleksander smiled. "I don't do much reading in Polish; my Polish is just passable. But in French I do enjoy Marcel Proust and Emile Zola. Why don't you tell me about your book?" He pointed at *Insatiability* on the banquette.

She told him a little bit about it. He didn't dismiss it the way Bronka had. Instead, he asked questions and said, "The future is something that will soon be our present. We need to focus on it more than on the past."

She watched his symmetrical face as he spoke: perfectly shaped lips, even teeth, a deep cleft on his chin. Occasionally, she glanced down at his hands, strong and rough with rope-like veins, artist's hands. His eyes were intense, intelligent, and expressive; it seemed as if he listened not only with his ears but his eyes too. It was as if there was nothing else in the universe to think about except the words emanating from her mouth. No one, certainly never a man, had listened to her so attentively.

All along, she'd been wondering if she'd made a mistake not telling him she'd been robbed. He seemed respectable and understanding. He'd not take her for an ignoramus, not after the book discussion they'd had. But he must have read her mind. "I saw those bums loitering near your cabin. Did they steal anything?"

She lowered her eyes. "Yes, it's true. They took my bag with everything I had. I should not have fallen asleep."

"Sleeping is not a crime," he said, "How will you manage in Paris?"

She saw genuine concern in his direct gaze.

"I will have to send a cable to my business partner," Rifka mustered a response though she had no idea how, or where to get it done. Desperately, she didn't want to appear helpless and green.

"A businesswoman!" he whistled. "What kind of business?"

"Women's undergarments. My firm, Fit for Venus, is in Warsaw; perhaps you might have heard of it?" she asked playfully. Then a peal of laughter. "How silly of me, you are a man, of course you wouldn't know anything about such things."

He smiled and she thought he blushed, but it may have been the wine. "Your laughter sounds like bells," he said and poured another glass.

10 PARIS

The train pulled into the station at Gare du Nord early next morning. The night before, Rifka had agreed to have Aleksander take her to a small hotel where his friend was a proprietor.

Outside, Rifka squinted at the brightness, but didn't miss the hustle and bustle around her. Taxi drivers leaning on their horns, carriage drivers doing their best to outmaneuver them, horses neighing, newsboys yelling, passengers in a hurry dragging heavy suitcases and bundles—much like Warsaw, but somehow different.

Ahh... the smell of pastries from a nearby boulangerie. Paris at last! And those narrow-waisted women in dresses with padded shoulders, cheerful little Garbo slouch hats. She, a waif next to them, but she didn't care, she was accompanied by a count. If only Bronka could see her now.

Aleksander hailed a taxi that took them across the Seine to the left bank. She craned her neck as they crossed. So much to see: couples strolling the riverbank, artists lined up with their easels, boats, fruit vendors, even booksellers—everything she expected and so much more.

"Let's get out a bit before we reach Rue de Rennes and walk around so you can get the feel of this area," Aleksander suggested. With that, Rifka stuck her hand in her pocket fingering her small bundle of bills. She wanted to pay her share for the ride, but the count objected. "You are a guest in my city."

She blushed and said, "And you have a valise to carry. Won't it be too heavy for a stroll?"

"Not at all," he said, and she realized the suitcase would be a mere feather with his athletic build.

They walked several blocks. More car horns, hooves on cobblestones, chansons wafting from corner cafes, shoeshine boys, and cigarette vendors calling out their wares—all of it music to her ears. Aleksander pointed out statues, historic buildings, and churches along the way.

Rifka's eyes could hardly keep up. She looked up at a church spire, lost her balance, and tripped on a slick stone.

Aleksander grabbed her elbow gently, kept her from falling. "Thank goodness we have arrived; the hotel is almost next door," he said. "God forbid, if something happens to you, I won't forgive myself."

Shortly they entered Hotel Legende.

"Bienvenue, *Comte* Zabielski," the young receptionist welcomed Aleksander and looked toward Rifka, appraising her.

"Is Lionel here?" Aleksander asked.

"Of course, sir, I'll get him immediately." The clerk went into a back office.

Rifka looked around: ornate cabinets and velvet chairs with carved legs, an elaborate gold clock on a marble table.

Within moments, Aleksander's friend emerged sporting a huge grin. They hugged.

"Meet Mademoiselle Bluestone. I hope you'll take good care of her, old chap," Aleksander winked.

"Lionel Bisset, the proprietor," Aleksander introduced his friend to Rifka.

Rifka extended her hand and smiled.

"Your luggage, Mademoiselle?" Lionel asked.

She hated to explain. "It was stolen on the train," Rifka said in a barely audible voice.

"Promise me, Lionel, you'll offer Mademoiselle special rates given the... circumstances... and the fact she's a friend," Aleksander said with emphasis.

"But of course!"

"Well then, I have an urgent appointment. I must leave. Please, Lionel, explain to my friend where she can pick up a few necessities around here." With that, Aleksander promised Rifka he'd be back next morning.

———

Rifka watched Lionel as he studied a row of small wooden compartments behind the reception desk. She could see keys with tassels hanging out of some. Now that Aleksander had gone, she felt uneasy.

Lionel turned back and consulted a thick guest register then took out a key from one of the compartments. "I found the perfect room for you, Mademoiselle, come with me."

He led her up a wide curving polished stone staircase whose mahogany banister was too thick for her small hand to grasp. "I hope you will be happy staying with us," he said, opening the door to her room. "How many days will we have the pleasure of hosting you?" he asked as they stood at the threshold.

She didn't like the gleam in his dark eyes, and he stood so uncomfortably close to her she could smell his pomade.

"Just one... or two," she said almost curtly, not wanting to engage him in conversation.

He pointed to a local brochure. His tone stiffer now, he said, "It shows the area's shops. You can find your necessities nearby."

She thanked him and shut the door quickly. For a few moments, she stood in the middle of the space, not knowing what to do.

Though the room was small, it was quite enough for her. A tiny green velvet loveseat in the corner, a small writing desk, an ecru lampshade with small crystals around its rim and a bed dressed in crisp white linens. She'd never had a space of her own. She felt worldly. If only it weren't for just one night. She walked over to the window and looked down at the street pulsating with activity. Bicycles zig-zagged in and around the crowd; an artist with his beret askew hawked a canvas; a woman with a baguette under one arm walked her bulldog; a musician at the corner played a violin, and bystanders tossed coins in his hat. None of them seemed to have a care in the world. And cats everywhere, so many cats.

All of a sudden, the long train journey, the shock of the robbery, and a heady mix of Paris and Aleksander had their effect. A wave of exhaustion enveloped her. If she didn't venture out to buy a few things right away, she'd fall asleep. She splashed cold water on her face in the tiny bathroom and went out.

First, Rifka traipsed around the neighborhood looking for a bank to change her few zloty into francs. Luckily, *Banque de France* was nearby. She understood the kindly look on the bank clerk's face when she handed him her crumpled bills. She didn't care if he pitied her, she'd would not let it get to her. Around the corner she found a shop on a narrow side street where she bargained for a cheap rucksack, then trying to find a place to buy at least a toothbrush, ventured so far outside the area of the hotel she worried she'd be lost.

She returned to the hotel with some inexpensive underwear, a thin nightgown, basic toiletries, and a copy of *Le Figaro*. The little money she had was now down to just a few bills. Despite feeling overwhelmed by her dismal financial condition, she lay down and let the feeling of being on her own at last wash over her.

Laughter from the street below, excited voices and cars honking. So much life and freedom. She definitely belonged here. She picked up the paper, reading the headline about Leon Blum's reforms, but was too tired to focus.

Rifka closed her eyes, then suddenly bolted upright, and sat shivering, her feet anxiously rubbing the worn Persian runner. Who was this Aleksander and what were his intentions? Why had he bothered with her at all? The image of the stranger in the dining car and his ominous warning rang in her mind. She had no idea what to watch out for. She took a deep breath, reached for the carafe at the bedside, poured some water and drank greedily. A few minutes later, she fell fast asleep.

———

When Rifka walked down to the hotel lobby next morning, she could tell by his rambunctious laughter that true to his promise, Aleksander had, indeed, shown up. When he noticed her, Aleksander paused his conversation with Lionel, stood up, and flashed her a radiant smile. "You look refreshed this morning. You must have slept well."

"Nice to see you," Rifka replied, still enveloped in a haze of disbelief.

A half-dimple formed on his cheek, a small imperfection on his otherwise symmetrical face. It absolutely endeared him to her. His shower-damp wavy hair glistened, and Rifka thought again how extraordinarily handsome he looked. He filled the small hotel lobby with crackling energy. "Let me first take you for a quick bite, just like a real Parisian."

"Thank you." Rifka all but forgot the admonition from the stranger on the train.

They entered a boulangerie down the block. Rifka inhaled the aroma of fresh bread, vanilla, and sugar. She stood flabbergasted before the mouth-watering display of baguettes, croissants, tartines, various breads with raisins and assorted eye-popping pastries.

A portly baker behind the counter recognized Aleksander immediately. "Welcome, welcome, *Comte* Zabielski, I just pulled your favorites from the oven." A huge smile bloomed on his fat cheeks. The baker turned his gaze to Rifka. "Who is this emerald-eyed beauty with you? Watch out, young lady, the man is a heart thief." The baker chuckled.

"Now, now, don't burn any baguettes," Aleksander reproached the baker playfully then turned to Raquela. He pointed to a small white marble table near the window. "Why don't you have a seat, and I shall bring you some treats to taste."

She accepted his offer and sat looking out at the street kaleidoscope.

"Please, taste one of my favorites, croissants *aux amandes*." Aleksander placed a tray on the table: a plate of croissants and two white porcelain cups filled to the rim with steaming hot chocolate. She took a bite and felt Aleksander's eyes on her face. A heavenly taste of warm almond paste and powdered sugar melted on her tongue. She couldn't tell if she was in love with the pastries or the man who brought them. She'd never experienced such a heady feeling. Everything seemed bathed in a golden light, the customers in the bakery more elegant, the air lighter, the pink ranunculus in the little table vase brighter. It felt as if a magician had waved a wand transforming everything into its better version... even herself. "So delicious, thank you," she smiled.

Aleksander returned a satisfied grin. "Today, I can only show you a sliver of Paris. I have to get back to my studio to meet with a prospective client."

"Well, a sliver of Paris is better than a *croissant aux amandes*. And after that I shall manage by myself," she said cheerfully.

They hurried out of the boulangerie and headed north because

Aleksander said, "My appointment is on the other side of the Seine, so today I'd like to show you the most important plaza in Paris, Place de La Concorde."

Alright, who was she to argue with a count? And did he just imply he'd show her Paris the next day too? Her heart skipped. Rifka walked so lightly she might have floated if it weren't for gravity.

Before they reached the Seine, Aleksander pointed out a huge building, Musée de l'Armée. "There's no time to visit here today," he said. "The collection is huge. Maybe another time."

"What kind of a museum is this?" Rifka felt alarmed by the name.

"A marvelous collection of all things military: weapons, uniforms, old armor, even cannons, howitzers and mortars," he said, looking at her in a bemused way.

"Definitely not my cup of tea," she shook her head.

"I didn't take you for a pacifist."

"But trust me, I am," Rifka said earnestly. "The very thought of blood makes me ill. All those weapons of war only serve those who sell them. Certainly not everyday people... and not even the soldiers who end up dying... for nothing."

"Oh, la la! Didn't mean to step on your toe." Aleksander chucked.

"I am quite serious," Rifka said, then stopped herself from pursuing the subject.

Half an hour later, they reached the Seine. Neither the pictures she'd seen in books, nor her beloved French teacher's stories were a match for what she saw. Aleksander pointed out artists leaning toward their easels, absorbed in their creations. Just as generations of artists had been, Rifka was mesmerized by the images shimmering in the water: languid clouds floating with the current, upside-down roofs of grand buildings, reflections of Art Nouveau street lamps, tree branches and floating leaves.

"Look at his singular focus," Aleksander pointed toward an old man in a beret, standing motionless in front of his easel. "He is oblivious to everything around him."

She dared to disagree. "Not oblivious; he is responding to an inner voice driving his hands. Aren't you as focused on your sculptures?"

Aleksander nodded.

"We all respond to our inner voices," Rifka said quite seriously, still observing the painters at work.

"I'd like to know more about your inner voice." Aleksander moved closer to her.

For some reason, she thought he'd reach for her hand, but he just looked at her as if she were an object to be painted or sculpted.

"What a proper gentleman you are," she said.

He stepped back, looked at her and said, "You seem irritated."

She blushed and protested, "No, not at all."

"Well then, let's move on."

After a walk through the Tuileries, they emerged onto Place de la Concorde where two stunning fountains greeted Rifka. They caught her by more surprise than other landmarks.

"Did you know that a dozen sculptors worked on these two fountains?" Aleksander asked.

"No, how could I have known?"

Her own brusqueness surprised Rifka; she still felt a bit miffed. But it wasn't because of anything Aleksander had said. It was her annoyance with herself for wishing he'd been more physical, perhaps holding her hand, brushing an errant hair off her cheek, or looping his arm through hers. She was perfectly aware of the madness of this desire; it was strictly forbidden for a young woman of her upbringing. Maybe that was the reason she wanted it, craved it. Her unexpected response to Aleksander's attentiveness bewildered her. She'd never felt such surges of emotion.

"You *are* irritated," Aleksander chuckled. "Look, closer to the Seine, is the Maritime fountain and nearer to the Madeline church, the Fountain of the Rivers. Aren't they magnificent?" Aleksander gestured in each direction.

Rifka didn't reply. She stood agape, staring. The monumental women so spectacular in their half-nakedness took her breath away. "Did real women pose for these sculptors?"

Aleksander took her question very seriously. "Hard to know, but at the start of the nineteenth century, when these sculptures were made, nude female models weren't common. The few women who dared to pose were thought of more as prostitutes."

"I sculpt women too," she revealed suddenly.

Aleksander looked surprised. "You have withheld yourself from me, Raquela!"

"Never mind, look at those shells and corals, fruits and flowers," she pointed, feeling a little exposed. "Maybe one of these days I can visit your studio and see your work for myself," she said.

"Perhaps on your way back from the Levant."

Of course. What was she thinking? In a day, she'd be boarding the train bound for Naples. Had she already forgotten she'd embarked on a mission?

The afternoon crowds became thick in the plaza. Tourists crowded around the fountains, posed for photos.

Aleksander glanced at his watch. "I have so much more to show you, but now I must head back. This afternoon a client meeting at my studio and in the evening a meeting in a bar, no place for a lady."

With that, Aleksander left her in the square, suggesting she take a closer look at the Egyptian obelisk and hurried off. She was half-disturbed he hadn't invited her along, but a studio seemed like an unladylike place to end up in any case.

Rifka spent the rest of the day wandering the streets of Montparnasse, noticing people. A young woman at a corner café sat with a demitasse cup in one hand, a cigarette in another, sending smoke tendrils into the air. Well-coifed matrons rushed past her with Bon Marché and Printemps packages dangling off their arms. In a brasserie window, two men, wine glasses in hand, argued animatedly. A woman on a bench flipped through a newspaper while her small dog waited curled in her lap. Rifka sat next to her and rested because she could feel a blister forming on her heel.

She walked some more, watched a group of small boys skipping from school, teasing one another, so charming in their prissy uniforms: berets, smocks, short pants, and white knee-highs. Back along the Seine, she stopped to watch painters at work. The creative energy around them electrified the air, making her thirsty for art in all its incarnations.

At another sidewalk café, she noticed an intense young man writing in a notebook, ignoring the noise around him. Who knew? Maybe an author. When she next passed a stationery shop, she bought a pencil and a moleskin-bound journal similar to his. The rash purchase diminished her cash to a critical level, but at the moment it did not concern her.

So much joie de vivre in this city. What was it that made people and sights here different? It wasn't as if Warsaw didn't have a vibrant life; it was a capital after all, but here everything and everyone seemed more interesting. Perhaps it was she who was changing.

She felt hungry, but her money was almost down to nothing. Unable to resist an exquisite display in a pastry shop window, she walked in and made woozy by the scents bought a single chocolate macaron.

She was tired now and headed toward her hotel. On the way, she passed the oddly named Dingo Bar. Struck by the soulful sounds wafting from the open door, she entered. Immediately, Rifka noticed the atmosphere here was different. Two musicians—one playing a golden trumpet, the other, a piano—entertained a swarm of men at the bar. She'd never seen people with dark skin, or so many men drinking liquor!

The place was filled with men. She could tell by their height, their rowdy laughter, and the different language they spoke they were not French, probably American expatriates. She'd read that many American authors and artists flocked to Parisian bars. She wondered if any of them were famous.

But she'd been noticed. She became aware of all the eyes on her. Lascivious grins. Catcalls from the left and right. This was no place for a woman, she realized. Who did they assume she was? She slinked out. Suddenly she was gripped by intense loneliness, and the laughter that followed her made it worse.

She returned to the hotel in the dark, exhausted, and miserable. She wanted to flop into bed to sort out her jumbled feelings and thoughts— not the least of which was her dire financial state—but became aware of the big blister on her heel. If she ever traveled again, she'd need more sensible shoes. She wished she had a pin to break it, but since she had none, she washed her foot and patted it dry, hoping it would shrink overnight.

———

Next morning, Rifka decided to walk and think through her wretched financial situation. She had only a few francs left, not enough to waste on a cup of coffee. Without money, she'd have to find a way to contact Bronka or do something distasteful: ask Lionel at the hotel to extend her credit. She chewed her lip so hard it bled.

Yet despite her worry, she couldn't help being buoyed by the beautiful day. It was early. The sun shone brightly; the late March air was crisp. Not many pedestrians, just a woman with a baguette under her arm walking her puppy, sweet. She passed the same boulangerie where Aleksander had taken her the day before and hurried past it. What a magical day it had been; she'd felt freer than ever before. Paris had fallen into her lap, and now she had to give it up. This afternoon she'd been planning to see Aleksander one last time before boarding the Naples-bound train. She didn't want to leave.

Without warning, a man tapped her on the shoulder. "Excuse me."

She turned around, shocked to see the man from the train whose warnings had so alarmed her. "Raquela Bluestone?" he said. "I have some news for you."

Stunned, she exclaimed, "Are you following me?"

"Shh, let's not speak to the entire city." He took her arm and pulled her aside toward a nearby bench. "We need to talk. Let's sit here for a few minutes."

"I most certainly will not sit with you! Who are you? Leave me alone!"

The man leaned toward her. "I represent a Jewish organization; I'll be your guide to Palestine. You must follow my directions if you want to get there."

She just stared at him in disbelief. "But who are you?" she repeated.

"Sorry, I should have introduced myself. I am Uriel Rozenberg, but you can call me Uri. You can trust me. Nudelman, you know him—the big *macher* at the Jewish Agency—works with us; he asked me to take care of you. It's my job to get you to your ship in Naples." The man sounded serious.

So, this was what Morris Nudelman meant. She hadn't realized he was so influential. She looked at Uriel closely, noting his sunbaked craggy face, surprisingly appealing in its ruggedness now that she saw him up close.

His gaze was hard, but his demeanor, at least for the moment, gentle. "The problem is the vessel has been delayed," he said after a long pause.

"Delayed?"

Rifka's stomach lurched. It was too much information to absorb all at once. "I don't have enough money to hang around waiting. Isn't there another way?"

Uriel patted her shoulder in a gesture of consolation. "You'll get there. Trust me, just be patient." He handed her an envelope, stood up, and began walking away. Rifka noticed his broad shoulders, compact build, and energetic gait. His parting words, "I'll contact you when the vessel arrives in port."

"But wait, wait," Rifka called after him. "You don't know where I'm staying. How will you find me?"

Uriel turned around. "Don't worry. I found you, didn't I? He walked away briskly, leaving Rifka baffled at the turn of events so early in her journey.

She opened the envelope, hoping it had the man's contact information: crisp fifty-franc notes! Were they real? She took one out and inspected it closely. It was adorned with an angel on one side and a woman who resembled her sister Leya on the reverse. Then she counted the bills: 500 francs! A stranger had given her money; had this all been prearranged by Nudelman? But Nudelman had asked her for money, for her passport and papers. At the time she'd seen it as a simple business transaction, but now it was apparent there was more to it. For the moment, she felt relief. And she became aware of something else. The mere mention of Nudelman's name brought Uriel's warning on the train to the front of her brain. He knew people, probably all sorts of people. What exactly did he know about the count? She cautioned herself to be more careful and to stop thinking of herself as Rifka.

In her mind, she'd been clinging to her given name but knew it would cause a lot of trouble if she didn't let go of it. From this moment on she resolved not only to think of herself as Raquela. She would *be* Raquela. Rifka is dead, she thought with a twinge, at least for now.

It was almost noon when she realized she'd been sitting on the bench far too long. Her unexpected gift of extra time in Paris cheered her; she'd take advantage of serendipity. She stood up and headed straight toward the Luxembourg Gardens where she'd agreed to meet Aleksander.

11 PARIS: THE GIFT OF TIME

Raquela sat near the Statue de la Liberté, waiting. She saw Aleksander approach. It struck her how handsome and confident he looked. Beneath his open, double-breasted tan trench coat a stylish navy suit, a chocolate brown fedora jauntily cocked on his head, pure elegance, Hollywood style. There was a bounce in his step. Now she'd spring her news on him.

He saw her and speeded up with a huge grin. "I couldn't wait to get here."

"I have some news," she said.

"News, so soon?"

"My ship has been delayed in Naples. I have to wait here for a while."

His eyes lit up. He grabbed her hand and exclaimed, *"C'est génial!"* then twirled her right there, on the path, near two elderly women who sat on a bench smiling and watching them.

Her heart beat furiously. She could swear a warm electric current was fusing her hand to his.

"You are a lucky man," one of them called out. "Your girl is a beauty."

Aleksander tipped his hat, acknowledging the ladies.

"Let's go. Now that we don't have to part, let me take you to the most iconic spot in my city," he said.

"The Eiffel Tower?" she exclaimed. "I'd love it."

Aleksander hailed a cab. Even as they approached, she could see from a distance the blinking signs near the top advertising Citroën cars. The ascent in the lift made her dizzy. She'd never been at such an elevation. But she knew the height wasn't the real cause of her dizziness. Afterward, they stopped at the base to buy two postcards with images of the wondrous tower. She'd write Momma and Bronka a heartfelt apology for delaying her return by a few days.

When Aleksander inquired about how she'd spent the previous afternoon, she told him about her meanderings. "The thing that struck me most was the artistic energy wafting from every open door, window, and café." She decided not to mention the Dingo bar. Instead, she said, "I watched the painters by the river for a long time."

"Most of them are very poor, willing to sell their works for a few francs to buy a hot meal."

"Yes, but it doesn't seem to matter to them. There's a zest for life and a quest for truth glowing in their eyes," Raquela said.

"You are such an idealist!" Aleksander smiled and glanced at his watch. "Speaking of hot food, it's too early for dinner, but would you like some ice cream? We make it with egg custard, you'll love it."

Apparently, he'd noticed Raquela looking at a group of giggly girls licking their cones.

There was no question she was hungry, having been so careful with spending her measly change. "I'd love some," she said.

He bought two vanilla cones. They walked and talked so much Raquela's ice cream began to melt and drip down her jacket. She felt like a careless girl, yet giddy.

"What was I thinking?" Aleksander said. "We are gallivanting, instead of attending to serious matters," Aleksander pulled out a silk handkerchief square from his jacket pocket and handed it to her.

Embarrassed by her clumsiness, she dabbed at the drip. "What do you mean?" she asked, startled.

He laughed out loud, a deep belly laugh. "I haven't taken you shopping to replace what you lost."

"I already bought some essentials yesterday."

"Pshaw! Essentials? You need more than the basics."

"Well then, since I'll be here a few more days, why don't you take me to a flea market tomorrow. I've read that Paris has some great ones."

Aleksander looked appalled. "Let me take you somewhere special. *Une femme comme vous a besoin de quelque chose de mieux*," he exclaimed.

"But..." she began to protest.

Aleksander interrupted her with a twinkle in his eye and an index finger across his lips. He looked so excited she didn't want to snuff out the obvious pleasure this idea of shopping with her gave him. He turned toward her, winked, then pushed open the door in the storefront nearby with panache.

The shop was modest in size, but Rifka was struck by its elegance: a crystal chandelier, floor- to-ceiling beveled mirrors, richly upholstered settees, colorful floral arrangements, and a few mannequins sporting the latest fashions.

As soon as they walked in, the shop's manager, Madame Gagne, greeted Aleksander warmly, "Comte Zabielski? Are you here to meet Comtesse Zabielska?"

"Ahh... I didn't realize she was here."

"She's in the back, looking at our latest style books and fabrics. Shall I get her?"

"Yes," he muttered.

Moments later Countess Zabielska made an appearance. Now Raquela, awed by the woman's striking beauty—same deep blue eyes as Aleksander's, high cheekbones, flawless skin, and fashionable dress—felt self-conscious. A countess! The woman could have easily been mistaken for his sister, but she must have been, what? At least fifty!

"Aleksander, dear, what brings you here, to my sanctum sanctorum?" She smiled pleasantly, then hugged her son and pecked him on both cheeks.

"Mother, I want to introduce you to this wonderful girl," he pointed at Raquela who stood shyly a step behind him. Raquela hung back, so Aleksander took her hand and drew her forward. "Meet Mademoiselle Raquela Bluestone."

Raquela extended her hand. She had no idea what to say.

Luckily, Aleksander jumped in. "Raquela has come from Warsaw. She's on her way to Palestine. I wanted to gift her something stylish. I know you hold this shop in high esteem, Maman."

"I certainly do. But Warsaw, my birthplace. Goodness, you have made me nostalgic, dear," the countess said and smiled, revealing a pearly set of teeth. She turned toward Madame Gagne, "Please, show the young lady the newest styles, something suitable for a woman in the flower of youth."

Raquela's cheeks flushed as she listened to the woman's lilting tone.

"How about those suits with broad shoulders and narrow waists?" Aleksander suggested.

Raquela found his idea amusing. "To wear in the swamps of Palestine?" she quipped.

That brought out a lighthearted chuckle from the countess.

Aleksander looked confused. Chastened, he asked, "What then?"

"All of the fashions here are the latest. Perhaps Mademoiselle Bluestone would like to try on some blouses, or a sundress?" Countess Zabielska suggested. With that she excused herself graciously, "I must continue to peruse the fall fashion catalogs otherwise I shall have nothing to wear for the opera season."

Raquela watched her amble away, admiring the way she carried herself on her narrow ankles, tall and dignified as behooved nobility. "Alright, something simple..." Raquela finally consented.

"In that case, come with me to the fitting room," Madame Gagne said.

When they emerged with the winning selection, Aleksander insisted on paying for three smart blouses and a skirt. They walked out hand in hand, he, holding the box with her purchase, Raquela as happy as she'd ever been. Was Aleksander the man who'd save her from an arranged marriage? Until now, the notion of any marriage had been repugnant to her. She observed herself as if in an out-of-body experience. Who was this exultant young woman? She didn't know her... and she frightened her.

"Mother is a fashion hound. She bought this store and two others. I doubt she's satisfied, may buy yet another," Aleksander said.

Raquela didn't reply, but her mind raced. A working girl hobnobbing with nobles. It could bring nothing but trouble. And yet, Countess Zabielska shared her birthplace and owned a shop. She was ambitious. Perhaps they weren't completely different.

By evening, Paris took on a different glow. The light reflecting off the cobblestones, the distant strains of music, the smells wafting from the cafés, all of it inflamed her senses. Raquela walked alongside Aleksander as if in a dream. She became tired and slowed her pace.

He looked at his watch. "It's past nine, time for dinner. You must be ravenous."

She agreed.

"Why don't we have a something to eat at Brébant, it's typical French fare," he suggested.

"Alright, your choice," she said, and it dawned on her that she'd been entirely too acquiescing. That was exactly what the Raquela she didn't know would do, not the Rifka she'd been.

Brébant turned out to be a chic restaurant on the Champ-de-Mars side of the Eiffel Tower. The waiter here, like the baker and owner of the clothing shop, recognized Aleksander. *Bonsoir.* Welcome, Comte Zabielski!" he greeted him enthusiastically and led them to a discreet table near a huge window. "Your favorite view, isn't it?"

Aleksander nodded. He ordered *coq au vin*, a dish Raquela had never tasted. All she knew was boiled chicken served in soup on Fridays.

The waiter set the platter on the table and lifted the silver dome ceremoniously. Steam rose from the dish.

Raquela eyed the mushrooms around the meat swimming in a velvet sauce. She took the first bite cautiously. The unfamiliar flavor coated her mouth. "Mmm... it tastes savory with a touch of sweetness," she said. "What's in it?"

"Here they add a secret ingredient in addition to burgundy wine—cognac," Aleksander explained.

She'd never experienced anything like it! She took a few more bites, then she noticed Aleksander watching her. "Do you like it?"

"Yes, it's very tasty," she said.

Was he trying to seduce her with this meal? She set her utensils aside, lest she appear too eager.

"You've barely eaten any of it."

"I am not a big eater, but it's delicious."

The most interesting part of the dinner was their wide-ranging conversation. She found it easy to talk to him and, better yet, to listen to his rich, melodic baritone about anything and everything from art to literature or politics.

Raquela's gaze fell on the blinking Eiffel Tower lights. Awed, she said, "Such a magical display."

"You'd never think the tower was used to send signals to the troops during the great war. In the Battle of the Marne, it sent signals directing our men to the front lines."

Raquela frowned. Aleksander was still oblivious that war was the last thing she wanted to talk about. She'd never quite gotten over the pointless death of Paul Baumer, just before armistice, in *All Quiet on the Western Front*, a novel that had influenced her pacifist stance more than anything else. The spell broken, she said, "Yes, but didn't the Allies lose more than 100,000 men?"

"True, but we won," Aleksander replied, taken aback by the intensity of her response.

"Winning isn't everything," she said. "It can destroy your soul."

"But wouldn't you fight for something you truly cared about?"

"I've thought about it, but I don't think I would. Battles are so primitive... barbaric really... Soldiers are just pawns on a chess board." Raquela realized her voice had risen as a couple sitting nearby cast irritated glances in her direction.

"Alright, let's not dwell on war." Aleksander gave in, poured another glass of wine and changed the subject. He spoke of an international photography exposition at the Louvre that took place early that spring and captivated her with descriptions of his favorite images.

Raquela felt relieved. She had her artistic Aleksander back.

They returned to her hotel well past midnight. Neither wanted to break the magical spell of the evening, so they stood a long time in front of the ornate wooden entrance doors, unable to finish their conversation. She made the first move to walk inside, but he pulled her to him. She submitted to his embrace and gentle kisses on both cheeks, Parisian style.

He *is* a proper gentleman, she thought as she opened the heavy door and walked inside quickly. In her room, she undressed and opened her new journal seized by a yearning she couldn't articulate. Despite the late hour, she sat at the little desk and scribbled notes on every place she'd seen with Aleksander, exactly what he'd said and how it made her feel. Loud shouting from the street woke her. It was two in the morning; she'd fallen asleep at the desk.

Next morning, she awoke in a fog. A dream with Aleksander and another shadowy figure clung to her eyelids. It was oddly disturbing, though she couldn't recall any details, and the more she tried to wrest them from her brain, the farther away they slipped.

They had arranged to visit the Louvre together, and Aleksander was already waiting for her in the lobby. As soon as she saw him, the last troubling echo of her dream disappeared.

"*Bonjour*, you look stunning!" he exclaimed.

"It's just a simple blouse," she blushed.

"My point exactly: simplicity showcases your beauty."

Outside, he reached for her hand naturally, as if they'd been intimate for a long time. Just what she'd wished for! The warmth of his grip flooded her entire body. When they arrived at the Louvre, she stood awed by the sheer size of the complex, still holding his hand like a lifeline.

"Prior to the revolution, these treasures had been here only for the pleasure of royals. Today you'll be a royal," he smiled.

An image of her momma stooped over the sewing machine flashed before Raquela. Abruptly, she said, "I have no use for royals."

"Why so testy? Does my noble title offend you?" he asked.

"No, not at all. You've misunderstood," she said.

They walked through the entrance without further discussion.

"Let me show you my favorite ladies," Aleksander said when they reached the sculpture pavilion. He led her to the *Winged Victory of Samothrace.*

The headless woman, wrapped in a clingy, wind-blown fabric, made an overwhelming impression. "She looks so determined, as if nothing can stop her..." Raquela said.

"Not even a missing head," Aleksander joked.

They walked the crowded exhibit halls, skirting clumps of visitors. So many naked, perfect marble bodies and none resembling her customer's shapes, Raquela thought.

"Take a look at this goddess of love," Aleksander pointed out the armless *Venus de Milo.*

"She's so sensuous," Raquela whispered, made uncomfortable by all the nakedness. It flew in the face of her upbringing, yet she couldn't help but appreciate the beauty.

"Not a bad body for a 2,000-year-old lady," Aleksander quipped.

"Aleksander! What's the matter with you?" she said, then immediately chastised herself for being a prude.

"I'm just teasing. She represents Aphrodite, the goddess of love. The hand of a great master, Alexandros, rendered her to perfection."

"My goodness, he's your namesake," Raquela said. "It must mean you are a very fine sculptor too," she chuckled.

The last statue Aleksander showed Raquela was *The Psyche Revived by Cupid* by Antonio Canova. "There are no words to describe the tenderness between them." Raquela blinked trying to fight the forming tears.

"The story says she'd be awakened only by his kiss," Aleksander said.

"But who gave her the kiss of death? I don't know much about Greek gods... any gods, really."

"It was Proserpina who filled a flask with a dark potion. But don't think about that, look at the amazing rendering of the sheet's texture as compared to the rock. Masterful."

After the sculpture pavilion, they stopped for lunch and chatted about their impressions.

"Tell me about your sculptures," Raquela said. "Or better yet, invite me to see your studio."

"My work is very different, modernist, not classical at all. Very rough. I'm not sure you'd like it."

"Let me decide," she said, wondering about his studio. Was it full of nude sculptures? Was he eyeing her as a possible model? "Maybe I'll get to see it one of these days," she said out loud, though she hadn't intended to.

"I must finish a piece for the Tuileries exhibition coming up next month. Your presence would be too distracting. Next time you are in Paris, you'll see my work, I promise."

"An exhibition? So, you are famous!"

"Not quite," he said wistfully. "Maybe one day. And speaking of time, I need to return to the studio soon. Why don't I take you to Gare de Lyon where you said you needed to validate your tickets, then I shall leave you, albeit very unhappily, until tomorrow."

She agreed reluctantly, wishing for more time with him.

Outside the train station, Aleksander said he had a small errand to attend to and would meet her when she was done.

101

Raquela walked into the bustling station. The long queue at the ticket window frustrated her. These people were stealing her moments with Aleksander! There was no telling when she'd have to leave, or if she'd ever come back.

She looked for him when she hurried out. A pang of anxiety when she didn't see him, then his voice, like a salve on her nerves, "Raquela, Raquela, I'm here." She ran toward the bench where he sat with a package on his lap and joined him. He handed her the box in a most casual manner. "Here, a little something for you."

"It's not my birthday," she said, taking it from him, wanting to remember the moment, the precise angle of his head, his genuine smile, the whiteness of his teeth.

"You can take off the outside wrappings but promise me you won't open it until you get to Palestine."

Her eyes widened. "But why?"

"Just trust me, not now," he insisted.

She looked at him, not comprehending, tore open the wrappings and saw a train case in rich tooled brown leather. "It's exquisite. I've never seen anything like it," she turned it around, looking at the designs on all sides.

"We met on a train, so I thought it an appropriate souvenir."

"But Aleksander, I have hardly anything to put in it," she laughed and felt the warmth of blush reaching her ears.

"Just as well, another reason why you needn't open it yet," he said with a wink.

She felt her cheeks getting hot.

"When is your birthday, Raquela?"

"I might tell you when I get to know you better," she said, feeling giddy and uncharacteristically coquettish.

"But you know me already. I feel as if I've always known you." Aleksander touched her hand. The gentleness and warmth of his touch melted something inside her. She felt as if she stood on the edge of a high cliff in the Tatras, a stunning vista before her; below, turbulent waters swirling. If she wasn't careful, she might fall in. "How can I ever thank you?"

He pulled her close, so close she could no longer focus on his face. She closed her eyes and felt the warmth and pressure of his lips on hers. "That's how," he said, coming up for a breath.

Her head spun. Would she faint from pleasure—or dread that she'd unleashed something dangerous and unstoppable?

Aleksander said, "I am truly sorry, but I have to go, and there isn't any time now, but let's just peek inside the restaurant at the station. If you like it, we will stop there for a bite before you get on your train and leave me."

A bit peeved, she said, "It's not like that. I am not leaving you; I am going to find my sister." It occurred to her that she'd told him almost nothing about her family or life in Poland and that he hadn't asked. With that, she stood up resolutely, straightened her jacket, brushed the curls off her face, and picked up her train case.

Aleksander stood up too. "Now, now, I didn't mean to ruffle your feathers." He took her hand and they walked toward the restaurant. "I wish I had more time to show you all of my favorite Parisian places," Aleksander said.

"Maybe one day if you visit Warsaw, you'll allow me to show you my favorite places," she said.

They arrived at the entrance to the Buffet de la Gare de Lyon and stood in the doorway. Her head spun looking at the lavish interior, every inch an artwork. "Such a pedestrian name for a place so stunning," she said. The rococo mermaids, caryatids, gilded chandeliers, murals! The place looked more like a palace, not an eatery at a train station. She became aware of Aleksander watching her.

"So, do you like it?"

"Very much."

"Great. We will eat here next time," Aleksander said checking his watch. He planted a rousing kiss on her lips and rushed down the steps toward a taxi rank.

———

The minute he left, she felt lost. She stood in the vastness of the station, clutching the train case, completely unable to move. Passersby jostled her as if she were a boulder in a swiftly running stream. A policeman touched her shoulder, "Are you alright, Mademoiselle?"

Startled, she said, "Yes, yes, I am fine."

Thankfully, her heel blister had shrunk enough so she could walk and keep walking until she regained her composure. She meandered toward the Seine, at first not conscious of the direction, except vaguely aware that her hotel lay on the left bank. When the haze around her head lifted, she found herself on Boulevard Arago and kept walking.

She passed the Observatory Garden and turned to walk its broad, bench-lined path, all the while the image of Aleksander in her mind, the feel of his lips, the sensuous fragrance of his musky cedar cologne in her nostrils. Eventually, she arrived at a gate behind which stood an imposing two-story building with tall arched windows. The gate was closed.

Soon all of Paris would be closed to her. She couldn't stand not knowing how much more time she had here. Was there a way to plan her return from Palestine via Paris? No, that would be wrong. Bronka was waiting for her. She had to find a way to see him again. She sat on a bench for a while, thinking how the last few days had turned her world upside down.

After a while, Raquela strolled along Boulevard Arago to the hotel to record her impressions in the journal before their freshness faded. As she rounded a corner, an old musician leaned on a lamppost and played so passionately she threw a franc into his opened violin case. The rheumy-eyed violinist gave her a toothless smile. Her morning walk with Aleksander swept into her mind. He had thrown several bills into a hat of an accordion player and had said, "Anything to see you smile, Raquela."

"You are an incurable romantic," she recalled teasing him. "Just like a friend of mine."

"And you?" he'd grinned.

"Oh, I am quite curable," she'd kidded him, but now she realized how foolish she'd been. The way she felt now, it seemed impossible she'd ever be cured of him.

It began to rain, at first a thin drizzle, more like a fine mist, then the drops grew fat and bounced on the cobblestones, sending trash down the gutters along swollen rivulets. She bought an umbrella from a vendor under an archway and hurried.

———

When she arrived at the hotel, the deskman held out an envelope, "Hand-delivered, for you, Mademoiselle."

She took it from him and ran upstairs, tearing open the envelope as soon she was through the door.

"The ship is leaving Naples. Make your way by the 6:30 a.m. train tomorrow."

Though it wasn't entirely unexpected, the message overwhelmed her. Fewer than twelve hours in Paris left! Every fiber of her being resisted the abrupt ending.

She cursed Uri, resented him. She'd been walking with her head in the clouds, her heart wide open, and her feet above the ground. Now he was forcing her to end that state she'd never wanted or expected. She'd been rudely pulled down to earth and did not like the feeling at all.

There was nothing to do about it except calm down and remember the reason she'd left home: to find Golda. It occurred to her, guiltily, that she'd nearly forgotten the purpose of her trip. She blamed herself for falling under Aleksander's spell and nearly forgetting everyone and everything like a stupid schoolgirl, like something Bronka might have done.

She'd make herself feel better if she could record in her journal all the things she'd seen, from the painters at the riverbank, to Venus de Milo, to the rheumy-eyed violinist. She sat down and wrote and wrote and wrote until the pencil became so dull, she could no longer even scribble. She wished she had a sharpener, but it was too late now.

She'd have to wake up early to catch the Naples-bound train. There wouldn't be time to contact Aleksander, not that she had his address anyway, but perhaps she could mention it to his buddy, Lionel. Despite the late hour—nearly midnight—she tiptoed downstairs to see if the office was still open. The hotel was completely silent. The office was closed. The night watchman gave her an odd look.

She returned to the room wretched, packed up her things in the new rucksack, checked that her papers were secured in the secret brassiere pocket, then took a long bath.

She walked toward the window wrapped in a towel and shivering. The rain seemed to have stopped, and nocturnal revelry from the block below wafted into the room. This evening, unlike the others, it annoyed her, so, she closed the window, slipped on her nightie, and turned out the light. Soon she'd be seeing her sister, she consoled herself. Best to focus on their joyful reunion. Golda was sure to be surprised but thrilled to see her.

Calmed by an image of Golda's bemused welcoming smile, she fluffed the pillow and turned to her sleeping position, on her side, but thoughts of Aleksander, kept intruding. He'd hijacked her mind.

After a while, a knocking at the door woke her from a deep sleep. She lifted her head off the pillow, feeling disoriented. At first it was gentle, but soon the sound became louder and more insistent. "Who is it?" she asked, full of apprehension. She didn't know anyone in the hotel and had seen the night watchman shutter the entrance door when she went downstairs.

"It's me, Aleksander."

At first, she heard a voice just above a whisper, wasn't sure it was him. "What happened? Why are you here?"

"I want... to... to... come... come in."

The slurred words and high pitch made no sense. Was he intoxicated? She could not very well open the door in her thin nightgown. Her mind raced.

"Please, please... Ra... Ra... Raquela, I must see you now, right now." The urgency in his voice and the growing harshness of tone made him a different man from the one who'd introduced her to almond croissants.

"I am tired, maybe tomorrow," she said, stalling, but unable to fathom how he entered the locked building, her anxiety turned to panic. Her palms became sweaty, her temples pounded. An overwhelming nausea and anxiety flooded her. She didn't really know this man after all.

Aleksander became enraged. He growled curses and pounded the door. "Open up, now! Why are you treating me like this? Damn it!"

Then she remembered. He had been planning to meet a buyer of his work at the bar this evening. He was completely inebriated! An image of a Warsaw drunk lying on the sidewalk, spouting profanities, sprang to mind.

Uri's warning on the train came rushing back with frightening intensity. Yet somewhere deep within, a desire rose. What if she did let him in? Would he see her firm breasts through the gauzy nightgown and desire to touch them, perhaps later sculpt them? Gooseflesh covered her bare arms. Torn between yearning and fear, she felt disgusted with herself. "Go away. I am going to sleep," she said as resolutely as she could muster, pulled up her covers and lay shivering, hoping for the banging to subside.

Eventually—how long was it?—it seemed like eons—she heard footsteps receding down the stairs.

Her guts churned. She tossed and turned on the bed as if it were filled with gravel. For a long time, she lay dismayed with his behavior and with herself too, trying to convince herself she'd done the right thing. A bothersome thought pushed through all the rationalizations: she should have trusted him, opened the door, and taken a chance. She punched at the pillow until exhaustion knocked her out.

12 NAPLES

The hands of the clock on the imposing tower at Gare de Lyon clicked to six. Raquela hurried, still thinking of the night before. When she passed the Buffet restaurant, she thought, if we dined here today, no one would mistake us for lovers. They'd pity me for being with a shameless drunk. It comforted her to think of him that way, helped rationalize her refusal to let him in.

Five minutes to departure! She'd miss the train if she didn't stop moping. She ran. Her bag, overstuffed with clothing Aleksander had bought, hung off her shoulder, bumping into people moving past her on the crowded platform. Pushing her way past a group of students, she nudged a burly traveler with the train case. "*Merde!*" he said, furious.

"Pardon," she said.

Why was she even carrying this useless thing?

The old coal engine on the track hissed, sounding angry. She wished she had a way to let off steam like that. Seventeen hours to Naples! How would she manage to evade the memory of the previous night?

She climbed aboard the train with only moments to spare and entered the nearest compartment. It was empty. She intended to catch up on sleep, hoping that with good rest her last night in Paris might not seem as confusing.

This time she'd be more careful and use her overstuffed bag as a pillow. She laid it on the long, upholstered seat and shoved the train case far under it. She didn't want to be reminded of him. She hung her jacket on the hook by the window, took her shawl out of the bag, wrapped it around her shoulders, and lay down.

Now she'd have plenty of time to think and rethink the events of the days before, to beat herself up for being an inexperienced prude and someone unfit for the worldly pleasures of Paris.

Damn that *shomer negiah* rule! Now she could not forgive herself for stubbornly refusing to open the door to Aleksander. It was childish. She knew exactly what Poppa would think of all this; she could see the blood vessel close to bursting, pulsating on his temple.

For a while, she listened to travelers walking up and down the corridor, closing doors, the train's whistle, the calls by the conductor. If only she could sleep, she'd forget the man who had been possessed by a dybbuk last night.

She woke up after some time and glanced at her watch. She must have fallen asleep after all. It was almost noon. She sat up, dug the brush out of her bag, brushed her hair and smoothed her skirt. Where exactly was she now? Looking out the window, all she saw were fields. The sharp train whistle told her that shortly they'd be arriving at a station. Soon a sign came into view: Saint Etienne. Raquela coaxed her brain to bring up the map of her route. She must be somewhere in central France, still hours until Naples. She felt hungry and out of sorts. She was too distracted to read.

Her heel brushed something hard under the seat. The train case! The stupid thing was still there to taunt her. She pulled it onto her lap and stared at the fancy tooled design. She ran her fingers absentmindedly over the incised flower pattern. After a while, the devil tempted her to open it. Silly, she thought; it was brand new, and she still hadn't put anything in it.

She lifted the brass latch. It opened with a small pop. An envelope lay at the bottom of the case. She closed her eyes and tried to make her mind go blank. Here she was, miles away from family, and she hadn't given them more than a moment's thought. How did she become so callous, so wrapped up in this man, this stranger whose intentions were now in doubt?

Her face was wet. She was glad no one saw her in this state. She lifted the envelope from the train case. A tear dripped on it. Wanting desperately to pull herself together, she wiped her eyes with her fists and tore the envelope open. The note, probably scribbled hastily while he waited for her, was nevertheless neat, the letters uniform in size and leaning to the right at the same precise angles.

My dear Raquela,

Forgive me for being so forward, but I couldn't help myself when I spotted this travel case. I knew you had been relieved of your rucksack by the thieves and thought you might like a proper carryall for your personal items. I have to be totally truthful with you. I've often been called a ladies' man by my parents, a cad and a womanizer by my friends. It may have been true until my eyes beheld you. Immediately, I could see you were an extraordinary woman, courageous and a free spirit. You have captured my heart. I haven't met anyone like you, and I want to know you better.

 Enclosed is a small sum to help you on your forward journey. Don't worry about repayment. I am lucky in that I have no concerns about money, but if I have some measure of you already, I know you'd say I shouldn't have done it. It was only my concern for your well-being. Forgive me if I have caused an offense. If ever you feel compelled to repay me, it'll be entirely your choice.

 I miss you already and you are still at the ticket counter.

Respectfully yours, Aleksander

Raquela's hands shook; her heart pounded so hard she heard blood pulsing in her ears. Yet some part of her glowed. Now that she was on the way to such a remote land with no prospect of returning to Paris, she didn't know what to think or how to quiet her mind. What if he wasn't drunk and simply ill? What if someone—Uriel?—tipped him off she had to leave in haste, and he wanted to say goodbye? She was angry with herself for her fearful, immature response. She might never see him again. She wished there were travel companions in her car, anything to keep her from thinking of Aleksander.

The train rolled on with a steady clatter. After a long while, Raquela folded Aleksander's note carefully and pushed it deep into her skirt pocket. She pulled out a twenty-franc note and placed it in her pocket, tucking the rest of the bills into her brassiere. She didn't have the nerve to count them, not yet.

Her stomach growled. She stood up, stretched, and made her way to the dining car. It was more crowded than her first dining car experience. It was lunchtime, and the waiters scurried around busily, navigating nimbly between the tables. She admired how they carried the large silver trays, apparently not bothered by the swaying of the train.

She chose a discreetly placed corner table for two so she could dine alone, undisturbed. A large, heavy menu lay on the table. She scanned it, but her mind was elsewhere. She decided on Croque Madame nearly at random, even knowing it was not kosher. How easily one transgression led to another! She was so engrossed in her thoughts; she hadn't noticed someone sitting down at her table. When the man lowered the tall menu, she gasped. Uriel sat directly opposite her! "Mr. Rozenberg!" she exclaimed, remembering his name.

"Calm down," he answered kindly in a steady, low voice. "Call me Uri."

"Are you following me?" The man made her extremely uncomfortable.

"I am sorry. I didn't mean to frighten you. I'm here to make sure you get to your destination."

Uri smiled broadly. The warmth of it made him look somewhat friendlier. He had a chameleon-like persona, one moment menacing, another approachable.

She decided to ask him the question that had been niggling at her. "Why did you warn me about Count Aleksander? Do you know him?"

Uriel grimaced. "Not something I care to discuss, not here anyway," he said. "But yes, I know him." He changed the subject. "I think you'll actually be glad I am traveling with you," Uriel said.

Raquela's heart pounded. "You, traveling with me? Indeed!"

He leaned close and whispered, "Have you forgotten already? I will lead you onto the clandestine ship bound for Haifa. Without me, you might end up roaming the streets of Napoli on your own. Good luck with that," he chuckled.

"Hmm..." Raquela swallowed hard.

Uri sniggered. "You thought you'd sail into Palestine just like that?"

"Why not? I paid for passage."

Uri looked around to see if anyone was listening, then he leaned over toward Raquela. "There are a few things you need to know. Firstly, to answer your question, the British don't want us there. Second, you only paid for your train tickets. You can thank the Jewish Agency for funding the sea passage."

"Jewish Agency?" A vague recollection of hearing about it from Golda came to mind. Maybe they had paid for her passage as well.

The waiter arrived with her meal and placed it before her.

She eyed the slice of ham suspiciously.

"And what about Monsieur? Will you be ordering anything?"

"No, thank you." Uriel seemed ready to leave her at last.

The waiter moved on.

Uriel looked around, waited until a couple near them left their table, then said to Raquela, "I don't much care what you think of me, but when we get off this train in Naples, stick close. Watch out for the police and don't lose me in the crowd."

Great, now it was she who had to follow him. Raquela gulped.

Uri stood up.

She wasn't sure if she wanted him to stay or go.

"You are not the only one. I have to keep track of the others," he said and walked out of the dining car. Others? Were there more people on this train traveling to Palestine? And who exactly was Uri that he was in charge? The journey was proving to be as mysterious as her destination.

Raquela picked at her food, left most of it uneaten. She motioned to the waiter for the bill, paid and walked down the long corridor toward her cabin. She noticed Uri in one of the compartments with several passengers, but she passed it quickly, didn't want to stare.

With many more hours of travel ahead, Raquela needed a distraction. She sat for a while trying to think of how she'd follow Uri in Naples, close as not to lose him, yet not so close he'd get the wrong idea. But her mind couldn't stay still. Suddenly, she could have sworn she heard Aleksander's voice. Her hand found its way to her pocket where she'd stashed the envelope. Slowly, incapable of resisting the urge, she unfolded the paper and read then reread the note, gliding her eyes slowly over some of the words: "... extraordinary woman," "... captured my heart." She blushed though there was no one there.

Her thought was interrupted by a train on a track across from theirs, rushing in the opposite direction. She heard the sound of brakes, then sparks in bright orange arcs flew from beneath the wheels. A trail of smoke from the engine wafted into the sky, mixing with the clouds. It was a pretty sight, but disturbing. What if the dry grasses beyond the tracks caught these sparks?

After a time, the motion of the train lulled Raquela into a dream. A slam of one of the compartment doors woke her. She was covered in sweat and dug in her pocket for a handkerchief to wipe her brow. The dream clung to her mind, though she tried to banish it. She hoped it did not presage bad news. In the dream, her momma and sisters became engulfed in a fire that consumed the buildings on her block. She returned from her shop to find the charred remains and couldn't stop scolding herself for having been away. In the dream, she sat on a curb and wept. Thank goodness for the noise. If she hadn't been wakened, she might have died of the pain of loss. She got up and stepped out into the long corridor to find the restroom and wash her face with cold water.

It was already dark when the train pulled into the Napoli Centrale station. Raquela felt the train slowing down and gathered her belongings as the station came into view. She had to find Uriel and quickly.

Travelers spilled out of every compartment, filling the narrow train corridor with bodies, overstuffed suitcases, and bundles of every shape. Everyone looked impatient to get off. Raquela craned her neck, trying to catch a glimpse of Uriel, but she was too short to see over the heads of the men in front of her.

What if he had already gotten off? Terrified, she rushed back into an empty adjacent compartment and looked out the window, checking the platform. Here the crowds were worse. Porters rolled stacked luggage carts, dispersing people in all directions. She didn't spot Uriel and walked back out to the corridor only to find it even more packed. Panic filled her.

She stepped off the train, stopping every few steps to look around, desperately trying to spot a man in a Sherlock Holmes cape—that was her only marker. Not seeing him, she flowed with the crowds toward the exit. Outside, groups of ragamuffins accosted travelers for change. She walked back into the station, found a toilet, and moved the money from her pocket to her shoe. The rest remained secured in her sweaty bra.

The area around Piazza Garibaldi teemed with vehicular and pedestrian activity. A bewildering number of narrow streets radiated from the plaza. Raquela had no idea where to turn. Men leaning against buildings, smoking, eyed her, whispered words she didn't understand. She approached a grizzled woman selling trinkets and asked her for the direction of the port, but the woman simply shrugged her shoulders. Desperate, Raquela repeated *port de mer* several times, and it must have finally dawned on the woman what she meant. The woman pointed the direction and said, *"Non andare a Spaccanapoli,"* shaking her head energetically. It seemed like a warning, but Raquela did not understand its meaning.

She'd lost Uri. For a moment, she stood frozen with fear, but when she noticed a gaggle of rowdy men approaching, she moved ahead purposefully. She rounded the corner to get away from them and there, to her enormous relief, a group of people with small bundles followed Uriel like a row of geese. Raquela breathed a sigh of relief. She'd never been so grateful for a man in an odd cape as now.

He turned when he heard her call his name. "If that's the best you can do, there'll be trouble ahead."

All she could say was, "Sorry."

The women parted ranks and pulled her in. They walked a long distance to a remote jetty in silence.

13 STILL WAITING

Bronka walked the ten blocks from her home to the shop on Marszalkowska briskly. This year's June days were exceptionally warm; Bronka yearned for some breeze. She felt sweat patches forming under her arms, always a dreadful concern, but more so when she had to face customers.

Before opening the shop, Bronka checked the mailbox in the back corridor. Still empty. Weeks had passed since Rifka had embarked on the mission to find Golda, but there had been only one postcard from Paris. No letter, no message sent with someone returning from Palestine. The worry about her friend had consumed Bronka for a while, but now something akin to deep annoyance crept in, albeit mixed with genuine concern.

Just like Rifka—always pushing the limits—to leave her here all alone to mind the business. And Leya, who was supposed to help, turned out to be useless. She stuck her fingers under the needle and messed up a silk brassiere with blood on her very first try! So, what that Rifka left patterns and notes on customers? There were so many orders! Bronka's initial secret pleasure of being in charge evaporated under the crush of work. Perhaps she shouldn't complain because business had been decent, but she desperately needed at least another pair of experienced hands. Leya turned out to be only good for grunt work, always having to leave early to help her mother.

It was getting late. The rush-hour crowds on Marshalkowska had thinned. Lights began to glow in the buildings across from Fit for Venus. A tall, skinny client with perfect posture and piercing dark eyes, Mrs. Stern, walked into the shop.

"Hello, anyone here?" she called out.

"I'll be right with you," Bronka responded from the back, closing the account book she'd been working on. She emerged, apron in hand. "I'm just about to close."

Mrs. Stern said, "I know it's late, but I'd like to pick up my brassieres. I won't take too much of your time. I'm rushing to my Bund meeting."

"A meeting? Sounds interesting. I've never been to one," Bronka said.

"I'd be happy to sponsor you if you'd like to come next time I go," Mrs. Stern replied with a charming, crooked smile, the only feature of hers that was irregular.

"Well, I'm just being silly. I have plenty to do with my time."

Bronka felt ashamed. She didn't know much about meetings, organizations, or politics. She only knew she didn't care about them.

"The Jewish Labor Bund is very welcoming to women. Women's rights are part of our political platform. Really, you should come," Mrs. Stern smiled. "We don't talk politics all the time we have fun too. And you should call me Zvia. We, Bundists, aren't formal. We have no use for honorifics."

Bronka had no idea what to say. She didn't even know what 'platform' meant. She'd smiled and said, "You are very kind, Zvia. Let me think about it and check my schedule." Immediately Bronka felt clever for thinking up an excuse.

"I hope you'll consider my offer," Zvia said, picking up her order.

After she left, Bronka rushed to close. She had no patience for yet another straggler. She swept the shop, got it more or less presentable, pulled down the metal safety door and locked up.

Bronka arrived home bone tired. And all that smiling at clients left her cross. The muscles of her jaw felt tight. She was sick of customers asking after Rifka, hoping Rifka would be back soon: "I need her to do my fitting, you know my figure isn't easy to work with," Mrs. Lisowska had said more than once, meaning the woman was hugely overweight and only Rifka knew how to fit a corset that would do a credible job flattening out the bulges without displacing the fat elsewhere.

At home, the kitchen sink was filled with dried-up dirty dishes. Again! Mendl sat at the table, bobbing up and down over the Torah, pretending to study. Bronka pushed his chair as she passed it and threw her jacket on the worn easy chair that used to be Poppa's. Mendl pretended not to notice.

Her younger siblings' squabbling coming from the back bedroom got on Bronka's nerves. They fought over everything; the brothers pulled the sisters' hair, the girls schemed how to get them in trouble. Havoc all evening. Momma took it all in calmly, but it reminded Bronka of Poppa's absence. Why did he have to die even before seeing them grow up? She might have asked this question of God, but she had little belief in him, and after Father died so suddenly, falling on the street as if struck by lightning, her faith had dwindled to nothing.

Bronka pushed up her sleeves and stood at the sink, scrubbing a pot with baked-on cholent. She wished Momma had at least filled it with water to soften the baked-on potatoes and beans. Her knuckles were getting red, the hands chapped. She couldn't afford to have the hands of a washerwoman. Her clients would be appalled. Suddenly she became sharply aware that she'd begun thinking of them as *her* clients. The notion pleased her. No more feeling like a subordinate. How long would Rifka keep her as the drudge?

Bronka felt her face flush. Embarrassed by such thoughts, she threw the dishtowel on the kitchen table instead of hanging it to dry on the hook. Tired, she sat down for a while, fully aware that in a few minutes she'd have to attend to yet another chore. She had to find something to do other than the shop and dishes.

"Bronka! Where are you? Help me thread the bobbin on the sewing machine. My eyes aren't as good as they used to be!" Momma's call interrupted her thoughts.

Bronka slumped to the bedroom as if her feet were stuck in tar. "How long did you think I'd wait?" Momma was annoyed. "I have to finish these embroidered handkerchiefs by the week's end before the factory will give me another order."

After her brothers and sisters fell asleep, a delicious hush finally descended over the household. Bronka sat at the kitchen table, sipping the last of her tea, trying to recall all of the next day's appointments. It was a relief not to hear the constant whirring of the sewing machine, Mendl's muttering, and her siblings' warfare. The only sounds now came from outside, someone dragging trash cans, stray cats mewling their amorous serenades, and the neighing of horses pulling the carriages of those who had the luxury of late-night assignations.

By this hour, Momma was usually fast asleep, emitting her familiar gentle snores and whistle-like sounds, but Bronka heard slippers shuffling in the bedroom. "Momma, are you up?"

"Wait, I'm getting my robe. I'm coming to speak with you."

Bronka's heart sank. She was in no mood for a chat, not at this hour. And frankly, these days, a talk with Momma at any hour wouldn't be pleasant. Bronka was well aware of her mother's anger at Rifka's abandonment of the shop. Hinda walked in slowly, dragging the slippers across the linoleum floor and sat heavily in the kitchen chair.

She looked Bronka over. "My poor, poor girl," she said looking directly into Bronka's eyes. "Dear daughter..." she continued.

Bronka felt alarmed. Momma was never so formal. She looked at her mother and for the first time in a long time saw her. Hinda had big puffy bags under her eyes, her hair was thinning, and her shoulders were so stooped that a small hump had formed at the back of her neck.

"What is it? Why are you up so late, Momma?"

"Well... it's money. I want to talk to you about money, my dear daughter."

"I don't know what you are thinking, Momma."

"I was thinking. Thinking keeps me from sleeping. In the daytime, I have no time to think."

"Just say what's on your mind. It's very late."

"Well, you do all the work now; Rifka has been gone for weeks! And while she is exploring the world, you take money to her mother. We sure could use that money."

Bronka blanched. She spit, "Momma, how could you?"

"I am just telling the truth. You are blind to it, Bronka. That girl is pulling the wool over your eyes even when she's not here."

"Her mother is a widow with ten mouths to feed. She needs the money as much as we do!"

"Widow? When did Hershel Berg pass away?"

"It happened shortly after Rifka left. He was kicked by a horse. The poor man fell and never regained consciousness. Mrs. Berg had no way to contact Rifka, so she missed the funeral and the shiva."

"That is appalling. That girl has no decency. The sooner you drop her, the better off we will be."

"Momma! Don't forget, Rifka is my best friend. I'll never do anything to betray her."

"Ach... you are such a child." Hinda waved her hand in disgust and rose from the chair. "You'll never learn. You are just like your father; may his memory be blessed."

"Momma, have you forgotten? Rifka is the one whose money paid for the shop, for the sewing machines and supplies, and it was her connections that brought us the first customers. She owes her grandmother a lot of money."

"*Bist a groyse naar*, you are a big fool," Hinda said and walked out without acknowledging her daughter or turning back.

Soon her snores restored the order.

14 SHIPBOARD

The SS Atzmaut engine quit suddenly, making the vessel roll, waking Raquela. All she could hear in the eerie quiet were the breathing sounds and snores of her cabinmates. Her body felt stiff from the hard mattress of her berth. The coarse wool blanket made her skin itch unbearably.

She tried to remain still though she badly needed to relieve herself. She didn't want to wake the three other women. Uri had said they'd be arriving in Palestine today, but the ship appeared to have stalled. She hoped it wasn't engine trouble. Raquela's nerves tensed with each passing minute. We have come this far, please, let's not have a disaster now, she prayed silently though she'd long given up asking God for anything.

Uri had told her the British patrolled the waters constantly and stopped any ship carrying illegal immigrants. He said two years before, the SS *Vallos* had made exactly this perilous journey toward Haifa and its 350 passengers had managed to make it to shore, but other ships had been stopped and their passengers arrested. Raquela hoped this captain was lucky in evading the British. Everyone who had boarded the ship in Naples knew well that arrival in the ancient land was not assured.

Gradually, Raquela's cabin mates began to wake and take turns in the minuscule head, dressing and chatting in hushed tones. The two Russian sisters, Chaya, and Mara had decided on making *aliyah* after their parents died. Raquela judged them to be thirtyish and provincial by their dresses and old-fashioned shoes.

"Good morning," Mara broke the awkward silence. "We are going to kibbutz Degania. Where are the rest of you going?"

At first there was no response so Raquela jumped in, "Where is this Degania?"

"It's on the shore of the Sea of Galilee and the Jordan River," Chaya chimed in.

Raquela closed her eyes trying to imagine it. "Those names sound so exotic; almost mythical," she blurted out and felt her face flush. It was a stupid comment.

Mara laughed. "Yes, they're quite real. If only we can keep the snakes, scorpions and mosquitoes at bay."

Menucha, a heavy-set woman with a thick braid crowning her head, the oldest of the women in the cabin, said, "I am going to meet my daughter in Jaffa. I have never seen my grandson."

"What about you?" Chaya pointed at Raquela.

"Me?" Raquela hesitated. "I am not sure yet. I have to find my sister, but I don't know where she lives."

Chaya and Mara looked at one another in disbelief. "How will you find her if you don't know where she is? Palestine is a big place."

"I will figure it out once I get there," Raquela replied, but the question stirred her unease.

"You mean *if* you get there," Menucha said, shrugging her shoulders.

Raquela wished the women would stop talking. She'd have to ask Uri. He seemed to know a lot about Palestine.

Low voices and shuffling footsteps on deck interrupted the women's conversation. They couldn't make out what was going on. Hearing a knocking on the cabin door, Menucha opened it and Uri stepped into the cramped space.

Raquela barely recognized him. He had transformed overnight into a younger, more vital version of himself. Dressed in khakis, no cape, he was a different man, erect and robust, firearm in a holster at his side.

"Get ready," he said, urgently. "I will be coming to get you as soon as the rowboats get here."

"Rowboats!"

"It will be all right," Uri reassured them and walked out.

The tension and exhaustion overwhelmed Raquela. She'd never

been in any situation like this, not even remotely. Much to her own surprise, she began to sob. She didn't know how to swim. What if the waves inundated the rowboat? Would she die, and no one ever know? "My... my sister. I have to find her." She could barely catch her breath between the sobs.

Menucha moved over toward Raquela and put her arm over her shoulders, hugging her close. "It won't be easy, but you'll be fine. This ship can't take the risk of reaching the shore. They will smuggle us, a few at a time, in the dark. The rowboats are quiet and can slip through unnoticed. Well, most of the time."

Raquela couldn't calm herself. The combined stress of everything that had happened since she left home hit her like thunder.

"Here, child," Menucha handed Raquela a handkerchief. "Wipe your eyes."

"I am not a child," Raquela burbled as she wiped the snot oozing out her nose. "I am not that emotional usually; I just don't know what's come over me."

"You are not the only one nervous here," Mara said and patted Raquela's hand.

After what seemed like a long time, they heard loud popping sounds.

"Shots?" ventured Chaya.

"The British might be very near," Mara whispered, her eyes wide with fright. After a while it was quiet. The women sat in silence, exchanging terrified glances, unable to see what was going on.

We are helpless here, Raquela thought. If she had to die, she'd rather be with her family, not here with strangers.

A furtive knock at the cabin door. Before they responded, Uri snuck in. The women began to clamor for answers, but he signaled silence with a finger to his lips then addressed them in a low voice. "I am taking a few at a time on deck. Be ready when the first rowboats arrive. You come first," he pointed at Raquela.

"Why me?"

"Just do what I say. And as there may be room for one more, you come up too." He pointed at Menucha.

"No, I'm not ready. Please, take one of the younger sisters," she said visibly distressed.

"Too much fussing. Who is coming with Raquela?" Uri's voice grew stern.

"Take the two sisters, I'll go on the next boat," Raquela volunteered.

"No! You are coming now. The British have stepped up their patrols. If you ever want to set foot in Palestine, you'll do what I say."

"You go," Chaya said to Mara.

Mara hesitated, but her sister urged, "Go, go now, I'll meet you on shore. It's fine."

Raquela looked at the sisters. Despite the calm in her voice, Chaya was on the verge of tears. Raquela picked up her bag and train case, but Uri gave her a withering look. "Leave this damn box. Whatever it is, it isn't coming with you."

Uri guided Raquela and Mara up the narrow, circular staircase ending at the deck. Raquela couldn't get Uri's new image out of her head.

On deck, Raquela's eyes swept the churning waters of the Mediterranean. A cold easterly wind gusted fiercely across the swells. A few distant stars illuminated the rough waters, but it was dark, the darkest night she'd ever seen. She pulled her shawl tighter and checked her glowing watch: well past two in the morning. The slapping of the waves against the hull of the ship added to her unease. Every now and then distant British searchlights swept the waters. Her breath quickened. What if they were spotted?

Uri led them toward the others who were to share the first rowboat. One of them was an old, frail man. Raquela could not fathom how he could manage the boat in the dark, sneaking onto shore. Their chosen companions stood in silence. Several other small groups huddled quietly nearby.

At the horizon, water and sky merged into an inky curtain. Raquela kept scanning it, terrified a British ship might emerge out of the blackness at any moment. She stared so hard into the darkness her mind conjured shadows that became vessels that weren't there.

Uri paced up and down the deck, illuminating the water with a small flashlight for seconds at a time, looking for the rowboats. Each time he lit up the water, she held her breath and prayed for him to turn it off quickly.

Soon, something bumped the side of the ship. Raquela gave a start, her heart beating like a trapped bird. Uri leaned over the railing and gesticulated to someone below. The moment had come. Uri approached Raquela first; she hardly had time to react. Expertly, he slipped a harness over her. She was about to say it was too tight, but he hushed her with a hiss, tossed a rope ladder down the side of the ship, and lifted her overboard, gripping her waist, as if she were weightless. "Be careful; the rungs are slippery. Hold on tight as you descend. It'll be all right, I'm holding on to the harness."

She squeezed her eyes shut in terror. Frightened enough to scream, Raquela held her tongue as she dangled over the ocean, primeval dread filling her lungs. Her foot found the first rung. She held the rope between the rungs so tightly it burned her hands. The swaying unbalanced her, so her foot, searching for the second rung, slipped off, waving about blindly. Against her will, Raquela glanced down and saw herself descending into the depths, the black waves just waiting to swallow her.

Two men balanced on the swaying boat, their arms lifted, waiting to catch her. They grasped her without a word, put her down gently, and slipped off the harness. Raquela was too startled by what had just transpired to say anything. All she could hear was the blood pumping in her ears and the sloshing of the water.

Only when she looked up and saw Mara being lowered did she feel a small measure of relief. They'd make it. The others waited their turn patiently on deck.

"Yalla!" The taller of the two men in the boat said sharply to the other as soon as the older man came down the ladder. He breathed so hard Raquela was concerned he'd have a heart attack; her mind swirled in fear and confusion. The boat's undulating movements made her more nauseous. Suddenly, the boatmen lowered the oars into the water, and the boat lurched forward. They dipped the oars in and out of the waves in synchronized rhythmic movements and quickly left the ship behind. Soon swells of sea water sloshed in the bottom of the rowboat and soaked Raquela's shoes and much of her skirt. She began counting to quiet her fear, just as she'd done as a little girl. Randomly she picked a number: 200. They'd get to shore as she reached it.

The passengers squatted on their haunches, too shell-shocked to converse. Two rowboats appeared out of the darkness, gliding toward the ship. Good, maybe they can pick up Chaya and Menucha. Out of the blue, Raquela squeezed Mara's hand, startling the woman, and whispered, "It'll be all right. I think your sister and Menucha will get on the next rowboat."

She continued counting. When she passed 300, she realized she was shivering. No, no, this was the Promised Land; bad things weren't supposed to happen here. But every time she glanced at the water, intense nausea threatened to spill her churning guts.

The boat must have bumped a sand bar. Abruptly, the boatmen stopped their rowing, waved their arms, called *"Yalla, yalla,"* into the darkness.

Raquela took the offered hand, clambered out into shallow water, and waded a short distance toward the lights on shore. Her bag hung limply off her shoulder, soaked. She held her shoes in one hand, Mara's hand tightly in the other as they propped up one another. The waves made her skirt billow out. The cold water was up to her waist. She stepped unsteadily over slippery rocks.

A small contingent of rescuers waited on shore. A young woman approached wearing slacks and a khaki shirt similar to Uriel's. A rifle hung off her shoulder. "I am Sara," she said brusquely, then a brief welcome in Yiddish and another in Hebrew. "Soon as the next rowboat arrives, we move to Kfar Vitkin. People? Are you listening? Be ready to move out!"

Other women greeted the arrivals with blankets and hot coffee. As soon as one of them wrapped a blanket around her, Raquela realized just how cold she was. She drank the bitter warm liquid greedily. A chill wind sweeping from the water went through her bones, making her teeth chatter. Sand, as fine-grained as sugar, coated her wet legs and palms and stuck to her skirt. She reached for more coffee. Before her, a stretch of inky water, occasionally interrupted by flashes of neon on the waves and rescuers busily dispensing succor; behind her, dark mounds of sand.

"Drink this quickly; we have to get you over the dunes. The truck is waiting," the woman serving coffee said with urgency in her voice, then refilled Raquela's cup. "Sometimes the British stop the rowboats, or board the ship and take everyone back to Cyprus."

Raquela gulped the coffee, breathed, inhaled the salty air. She was finally here, in the Holy Land! Suddenly, she noticed bursts of light in the distance.

"British flares," Sara muttered.

Then there were engine sounds, voices shouting, and pops like shots.

Young men with rifles slung over their shoulders appeared. "Stay calm," they said. "And quiet." And finally, "This way, toward the dune."

Raquela turned back and noticed men readying more rowboats, dragging them close to the shore. "For the next contingent," the young woman who doled out the coffee explained.

Sara and another woman, also equipped with a rifle, guided the group up the sand dunes, leaving a few others to wait for the next set of arrivals. The climb was difficult. Stress and fear made Raquela's legs leaden; the coffee had little effect. The sand-laden skirt weighed her down. The grit in her wet shoes rubbed her skin raw, and her feet kept sinking into the sand. Whenever she could, she grabbed a sagebrush branch to hoist herself up.

With every few steps she turned back to see that Mara was still behind her. The sky lightened. Raquela could see Mara's terrified eyes. She stopped at one point, wanting to tell her not to lose hope, but Sara, now standing at the top of the dune, called out, "No stopping. Hurry."

When they arrived at the road, a wiry, dark-haired driver hopped out of the first of four waiting trucks. He saluted Sara and the other woman. He, too, was armed. "Quickly, quickly, get in!" He motioned the group into the truck. Sara and the other woman kept a lookout for Arabs. Everyone got the message: danger lay ahead.

It wasn't until they were on the road that Sara began to relax. "Okay, my beauties," she said. "We are going to a moshav. That's a communal farming village. You'll be able to get a shower, dry your clothes, and eat some warm soup."

A chatter of relief swept through the group.

15   THE PROMISED LAND

The first thing you smelled in Kfar Vitkin was manure.

"Don't crinkle your nose," Mara said, and the first half-smile formed on her face.

"I have never been near cows," Raquela said, yawning, turning her head all around.

By now the sun had risen, and she could finally get her first glimpse of the Promised Land. The darkness, nausea and fear of the voyage had been replaced with blinding light, palm trees and hope: they hadn't been caught.

Waiting for instructions, Raquela noticed several wooden barracks and, behind them, rows of tents. Nearby, crude wire fencing surrounded plots of ground with plantings. Unfamiliar with the countryside, she couldn't tell what grew there. Snow-white chickens with scarlet combs pecked energetically at the ground; skinny cats traipsed all over the place.

Once everyone got off the truck, Sara led them inside one of the barracks that turned out to be a dining hall filled with rough-hewn tables and long communal benches.

"You'll find some used dry clothes over there; there won't be enough for all of you, and what there is may be the wrong size. It's the best we can do." She pointed to the rear of the barrack toward a table piled with neat stacks. "Take whatever you need, then proceed to the showers and come back here when you are done. You'll get something to eat." She distributed bags for the wet clothing and cautioned everyone to shower quickly. "Water is more precious than gold here," she emphasized.

The shower stalls, just behind the dining barrack, turned out to be nothing but a row of spigots outside with soap holders fastened precariously to the water pipes by wire. The women's section was separated from the men's by a sun-bleached wooden partition. Raquela shed her wet clothes and massed them in a small pathetic pile on the ground nearby. Her nakedness shamed her. She'd never disrobed before anyone, not Bronka, not her sisters, not even her mother. Yet here she was with Mara and a bunch of other women, all naked as the day they were born.

She turned on the water. A sparse, cold spray sputtered out. She washed the sand off quickly, avoiding looking at the other women, rinsed the sand out of her shoes, and pulled on the dry donated clothing. Then, she collected her wet stuff, placing it in the bag Sara provided, being careful to first pull out her documents and money and tuck them back into her damp bra.

When Mara was dressed, the two walked along a gravel path back toward the dining barrack, passing a pair of speckled chickens with impressive crests and a large, ghostly gray dog with menacing blue eyes. The dog followed too close for comfort and sniffed at Raquela's legs. Not being used to pets, she sped up.

They entered a crudely constructed, dimly lit dining hall. Huge sooty pots, pans and buckets hung on rusty nails along the long walls. Spoons clattered against metal bowls, and trays stacked in a pile near a huge sink looked ready to topple. A multilingual cacophony of conversations assaulted Raquela's ears. Women in long white aprons, wearing hairnets or scarves, served hot soup and bread to the arrivals.

Raquela and Mara sat next to one another at the end of a bench. The newness of the environment was overwhelming; neither spoke.

A stout woman with a pot approached and ladled in the soup. She smiled and said, "We don't have much, but we are happy to share."

Raquela swallowed her vegetable soup greedily and wiped the bottom of her bowl with her last piece of dense, yeasty bread. Judging by the slurping sounds, her fellow travelers appreciated the hospitality as well.

After the meal, Sarah strode in, banged pans together, announced some trouble with the British, but gave no details. "We will know more in the morning and share it with you before training."

One of the Russian women who had been on the boat with them called out, "What kind of training?"

"You'll soon see," Sara said. "You've all been through a rough voyage, I realize that, but now you are safe. Get some rest. You will be very busy tomorrow."

Training? Raquela, still in a state of astonishment that she'd arrived safely hadn't given any thought to what would happen next. She was exhausted. Fear and tension seemed to have erased everything in her brain. All she wanted to do now was to sleep.

Raquela awoke to voices. It was a first for her, starting the day in a tent. She rolled up the fabric flap serving as a window. And with that, everything was bathed in yellow light. Brilliant sunshine, stronger than she'd ever seen or felt, made her squint.

"Still tired?" Uri poked his head into the tent, grinning and startling Raquela. "Get ready, we have arms training this morning. See you in fifteen minutes in front of the long barrack next to the dining hall."

His sudden announcement left Raquela dumbfounded. No way, I am not doing any such training! She'd have to find a way to avoid it. She understood the danger, but had not considered, even for a moment, that she'd be involved in any defensive activity. That was a necessity for settlers who *chose* to live here. She was only a transient.

"Look, Uriel made it off the ship! We will see Chaya and Menucha soon," Mara said excitedly sporting a wide smile.

Raquela noticed how pretty she looked with the burden lifted. "I thought all you settlers were here to learn how to work the land," Raquela said.

"I thought so too," Mara said. "No one ever mentioned arms training."

"Well... there are Arab marauders, Mara. I suppose someone has to protect the land."

"That first night on the ship when we had the briefing, Uri said the settlers bought this land from the Arabs. Jews own it now," Mara reminded Raquela.

"Don't you get it, Mara? We aren't wanted here, or anywhere." Raquela thought of the assault on her shop.

She washed her face hastily in a basin perched on a chair in the corner while Mara waited her turn, brushing her hair. Raquela pulled on the blue skirt she'd fished out of the pile the day before. She shook the sand out of her own now dry but dirty skirt, unrolled it, and pulled out Aleksander's letter from the pocket. It was damp and crumpled. She smoothed it as best she could, folded it carefully and placed it in the pocket of the hand-me-down skirt.

Soon they met a motley cluster of others who must have arrived after Raquela's group. In contrast to the grayness of the group on the ship, these people—dressed in donated clothes from the pile—resembled an assortment of wildflowers. Now they formed a platoon of more than three dozen. After surveying the newer arrivals, it became painfully clear Menucha, and Chaya were not among them.

As soon as she noticed their absence, Mara's eyes filled with tears. Raquela felt wretched. If Uri hadn't insisted, she go first, Chaya could have been here with her sister. Why did he insist Raquela go first?

Before the arms training session began, Uri arrived and addressed the group. "We have had a setback. A number of people were intercepted and deported. The SS *Atzmaut* was impounded."

"No!" Mara called out. "Where are they?"

"Sent back to Cyprus by the British."

Raquela gasped then clamped her hand on her mouth. She had to remain calm, if only for Mara's sake.

"What will happen to them?" Mara asked.

"They'll remain in an internment camp, and we will do our best to liberate them."

"Are these camps like prisons?" A woman in the group called out visibly agitated.

"Not exactly, but I'll be honest, they are no picnic. The conditions there are harsh," Uri said.

"So when will you get them out?" Raquela spoke out. Her voice sounded small and tremulous.

"When we become our own country," Uriel responded with such

130

strong determination that Raquela believed him, or rather wanted to and hoped that Mara and the others believed it too.

———————

Sara led the weapons demonstration and distributed the machines they'd learn how to use and clean: bolt action rifles, semiautomatic pistols, and the lone, rusty-looking infantry mortar. The pacifist stand Raquela had been cultivating made it more sickening to contemplate participating in this activity. She brightened when Sara said in response to those who complained they hadn't gotten a weapon, "The weapon and ammunition supply is short. You must share and if you find yourself in a bad situation without weapons, remember, you still have your fists and your wits."

Despite her deep discomfort and iron determination not to take part in the training, Raquela was impressed with the take-charge attitude of this small, wiry woman with tight black curls and a determined mouth. She had such a composed and efficient air about her. "Who is she?" Raquela whispered to a man standing nearby.

"She is a *sabra* and our local Haganah commander," he replied matter-of-factly. "Once you learn how and when to use these arms, you'll have to teach it to the youth of the village. We train everyone," he said. "By the way, my name is Ben. Sara is my cousin. My parents came from Berlin when it was obvious that Jews weren't wanted there."

"I hear the Arabs don't want us here either," Raquela stated the obvious.

"Well, we will show them..." Ben said.

"Ben, can I ask you for a favor?"

"What kind of favor?" Ben looked wary.

"Could you ask your cousin if I could do something else, be excused from the weapons work? I am a pacifist, can't imagine killing anyone, not even an Arab marauder. I'm here to find my sister."

Ben's eyes crossed. "Are you crazy? The British and the Arabs will slaughter us if we can't fight. Cut the crap and listen to the instructions, woman!"

Luckily, Uri interrupted the exchange. "We need a few volunteers to dig irrigation trenches around recently planted orange groves nearby."

Raquela's hand shot up first. This time, she'd get to skip the weapons training.

Most newcomers followed their respective leaders to shooting practice. A small group headed toward the orchard. Raquela hung back, hoping to catch Uri privately—he seemed to be one of the people obviously in charge here—to find out where she might begin her search for Golda.

She sat on a large rock, gathering her thoughts. By now, the sun was high in the cloudless sky, whitewashing the barracks. A single palm, nearby, cast a scant shadow. She felt hot; drops of perspiration covered her forehead.

Chickens crisscrossed the path, and the area, so filled with voices and commands moments ago, fell eerily silent. Raquela recognized Uri from some distance by his confident gait. The rifle on his shoulder seemed somewhat reassuring, given the morning's lecture, though it conflicted with her own feelings about violence. She called out to him when he came nearer.

He recognized her and smiled, his white teeth contrasting starkly with his tanned, stubbled face. "You have a question written on your face," he said, motioning for them to move into the shade.

"I need advice from an experienced man like you on how to find my sister."

Uri looked surprised. "I thought you wanted to be a pioneer, work the land, make it bloom one day. Now you want to be detective?"

"Seriously, Uri, we haven't heard from my sister in months. My mother in Warsaw is worried sick, and so am I. That's the main reason I came. I didn't come to settle the land. I'm sorry if that was not understood, but nobody asked me. Will you help me? I have her old address here in Palestine. Maybe that's a starting point."

"Well, if she's made *aliyah*, we move around a lot, get sick a lot." He paused, took a pack of Woodbines from his pocket, lit one, took a long drag and said, "Many get killed or die of malaria."

Raquela's eyes filled. She pressed the back of her fists to her eyes to stanch the tears. This was not a place to bawl. She hated herself for showing such an excess of emotion.

Uri put his arm around her shoulders.

She was shocked at this familiar gesture but didn't dare offend him; she'd be depending on him.

"Look, I'll do what I can. Tomorrow we are heading toward Jaffa. If your sister Golda is not much of a farm girl, she may be in the Tel Aviv area. Let's see."

"But going all the way to Jaffa, for me?"

"Don't flatter yourself; we make the trip weekly to get supplies."

No matter his brusqueness, Raquela felt satisfied. How could she have so misjudged this man? Now, thanks to him, her quest would begin in earnest.

"You've missed your group leader. Let me take you to the orange orchard; you won't find the way yourself," Uri offered. "We need all the help we can get."

So did she. Raquela returned Uri's offer with a genuine smile.

16 JAFFA

On her second day in Palestine, Raquela became even more acutely aware of how different the place was: scorching sun, moisture-laden air that didn't let her armpits dry, and—worst of all—a constant anxiety about snipers. All of it added to her unease about Golda's whereabouts. Maybe Jaffa would provide the answer.

After breakfast, Mara went to her arms training session, and Raquela met Uri and Sara on a long stretch of road behind the dining hall. She climbed into the back seat of Uri's beat-up sedan; Sara would be riding shotgun. A truck from Kfar Vitkin with a half-dozen armed men would follow them.

Under normal circumstances, the thirty-mile trip from Kfar Vitkin to Jaffa might have been pleasant. Raquela had never seen the sea in Poland. For her, seeing stretches of pristine beaches, gently swaying palms and the azure waters of the Mediterranean Sea should have been enchanting. But as they bumped along a deeply rutted coastal road with clouds of dust kicked up by vehicles in front and behind them, it was hard to feel anything but anxiety. Paris and Warsaw now seemed farther than the moon.

At the dining hall breakfast, Uri and Sara had spoken of how the entire community was still in a state of shock since the Arab revolt kicked off in April. Until then, they'd been coexisting in relative peace.

"They were the ones who started it!" Uri had said with a sardonic laugh. "Somehow we thought we could live peacefully side by side."

The situation confused Raquela. She said, "But you bought this land from the Arabs and now they want it back?"

"Money isn't the same as land," Uri replied, shaking his head.

The bouncing and swaying of the vehicle made Raquela regret she'd eaten salad for breakfast. Even the food here was strange. She felt nauseous. Uri and Sara seemed sullen. Still, Raquela wanted to talk. "So, tell me about the Arab revolt," she asked Sara.

Sara craned her head toward the back seat. "Six weeks ago, our drivers, Israel and Zvi, were killed leading a convoy of trucks."

"Was it an accident?"

"No, it was the Arabs," Sara said, clearly irritated, glowering pointedly.

"Don't worry, we will get the bastards," Uri spoke up.

Sara said, "They must have learned about the shipment that came in last fall."

Raquela wanted to know more. "What kind of shipment?"

Sara was too annoyed to reply.

"Arms for the Haganah," Uri responded.

Haganah, there was that word again. It was good Ben had mentioned the Haganah was a military organization and that both Sara and Uri were its commanders. She felt foolish for asking.

As the sedan rolled on, Sara must have gotten over her irritation because she continued to speak about the politics of conflict with the Arabs. And Raquela listened, trying not to miss a word. Sara said Amin al-Husseini, the Grand Mufti of Jerusalem—an avowed hater of Jews—did everything to foment rebellion, even getting support from Mussolini. Raquela was awed by Sara's knowledge and became acutely aware of her own naivete. She hadn't been involved in politics back home, though she'd read a lot and was interested. Both Jews and Arabs cradled such a deep belief in the rightness of ownership to this miserable land. How would this fight end?

When the conversation died down, Raquela stopped asking questions, not wanting to highlight her ignorance. She began paying more attention to the road. Every few miles she saw old Arabs in traditional garb walking alongside donkeys laden with bulging sacks or huge baskets. How different they looked in their long robes and *keffiyehs*

—checkered headdresses held in place by black cords—from the Jewish pioneers in their khaki shorts and small-brimmed cotton hats. No wonder these people had a different world view. Yet some of the Arabs looked friendly. Fellahin in *galabiehs*, simple cotton robes, paused at their plows and waved at the passing vehicles, shouting, "*Salam Alaikum.*"

"What are they saying?"

"Peace be unto you," Sara replied.

Uri snickered. "Just don't go looking under their robes. You might find a grenade."

Then it was quiet. Hot wind blew through the open windows; Raquela closed her eyes, still not sufficiently rested from the sea journey. How far had she come from her shop. The thought brought Bronka with such force. She had left her friend alone to do all the work. And who knew for how long? Now it didn't seem fair. And what about Momma and her sisters?

Even Paris—her dreamlike interlude—seemed remote and unreal. There, people lingered in cafés and strolled along the Seine; here people struggled to eke crops out of parched soil, practiced using guns and listened for intruders. How could it all be happening at the same time, in the same world? It struck her that what she had thought of as one world was really a collection of kaleidoscopic slices of the planet, one more different than the next. She wished they'd get to their destination already; she didn't want all this time to just think.

The vehicle stopped suddenly, jerking Raquela forward. Her bag fell to the floor scattering the contents. "What?" she asked.

Uri shushed her. "Didn't you hear the shots? They are distant, but we have hearing like bats, always on the lookout for snipers."

Raquela sank into her seat and said nothing. There was nothing to say; she'd gotten herself into this situation. She picked up the fallen items.

Sara navigated. "Uri, get off the main road. Let's take the back alleys."

"We have to get to Jaffa before dark, but it will take much more time. You know this area better than I, so guide me."

It impressed Raquela that Sara was treated with such respect. Despite the rough conditions, women were valued here.

Uri maneuvered the car skillfully over rough terrain, swerving sharply every now and then to avoid ditches and ruts on dusty back roads and alleys. The moshav trucks followed close behind. Uri and Sara remained silent, concentrating, and Raquela's anxiety increased. Small beads of sweat formed at her temples. She couldn't tell if it was heat or fear of impending attack.

As their vehicle rolled past the village of Ra'anana, a volley of shots pierced the silence. This time even a deaf person could hear them. A few yards into the settlement, the shots died down, but in the center, bodies lay scattered near the well.

"Damn that bastard al-Husseini!" Uri mumbled under his breath and scrambled out of the car.

Raquela rolled down the window; she could hear the injured man nearest the car moaning for help.

Sara reached back for a first aid bag. Now she, too, clambered out and ran toward the grisly scene. Both she and Uri tended the wounded. The trucks caught up moments later. Men jumped out like lightning; weapons drawn.

Uri shouted commands. "Spread out, look for the bastards, protect the perimeter."

Raquela remained in the car in a state of shock, hands shielding her eyes. When she mustered the courage to look, she saw blood oozing from wounds of men moaning in pain. Some lay silent, staring skyward with limbs in odd positions. Maybe they were already dead.

Sara tended the wounded efficiently, moving briskly from one to another. Raquela just sat terrified, sobbing. Uri and two of the men lifted the dead and carried them to a nearby shelter. It was Friday; according to Jewish tradition, they'd have to be buried before sundown. Her mind conjured the sound of spades hitting parched soil, mothers and wives wailing, their cries drowned out by more shelling. Their bodies would still be warm, she thought, horrified; it made her physically sick. She opened the car door and threw up violently.

She dug in her bag for a handkerchief, wiped her mouth, then closed the door and slunk down on the seat. At a sudden new burst of gunfire, she sat up and saw Uri collapse, watched him going down in slow motion. Uri! Sardonic, capable, knowing Uri. How could this be happening? Her chest tightened, her hands shook; she was too paralyzed with fear to think of helping, not that she would know what to do anyway.

Sara ran toward Uri and bent over him. After putting something in his mouth, she stripped off his shirt. He sat up and she wrapped a bandage on his upper arm. Raquela was dizzy with relief.

Just then, one of their men emerged from behind the shelter building. "I got them. *Kinim*," he spat out. Lice.

Raquela knew the word from the Passover service. That told her more about the Jewish-Arab conflict than any conversation.

Hearing the attackers had been neutralized, Uri stood up slowly and put his shirt back on. Sara tried to take his arm, but he brushed her off and hurried toward the sedan.

"You continue here, deal with the families. We have to move on," he shouted to his men. "Meet Sara at seven in the morning at the warehouse, you know, the usual one. I have other business to attend."

Sara looked at Uri's pale face and insisted she'd drive, but Uri said, "Nonsense, it's a small wound." And he revved the engine. After a while, Raquela could see that Uri's injury wasn't so minor; blood oozed though the bandage and down his shirt sleeve. She feared for his life and even more so, for hers. What had she gotten herself into? One day in Palestine and already this?

How had her sister managed in this land of constant danger? In her mind, Golda was happily tending the land, but she realized what a foolish vision that had been. Naive. Till now, Raquela worried about her sister's whereabouts, but was she even alive?

———

They arrived in Jaffa past midnight. The inky sky hung like a thick curtain obscuring the surroundings. It was difficult to make out buildings or tell what or who might be lurking. Throughout the meandering journey on the back roads, distant shots rang out in the dark, but Uri pushed on.

The car stopped in front of a stone wall that surrounded a compound. It was difficult to discern its details in the dark.

"Where are we?" Raquela whispered.

"We will try to rest here for the night," Uri replied.

Scared as she was, Raquela was intrigued. "Whose place is this?" It looked nothing like Kfar Vitkin's primitive barracks and tents.

Uri did not respond. He stepped out of the vehicle and approached the ornate metal gate, knocking several times. They remained completely silent, waiting.

A few minutes later, after some fumbling with the lock, an old Arab emerged wearing a loose, white ankle-length robe, which seemed to glow in the dark. A keffiyeh on his head was just like the ones Raquela had seen men on the road wearing. To her shock, the man hugged Uri. An Arab? And here she thought they'd mistakenly knocked on the wrong gate. What a crazy place this was; one couldn't tell who was an enemy and who was a friend.

The Arab, who was introduced as Sami, took them inside and offered them bedrooms on the second floor. Raquela stood in a large, square room outfitted with ornate furniture and a bed covered in white mosquito netting—at least, that's what she surmised it was. For the moment she was safe; relief washed over her. After the intense emotions of the day, she was practically comatose, and fell asleep immediately in her sweaty clothes.

17   THE ATLIT COLONY

Uri knocked on her door early next morning, rousing her from deep sleep. Raquela woke up disoriented.

"We have to leave now," Uri said through the closed door.

"Wait," she said and ambled over to the door opening it a crack, her hair mussed, her teeth fuzzy, her breath no doubt foul.

He told her Sara had already been picked up by their back up truck and was on the way to the warehouse.

"We just got here, why are we leaving already?" Raquela asked.

"Our host is an early riser; my business is done."

"But what about my sister?" She had gone through such a nightmare to get here and now... nothing?

"I have a little plan. Now hurry." With that, Uri disappeared, leaving her with a sense that nothing in this country would ever be clear.

Raquela washed in the spacious, well-appointed bathroom, taking pleasure in the first real shower she'd had since Paris. Dressing, she noticed out the window that the compound surrounded a small orchard and several outbuildings. At the far periphery, two men in Arab garb stood chatting. From a distance, she couldn't tell if they were guards or farmworkers. The stone wall around the compound was clearly meant as protection, but from whom?

Downstairs, all ready to go, Raquela admired the colorful geometric patterns on tile floors and ornate, carved furniture in the hallways. How different this place looked from the Spartan barracks of Kfar Vitkin. The place was exotic, unlike any she had ever seen. But the most perplexing thing about this stopover was the Arab's hospitality.

Uri's car waited for her just outside the gate. A profusion of bright pink flowers hung over the car, a pleasant image after the previous day. Uri looked impatient, tapping on the dashboard with one hand and waving her over with his other, from which a lit cigarette dangled. "Get in. Let's get you to Atlit."

She climbed into his beat-up Austin, feeling miserable that she had no clean clothes to put on after the shower. "Where is this place and why are you taking me there?"

"You asked for help, didn't you?"

She didn't answer right away; she noticed he was wearing a different shirt, and the bulge on his upper arm meant he had on a thicker bandage under the sleeve. She decided not to pursue it for fear he'd think she was too soft. "What's in Atlit?"

"Who knows? Maybe your sister."

Raquela swallowed hard. "What makes you think she's there?"

"Many newcomers land in Jaffa and my friend Sami has all kinds of contacts. He suggested we try Atlit first."

"The Arab?"

"We don't judge people by labels; we pay attention to what they do. Sami Hadawi is a friend." Uri went on to tell her how he and Sami had become close friends years before. Uri stressed he could always count on Sami to brief him on local developments, both good and bad. He knew so many people because he owned a cinema and a café popular with Arabs and Jews. "This time he might just be right about your sister."

"So where is this place?"

"You'll see soon enough," Uri said, hitting the gas pedal with excessive force. Despite the gunshot wound he'd sustained the day before, Uri's spirits had picked up. He whistled a tune as he navigated onto what looked like a main road.

Raquela was so appreciative of his efforts to assist in her search so soon after arrival. It felt like a good omen. "I am sorry for taking up your time," she said.

Uri stopped whistling. "It's not a problem. I have to see someone in Atlit anyway."

"It would have been so much harder without you," she said, feeling genuine gratitude.

Thinking of how Uri had frightened her on the train made her think how easy it was to make mistakes about human nature. She thought now might be a good time to get more information about Aleksander. After all, he'd said he knew him. "Can you explain exactly what you meant about Count Aleksander?"

Uri responded with a sardonic chuckle. "Aleksander? A spoiled momma's boy. A scoundrel."

His snide dismissal made her hackles rise. Despite her disappointment with Aleksander, she didn't like how Uri described him. "How do you know him?" she asked.

"His mother, Madame Zabielska, is a big contributor to our cause. Good woman. That's all I'll say. Don't ask for more."

Raquela didn't respond.

The car bumped along the rough road sending clouds of dust around them. At times it hit huge potholes. She worried it might break down in the middle of nowhere.

After a while, Uri said, "Keep your head down."

It was eerily quiet on the road; the silence added to Raquela's anxiety. She didn't feel like speaking or asking questions. Her mind turned to the practical: the possibility of getting clues to Golda's whereabouts. How would it be to finally find her? Had life in this harsh land changed her?

Now, they drove along a desolate coastal road with nothing but ocean on their left and sand dunes on the right. Raquela stared at the turquoise water, unable to think of anything else in nature that had such an arresting color. Her mind drifted, though she should have been alert.

She began thinking of Uri and the strangeness of riding with him solo. She had been so consumed with her desire to leave home, preoccupied with managing her shop and before that, with school, she'd hardly considered men. They were no more on her radar than air, of no more consequence than the water she drank. If she ever felt twinges of sexual stirrings, they were squelched by her strict religious upbringing and her single-sex school hadn't allowed her attention to be pulled by boys. But recently, something had begun to happen.

She didn't so much know as feel it in her gut, in the way her breath quickened, the way her eyes swept the faces and bodies of men. It may have been Aleksander or the intoxicating atmosphere of Paris, or perhaps the anonymity of being in a foreign land that had awakened her senses, loosened her inhibitions. She couldn't exactly say how she'd transformed, but she knew that back home she'd have never allowed herself—or been allowed—to ride alone with a man like Uri.

She reflected on how solicitous he had been with her—giving her money and making sure she was first in the rowboat—and now taking her here and there, trying to help. Was there more to his attention than simple kindness? Would he expect something in return? And her own reactions to him were something to ponder too. Sitting so close to him, she inhaled his scent. It did something to her body, made her feel liquid, as if she were carried on warm currents. She'd never tell anyone, but the thought he might have been detained by the British made her more upset than not knowing what would happen to Chaya and Menucha. Now she was concerned about the wound on his arm. She found his stubbled, brown face arresting. Maybe her sister would not be found in Atlit. Where would he take her then?

Uri's voice startled her. "With the shootout yesterday, I never answered your question."

She didn't remember it.

"You wanted to know why the Arabs refused to respect the Jews' ownership of land."

"Didn't you say they had good relations with the settlers before?" she asked, perplexed.

Uri laughed, a sardonic laughter that she didn't care for. She liked him better as her kind protector. "As soon as our numbers here grew, we scared them. We were no longer neighbors; we became intruders."

A screech of tires, then an abrupt stop. The conversation ended. She froze. They idled at a British checkpoint. Uri had said they may run into one, but he'd try his best to avoid them. "And should we come upon one, just let me do the talking," he'd said. "But I have my papers, why would it be problem?" she'd asked.

Now a tall, thin British officer with a blond mustache approached the Austin. His name was Ainsley, plainly displayed on his uniform. He motioned for Uri to get out. Raquela only watched. She noted Ainsley's shiny black knee-high boots and well-cut jacket, British elegance. He pointed at her. Uri opened the door and asked her to step out and show her papers. She climbed out of the low car, her heart in her throat, turned sideways to dig the passport out of her brassiere, then handed it to the officer.

Ainsley looked her up and down, then inspected the document, holding it up to the light and squinting. "Bloody hell," he exclaimed. "She's some Brit," he laughed.

Having absolutely no idea what he meant, she stood silent, her cheeks aflame.

The man shook his head and returned the passport to Raquela. Then he turned toward Uri. "You should be able to do better than this."

Better than what? But Uri only nodded, said, "Thanks Ainsley."

"The camel jockeys are tooled; gun your machine and scram," Ainsley called out as they got into the car.

Raquela put her hand on her thumping chest and breathed hard; her mouth felt dry as sand. "I thought that would be it," she said.

"We have an understanding," Uri said and gunned the engine.

He did not elaborate, but Raquela understood that Uri's and Ainsley's cryptic talk had something to do with the gathering Arab storm.

***

By noon, Uri announced they'd soon arrive in Atlit—a colony founded by Baron Rothschild in 1903—now home to several hundred Jewish settlers and a few hundred Arabs. Raquela could see terraced fields almost as soon as they passed the colony gates. In the distance, people worked the fields; this was a place where the land was cultivated.

Uri saw her craning and explained that the neat rows of plants were cucumbers, peppers, and tomatoes.

"What an amazing sight!" Raquela exclaimed. Not that she ever gave it much thought before but seeing a farmed area in this land of sand and marshes seemed miraculous.

Soon they approached a low cement building. Some men and women stood in a queue right up to the door. "New arrivals," Uri observed.

"They look so hot and tired baking here in the sun," Raquela said.

"Have to get used to the heat if you want to survive here."

Uri came around to give Raquela a hand out of the low car.

She was surprised at his courtly gesture. "What now?" she asked.

"Let's go inside and speak with Gad. He might know something."

She followed Uri into the building and listened for a few moments while Uri chatted with Gad in Hebrew. Though she could read Hebrew prayer books, she had never imagined it a language of daily discourse and had no idea what they were saying. She observed Gad's bulging muscles and an air of efficiency. Like other men here, he was deeply tanned.

Uri turned to her, "Gad here, is asking your sister's name."

"Golda."

Gad understood. He arched his brows and replied in Hebrew.

"Hmm... They have two Goldas here," Uri reported. "Golda Frydman and Golda Har."

Raquela's heart sank. "My sister's last name is Berg, like mine."

The minute the truth escaped her lips, Raquela clamped her hand to her mouth.

Uri gave her a stern look, but Gad hadn't noticed the blunder.

"Well, maybe she has taken a new Hebrew name, or maybe she uses a married name," Uri conveyed Gad's suggestion.

"No, she'd not marry without informing her family." Raquela took righteous offense at the suggestion, trying to cover her blooper.

Gad spoke to Uri while the new arrivals waiting to be processed cast annoyed glances. What looked like a brief disruption, initially, was now taking too long.

"Gad invites us to stay for their supper and *kumzits*." Uri looked at his watch and added, "There's no time to make it back before sundown and more dangerous to drive in the dark. I think we should take them up on the offer. What do you say?"

"All right," Raquela agreed reluctantly. "What's a *kumzits*?"

Uri smiled. "It's a big bonfire and sing-along. Settlers do it on Shabbat. I think you'll like it."

Learning they'd be staying in the area dedicated to new arrivals, as the permanent resident housing had no spare rooms, Raquela said, "All this hospitality. I am a total stranger here."

"You don't understand, Raquela. Here, we Jews are all brothers and sisters."

They walked along a gravel path lined with palms; it ended abruptly as they came closer to the tents. A few dozen white peaked tents stood in neat rows on an expanse of sandy soil. Uri showed her to a tent. He said, "Get some rest. I'll come get you when it's time for supper." She saw him striding to the farthest row of tents close to the barbed wire fence.

The tent was basic, but it had a straw mattress on the floor and some old crates on which stood a pitcher of water next to a rusted basin. Raquela was glad to see a towel and a small cake of soap nearby. Grimy after the long, dusty ride, she washed up and lay on the mattress and soon fell asleep. She dreamed of meeting Golda, but in her dream her sister was a withered old woman leaning on a cane, her single-toothed smile frightening. Awaking in the dim tent, Raquela felt sweaty and disoriented. Her head hurt.

Seeing an oil lamp on a low stool in the corner, she thought about lighting it, but she opened the tent flap and saw people streaming in the direction of a large building in the distance. She stood up, smoothed her hair and skirt and stepped outside.

"Raquela!" Uri's voice came from behind. "Wait up. I'll show you to the communal dining hall."

She felt happy to see his familiar face in a sea of strangers, but her temples pounded.

The colony members sat on long, rough-hewn wooden benches, similar to the ones in Kfar Vitkin, and ate their meals off metal plates, at equally Spartan tables. The place was filled with voices of a hundred conversations. The noise made Raquela's headache worse. She followed Uri to the food station where bowls of salad and containers of hard-boiled eggs stood alongside tubs of yogurt. She filled her plate modestly and tried to follow Uri, but he made frequent stops to chat with people, so Raquela sat by herself, hoping he'd find her and direct her to the bonfire. So far, he had not failed her.

The smoke of the bonfire curled into the darkening sky, giving the gathering an aura of mystery. Now and then, sparks rose up, making the evening feel like a grand celebration. Yet she knew not to let go of her anxiety when she spotted armed sentries on the periphery: those ever-present rifles.

Uri had disappeared somewhere. He knew many people here. Raquela felt like an intruder. She walked cautiously toward the circle of settlers ringing the fire. When she reached it, some women moved over and made space for her.

When the familiar strains of *Po ba'aretz*, "Here in this Land" wafted into the air, Raquela's discomfort diminished a little. She remembered Golda humming it at home after her HeHalutz meetings. The song made her long to see her sister and brought tears to her eyes. She was glad it was dark so no one could see them. The voices of the singers rose up in unison. These people were all a part of a cohesive whole. She felt a little jealous.

A man on the other side of the huge circle led the sing-along. In the smoke, she couldn't make him out or anyone else on the other side. Even though she wasn't fond of group activities, the communal meal and singing awakened a warm feeling toward the life these people led.

She tried to picture her sister in this rough land. Golda was most comfortable preening in front of a mirror and making sure she was as attractive as possible, not exactly the kind of woman you'd think would enjoy a pioneer life. Well, you could never figure out people's inner desires and motivations, not even your own sister's.

An older woman with a broad face and wide mouth, sitting next to Raquela, closed her eyes and smiled blissfully each time the group erupted into a new song. She swayed to the tune, her arm around the shoulders of the woman beside her. Raquela strained to make out the faces of the others in the circle through the darkness.

Just before the *kumzits* ended, the group leader asked if there were any questions. Raquela's ears pricked up; the man's loud voice had a vaguely familiar ring, deep and resonant. It bothered her that she couldn't place it. She'd heard this voice somewhere. People speaking over one another, getting up and shouting greetings, soon drowned out the voice.

As the celebration broke up, small groups of settlers began to stream home, like a school of fish, all heading in one direction. Raquela looked around for Uri but could not find him. She was concerned about locating her tent in the dark; they all looked the same. Soon a group of women laughing and chatting passed her on the path. She could have sworn she heard Golda's unmistakable throaty laugh. Her heart

147

quickened, and she ran after the group. Surely, she was imagining things.

When she caught up with them, she tapped the woman closest to her on the shoulder. "Shalom, I am looking for..."

The woman turned around to face her. Her companions stopped.

Raquela and the woman stared at one another for a moment, recognition lighting their faces. Then the woman threw her arms around Raquela. "Rifka! *Got in himmel!* Never in a million years would I have expected to see you here!" She stepped back, then put her arms on Raquela's shoulders, holding her at arm's length.

"Let me look at you. When did you get here, Rifka?"

"Golda! I recognized your laughter. You look so different; you've cut your hair!"

"Look, everyone, this is my sister," Golda announced to her friends, stepping back from Raquela, and introducing her anew with a flourish. "My little sister Rifka made *aliyah*, followed my example. Finally!"

"No, you don't understand... I haven't exactly made any decisions... I was just looking for you, and I am Raquela now. Please use this name from now on, Golda."

"Tsk, tsk... You've acquired some haughty airs, sister."

"I'll explain it all later. The most important thing is that I found you!"

"Aha, so you've missed me! How are Momma and the little ones? What are you doing here?"

The sisters hugged again, their faces moist with tears. Words tumbled out of them helter-skelter, each talking over the other. The women stood around them, taking in the sisterly reunion and clucking at the miracle of it.

A woman in the circle said, "Wait till you see Maya and her father! Like two peas in a pod."

Golda pulled Raquela's hand. "Come to my place, sister, I'll make tea, then we can talk. We have so much ground to cover. It'll take us ages to catch up."

The bystanders were no longer included in the emotional meeting. Giving Golda and her newly found sister space, the women began dispersing, bidding one another goodnight. "*Layla tov, Layla tov!*"

The sisters locked arms and walked on a gravel path.

Golda pointed at the cluster of low cement buildings. "See, we are out of the tents now. We have a real apartment."

"That's good. I'm happy for you," Raquela said. "I'm staying in the guest tents."

"Me? I've had it with living in a tent. It's bad enough I have to work the fields. I couldn't wait to get a place with running water."

Raquela didn't respond. It was just like Golda to seek creature comforts. It was truly a puzzle why she'd chosen this life. But Raquela felt elated to have found her alive and in good health. It was worth all the trouble to get here just to see her dear face.

Distant sounds of hyenas and owl hoots mixed with occasional shots coming from a nearby Arab village. Raquela was startled and gripped her sister closer.

"You are shivering in this heat." Golda let out a quiet titter. "Don't worry, the shots you hear are most likely sounds of celebrations, a birth or a wedding. That's how some Arabs express happiness."

They walked silently for a while, searching for the right thing to say. The separation had made them strangers. They had never enjoyed a closeness because of the six-year age difference. Raquela was twenty, Golda twenty-six.

"Let's stop at the Children's House before we get to my place," Golda suggested. "That way you'll see your new niece, Maya."

"You've had a baby?"

"Yes, why not?"

"You don't share the good news?"

"You heard one of the women mention Maya just before; you've been informed. Let's go see her now."

The crying of infants and squealing of babies signaled the approach to the children's place. Golda led the way in. She walked straight toward a bassinet, picked up her pink swaddled bundle and handed her ceremoniously to Raquela. "Meet Maya, the future President of our country."

The tension relieved, they laughed in unison.

"Your momma is ambitious," Raquela said, handling the wriggling bundle awkwardly.

Soon Nurit introduced herself. "Glad to meet you, Maya's auntie. I'm the caregiver. Pardon me, but I have to get all of these young ones to settle down. It's been a long day."

Golda kissed her baby and placed her gently in the bassinet, then the sisters walked out into the dark. "Hold on to me," Golda said. "I don't want you wandering off. Despite the celebrations you heard, there are plenty of marauding Arabs too."

Until they reached the apartment block, they walked in awkward silence. Golda led Raquela though a dim hallway stashed with baskets, a beat-up bicycle and gardening rakes. They entered the first-floor apartment, and Golda lit an oil lamp that cast long shadows on the walls. Colorful pillows strewn on the straw mattress provided a bit of hominess in the otherwise sparse room, but an odd musty odor hung in the air. Raquela crinkled her nose. Golda must have noticed because she explained, "We had a torrential rain recently, badly needed, but we left the windows open, and everything got soaked. Things take forever to dry in this humidity, yet we were pleased because we have so little water."

"Are you happy living here? It's so different from our home," was all Raquela could muster.

"I'm all for differences," Golda snapped.

Raquela retreated. "Why haven't you written home?"

"With the baby and all the work around here, who has energy to write?"

The acid in her sister's tone disturbed Raquela. After all these months of planning and her eventful trip here, now that she found Golda, Raquela had no idea what to do or say. She wasn't sure if Golda would find her travel adventure of interest or if it would seem like childish nonsense. She searched her mind for something non-confrontational to say. Back home, Golda rarely had time for Rifka, but Rifka was so impressed with her sister's savoir-faire that she swallowed some indignities.

Golda, apparently now aware of her unkind welcome, broke the tension. "My Eli should be coming home soon; it's late. He's always the last one to wrap things up. I'll put on the tea I promised you."

"Who is he?" Raquela vaguely remembered a cousin Eli from Poland.

"Didn't you see the man leading the sing-along?"

"I couldn't see much in all that smoke and darkness. His voice rang a bell, but I couldn't figure out where I might have heard it."

"You'll see him soon enough," Golda said with a smug expression and filled the teakettle with water.

"While we wait, let me tell you a little about my journey to find you," Raquela said, trying to lighten the edginess that had crept between them.

"Find me? I wasn't lost," Golda chuckled.

"Believe me, Raquela, I know all about rough journeys. Can't think what you can tell me that I haven't experienced."

"But I ended up in Paris of all places. Can you imagine, Golda? *Me* in Paris?"

Golda's brow crinkled. "Don't tell me you had some tawdry affair with a *goy*."

Raquela hoped her letdown at her sister's cutting response didn't show on her face. "No, nothing like that. It was just a change in trains."

The tea kettle whistled.

"Let me help you make the tea." Raquela attempted to get on a better footing with her sister.

Golda turned off the burner, pointed toward the cupboard and sat at the table.

Raquela took down three mismatched cups and saucers, placed them on the table and poured the tea. Was her sister pleased to have been found? Raquela began to seriously doubt it.

Golda sat in silence with an absent expression, watching the steam rise from the cups, then glanced at her watch. "Eli should have been home by now. Women always stop him to chat... and he just can't help himself, has to yak with everyone." She looked irritated. Golda picked up a cup, took the saucer from beneath it and used it to cover the cup. "He doesn't like cold tea," she said.

Just a few minutes later, a handsome, stocky man stood in the doorway.

Instantly, Raquela knew who he was. She popped up to greet him. "Eli? Eli?" was all she could utter.

"Is that you, Rifka?"

Golda said, "Well, it's about time you showed up. We have a guest."

"It's me," Raquela said.

"The baby sister!" Eli laughed in his rich, resonant voice. "What the hell?" He hung his hat on the hooks near the door.

Raquela didn't like his tone—her presence here was no joke. She said, "First, I am no baby. Second, I am Raquela now. I set out to find Golda because we hadn't heard from her in months."

Eli raised his eyebrows. "Golda, you haven't written home?"

Raquela saw that Golda gave him a look of caution.

Soberly he said, "You came by yourself?"

"Yes, by myself to find Golda."

"Come here, come here, little girl. Let me squeeze you!"

Such informality! "Cousin, squeeze yourself," she said.

Golda laughed. "She's really not a child anymore, Eli. What's the big deal? So, she traveled here, she'll be another one of us, a pioneer. Look at her thick arms and legs, perfectly cut out to tame the land."

Eli laughed.

Raquela huffed. "So, you two... You two are what? Married first cousins?"

"Who said anything about marriage? Such a bourgeois idea," Golda puffed out her cheeks, removed the saucer off Eli's cup and moved it toward him.

Eli sat down at the table, chuckling. He took a sip of tea and said, "This is a new country; we make new rules."

"New rules?" Raquela's eyes widened.

"Listen to my Eli. He knows what he's talking about," Golda said.

Her possessive tone annoyed Raquela. "So Maya is your child. You made her together," Raquela stated the obvious, nodding and chewing her lip. She still had a hard time believing it. She stood up unsure what to do next.

"It does take two to make a baby," Eli said, laughing heartily. He got hold of Raquela, wrapped her in a bear hug. "Don't worry. It's all right. She's fine, a great little *sabra*, and the light of our lives. You'll meet her tomorrow."

"I met her. She's beautiful. But now I am tired. I hope you don't mind if I skip the tea, and we catch up tomorrow. You'll understand if I'm a bit touchy. It's been a shocking day... Very emotional."

Eli said, "Whoa, whoa, girl. Take it easy on your sister. She's not well."

"Not well?"

"Golda, baby, tell her: you have an appointment at the Afula hospital tomorrow."

"Why? What's wrong, Golda? Not well?" Raquela put her hand on her sister's shoulder.

"Oh, it's nothing." Golda shrugged off her sister's arm.

152

Eli said, "Nothing? It's her breast."

"Yes, okay. It seems I have a nasty abscess that needs to be cut open before the infection spreads."

"Ugh! I am so sorry," Raquela said, pushing aside her own discomfort, her shame at being so angry. "Is there anything I can do to help?"

"Yes, you can spend the day with Maya. I was just about to ask, in fact," Golda said.

Eli explained. "Nurit, the woman who cares for our babies, has a child in the nursery who needs medical attention. And I told her I'd take them to the hospital along with Golda. It's a day-long affair. What do you say, Auntie?"

"I'm no expert with babies," Raquela said. "But, of course, I'll do it."

"There have been plenty in our home; surely babies aren't too daunting for you," Golda teased.

A pale moon illuminated the narrow gravel path to the outskirts of the colony. The sisters chatted as they walked toward Raquela's tent.

"What was that business about marriage being bourgeois, Golda? I never expected such a radical statement from your lips."

Golda paused on the path and turned to her sister. "Don't you think we should change as we grow?"

"I suppose, but I need to think more about that," Raquela said. "Let's be honest with one another," she said suddenly. "Did you come to Palestine only because of Eli?"

"What do you think?" Golda said.

"Hmm..." It was too dark to see Golda's face clearly. "You had Maya, so the answer is yes."

When they arrived at the tent area, Golda said, "Here you are. Get some sleep. It's not a palace, but I've slept in worse!" With that she walked away.

Not even a hug? Raquela felt abandoned. The white tents looked like an encampment of ghosts. Raquela stared at the sky for a while, trying to identify the stars. Same stars as back home and in Paris; the world seemed both small and enormous.

Deep in the middle of the night, Raquela woke, her head swimming with emotion: Eli and Golda. Baby Maya. Distant shots still peppered the silence. After an hour, hopeless, she got up and groped for the lantern. She lit it and stared at her shadow on the tent's fabric. Now that she'd found Golda, Raquela's mind returned to the drama with Aleksander. Yes, only Bronka would understand. She'd write her a brief letter. She rummaged in her bag and found the pen, some paper, and the envelopes she'd bought in Paris intending to write.

Hello Bronka, my dearest friend,

I'm writing to share some good news. I shall be home very soon now that I have found Golda. Remember how worried we all were about her? But she is well and has a beautiful baby girl, Maya.

I can only imagine my absence has made your life difficult, but I shall reciprocate. I promise. Tomorrow I must be up early to take care of my baby niece, so I'll be brief.

Knowing you as I do, I think you'll be happy for me and... surprised to hear of my marvellous adventure. On my way to Palestine, I met a fascinating man. I know you won't believe this, but he is a count. His name is Aleksander, just like Aleksander the Great and Pushkin! He lives in Paris and has been kind enough to show me a bit of it. This incredible man has made me forget everything I thought I knew. I never expected it. Never. But I am smitten.

How is that for discovering a new facet of your old friend? I can just imagine the look on your face as you read this and hear your peals of laughter. Now I feel guilty about saying those things about Kazio. More on the romantic front, do you remember my cousin Eli? He lives with Golda, and Maya is their baby! People here aren't as conventional as back home.

Can't wait to talk with you and see the shock in your eyes, or maybe it'll be amusement.

Your ever faithful,

Rifka

P.S. The situation with the Arabs is tense. I'm not so sure about any of us considering aliyah. Don't tell my Momma, she'd worry too much.

Raquela felt good, if a bit embarrassed, to have penned those words, but Bronka would understand. Now, Raquela felt fully awake and not even tired. As long as she couldn't sleep, she'd write to Momma. She opened the window flap for some fresh air and began.

Dearest Momma,

Believe it, or not, I found Golda! I am so sorry I worried you with my abrupt departure into the unknown, but I told you I'd find her. You were so upset; I could see it in your eyes. I sent a postcard from Paris, but I hadn't written a letter before because I just couldn't. Trust me. It's a long story. One day I'll tell you in person. What can I say about our ancient land? It's quite primitive, but...

Raquela paused and considered just how much to tell Momma, then decided.

.... nothing worrisome is happening here. Golda is well and you wouldn't believe it: she has a beautiful little baby named Maya. You are a grandmother!! Your very first grandchild. Mazal Tov! I'll be home soon.

Your ever-loving daughter,

Rifka

155

Whew! Raquela sighed with relief that the unpleasant task was done. No need to mention Eli or Golda's abscess, she convinced herself, but she didn't like keeping things from Momma. She had no idea where to post the letters and hoped that Eli would take them with him to Afula. If they had a hospital, surely, they had a post office.

The finished letters gave her mind a measure of peace. Raquela lay down and finally fell asleep.

18 MAYA

A rooster woke Raquela early; small miracle she caught any sleep at all. She opened the tent's window flap and saw chickens pecking the sandy ground. Her mouth felt like cotton, but she had no idea where to go to get something to drink. More urgently yet, she didn't remember where the latrine was. The location of Golda's apartment was a complete mystery too. Raquela wished she had paid more attention to the path, but she had been preoccupied.

The tent became brighter as the sun rose. Raquela found the basin and water pitcher, and washed her face and hands. The lukewarm water did little to wash off the previous night's shock. She ran her fingers through her curls to tame them a bit and straightened her rumpled skirt. She hoped Eli or Uri would appear soon and direct her to the latrine. Just when she thought she'd have to pee in the basin, she heard voices.

"Open up if you are decent," Eli called.

She opened the tent flap.

Four men, plus Uri, gathered right behind Eli. "Good morning!" Eli said with a broad grin. "We have already managed a few hours of work, coming back from the fields. Starving for breakfast."

Uri said, "*Shalom*, Raquela. I heard you've found your Golda. Soon you'll be one of us."

"No, soon I'll be going home."

A tinge of irritation crept into Uri's voice. "You are acting like a tourist. Haven't you seen what's going on here? We need you to work with us."

Raquela felt a pang; he was expecting her to stay.

"But today she's spending the day with our Maya," Eli interrupted. "Don't forget to pick up some bottled milk for her when you go to the Children's House. She may not be used to it, but it's all we can do for now, no wet nurses around. And grab a bunch of diapers too."

"I'll do my best," Raquela said.

"I have no doubt. It's an instinct. Women just know how," Eli said. "Uri will show you the way to the Children's House. I have to get on the road."

"Yes, as we discussed," Uri agreed.

"One more thing, Raquela; keep Maya in our apartment. A few of the children are sick. We don't want her catching something," Eli instructed.

It touched Raquela how he cared for his little girl. It was nice, surprising even, to see such tenderness toward a baby in a man. She'd never seen it in her father.

"A favor for a favor, Eli. Can you post these two letters for me?"

Eli whistled. "Writing about your adventures in Paris?"

"No! What did Golda tell you?"

"Nothing, nothing. She has a wild imagination," Eli laughed.

Raquela couldn't help noticing the stubble on his tanned face or the playful expression in his eyes. The faster she walked off in the direction of the latrine she'd been shown, the better.

Maya was quite a chubby baby. Raquela's arm ached from trying to hold her steady and make her comfortable. Every now and then, Maya made little noises and sucking movements with her sweet rosebud lips. "Sorry, baby, I'm not the one with the milk." Raquela felt ill at ease. So many babies at home, yet Raquela never gained much experience caring for them. She evaded diaper changing. It was the least enjoyable aspect of baby care. She'd always been too squeamish. Babies had a way of hooking you with their cuteness and once that happened you were at their beck and call. She preferred to help Momma by washing dishes, shopping for groceries, or doing the laundry.

She put Maya down on Golda's mattress and warmed the bottle in a small pot on the hot plate. Momma never bottle fed any of her children. Luckily, Raquela had seen a neighbor bottle feed her youngest. After testing the temperature of the milk on her wrist, she offered it to the baby. Maya grabbed the nipple eagerly, spit it out immediately and began wailing, long piercing shrieks.

Raquela sat the bottle aside and rocked Maya in her arms. Innate behavior? Eli was a fool! She tried the bottle again, hoping the cooler milk would be more acceptable, but Maya took a swig, began coughing and turned red in the face. She continued fussing with each of Raquela's feeding attempts. Suddenly, it occurred to Raquela that cow's milk might taste very different from the breast milk to which the baby was accustomed.

"I am so sorry, Maya." Raquela gave up trying to make the baby drink the milk. She dumped it out and washed the bottle, fearing cow's milk could hurt Maya's delicate stomach. Then Raquela looked for sugar in the cupboard to make sweetened water for the baby, but there was none.

Next best thing was to sing from her meager repertoire of lullabies. Raquela's gentle voice calmed Maya. Eventually, she fell asleep, and Raquela began feeling bored. Her first flush of pleasure in caring for her baby niece evaporated. Her eyes drifted closed, and she realized how much she needed sleep, but Maya awoke, crying fiercely. Raquela decided a diaper change might be in order. The mustard-yellow poop made her gag, but she washed Maya's bottom with warm water and patted it dry with a towel. She wrapped the diaper carefully, fastening the diaper pin with care, but Maya continued wailing.

By now Raquela had run out of lullabies to sing. Her irritation at Golda's long absence increased. She felt sorry for her niece. Why, the poor baby must be starving! At last, exhausted by all the crying, the child fell asleep. Raquela laid Maya next to her on the mattress, covered her snugly, and patted her back. She decided to take a nap too. Might as well catch some rest before the little tyrant woke again.

The sun hung low on the horizon when Raquela woke up. It was quiet inside and outside. Where was everyone? Golda? Eli? She turned toward Maya. Thank goodness, the baby was still asleep. Raquela stretched and thought about making some tea. Then she looked at Maya: the baby lay completely still.

Disturbed by the baby's stillness, Raquela turned Maya over. Her face had lost its delicate pink hue; it looked pale, grayish even. With dread growing in her chest, Raquela put her ear to the baby's mouth and listened for her breath. Nothing. She picked her up, hoping for a movement, a kick of the little fleshy legs, a twitch, a cry, anything.

Nothing!

For a moment, Raquela sat completely frozen, then screamed, "Maya! Wake up! Maya!" Terror seized her entire body. She shook the baby, then shook her some more. Maya's limbs felt floppy, but warm. "Please, baby, wake up!" Raquela pleaded.

Maya wasn't waking up. Raquela hoisted the inert infant on her shoulder and tried patting her back, praying to push a single breath into her lungs. The baby hung limp. Each pat increased Raquela's terror. She lay Maya down and tried to breathe air into the tiny mouth, to no avail. She grabbed Maya in her arms and ran out of the apartment, screaming. She didn't even know whose name she was calling out. "Golda! Eli! Someone, anyone, help!"

Men and women returning from the fields came rushing toward her. "What happened?" they called to her, but she had no answers. She heard someone yell, "Call for the doctor." In her wild run, she stumbled upon the Children's House. She ran inside, still screaming.

An older woman, the substitute caregiver, ran toward Raquela. "What's wrong? What's wrong?" She extended her arms to grab the lifeless bundle from Raquela.

Raquela was so hysterical she couldn't respond, but the answer was immediately obvious. Others ran in and stood silently, staring at the caregiver's ashen face. She lay the baby on her back, on the table in the center of the nursery, and tried to blow air into the tiny mouth and nose. Maya's face began turning bluish.

After several more attempts at reviving the infant, the woman turned to Raquela and asked, "Did you happen to fall asleep and perhaps overlaid on her?"

"I don't know!" Raquela screamed. "How can I know what I did while I slept?"

"The doctor has been called," a man said.

"I'm afraid it's too late," was all the caregiver said and wiped a tear rolling down her cheek.

By now the word had spread, and people began pushing into the room.

An old woman in the back of the crowd pointed at Raquela, asked, "Who is this Angel of Death?"

"Stop it," the caregiver said. "She's Golda's sister and she's innocent; things like this happen."

Raquela's sobs turned to wrenching howls.

"Calm down; your hysteria isn't helping," the caregiver pronounced. She laid the inert baby in her bassinet and asked the gathered group to leave.

Raquela continued weeping. Her body shook uncontrollably. The horror of the situation had barely sunk in, but a singular thought hijacked her brain: I can't face Golda and Eli. I can't. I can't. I must leave before they return. She had never felt so frightened in her life. She could not do this... She didn't know what to call it. She was cursed and she'd cursed them.

She wiped her swollen eyes and nose with the edge of her skirt and looked directly into the caregiver's face. "I need to find Uri, the man who brought me here yesterday. Do you know how to find him?"

The woman didn't respond, just stood, shaking her head. "I don't have much that is useful to say except that if you think of a chapter in Kings about King Solomon, there was a verse about a mother who overlaid on a baby and snuffed out its breath—accidentally," the woman said with emphasis, to console Raquela.

"But I am not the mother." Raquela's stream of tears started again.

"I suppose if it happened with the mother, it would be worse. At least now she has someone she can blame."

Raquela gasped.

"Let me see if Uri is in the office with Gad." The woman dialed the phone then went to tend her charges.

Uri appeared shortly. "Not good, not good at all," he said.

"Please, Uri, I beg you, you got me here, now you must take me away. I cannot stay here, not another moment. Please."

"Don't you want to tell your sister what happened? Apologize to her at least?"

"No!" Raquela's sobs began all over. "I can't. I can't. You are insane.

How can one apologize for killing a child? There are no words, no words..."

Uri looked at his watch. "They'll be returning from Afula any minute now. You'll have to face them. I won't let you leave like a coward without telling them."

Overhearing Uri, the caretaker said, "Look at the girl, for God's sake, she's no coward, she tried to get help. It's a tragedy, but things like this happen. She's not at fault."

Her eyes almost swollen shut, her nose stuffed, her throat raw, Raquela continued weeping. Shortly they heard a honk and heard voices. Eli and Golda walked into the nursery briskly. Even before he was over the threshold, Eli said, "Sorry we've been gone so long."

Immediately, he and Golda noticed Raquela sobbing in the corner of the room.

"What happened?" Golda asked. "Is she hurt?"

Then Golda and Eli looked at Uri's and the caretaker's grim, silent faces. "What's going on here?" Eli asked, his voice rising with alarm.

"It's Maya," Uri said.

Golda's face went white, "Is she sick? Where is she?"

The caretaker approached, put her arm on Golda's shoulder, whispered something and led her toward the bassinet. Golda's wrenching screams filled the nursery. It was as if her guts had been ripped out by a rabid beast. Eli froze momentarily, spat in Raquela's direction, raced over to Golda, who'd already collapsed to the floor, rocking Maya's inert body, saying over and over, "She's a sound sleeper, she'll wake up, she'll wake up."

Eli dropped to his knees and embraced Golda and his daughter.

Raquela moved toward them tentatively, unable to find the words. But Eli shouted with so much rage that spittle flew from his mouth, "Get out and never dare to show your face here again! Golda always said you were trouble. Out! Out!" he screamed.

"I... I don't know what happened," Raquela tried to speak, but overcome with grief, only managed, "I... I am so sorry," through convulsive gasps.

"Leave them now. This is no time to—" Uri said. "Come with me."

And Raquela followed him in a trance, unthinking, totally numb.

19 TASTING POLITICS

It was an unusually warm spring in Warsaw, but when the evening air had cooled, Bronka decided she'd go to the Bund meeting after all. She walked briskly past crowds clogging the street on their evening strolls. Her mind still lingered on Rifka's letter. Its contents had startled, even upset her. Romance was her specialty, not Rifka's! It stung to recall how her friend belittled her romance serials, and now she was living one of her own... in Paris of all places! She shook her head. How unpredictable Rifka could be! The man had to be someone out of the ordinary. And where was Rifka now? Would she have the decency to return by Rosh Hashanah?

For several weeks Bronka had been attending the Jewish Labor Bund meetings after Zvia Stern introduced her to the group. She still remembered how nervous she felt that first Thursday. She chose her nicest white blouse with frills around the collar, the one she wore to a cousin's wedding, her best black skirt that clung snugly to her wide hips and flared out at the bottom to compensate. She'd spent at least an hour in front of the mirror, making sure she looked her best.

The only feature she didn't need to worry about was her hair. People always commented on her luxuriant, honey-blonde braids. Come to think of it, that was the only aspect in which she knew she had surpassed Rifka, whose hair was short, thick, and unruly. In fact, Rifka's hair matched her personality. Bronka smiled at the thought as she pinned the braids in a neat crown around her head. Rifka, you exasperate me like no one else, but I miss you like crazy. There is so much I need to tell you.

The first time Bronka had walked into the meeting space—a classroom at the Sholem Aleichem Bund school—men had eyed her. There must have been at least a dozen staring at her. She felt self-conscious. The crowd was a mix of men in blue-collar workaday clothes and women who looked as plain as a meal of boiled potatoes. Zvia Stern appeared to be best dressed among them. Bronka felt as if she'd walked into the wrong room. She thought it would be different, though she couldn't say exactly what it was she'd expected. Zvia introduced her as the manager of a ladies' undergarment shop, and they all broke into applause.

"She's one of us," a man in dark blue overalls exclaimed with a huge grin on his pockmarked face. "And a manager!"

Bronka squeezed herself into a low seat behind one of the desks and ran her fingers over carved Yiddish letters on the wooden top, marked up by the students whose language of instruction was the language of her home. The Jewish Labor Bund school was free, but it had opened only recently, past her days as a schoolgirl.

Despite her initial misgivings, Bronka liked the ordinary, impassioned folk at the Bund meetings and continued to attend every Thursday. She quite enjoyed chatting with some of the regulars before the program started.

A gray-haired woman who stood removing her apron greeted Bronka, "How did your day go?" Then, "Oh my, I was in such a rush to get here, I walked out of the factory still wearing my smock." She smiled.

"I had a long day myself," Bronka said and sat near the woman. The woman was genuine; Bronka felt her greeting wasn't just meaningless small talk. She cared. There wasn't much time to socialize. Just as Bronka was about to chat with her, the meeting began.

The leader, the thirtyish Mordechai who'd been so enthusiastic when Bronka was introduced, led the discussion. It focused on analyzing the successes of massive protests organized by the Bund in the wake of the antisemitic riots in the city of Przytyk. A heated discussion erupted when a young woman in the back of the room called out, "Maybe Jews shouldn't have been using weapons."

"What's wrong with you?" an outraged young man in overalls said. "You want us to be like lambs going to slaughter?"

In the end, most in attendance agreed with him. Bronka remembered the rabbi reminding her and Rifka on the day their shop had been vandalized to keep their heads down in the hope that the violence would pass, and the police would handle it. She needed more time to think it over for herself, but she was certain Rifka would never take the violent path.

Then the discussion turned to local elections. Bronka liked how smart and curious these people were. Surely, Rifka would appreciate their intelligence and intense involvement in precinct politics, but politics still wasn't very interesting to Bronka. It was Rifka's domain.

After the meeting, Mordechai, the meeting leader, approached her. She'd noticed him casting furtive glances her way more than once. "Would you like to take a walk in the park with me? It's a nice evening."

Was this what Zvia was thinking when she had encouraged her to go to these meetings?

Mordechai's crooked smile disarmed Bronka readily. It was true that he was missing a couple of teeth, but there was something so gentle, yet manly, in his manner that she agreed.

A light drizzle greeted them on the street.

Bronka stopped in front of the door and said, "Maybe a walk in the park is not the best idea for this evening." She felt relieved. This would not be the day for a first real date with a man. She didn't consider her sneaking around with Kazio to be real dating.

But Mordechai said, "There's a café just a few blocks from the school. "Nothing fancy."

And so, they walked. The street had darkened, but just ahead, the bright light of the café window and its well-lit coffee cup shingle were visible.

Bronka's mind churned uncomfortably. If she paid, it wouldn't really be considered a date, would it? Yes, a good idea. "Let me treat you to the coffee," she said.

"Sure, you can pay, but only if it won't take food out of your family's mouths. We Bundists like that women work. We believe in equality of the sexes." Mordechai smiled.

"No, no, it won't," she assured him.

A few late diners sat around square, bare-topped wooden tables. A waiter lingered at the bar, apparently waiting for customers. He gave them a cheery welcome, "Good evening, how's the rain; did it slow down yet?"

They sat in the corner, away from other patrons. The waiter approached, menus in hand and advised, "Have the liver with onions; it's the freshest thing tonight."

"Just a coffee for me," Mordechai said.

Bronka admired his modesty. "A coffee for me as well," she said.

As they waited, Bronka noticed that suddenly Mordechai seemed tongue-tied. "Tell me about your family and your job," she said.

And he began, shyly at first, "I live with my father and younger brother. My mother died a long time ago; I barely remember her. She died when I was five."

"Oh, I'm sorry," she said. "It must be rough." Bronka wondered who did the cooking and the cleaning. She looked at his animated face.

"We manage. I'm a pretty good cook."

"What about your job?" Bronka wanted to steer the conversation away from the personal.

"I work in a factory where we dye fabrics. The place is hotter than hell. All those vats of hot water where yards and yards of fabrics can become any color," he said.

"Sounds interesting," she said.

"No, not at all. I'm like a stewed prune when I come out of there after fourteen hours."

Bronka was shocked. "You can't mean that! Who works fourteen hours?"

"Anyone who wants to eat." Mordechai laughed. "That's exactly what the Bund is fighting for, to reduce the workday by at least three hours."

"I'm my own boss. I can come and go as I please, though if I'm to help feed my family and Rifka's, I have to work long hours as well," Bronka said.

"At least it's your decision. And who is this Rifka?" Mordechai asked.

"Oh, it's a long story. She's in Palestine now."

What she really thought was that Rifka had abandoned the shop. Still, it was her outrageous idea that made it possible for Bronka to be her own boss and not swelter in a factory. This, however, was something she preferred to keep to herself.

"Goodness! Where did the time go?" Bronka exclaimed as she looked up at the clock above the bar. It was past midnight. Her mother must either be pacing, going crazy with worry, or had fallen fast asleep, thinking her daughter was in bed.

"You are a fascinating woman, Bronka," Mordechai said and reached for her hand across the table. "I wouldn't mind staying here with you till dawn."

"I think they are about to close," she said and withdrew her hand. "Look, they are putting the chairs up on the tables. I think they are sending us a message."

Too bad Mordechai didn't have Kazio's killer looks or forbidden aura.

She stood up and walked outside, Mordechai, quite deflated, behind her. Just like a Bundist—all frankness and politics—Mordechai said, "If you don't want to kiss me, let's at least shake hands." He reached for her hand and held it a moment. "See you at the next meeting, we'll have the election results by then."

She lowered her eyes, her mind raced. He was thoroughly decent and hard working—solid husband material—but not someone she desired in her fantasies. He held zero potential for romance. Was she wrong to wish for a man who'd take her away from her mundane life, someone like a Hollywood star: a Paul Muni, Cary Grant, or Maurice Chevalier?

Bronka walked away feeling a little guilty for rebuffing Mordechai and wondering how to steer the next encounter.

20 THE ARAB REVOLT

Raquela scrambled into Uri's vehicle. Her head, an anvil pounded by a thousand hammers; her throat, coated with tar and sore. Maya's ghost filled the air, choking her. "Where are we going?" she asked, her voice raspy as a chain smoker's. It was dusk, this horrible day ending.

Uri put his hand on hers, held it, and said, "Quiet. Just let me think."

For a hard man, he, too, appeared shaken, yet his compassionate gesture felt to her like a salve. He gunned the engine and they sped off. Raquela had no idea where, and she really didn't care. Uri knew how to transform himself to fit the situation; she knew he'd save her.

For a long time, they drove in utter silence, occasionally interrupted by distant shots and Raquela's spasms that shook her entire body. She held her tears in check as best she could. Past midnight they arrived in a city. Uri's car wound its way through a warren of narrow streets.

"Where are we?" Raquela asked.

"Neve Tzedek," Uri said. "My grandparents' place. Let's go," he pointed toward a white, four-story building with no ornamentation. Its newness and clean lines seemed out of place. Rows of large windows stood dark.

"Are you going to wake them?" she asked.

Uri said, "Only if you can wake the dead. I stay here sometimes."

She followed Uri distractedly toward the entrance and up a wide staircase. Raquela's body felt heavy as if she'd eaten a giant meal, but she realized that she had nothing with her, nothing to carry except an overwhelming sense of guilt and shame.

Uri fumbled for keys. When he opened the door, her eyes fell on an exotic multicolored rug in the center of a spacious, sparsely furnished modern space. A few abstract paintings hung on white walls. She stood in the room, unable to remember how and why she'd gotten there; she had no idea what to do.

Uri dropped his satchel on a low sofa, took her hand and led her to another room. "You need to sleep," he said. "Tomorrow you'll be able to think more clearly."

"Sleep," she repeated, robot-like.

Uri rummaged in a bureau drawer and pulled out a man's shirt. "Here, if you want to change," he said and pointed toward the bathroom. It was then she realized she reeked of sweat. A pungent, sour odor filled her nostrils. She walked into the bathroom, undressed, and stood in the shower for who knew how long, the water just pouring over her, all the while aware she could never wash off the shame. She wrapped herself in a bath sheet, wanted to be swaddled like a baby. A baby. The first baby of this generation of my family. I killed her. How did it happen? How can I live with this? She remembered Maya's chubby pink face, her skin as soft as butter, the tiny eyelids, and knew she would never have a child.

She returned to the bedroom. Without thinking, she slid into bed, aware only of the crisp sheets. Uri lying there, smoking a cigarette, barely registered on her spent brain. He put out the cigarette in the bedside ashtray, then turned toward her. "Ready to sleep?" he asked.

"How can I sleep? My poor sister... her screams... they'll ring in my ears forever. What have I done? What have I done?"

Uri moved toward her and wrapped her in his arms. "Shh... don't do this to yourself," he whispered, now so close to her ear she felt his warm breath. It soothed her, made her feel safe. She could feel the roughness of his beard against her cheek. He smelled of tobacco and sweat, a manly scent, but not unpleasant. He stroked her hair. His rough hands caressed her body. "It wasn't your fault," his voice barely above a murmur. Her insides quivered. What happened then was so quick and so unexpected, she did not resist. At first, she thought she deserved being taken, like a hostage who needed punishment. But very quickly, Uri's weight, the taste of his mouth, his chest hair brushing her breasts felt like a protective shield. Like a dying person, she needed exactly this kind of absolution.

Uri was an experienced lover. On this heart-rending day he made her feel like a desirable woman, not a monster.

Afterwards, just before she gave in to sleep, she thought about how something as momentous as her first sexual experience should have happened under such tragic circumstances. Would the pleasures of sex, from now on, always mingle with death?

The morning light dawned thin and gray. When Raquela woke up, Uri wasn't in bed. She heard him rummaging somewhere. Her heart and eyelids were still heavy, but her body felt different, lighter, more womanly. She struggled to remember exactly how she had given herself to him—the previous night still in fog—but she didn't regret it. He had been gentle and kind. It cheered her a little to think that what had happened between them was such a stark demarcation between death and life.

She heard him calling, "*Boker Tov*, do you want some coffee?" His voice had the warmth of the sun. She tiptoed barefoot, still wearing his shirt, into the kitchen and sat on a high stool, watching him. His dark stubble, now darker, made him look like an Arab. He wore khaki pants and a white sleeveless T-shirt that showed his well-defined musculature. She noticed how hairy his arms were, like a bear, she thought. The bandage on his arm showed some pink. "If you have any gauze, I'll change your bandage," she said.

"It's nothing, don't make a big deal of it," Uri said. He turned on the faucet and put water into a long-handled pot. When the water boiled, he emptied the coffee grounds from a hand grinder and added them to the pot with plenty of sugar. Then, he poured the black coffee into two clear, small glasses and stirred in a powder.

"What is that?" Raquela detected a subtle woody scent.

"Cardamom. And just so you get to know our ways, that pot I used is the Finjan," Uri said. "If you stay with me for a while, you'll become a pro at this."

Her mind a swirl of confusion. "Stay with you?"

Uri took a sip from his cup, added more sugar, and twirled the teaspoon. "You can't very well go back to Atlit."

True. She knew that was not an option, and she couldn't see herself returning home to face Momma. Her first grandchild was dead. Dead under her—Rifka's—care. Nor could she ever explain to Bronka her sudden change of heart about men.

A knock at the door.

Uri pulled a gun out of his waistband and walked toward the front door. "Who is it?" he asked.

"It's me, Gad, open up." Gad walked in, looking agitated, and the men spoke for a while before Raquela noticed Gad had her bag in his hand.

"The trouble with our Arab neighbors has gotten much worse. I have to leave now," Uri said, handing her the belongings Gad brought back from Atlit. "Hurry, get dressed, I'll drop you off at Sami's." Uri dumped the coffee into the sink.

Raquela threw her clothes on, grabbed her rucksack, and ran downstairs to Uri's car.

"I wish I could help you more, but this is a bad time. You don't know how to handle weapons. You'd only be in the way," he said.

Raquela did not respond. Let me stay calm, she repeated over and over in her mind as Uri drove. An irrational composure came over her, but it didn't last long. Maya's plump little face floated before her mind's eye. Raquela willed it to go away, then felt guiltier.

"I have to make a detour before I drop you off," Uri said. "Maybe a couple of hours. I have to meet some people and get the goods."

It took much longer. By the time Uri picked up several crates from two bearded men behind a warehouse on the outskirts of another village it was late afternoon. She assumed it was a cache of weapons because Uri and the men looked very tense.

Throughout the ride, Raquela's mind swirled with inchoate thoughts. Death. Guilt. Golda. Momma. The emotions lay like a stone in the pit of her stomach. She went over every minute of the day spent with Maya, trying to find any act of omission or commission that may have contributed to the tragedy. What had she done wrong? Maya was a beautiful, healthy baby. Maybe the woman in Atlit was right; maybe she was the Angel of Death. She reflected on her initial unease with having to care for Maya and Eli's stupid statement that it was woman's inborn trait. Maya's death will prove him wrong, but at what cost? She'd always felt she wasn't cut out for motherhood.

Along the road, small armed groups of Arabs had gathered, prepared to face the Jewish settlers. Raquela's mind jumped from one extreme to the other. At some moments, she feared they might attack the car; at others, her eyes beseeched the men in keffiyehs to shoot her; kill her now and spare her the anguish.

Suddenly, Uri's Austin swerved so sharply it seemed it would crash into the ravine, but it stopped at the precipice. "Quick, jump!" Uri yelled to her and ran around the front of the vehicle to catch her. Now she became aware of shots coming from somewhere nearby.

"Bloody hell!" Uri spat out. "We are not too far from Jaffa now. Had you been awake you'd have seen what's going on."

"I wasn't sleeping. I was praying one of their bullets would reach me."

"Crazy woman!" Uri pushed her down into the ravine below the embankment and jumped in, pressing himself to the ground next to her.

They lay silent. After a while, when no shots were audible, Uri muttered in a low whisper, "As soon as the Arabs move on, I'll drop you off at Sami's and join our fighters. I must get the crates back to Kfar Vitkin tonight. Until I give you the signal, just stay quiet."

Her voice tremulous, she asked, "Will you come back to get me?"

He must have noticed her trembling because he said, "You had better get a hold of yourself."

"I feel so confused," she said.

"Nothing to be confused about. Stay and fight for our country; we need every able-bodied Jew. Make a life here... with me," Uri said.

"I can't stay here, but I can't return to Warsaw either. Maya's death changed everything... everything," she said quietly, unsure if he'd heard.

"Damn it! Do you have any idea how much effort was invested in getting you here?" Uri waved his hand in disgust. He was nothing like the night before. Had the impending battle with the Arabs unnerved him?

She marshaled all her inner resources to say it. "You took advantage of me at the lowest point in my life, but I'm not giving you a license to get into my mind too."

"Stupid girl." Uri turned away and waited till it was safe to leave.

No use asking how she'd manage at the Arab's house when Arabs seemed intent on killing Jews. She'd have to steer her own fate from here on, be the way she had been before she left home and stop depending on the Uris and Aleksanders of the world. It was a far more daunting prospect than opening a shop or deciding to travel to Palestine. Those were choices; this was something else.

The future seemed an open abyss when Uri stopped in front of Sami's compound on the deserted street. Dog barks shattered the stillness when he knocked on the gate in code. Soon, Sami shuffled out in his slippers and long robe. "*Salam Alaikum*," he greeted them in a gravelly voice. He opened the gate and embraced Uri. After a quick whisper into Sami's ear, Uri left abruptly without so much as saying goodbye.

Raquela stood for a minute, confused, but Sami welcomed her as if she were a long-lost friend. "Come in, come in, but quickly." Sami put his hand on Raquela's shoulder, took her rucksack, and walked her into the sprawling house that had appeared so strange just forty-eight hours before. He led her to the same room she'd occupied before.

"We will sort things out in the morning. Now get some rest," Sami said as he departed.

She craved asleep, wanted to forget everything that had happened. She washed quickly and fell into bed.

When she woke up, Raquela was thirsty; she needed a cup of hot tea. After a quick bath, she dressed and walked downstairs to a large, well-appointed dining room where a beautiful copper samovar graced the center of a buffet. Except for an old Arab woman, Raquela was the first guest. She noticed the beautiful embroidery on the woman's loose, long dress with its eight-pointed star, birds, and a moon. The woman smiled and gestured toward the buffet where many attractive small dishes stood on the cloth-covered surface.

Raquela did not recognize most of the foods. She gestured an inquiry toward the woman about a bowl closest to her, but the language chasm was too great. Raquela tried to use her German, then French, but it was no use. Cautiously, she sampled a few spoons. The porridge had an unfamiliar fermented taste, but Raquela's willingness to try it seemed to please the woman because she smiled kindly.

A few guests began arriving for breakfast. Most headed straight for the buffet, reached for the china cups, filled them with tea, then piled their plates and sat at the small tables scattered around the room. Raquela looked around the room, trying to find a seat.

A swarthy man with a lean, wiry build caught her eye. She couldn't help noticing the scar crossing his temple and upper cheek. With a self-assured air, he approached and pulled out a chair for her. He addressed her in Arabic, but her blank expression made it obvious she didn't speak it, so he tried a different tack, *"Puis-je me joindre à vous?"*

His French surprised her. He wanted to join her. Good. He didn't see her black heart; the sham smile she'd plastered on her face had disguised her well enough. The man sat his cup on the table, spilling a drop.

"Yes. Why not?" she replied, her brows raised in surprise. "Not a language I expected here."

He smiled warmly. A cleft on his chin softened his angular face covered in dark stubble, though it looked as if he had shaved. She detected a playful spark in his intense black eyes. "What brings you here, Mademoiselle?" he inquired.

"Business," she answered quickly and changed the subject. "And you?"

"First tell me your name," he said in a warm tone, inviting conversation.

"Raquela Bluestone." She extended her hand.

His palm felt warm and dry in contrast to the coolness his body projected. He shook her hand and held it a moment longer than she thought proper for a stranger. "So now it's your turn to tell me about yourself."

"I am Jacob Ben Maimon. I hope we will have plenty of time to chat."

Presumptuous, she thought, but didn't respond. She was so alone now it was no use discarding potential friends. Already, her resolve to be the captain of her own ship began to weaken.

There was something about this man that seemed odd, though she couldn't quite put her finger on it. His sunburned face resembled the

Arabs and he spoke Arabic, but he didn't wear Arab headgear. Unlike the Jewish settlers she'd seen, he didn't wear either khakis or shorts. Dressed in neat white shirt and gray slacks with a sharp crease, he looked more like a foreign businessman.

They sat next to one another, paying no attention to the others in the dining room. "So where are you from?" he asked. "I can see you are not a local."

"Warsaw," she responded laconically, wary of engaging him.

"I am from Morocco," Jacob said.

"Morocco?" She arched her eyebrows. "I've never met anyone from there."

He chuckled. "I don't know your plans for today, but I am heading to Sami's café. I promised to give him a hand for all the help he's given me. If you want to come along, you can."

Raquela was puzzled. "But we are at Sami's, right here."

Jacob clarified. "This is his guesthouse, but he also owns a café in the center of Jaffa."

"Alright, I will come. I have some things I must figure out," she said slowly, unsure why the café would be a better place in which to think.

"Good," Jacob smiled.

She decided that despite the scar, he was attractive in an exotic kind of way. He exuded confidence, something she now lacked completely.

Jacob stood up. "I'll be right back," he said and walked over to the buffet. Moments later, he set before her a plate of unfamiliar foods. "For us to share."

"I have no idea what these are," she said.

"Delicious food," he said, pointing at each item. "Pita, labneh with olive oil, green olives, baba ghanoush."

"I'm not very hungry, but thank you," she said.

Jacob looked disappointed and seemed to lose interest in the food since Raquela didn't touch any of the dishes, only sipped her tea. An awkward silence ensued. He picked at his pita, ate a couple of olives, and said, "Let's go."

She stood up quickly. Both of them left as if neither had the patience to wait to learn more about the other.

Getting through the packed streets of Jaffa with a sputtering Jeep was a challenge. Ever since she'd landed, Raquela noticed that nearly everything in this place was jerry-rigged, assembled with spit and glue to make it work. Everything, clearly, was in short supply, except perseverance and nerve. The stop-and-start traffic caused the engine to buck, but Jacob drove skillfully, babying the clutch and brake to keep the vehicle from stalling. Raquela watched people running hither and yon, heard distant grenades.

"Where are these explosions coming from?" she asked.

"Can't tell."

"So why are you so calm?"

"Can't get too rattled. Soon the Arab rebellion will be in full swing. It'll get worse. For now, they are just practicing."

It was lunchtime when they finally made it to Sami's café. Sami was officiating, a generous host. A stained red apron hung on his rotund belly, over the caftan. Immediately, Raquela was struck by the music. An older man with graying hair peeking out from under his headdress and wearing a long white caftan played an odd, pear-shaped string instrument. A very young man, a teenager with an incipient mustache, provided accompaniment on a tambourine. A multilingual crowd partook of large pitas and bowls of hummus and tahini, platters of juicy red tomatoes and small plates of olives. A foursome of British officers sat at one of the tables, laughing and drinking PEP beer out of bottles. Like other guests, they appeared to be here to enjoy, to forget the chaos outside, if only briefly.

The upbeat atmosphere here was such a sharp contrast to the confusion outside the door. It was difficult for Raquela to comprehend how such two different worlds could exist side by side. "Grenades outside, music inside?" she said.

"Yep," Jacob said, walking toward the rear of the restaurant. "If we didn't have music and laughter, we'd cry. It's the calm before the storm."

Strangeness was becoming the only permanent feature of this godforsaken place.

Jacob disappeared somewhere in the back, and for a while Raquela stood uncomfortably among the few empty tables. Disheveled, she felt like a stray dog who'd wandered in off the street looking for scraps. Her stomach rumbled. She knew the few Palestine pounds in her pocket would not cover a meal. The money from Aleksander was stashed with her belongings back at Sami's house. She'd decided to save it for grave emergencies.

An idea took hold, grew into a fervent desire: maybe Sami would agree to hire her as kitchen help until she figured out her plan. No way. What would he want with a stray Jewess? Everyone suddenly seemed to stare: Arab or Jew, she couldn't tell.

Luckily, Jacob bounded out of the back with a tray. He plopped it on the table near the musicians, nearly letting the small plates of hummus fly off. "Our lunch! Courtesy of Sami. He says we can work it off washing the dishes and the floor, emptying the ashtrays, and swabbing the counters at the end of the day. Don't be so glum, at least we get to eat. Sit! Sit!"

She sat down. Relief washed over her. At the moment, Sami and Jacob were the only friends she had. She glanced at other diners to figure out how to scoop up the hummus. Its surface glistened with an oil slick and red peppers. She picked up a piece of warm pita, tasted it cautiously and liked it. Jacob plunged into his meat kebab.

As they ate their meal, Jacob explained he'd been staying with Sami for several weeks working odd jobs. He leaned closer and whispered, "Ever since my prison escape."

She said, "Stop it! I'm not in the mood for jokes. Why are you here and where have you come from, really?"

Her outburst took him aback. "The blue city," he said quietly.

"Please, if you mean to have a conversation, don't speak in riddles."

"I'm perfectly serious, my little fire-breathing dragon. The blue city is Chefchaouen."

"I've heard of neither," Raquela shrugged, embarrassed.

The musicians, now joined by a third man with a long wind instrument, began to play a new set, drowning out the possibility of conversation. The music was exotic, oddly soothing, much needed. They listened to the music. Raquela watched the musicians and their exotic instruments, then noticed Jacob watching her.

"You look sad," he said. "What's wrong?"

"Nothing that can be fixed," she said. She was glad he didn't press.

They turned their attention to the food, finishing the last few pieces of pita and wiping their plates clean of any remnants.

"So just how did you end up in prison? Did you kill someone, or are you just a common thief?" Raquela said, half in jest.

"Let's just say it had something to do with preparedness," Jacob said.

She raised her eyebrows, unsure what to make of that remark.

"If you'd gotten a small taste of what's going on here, you'd understand," he said.

Raquela closed her eyes and saw the shootout scene where Uri was injured. "I did... more than a taste," she said.

Jacob said, "Let me just say that getting out alive from an Ottoman era fortress surrounded by a moat is not for the faint of heart."

"Now you are just bragging," she said.

The man knew how to get out of a tight spot. Maybe she'd stick with him until she found a path forward.

"Shall we?" Jacob said, rising.

And they began to clean the tables where diners had left coffee cups, plates, crumpled napkins, and cigarette butts and kept at it through the afternoon. All the while, the work itself, coupled with the soothing music, kept Raquela so distracted that for the time being she didn't think about anything else.

It was dark outside when the clanging of dishes, rattling of pots and voices of diners had fallen silent at the café. Sami came out from the kitchen carrying plates of food, a little of everything they'd been serving. "Let's eat," he said and flopped into the closest chair.

Raquela noticed the bags under his eyes seemed swollen.

She and Jacob joined him at the table.

Sami reached in his apron pocket, pulled out a cigar, and lit it. "You two really earned your keep today," he said, puffing out his cheeks and sending a swirl of earthy smoke into the air. "I think all my customers are hiding from reality. It's why they flock here. My musicians drown out the real world and it's just as well. There'll never be peace here."

Jacob and Raquela looked at one another in alarm.

"Don't look so surprised," Sami chuckled. "I mean, we Arabs and you Jews, we are like brothers who won't share. Our mothers didn't raise us well. But I've got no hate for anyone." He rested his unfinished cigar on the ashtray, stood up and reached for a bottle at the bar. He brought it over, then set three ice-filled glasses on the table. "My evening ritual," he said. "Helps me unwind. Would you like some?"

"What is it?" Raquela asked, looking at the clear liquid in a nearly empty round bottle.

"Arak, milk of lions," Sami grinned, licking his lips as if he were tasting it already. "Strong stuff."

"I'd love to try it," said Raquela. The notion of remaining in her currently insensible state appealed to her.

"Yes, please," said Jacob.

Sami poured a smidgen into each of their glasses, then added water from a pitcher. The drink turned milky.

"The stuff will knock you out if you aren't used to it," he said, smiling, then filled his own glass to the top and stirred the ice with his finger.

A question scratched at Raquela's brain. Wasn't there a prohibition on alcohol for Muslims? Never mind. She was eager to taste it.

The three sat huddled around the small rear table, sipping arak and chatting like old friends, pretending to ignore the ominous sounds of distant explosions. Revolts must have been on all their minds because Sami said, "Did you kids know about the Asturian miners' revolt in Spain? It happened... Let's see..." He looked up with his eyes closed. "About two years ago."

"But don't we have a major revolt brewing right here?" Jacob said.

Sami frowned. "I'd rather talk about what's behind us because the future looks bleak." Sami was a man of the world. His awareness of events beyond Palestine surprised Raquela; her ears pricked up. "I followed the Asturian revolt in the Polish papers. Those Spanish miners were anarchists."

Jacob nodded and Sami let out a curling ribbon of smoke, both perhaps surprised that a young woman had familiarity with politics.

"The anarchists thought they could live freely guided only by their own sense of right and wrong. No authoritarian governments to tell them what to do," Jacob said.

"I loved their idealism," Raquela chimed in.

"Yes, but reality hit them in the face, didn't it?" Sami said. "Three thousand of them killed."

Sami's robe and headdress had given Raquela an entirely erroneous impression. She'd mistaken him for a man knowledgeable about camels, donkeys, tents, and sand. My own prejudice, she reflected with disgust, and became aware that the arak made her feel mellow, less preoccupied with her dark secret. She felt more comfortable with these strangers than with Uri, Eli or even Golda. She didn't have to explain anything; she could be someone else.

Sami was a spellbinding storyteller and now, his tongue loosened by arak, he had reawakened her old interest. His words painted the miners' bleak lives and made their passion for the rugged Cantabrian Mountains feel real. Raquela felt the romance of their righteous struggle, yet she, herself, had been cautious about jumping on causes.

Thoughts of the miners circled her brain like mosquitoes, but they were far better than thinking of her last day in Atlit. For the moment, the struggle of the miners succeeded in occupying her mind. The arak, helpful at first, now took its toll. Her head ached; her eyes burned. It was late. She yearned for bed.

After Sami had run out of steam, he closed the café, and Jacob drove the three of them back to the Jaffa compound. Raquela sat in the back with Sami. They rode in silence punctuated by Sami's snores and distant gunshots. When Sami's place came into view, Raquela was alarmed to see it surrounded by armed men. He opened his eyes and said, "These are our men, don't worry."

The three of them entered the gate, but Raquela couldn't understand why the armed guards hadn't been there the other night. The mood felt different, tenser. "Goodnight," Raquela uttered quietly and went upstairs unsettled.

For several days Raquela worked long hours at the café in the hope her nerves, shattered by the Atlit disaster, would be soothed by the mundane work and Jacob's commonsense presence. He was a hard worker and practical, always reminding her to save the meager earnings. "Got to be prepared for a rainy day," he'd say tucking the coins into his pocket, unaware that her rainy day had already come. He spoke about how he admired Sami's egalitarian stance and no reservations about hosting or employing Jews. Jacob's upbeat demeanor helped her get through the days when Maya's death overwhelmed her. She could tell Jacob recognized she was troubled, yet he never pried; simply smiled with understanding in his kind eyes. And right now, kindness was what she needed most.

One day, she awoke to a pink dawn and loud shouting downstairs. She threw on her clothes, grabbed her bag and ran down. It was Sami standing in the large dining room, gesticulating wildly, and calling out, "*Yalla, Yalla,* everyone out!"

Outside the compound, an angry Arab mob—a hundred men, at least—armed to the teeth with machine guns, clubs, and grenades, made it clear the guards wouldn't be able to hold off the rioters much longer. The revolt had arrived at Sami's doorstep. Even though Sami was an Arab, it was well known he occasionally harbored Jews. Doing business with them... Well, that was one thing, but protecting them...

Jacob flew out of Sami's building with his belongings. "At the very least, they'll loot Sami's place," he whispered and took Raquela's hand, squeezing it.

"If they hurl a grenade the whole place will go up in smoke," he said. "Let's get out of here."

They both knew from Sami's stories that the mix of land claims, counterclaims and emotions in this region was pure dynamite. Both peoples were obsessed with this barren piece of the world. In a flash, Jacob jumped into Sami's truck, parked just outside the compound gate, opened a door for Raquela and motioned her in. They sped off, leaving a trail of dust.

21 INTERNATIONAL BRIGADES RECRUITMENT HEADQUARTERS

Aleksander Zabielski was grateful for the short interval of quiet as he sat at a desk stacked with papers: false passports waiting for photos to be affixed and train tickets to be distributed. He put his feet up and lit a cigarette. Soon hordes of fresh young men and women from all over Eastern Europe would stream into this Parisian recruitment headquarters and swear allegiance to the cause. Some from as far as America, all young: Jewish girls from Warsaw with short-cropped hair, wearing slacks and ties to project an image of unfussy modernity; young Hungarians from Budapest sick and tired of the roaming bands of Arrow Cross promoting Hitler's racial ideology. Of course, Aleksander's fellow Frenchmen came in droves too, all eager to fight for freedom, to squelch Franco's fascistic moves before fascism spread all over Europe like an incurable disease.

He remembered the astonished look on his own interviewer's face when he quizzed Aleksander for this clandestine job. All those questions about his politics and commitment. He hadn't quite expected how difficult it would be to get through the interrogation. Karol Swierczewski—one could immediately tell from his stance he was a military man—walked into the room, bending stiffly to avoid hitting the low door frame. He sat at the desk chair without so much as an introduction and looked Aleksander over. Then the questions shot out of his mouth with machine-gun speed. Then this, with a big happy laugh:

"You, a count and a communist? That's pure nonsense! Count Zabielski, indeed!"

"No, comrade," Aleksander told him. "I may be of noble blood, but don't judge me by my heredity. I want to do everything in my power to help our Spanish brothers keep their peaceful, equitable life in the villages. I know how hard they struggled to win their freedom. No bosses! Who in their right mind would object to that?"

"Quite a lecture, Aleksander! But at thirty-five, you may just be too old to fight. We need fresh blood."

"Comrade Swierczewski, I can work as a recruiter. I have many connections in Eastern Europe, especially in Poland. I can deliver the fresh blood you are looking for."

"Poland?" Swierczewski knitted his eyebrows and seemed surprised.

"Yes, my family came to Paris at the turn of the century, before the constitution of the Polish Republic outlawed the noble class and titles."

Swierczewski leaned back in his chair, stretched his legs sporting black knee-high, spit-polished boots, and looked up at the ceiling.

"Ah, yes, I should have recognized your Polish name sooner. You Zabielskis were quite a prominent noble family, but someone like me who grew up dirt poor didn't know any nobles or gave a damn about them."

"I don't give a damn about them either, Comrade," Aleksander said. "My father and grandfather are long gone, so no more real nobles in our family."

"What about Countess Zabielski? How does she feel about you straying this far?"

"I need to tell you the truth," Aleksander said slowly and deliberately. "Now that you brought my mother into this."

"The truth, eh!"

"Mother never accepted the nobility nonsense. She is Jewish, comrade. Her nobility is in the Talmud."

Swierczewski burst out laughing. "Jewish! I was a Tenenbaum before I became Swierczewski, a fucking fir tree. Imagine that!"

"You too? You're a landsman?"

Comrade Karol pulled out the desk drawer and produced a bottle of vodka, passed it to Aleksander with a wink. "Here, take a swig. I've heard you take a nip now and then and that you like the ladies too. My kind of Jew, my friend."

Aleksander blushed, shrugged, took the bottle. No use offending Comrade Karol. The vodka burned pleasantly. He looked around the room. A pin-studded map of Spain and the narrow peninsula of Gibraltar connecting it to Morocco caught Aleksander's eye. He said, "Do you have any news about what's happening in Madrid?"

Swierczewski did not reply. He stood up, shook Aleksander's hand with a vise grip. "You are in," he said and marched out of the room.

Well, that was many months ago. By now, Aleksander knew they had to keep spies and informers out of the operation. He also knew how to conduct a real interview, how to detect a false note or insincerity in an applicant's response. Now he was the boss.

The noise of feet thundering down the stairs to the cellar sounded more like a stampede of wild horses. There'd be many applicants to screen. Aleksander pulled the chair closer to the desk, sat upright and made himself look official.

An earnest-looking young man came in and nodded when Aleksander motioned toward the chair in front of his desk. Probably a student judging by his plaid cap, open collar, and blue-striped shirt. Bright red suspenders.

Aleksander quizzed him for a while on the basics, then he threw the applicant a stern glare. "Are you willing to shed your persona, become someone else?"

"What do you mean?" the young man asked.

Aleksander leaned back in his chair, never losing eye contact. "You'll have to adopt a new name for the kind of work we have in mind."

"Oh, yes, of course." The reply came swiftly.

Good he isn't asking for details, Aleksander thought. He seems willing to do whatever is necessary. "Go next door, pick up your paperwork and take it to our office near Gare du Nord," Aleksander said. Then, "Next!"

A fresh candidate entered in a sprightly manner. If not for her buxom appearance, he might have mistaken her for a young man because of her close-cropped black hair, trousers, and tie. "Well, well, well..." Aleksander looked the girl over. "Ready to handle a weapon?"

"Are you saying we volunteers will have to kill? I thought there would be plenty of support work in Spain for girls like me."

"Girls like you? And just what kind of support work did you have in mind?" Aleksander chuckled.

The girl looked rattled.

"Try applying next time a country fights a civil war. You have some growing up to do," he said.

She shrugged her shoulders and walked out in a huff.

Aleksander shook his head in annoyance. He couldn't stand these kids just playing at war. The noise in the waiting area, just outside his door, reminded him to get on with the interviews. "Next," he called out.

A serious-looking, bespectacled man walked in. Neatly trimmed beard, confident gait. Aleksander judged him older than the students he'd been seeing, upper twenties, maybe older. Some standard questions, then the applicant asked, "Is it true Italy and Germany are supplying the Nationalist insurgents?"

"Aha, I see you've been keeping up with the news," Aleksander said.

"Of course. I've heard they are rounding up the civilians in bullrings and shooting them like fish in a barrel. Savages!"

Whenever an applicant sounded passionate, Aleksander pressed for more. He couldn't be too careful. He asked questions to elicit convincing attachment to communism, socialism, or anarchism.

This man passed muster.

Aleksander stood up and slapped the man's shoulder. "We need men like you. Welcome to the struggle."

By the end of the day, Aleksander stretched, lit a cigarette, and smiled though no one was watching. He, a sculptor shaping innocent civilian young men and women to be fearless, to learn how to function as a disciplined quasi-military battalion? At times, these interviews made him feel like a hypocrite. Sure, he reassured Comrade Swierczewski that he was aligned with the goals of the Republicans in the Spanish Civil war, that he wanted to do his utmost to serve the cause of democracy, yet the burden of his noble title weighed on him like a boulder. He worried his new comrades would shun him if they learned of his title. The honorific he wanted to bury surfaced like a bad penny. It was on all his legal documents. It was a good thing that now that Karol Swierczewski had been sent to Spain to command the Republican operation as General "Walter," the newer heads of the recruitment operation wouldn't look so closely at Aleksander's background. He passed muster with Comrade Karol; he should be untouchable.

It was good the volunteers had to take on new names, shed previous lives and personas. Who knew how the brutal combat would change them? The new names would ease that process, allow them to imagine themselves as soldiers.

After a long day spent in the stifling, smoke-filled cellar, Aleksander emerged onto a street pulsing with life and inhaled deeply. The Left Bank of the Seine was the intellectual and artistic part of Paris and its proximity to the Sorbonne assured a steady stream of applicants for the cause. Students were more open-minded, more attracted to the battle for freedom, yet blissfully unaware how much of their blood would be spilled.

On this August day in 1936, Parisians had to contend not only with unusually high temperatures but with scant rainfall. The dusty streets had taken on the appearance of a woman who has stopped caring for her looks. Aleksander's shirt felt damp on his back. Luckily, the walk to 13 rue de l'Ancienne Comédie was no more than ten minutes.

At Café Procope, the haunt of the greats, Rousseau, Thomas Jefferson, Ben Franklin, Dante and Voltaire, Aleksander ordered *Magret de canard* with mushrooms and polenta. Didn't his noble forbears have a tradition of duck hunting? And wine of course, an expensive Côte de Nuits Pinot Noir.

He tried not to stare at a black-haired beauty several tables over, but emboldened by alcohol, kept returning to her profile: something about her reminded him of Raquela. Simple as that. It wasn't the hair, but she had the same delicate features, same intensity in her eyes, the bearing of a determined woman, someone not easily distracted from her goal. Aleksander chuckled to himself. He finished his meal, his wine, blew out a melancholy breath: Raquela was the most interesting woman he'd ever met. She was worldly yet naive, tough-skinned at times, then vulnerable as a baby. And she was totally unaware of her allure. That's what made her so fascinating.

The violinist began to play Schubert's Serenade, but Aleksander's mood soured. The memory of the applicants singing the *Internationale*,

186

with an expression of reverence on their fresh faces, drowned out everything at Café Procope.

The woman never returned his gaze. He called for his check, paid it quickly, headed home to his studio and back to work on a sculpture he'd been reworking far too long. He liked working late at night, though these days, with all the hours spent recruiting and interviewing candidates for the International Brigades, he had become less productive.

In Jardin du Luxembourg, he took his favorite spot, a bench at the fountain built by Marie de' Medici, mother of Louis the XIII. The nobles were good for some things, after all! He watched errant leaves floating in the pool, the evening trees reflecting in the water, the play of the light over everything. He stared at the sculpture of Galatea in the embrace of her lover, Acis. Her perfect body reminded him of Raquela. Would that he'd seen that goddess naked! That last night when he'd gone up to her hotel drunk as a peasant and banged on her door, she must have thought him the Cyclops Polyphemus crouching above the lovers, trying to take Galatea against her wish. Well, she was gone now. He regretted his drunken hijinks. He pushed the image away. He'd never see her again. There were plenty of women but finding someone exceptional like Raquela happens only once in a lifetime.

He was about to get up and walk to his studio when the sound of heels announced a woman approaching. She was tall and stately, well dressed. She sat on his bench. "Do you mind if I sit here? I love this exact spot."

"No, not at all. Galatea belongs to all of us," Aleksander said. Now he had a dilemma. If he left now, she might think he really didn't want her to share this bench. Not wanting to offend, he decided to sit a while longer. She appeared to be deep in thought as she observed the fountain. Aleksander looked at her profile. There was no question, she was very attractive. Lovely long hair flowing in waves down her back, a delicate nose, full lips.

Suddenly Aleksander, never one to drown his impulses, interrupted her reverie and asked, "My apologies for being so forward. I see you appreciate the sculpture; you look at it as if your truly understand art."

The woman smiled and said, "Thank you, I do love sculpture very much."

"In that case, perhaps you might like to see a sculptor at work. I am heading to my studio right now."

She smiled.

He understood her answer, and it pleased him.

After a brief silence, they walked toward his studio, Aleksander's head filled with images of Raquela.

When they entered his building, a middle-aged matron who lived on his floor passed them in the hallway. She cast disapproving glances his way as if to ask, yet another conquest? Aleksander took the woman's arm and opened the studio door quickly. They entered into a clutter of half-finished plaster bodies, some on the floor, some nearly finished on pedestals.

The woman said, "So you only work on women's bodies."

"Yes," Aleksander said.

A narrow table under the window held an array of tools: chisels, mallets, rasps, bags of plaster and modeling clay. She walked around a nearby chair with an overflowing ashtray and stared at the Andre Renaud poster promoting the musician playing two pianos simultaneously.

"I see you like women and music," she said.

"Maybe you'd consider modeling for me one day," Aleksander said, approaching her. He took her hand and led her to the bedroom behind the studio.

The urgency of gathering volunteers from Europe grew daily in the summer of 1936 as Spain's Nationalist rebels received ever increasing aid from Germany and Italy.

"We must send the International Brigades in early fall, before our comrades are all wiped out," Aleksander's new superior announced.

It was clear that the rotund Frenchman, who had once been a coal miner, meant what he said. His ruddy cheeks turned even redder as he gesticulated and pointed at the map, highlighting for Aleksander the strongholds of the Nationalists in the south and the poorly defended Republican positions in the north.

"You'll have to leave for Warsaw immediately. Comrade Karol so instructed before he decamped for Spain. You have connections in Poland, and you speak that crazy, tongue twisting language."

"I expected this," Aleksander said. "I know French applicants are dwindling."

"New blood from the East, Comrade!"

"New blood," he said. "I will depart in the morning."

With that, Comrade Lionel handed him a portfolio of possible individuals and organizations to contact and train tickets. As for a false passport, Aleksander had created one for himself weeks before. Now he'd actually have to say his assumed name out loud, as if he believed it: Antoni Zak. He'd kept the initials so he could use his monogrammed shirts and luggage.

On his way home, walking through the lively streets of Saint-Germain-des-Prés, he reflected on how he felt French to his very bones. The motto 'Liberté, Egalité, Fraternité' was not just a collection of words. It was his religion. The sounds and smells of these streets were in his blood. How would he feel in his ancestors' haunts in Warsaw? He wasn't at all sanguine about that. Being raised in France by a Jewish mother who herself had abandoned the religious life, he was a cosmopolitan freethinker and, most of all, a free spirit and an artist. How would he relate to the strait-laced dogmatic Catholics in Poland? Well, they were not his only recruitment targets.

At home, he absentmindedly threw a few things into his leather Vuitton keepall bag, then poured himself a glass of wine.

22 CARMEL GUESTHOUSE, SUMMER 1936

When the Arab revolt reached its boiling point, Jaffa resembled a war zone. Jacob and Raquela, no longer under Sami's protection, had to find a safe haven. Like a demon, Jacob maneuvered around barricades the British had erected. Glass shard and nail-filled access roads racked Jacob's nerves. Raquela's heart stuck in her throat; at any moment, a tire could blow out.

"Shit! Shit!" Jacob yelled every time they had to evade burning tires.

When the vehicle reached a dead end with no chance of turning back, they scrambled out and ran, ducking grenades hurled through the marketplace. They skirted overturned stalls, tripping on fruit spilled everywhere. Screams of women running with babies in their arms filled Raquela with terror. Older children wailed and clutched their mothers' caftans for dear life. An acrid smell of smoke stung Raquela's nostrils. She gripped Jacob's hand as she ran. He pulled her into alleys to avoid British soldiers, angry as bees that their mandate over Palestine was being challenged by motley groups of ill-equipped Arabs. If it hadn't been for him, Raquela was certain she'd have died that day.

A chorus of stray dogs welcomed Raquela and Jacob when they arrived close to midnight at the Carmel Guesthouse. After two days on the run,

190

they were so exhausted they overcame their misgivings about the tumbledown neighborhood. The ramshackle building—a squat cement block structure with missing windows and a corrugated metal roof—bore all the makings of a dwelling for those displaced by life's misfortunes. A worn, chipped and dented assembly of chairs, barrels and buckets sat outside, huddled next to a trash-strewn yard. One sad-looking palm was a reminder this was still the Levant.

The guesthouse was located at the foot of the German colony of old Haifa, a stone's throw from the sea. Raquela knew that staying close to the port suited a plan Jacob had been hatching, and the place would be cheap.

Jacob knocked on the front door. No response. He knocked harder.

A sleepy looking old man cracked the door open, looked them over squinty-eyed. "Coming at this ungodly hour?"

"We are Jews," Jacob reassured him.

"Please, we need a room," Raquela chimed in, and Jacob opened his fist to show they could pay.

The man looked at the crumpled bills but didn't take them. "We will settle up in the morning." He handed Jacob a key, then directed him to a room down a long corridor.

In the tiny room, only one cot stood next to a low table with an enormous ashtray. A naked lightbulb glared from above.

Without thinking, Raquela asked, "But where will you sleep?"

"In the bed." Jacob kicked off his shoes and unbuttoned his shirt.

"And what about me?"

"You can join me, or you can sleep sitting up there," Jacob pointed toward a metal folding chair in the corner."

She looked at him, disbelieving. "And here I thought you were a gentleman."

"Quit it. I'm in no mood." Jacob dropped his trousers and slid into bed.

What a monster, she thought. This, after all they'd been through? Raquela closed her eyes tight to stanch the anger.

Soon the room was full of his buzzing snores.

She unfolded the chair. It squeaked, but he didn't wake up. She sat down and leaned her head on the wall, trying to sleep, but it was impossible. Her body ached. She'd hurt her ankle jumping off the jeep in Jaffa. Now it was swollen; she could hardly move it.

After an hour, perhaps two, she swallowed her pride and inched her way to the edge of the cot. Instinctively, Jacob moved over in his sleep and teetered on the other edge, giving her space.

When she woke up, she realized the weight on her shoulder was Jacob's arm. She didn't move, could hardly breathe. Again, in bed with a man! She closed her eyes. God, who have I become?

Warm, yellow light filtered through the grimy window. "Good morning," Jacob leaned over her, brushed the curls off Raquela's face, and looked at her close up. With a hangdog look he said, "I am sorry for being such an ass last night."

"I have no choice but to forgive you. You saved me from those... savages in Jaffa," she said.

"They aren't any more savage than we are," Jacob said.

After they got up and washed in the communal hallway bathroom, they returned to the room.

"So how long do you plan to stay here?" Raquela asked.

"I don't know. I'll find out if people here know anything about tramp steamers."

"Tramp steamers?"

"That's how I'm hoping to get out of here. Work my passage as a deckhand."

"Wait, wait," she said. "A passage to where? We just got here."

"Hold your horses, woman. I wasn't talking about you. It's my plan."

Raquela bit her lip. Why had she assumed he'd take her with him just because they shared a cot? Stupid. She wasn't exactly sure if he still planned to go to Morocco or Spain, something he'd mentioned obliquely when he spoke with Sami. Fear of facing Momma and Bronka still filled her, but she asked, "Do you think a tramp steamer would get me to Poland?"

All the awful things that had happened since she got here made her so overwrought, she had hardly given a thought to what came next. It was as if she were a hapless leaf floating on the current, powerless to determine her course. She wasn't herself, and she knew it, but saw no way of clambering out of the swift flow of events.

Jacob looked at her, perplexed. "I have no idea, but I rather doubt it." He must have noticed her crestfallen look because he said, "On second thought, if you could get a ship to get you to Athens, you might be able to get to Warsaw by train in three, or four days, but it could be very expensive. And a young woman alone on a tramp steamer might not be safe."

"Let me think about it," she said, keenly aware now of the hunger pangs in the pit of her stomach. Her mind swirled.

Before they had checked into the guesthouse, they pooled their money to pay for room and board. She'd held on to the money from Aleksander. It was her insurance policy. But depending on how long they'd stay at the guesthouse, even that insurance stash might be gone. And then what? Perhaps Jacob's agreement to combine their meager resources meant that he had given at least a fleeting thought to taking her along to his next destination. But then... What if her money was just a convenient windfall?

The sun shone brightly when they walked outside. Four men, apparently Carmel guesthouse residents, sat in front of the house. A bald, skinny one exhaled cigarette rings; an unshaven one with wild, white hair seemed to be mending a shoe, while the youngest of the group, a dark-eyed youth, watched. The old man who had opened the door when they first arrived greeted them. "Let me introduce myself properly; I am Moshe, a Jew from Russia. I manage this joint. And you?"

Jacob shook his hand. "Jacob, from Morocco."

"And who is she?" The manager pointed at Raquela standing off to the side.

"She... she is Raquela, from Poland," Jacob introduced her as she stepped forward hesitantly.

"Your girl?" Moshe grinned, but Jacob didn't respond so Moshe directed his gaze to Raquela.

"We need young women like you to build this country. Now, kids, what are you up to?"

"Any place around here to buy food?" Jacob inquired. "We are starved, haven't eaten in two days now."

The smoker took the cigarette out of his mouth and spoke. "Why not?"

"Don't be an idiot, David," Moshe said. "They escaped from Jaffa. We are lucky to be sixty miles north of the craziness."

David spit out a wad of phlegm and waved his hand in disgust, "Always fighting the Arabs; it'll never stop, not in our lifetime."

Moshe looked at David and said, "Our numbers here are growing; we're getting on their nerves." Then, he turned to Jacob. "Walk to the right and in about five blocks turn left, you'll find a place to get some pitas and hummus."

The white-haired man stopped fiddling with the shoe and cackled, "It's an Arab bakery, you can test your luck there."

Alarmed, Raquela looked at Jacob, but he said, "Let's just go."

By day they could see the area was heavily industrial: bulldozers, cement mixers, cranes. Jacob stopped a young, dark-skinned worker—they couldn't tell if he was an Arab or a Sephardic Jew—and asked in Arabic, "What's all this construction equipment?"

The man pointed proudly to the Union Jack flapping on a pole some distance away. "The British are building a modern deep-water port."

"Do you know anything about tramp steamers that dock here?" Jacob inquired, but the young man had no idea.

They kept walking. Soon they smelled the mesmerizing aroma of fresh bread. In the bakery, a middle-aged Arab with missing front teeth greeted them cheerfully, "*Salam Alaikum.*"

Jacob paid for a stack of warm pitas, a container of hummus, and a dozen labneh balls.

"Why are you buying so much?" Raquela asked.

"To share with our new neighbors."

Raquela began to suspect she had misjudged him.

Once the relief of having escaped the Arab mob wore off, Raquela sank ever deeper into depression over Maya's death. She brooded about the rarely mentioned deaths of Berg babies born before her. Was that why Momma smiled so rarely? Was she in perpetual mourning and would that now happen to both Golda and her? One thing was clear. The breach the death had caused with Golda was something that could never be repaired. The carousel of dark thoughts paralyzed Raquela. She slept too much or just lay awake; her body resisted getting up as if it had turned to a moss-covered boulder.

At her loneliest moments, Raquela saw her grandmother Sarah's smiling eyes, almost felt a papery hand on her shoulder and that sweet voice whispering don't despair, you won't always be so sad. It was that image of her grandmother that made her realize the worst impact of the baby's death: Raquela lost her courage, her confidence she could overcome any obstacle. She'd turned into an apathetic, powerless woman, someone she didn't recognize. She was definitely no longer Rifka.

The cramped quarters of the guesthouse, the dirty communal bathroom, the incessant noise of the port construction and the oppressive heat only added to Raquela's hopelessness. And the broken window screens increased her misery as mosquitoes feasted on her each night, and she scratched herself raw.

She couldn't bring herself to admit the abject fear of facing her family upon return to Poland, nor could she, if asked, say why she remained at the guesthouse with Jacob. But Jacob did his best to lift her spirits by telling her stories and bad jokes and bringing her oranges that she seemed to like.

She didn't react until he began telling her about his risky adventures. This Saturday, after she ate a few slices of orange, Jacob said, "Have I ever told you about my prison break?"

Grudgingly, she said, "I thought it was a joke when you had first mentioned it."

"Oh, but it is true. The Acre prison was so brutal, I'd have risked anything to get out."

"How did you manage that?"

"I left a poor facsimile of myself made of wet papers and a blanket, then slid down to safety on knotted sheets and ran like hell," Jacob said.

"But what were you planning to do if the British had caught you?"

Jacob grinned, "Run fast."

She came a bit more to life. "But how did you become a prisoner in the first place?" A small crack began to form in her depression.

"I was a merchant back in Morocco in my father's tool shop. Through our clients and their connections, I became involved in running arms to our brethren here. I was good at it, developed many contacts, but it didn't always end well. Maybe I was too trusting..." Jacob chewed his lip and reached for a cigarette.

"But weapons... How did that start?"

"My father had fought in the Rif War. Always spoke of how you need arms to win your freedom."

She was becoming more interested. "Did you fight here too?"

"There are plenty who want to fight, but too few weapons. This was my way to contribute."

"Where did you run to get away from your pursuers?"

"I made my way to Sami. Thank goodness for him. He sold me this," Jacob pulled up his pant leg and revealed a gun strapped to his calf.

Raquela's sharp intake of air startled Jacob. He put out the cigarette, stood up and straightened the pant leg.

Raquela smiled, probably the first time since Maya's death. "From now on I'll always wonder if you have a gun stashed somewhere on your body."

He shrugged, "Remember, Raquela, weapons are like any other tool. They can be used for good or ill."

After the first anxiety-filled night, Raquela reconciled to sharing the cot with Jacob, albeit on a completely platonic basis. She was grateful he was a gentleman; he didn't pressure her. In just a couple of weeks, the men of the guesthouse seemed like members of an extended family. Jacob was parsimonious with the little money they had left but still went out most days at dusk to buy pitas and hummus for everybody to share. They ate together and chatted, sitting outside to get the benefit of the sea breeze until it was pitch black with only sporadic glimpses of British patrol boat searchlights scanning the waters. They spoke of the fierce battles between the Jewish settlers and the Arabs who sold them the land and then regretted it. They spoke of the British and wondered what stake other than oil they had in this remote, uncivilized part of the world.

Rumors reached them that more than 1,000 British soldiers had marched into Jaffa, blowing up homes and trying to close the sea route. Raquela and Jacob were among the lucky ones. For them, the possibility of escape from the Haifa port was still an option. The world outside the Levant interested the guesthouse residents too.

"We aren't the only ones fighting for freedom. In Spain, Asturian miners have been clashing with the fascists," Moshe said one evening as they gossiped outside.

David lit a cigarette and spoke slowly, as if delivering a judgment. "They won the latest elections in Spain with a coalition of left-wing parties. With God's help, they may reverse all the damage the fascists have done."

"God has nothing to do with it," Moshe spat out. "If you really want something, you have to fight for it, and fight again if you lose it. They have to stand up for their beliefs, just like we are doing here."

The words reverberated in Raquela's head. She'd come here for Golda, not out of any sense of zeal to reclaim this land. She felt no connection to it. The Spaniards' fight for an ideology appealed to her far more than holding onto a piece of turf. She needed to just snap out of this... whatever it was, stop sleeping all the time and find the gumption she had back home. Maya was dead, and she couldn't change that. Her suffering helped no one. She wasn't sure how one could get past such a feeling—the shame and grief cutting so deeply, constricting her heart— but she understood that she had to. In Warsaw, she'd been like the prickly pear cacti that surrounded the guesthouse, protected, mostly solitary and resilient. Here she was more like a wispy dandelion, falling apart with the slightest breeze. Maybe she should join Jacob. If nothing else, it would show her solidarity with the Spaniards and be a way out of hopelessness. But was Jacob really bound for Spain? She wasn't certain of anything.

———————

For three months, Jacob continued his daily quest to get information about tramp steamers and David, a longshoreman from Odessa who'd emigrated to Palestine years before, proved to be a useful contact. Now that his wife had died, he made the inhabitants of the guesthouse his family.

"I'll do what I can to help you," he'd told Jacob right from their first day.

It was David's daily habit to sit at the shore for hours looking out to sea, dreaming of his old life. He seemed to know all the stevedores, mechanics, pilots, and warehouse workers. Jacob asked David to tell him if he'd spotted any steamers and to inquire with his port contacts if a given ship might be bound for Spain or Western Europe.

On this July evening, Jacob lay in bed, resting after a long day of hauling cargo at the pier. He had already filled the huge ashtray but reached for another smoke.

Raquela folded a few pieces of laundry she'd pulled off the line just before a rare rainstorm pelted the corrugated roof, making an awful racket. She could no longer remain silent. She had decided to tackle her uncertain status with him. "Assuming a tramp steamer shows up, where exactly are you going?" she asked.

Jacob sat up and took a long puff. "Remember Sami's talk about the military moves in Morocco and rumors about Franco's intentions to attack the democratic government in Spain?"

Raquela's brow crinkled. "Yes," she said slowly.

"Well, it's happened. I need to get to Albacete, Spain," Jacob said with emphasis.

"Why there?"

"It's the headquarters of the International Brigades. I'm leaving as soon as possible. I've heard they are recruiting volunteers all over Europe, and even in America."

"And what about me?" Raquela blurted out.

Jacob pushed his cigarette stub into the overflowing ashtray and said, "Come here, sit next to me."

She put down a blouse she'd been folding and sat by his side, half turned, facing him.

Jacob's eyes locked in on hers. "It's up to you. David says scuttlebutt is any day now the *Pharaoh* or the *Altajir Saeid* will be coming in. You can join me if you want to venture into a war zone, or you can look for a way back to Poland."

"Without money?" Raquela's eyes filled with tears. She sat cracking her knuckles.

"Money," Jacob echoed her words. "Unfortunately, always a basis for decisions." He pulled her closer and embraced her.

She sat motionless with her head nestled on his shoulder, inhaling his earthy tobacco scent until she realized her tears had dampened his shirt. She pulled away, but he grasped her hand and held it.

"Maybe fighting for democracy will give you a purpose, a

commitment to something larger. As for me, I'll fight till my last breath alongside the Republicans."

She spent the night awake, considering her options. There weren't many. Getting back to Poland after such a long, unexplained absence was not only emotionally terrifying; without money, it was not feasible. And she liked Jacob's gentle brown eyes, his honesty and kindness. She wanted to be needed. The more she thought of it, the more Jacob's comment made sense. Maybe joining the cause would help her climb out of her bottomless depression. She might go to help, but not—God forbid—to fight.

They awoke to banging on their door. It was David. "The *Pharaoh* just docked," he said out of breath. "I was sitting on the shore, waiting for sunrise and there it was. I heard it'll be moving west, but still no word on its cargo. Let's just hope it's not anything dangerous."

Jacob scurried around the room throwing his things into a bag.

"What are you doing?" Raquela asked.

"I'm leaving. Now. Who knows when it'll sail? I'm not missing this chance."

"Be careful and good luck," David said as he slipped out of the room.

It was still quiet in the guesthouse. To Raquela the room that had sheltered them all these months suddenly shrank to the size of a jail cell.

Jacob put his bag down and looked at Raquela, "Coming?"

"I suppose," she said. "If you'll let me."

It felt like her only choice.

23 THE RECRUITER. WARSAW, AUGUST 1936

The men mopped sweat from their brows with soggy handkerchiefs; the women fanned themselves vigorously with their notepads or the afternoon newspaper. This August day not so much as a whisper of a breeze came through the open windows. They were all in attendance—not one was missing—because the group leader, Lazar, told them as they finished the last meeting that this one would be special. Apparently, someone had traveled from abroad to speak with them, but the subject could not be disclosed in advance.

Curious to find out what the secrecy was all about, Bronka had canceled a late client meeting so she could attend. But Mordechai had become more insistent on spending time with her after the meetings, and it made her increasingly uncomfortable. She liked him, but not that way. She'd slip out early, as soon as she learned what the foreign speaker had to say.

The meeting began in the usual manner with the singing of the Bund anthem. The vow to rid the world of tyrants and fight till death clearly resonated, as many eyes glistened on that particular stanza. Lazar discussed the following week's demonstration to protest for wage increases, and Bronka's mind wandered to a special Chantilly lace brassiere she was making for a young woman's wedding day that was due for a final fitting the next day. Suddenly, Lazar's voice became louder, and his tone turned almost reverent. She sat up and listened.

"Our brethren abroad are struggling to keep fascism at bay. How many of you would be interested in helping?"

Many hands shot up in the air, though not Bronka's. She had a business to run.

"In that case, you need to meet someone, but I caution you, if you value your life and freedom, you must keep what is discussed in this room to yourselves." The murmur of surprised voices filled the room momentarily, then a hush fell over the room. Some people left.

Lazar opened the door. A stranger strode in with a stack of folders under his arm, stood near the desk at the front of the room, and addressed them in a resonant voice that might have belonged to a radio announcer.

Bronka glued her eyes to the exceptionally handsome man. He looked more like a stage actor than a worker. The man brushed the shock of wavy hair tumbling onto his forehead away from his face and began. "Comrades, I am Antoni Zak. I have come from the Paris recruitment office to find brave men and women willing to give their lives for freedom. I am recruiting for the International Brigades."

Bronka was surprised at the way he seemed to emphasize 'women.' His gaze roamed the room with incredible electricity. Passion for the cause of the simple men and women of Spain, fighting against Franco's brutal thugs, burned in his eyes. The man intrigued her. There was something beguiling about him: his well-cut clothes, his confident stance, the intelligence in his eyes, the passion in his voice. And his given name and surname, stretching from A to Z, conveyed the impression he knew everything in the encyclopedia. Bronka was hooked, if not necessarily on the cause, then certainly on the man making her feel as if his cause were a burning coal. She didn't care if he was Jewish... or even married. She had to meet him.

Antoni continued to detail the battles erupting all over Catalonia and the urgent need for fighters. He invited all those who were interested to remain after the meeting to enroll for screening interviews. It turned out you couldn't just sign up. There would be several interviews held in as yet undisclosed locations.

Bronka felt torn. She didn't know whether to slip out and hurry to the shop to finish the wedding brassiere or to get at the end of the line, wait till everyone was gone, including Mordechai, whom she saw queueing already. Within seconds, she realized it wasn't really a choice at all. She needed to speak with this Antoni and ask how she might help. She needed him to speak just to her, see if there was a way she could remain near him. She didn't think she could shoot anyone in Spain, but surely, there had to be something she could do. The line moved very slowly. All of the potential applicants had many questions. She could hear Antoni answer them with confidence and a sense of urgency.

For a while, Mordechai lingered. Bronka assumed he was waiting to see if she would join him for the movie date he'd been longing for, but after an hour, he gave up and left with a hangdog look. Bronka waited till everyone on the queue gathered their belongings and left the room. She approached Antoni, now seated behind the desk, with her heart pounding. She glanced at the wall clock above the desk. "Do you have time for yet another applicant?"

Antoni smiled, "I always have time for beautiful women."

Bronka felt weak at the knees. Her face flushed. This was much more than she expected. She fanned herself with the newspaper. "It's too hot here," was all she could manage.

"If heat bothers you, you may not be cut out for the hardships of battle," he responded with total seriousness in his voice, but his smile broadened and his eyelids drooped slightly, showing off his long eyelashes.

Bronka's gaze fell from those eyes to the dimple on his chin. "Is there any other way a woman like me can help?" she asked.

"Well... I have no idea what kind of a woman you are," Antoni shuffled the papers and folders on his desk. He appeared to be organizing them and preparing to leave. Then he looked up at the anxious, enthralled Bronka. "You know what? I'm heading back to my hotel now. Why don't you tell me about yourself over a drink? I am staying at the Polonia Palace because it reminds me of Paris. And it has a great wine cellar."

If it weren't for the fact that she had been supporting herself with one hand on a nearby chair, she'd have fallen. A drink? At the Polonia Palace? Why, that was a place for diplomats and aristocrats! They'd probably not let her past the entrance.

Antoni saw her consternation. "Why are you hesitating?"

"I don't know; my life is so different." Bronka wanted to stand up to his aristocratic boasting but had trouble finding the right words.

"If you are one with the people, you may be the ideal candidate," Antoni chuckled.

Bronka took offense, hot scorn rising into her voice. "Don't toy with me," she said, but knew right away that she came across as a hurt little girl. A naif. Not the sort of woman he was used to.

"Look, we can talk and then we can dance," Antoni tried another tack.

"Dance?" Bronka's mouth hung open, her pulse quickened. "Dancing is for fools," she pronounced with a wicked little smile.

"What?" Antoni knitted his eyebrows.

"Just a little personal joke, something a friend used to say."

"You keep strange friends," he said. "So, are we on?"

"Yes, yes," Bronka said quickly, lest he change his mind.

"The Polonia has a beautiful dance hall and I'm a pretty good dancer if I do say so myself," Antoni winked at her.

The man was impossible. How could she resist? "Just so you know, I have an appointment later this evening, so it can't be a long meeting," she said, feeling a hot blush rise on her cheeks.

"Well, I have to leave now, but you can meet me in an hour at the hotel bar," Antoni said.

"Alright, that'll give me time to take my package back to my shop," pointing to a bag of supplies she'd purchased before the meeting, grateful for the time to freshen up before the momentous occasion.

———

Bronka raced home, bumping into people on the street. She washed quickly and slipped on her best dress, a silky jade green number, bias-cut to accentuate the curve of her hips, ruffles at the midi-length hem and flutter sleeves. She wrapped her braids into a crown-like hairdo and dabbed on some lipstick, kept well-hidden from Momma. One quick look in the mirror and off she flew.

She felt excited and nervous but reassured herself that the steps to the jitterbug and foxtrot she'd practiced to the radio in the back of the shop would help. She'd never danced with a man! If she danced well this evening... who knew what good things could happen. Briefly, Kazio came to mind, and she dismissed him. How had she ever thought him good-looking?

Antoni waited for her in the bar, a place as alien to her as the moon. With a gentlemanly gesture, he ushered her to a small table where she fell into a plush velvet easy chair. Even in the dim light she could see couples nearby toasting with champagne flutes. In the background, she made out the muted strains of Jan Kiepura's *Sweet Melody of Love*.

"You look lovely," Antoni said. "What would you like to drink?"

Not wanting to make a faux pas, she hesitated.

"How about a glass of champagne?"

"Well, alright, but a small one." Almost immediately the drink made her lightheaded. She felt her face redden and hoped he'd not notice in the low light.

"You said you have a shop. Tell me about it," Antoni said.

"Oh, it wouldn't be of interest to a man," she said.

"Why not?"

"Our... no, I mean, my shop produces ladies' undergarments."

"What red-blooded man wouldn't be interested in those?" he chuckled. "So, you are a businesswoman. At the meeting I took you for a working girl."

"But I am a working girl," Bronka took umbrage. "I put in ten or eleven hours a day. It would be easier if my partner hadn't abandoned me... and the shop."

"Tsk, tsk... who is your fickle partner?" Antoni asked.

"Never mind, it's the friend who thinks dancing is for fools," Bronka lightened the conversation.

"Why did she desert the shop?" Antoni asked.

"She went to Palestine to find her sister back in April. It was supposed to be just a few weeks, but she's been gone more than four months," Bronka said.

Antoni's brow furrowed.

"What?" Bronka said.

"Hmm... I met a woman on a train to Paris who practiced your trade, only she called herself a sculptor of women's bodies. She was going to Palestine as well." Antoni looked up, thinking. "Yes, I recall now, it was definitely in the early spring."

Bronka felt the blood drain from her face. She struggled to stay calm, keeping her face neutral. "A mere coincidence," she said waving her hand dismissively, pushing Rifka's image away.

"The world is full of coincidences."

A momentary chill fell between them, but Antoni shook off his bewilderment and said, "You brought up dancing. Let's go and practice, but let's make sure we don't look foolish."

He took Bronka's hand and the two sashayed toward the dance hall. The upbeat sound of swing greeted them when they entered the spacious room: couples twirling, a female singer crooning a bouncy song. A good-sized band of tuxedoed male musicians played trumpets, saxophones, a piano, a guitar, and drums.

"Let's do it," Antoni seized Bronka's waist.

From the first step, it was obvious Antoni was an experienced dancer, but she kept up with him. Each time their bodies came closer, the scent of his cologne made her woozy. She danced in a trance. What she wouldn't give to have this man as her own! She'd leave her shop, volunteer for the International Brigades, suffer any hardship to be with him.

After several dances, Antoni paused, wiped his brow and asked, "So what do you think? Were we fools?"

"Not at all," Bronka said with genuine conviction.

Before she knew it, Antoni grasped her shoulders and planted a ferocious kiss on her lips. She was too startled to utter a word.

"I have to be up early tomorrow," he said. "Meet me at this office for an official interview." He handed her a card with an address and strolled away, leaving her speechless.

The drudgery of life had magically been lifted off her shoulders. Bronka felt more alive than at any time before. This man was nothing like Mordechai or Kazio, not like any man she'd ever met. Even Rifka, her fickle friend, would understand this feeling. After all, hadn't she met a man as fascinating as Antoni?

Bronka took the bus home and for the entire ride succeeded in pushing aside the memory of Antoni's passing comment about the woman he'd met on a train. Why assume it was Rifka? There must have been dozens of corset makers in country as large as Poland traveling abroad. Instead, Bronka dwelled on every step of their dances, the pressure of his hands on the small of her back and the tenderness of his lips. The worry about his remark evaporated completely.

As soon as she got home Bronka rummaged in her bureau drawer to find Rifka's one and only letter. She scanned it quickly and an enormous wave of relief washed over her. The man Rifka had met had a different name and he was a count. No nobleman would be mingling with working people, doing the kind of work Antoni did. Bronka would do everything in her power to be with him. She opened the closet and searched for her best clothes for the next day's interview.

PART 3

SPAIN

24 ALBACETE, SPAIN

On October 15, 1936, Raquela and Jacob disembarked the tramp steamer at dawn in the port of Valencia. They made their way to the imposing main railway station, Estació del Nord. From there, it would take about two hours to their final destination, the Albacete recruitment headquarters for the International Brigades.

Raquela noticed Jacob carrying a large canvas bag he hadn't had when they'd boarded the tramp steamer in Haifa. "What are you carrying? she asked.

He didn't reply. Instead, he gave her a meaningful glance. "Come here," he said and put his arm on her shoulder. "It'll be an adjustment for both of us. Here we won't be marking time. We will work harder than we have in our lives, but it won't be for money, it'll be for an idea."

He was so serious she decided not to pressure him for an answer.

They clambered onto the train. Raquela was careful to stow her bag where she could keep an eye on it, but Jacob insisted on keeping his canvas bag right under the seat, behind his feet. She realized she'd missed his company the many weeks they'd been separated on the tramp steamer. She watched him. Jacob had a faraway expression as he stared at the scenery flashing past the train window.

He turned to Raquela. "Would you like me to tell you about my blue city in Morocco, just to pass the time?"

"Why not? I know nothing of Jews outside Europe."

"My forefathers have lived in Spanish Morocco for hundreds of years," Jacob said.

"Blue, what an odd name for a city," she said.

"Oh, if you could only see it, you'd understand. Everything in it is blue." Jacob looked excited; his tiredness dissipated.

"Everything?"

Jacob laughed out loud. "Yes! The buildings, the staircases, the arched passageways, even the market stalls in the Medina."

"It must be beautiful." Raquela moved closer to Jacob, their bodies almost touching. "I would love to see it one day," she said.

"Maybe you will."

She mused on the mixed signals they'd been sending one another, like a cryptic mating dance of a species hitherto unknown to science. It struck her that coming from completely different worlds, the two of them couldn't be more different and yet, oddly, they fit together. Maybe Jacob had his secrets, as she had hers. Ever since he worked so hard to pull her out from her depression, she appreciated him more, though she still harbored no romantic ideas about him. He was a friend, that's all. It was never her way to muse about men in romantic terms, except for one impossible moment in time. Had her sojourn in Paris been a dream?

The train lurched to a stop. They'd arrived in Albacete. Raquela could hardly pronounce its name, much less absorb the notion that she'd drifted this far off the path her life was supposed to take. Jacob pulled a crumpled piece of paper from his pocket. "Here is an address the captain gave me. We can rent inexpensive lodging there."

"He wasn't as bad as I feared."

"The old salt was sharp. Did us a favor," Jacob agreed.

They headed to Calle Rosario just a few blocks from the International Brigade headquarters. Señora Fuentes—the corpulent landlady with pink cheeks and an apron reaching to just where her rolled-up stockings stopped at the knee—eyed them suspiciously when they first arrived at her street-side apartment.

"The captain of the SS *Pharaoh* sent us," Jacob said, standing in the doorway.

"*Un buen hombre, un buen hombre,*" Raquela heard Señora Fuentes.

A broad smile erupted on the woman's face; her crepe-like cheeks folded into a tapestry of wrinkles. "You must be here for the Brigades. Right?" she said.

Jacob nodded and translated Señora's words.

With that, she picked up a bulky keyring and her cane and lumbered up to the third floor with the young people following.

A quick walk-through and Jacob agreed to rent the apartment. A small parlor with severe Spanish-style furniture—all heavy, dark carved wood and leather—a basic bedroom facing the street and shaded heavily by the trees outside, and a good-sized kitchen. With its green and white tile floor, a large white sink under the window, cheerful percale curtains above it, a green enameled table at the center and cabinets to match, the space looked more inviting than the rest of the rooms. It was the hearth of this home. To Raquela, after the barren room at the Carmel Guesthouse, not to mention her cabin on the steamer, this place seemed palatial. She surveyed the apartment while Señora Fuentes chatted with Jacob in the kitchen. They paused when she came back in.

"What?" she said. "Sorry to interrupt."

"Señora tells me things are looking bleak in the southwest. The Nationalists have taken Badajoz, killed thousands in the bullring. But she also says we are lucky."

"Lucky? Why?" Raquela looked at Jacob.

He chatted with Señora some more. Their Spanish was so fast, Raquela couldn't make out any words at all.

Jacob translated: "Not so long ago, in this town, forces loyal to the democratic government had suppressed a coup by the brutal Civil Guard."

Raquela was shaken. "Has the fighting already reached Albacete?"

"Yes, but our side trounced them; they are gone. It's a good thing we didn't arrive when the bombs flew here, fast and furious," Jacob said.

Raquela was thankful for the tramp steamer's interminable meanderings with its many stops to deliver and pick up cargo in obscure ports.

Señora chuckled and said something to Jacob. He translated. "She says she stood at this very window watching a crowd of local people: peasants, factory workers and teachers storm the Civil Guard barracks and make citizen arrests."

"Ordinary people winning over such a force! Very uplifting,"

Raquela said. "I suppose at least for now Albacete is outside the strike zone."

"Yes, we are here to make sure it stays that way," Jacob said. "Let's head over to the Brigade headquarters to register."

Jacob paid the landlady and they hurried outside. Raquela noticed that Jacob took the canvas bag with him. They walked out onto the broiling afternoon street; the blast of heat surprising in mid-October. It was quiet, many residents still at siesta with shades drawn. The town of Albacete had the stern look of a gaunt old disciplinarian. It made Raquela think of Don Quixote. She didn't know if he had traveled this far north. The sun reflected off the whitewashed homes on the hillsides, turning them ghostly. She hoped the Spanish sun might fade her guilt in the same way. Perhaps here she'd have a chance to redeem herself.

"Why so quiet?" Jacob startled her as they walked side by side.

She stopped near the corner and moved under the shady awning of a shop closed for siesta. "Just thinking of how I can help," she said.

Jacob stepped toward the square of shade. He chuckled. "You don't need to think. We will join others and head to the front. They'll tell us what to do. Let's go," he said. "It's getting late." He pulled her hand to cross the street.

"Not I!" She pierced his casual assumption defiantly, trying to wiggle her hand free of his.

"What's with you, woman?" Jacob was nonplussed. "Then why are you here?"

A bus came to a screeching halt. The driver opened the window, yelled, "*Idiotas descuidados.*"

Jacob pulled her by the arm onto the sidewalk.

"I'll find a different way to help the war effort," Raquela argued, undeterred. "If that makes you angry, I'll get my things and go elsewhere, find a place to stay."

Jacob waved his hand in disgust. "Never mind, let's just complete the registration process."

The Gran Hotel appeared as they rounded the corner: an imposing five-story façade adorned in Renaissance and Gothic accents, arched triple windows with lacy stone embroidery nestled under a roof crowned with three spire-topped turrets!

"Oh, it's beautiful," Raquela said, but Jacob pointed to the line of people snaking around the building. "Volunteers, like us," he said. "There's no shortage of freedom-loving men and women."

As they came closer, a Babel of languages, conversations, laughter, questions, and jokes filled the air, a kind of nervous energy not seen in nature. Soon they learned from others on the queue, mostly young people, that the headquarters and training center saw these kinds of crowds daily.

"We will liberate Spain, free it from fascism," a serious-looking, bespectacled blond man, standing in front of Raquela and Jacob, said to his companion.

"If we don't, Franco's ideas will soon infect the rest of Europe... like a disease," the girl replied. Her heavy knapsack pulled her shoulders back, but she hardly seemed to notice, so passionate was she about the cause.

Raquela tapped Jacob's shoulder. "Let's sit there for a while," she pointed at a bench in a nearby small square.

"Why? What's wrong? We will lose our place in the queue."

"It's an idea I have. I want to talk it over before we go in." Raquela decided to spit out something that had occurred to her. No use incubating it like an egg. Maybe Jacob would agree. She turned to the dark-haired woman with the knapsack. "Would you mind keeping our place in the queue?"

The woman agreed and they walked over toward the bench on the square.

"Well, what is it? We need all good ideas to beat the fascists." Jacob looked peeved, impatient.

"Remember that group of raggedy children begging for handouts we saw at the railroad station?"

Jacob raised his eyebrows. "What of them?"

"I think there must already be children orphaned by this war. If I could volunteer to work in an orphanage that would be helping too. Wouldn't it?"

"Honestly, I hadn't considered it, Raquela. Is this your strategy to weasel out of fighting?"

Hot anger ambushed her. Her hands clenched into fists. "Who do you take me for? A coward?" she said.

"No, but I thought you were serious about this," he waved his hand at the still growing line of applicants.

"I am serious, but I want to do it my way," she said.

"Alright, alright." She could see Jacob was softening. "Let's first register, then we can speak to a comrade who heads our battalion," he said.

"Comrade, battalion—all this new vocabulary! I see you have already caught on to the war parlance, Jacob." She looked directly into his eyes. "Here's something you must remember about me: I hate war, I hate blood. I'll never kill another human."

"Don't get so worked up, Raquela," Jacob said. "It's our turn to go in." He pointed to someone in the queue waving them over.

For Jacob, the registration process began with a coughing fit. He was helpless to stop the hacking and stood in front of his interviewer with his face white, wiping perspiration off his forehead.

"Nasty cold," he said, worried the cough he developed on the tramp steamer would raise questions.

A bright-eyed young man wearing a khaki shirt with epaulets said, "Not to worry, we need everyone. If you can breathe, you are in."

"Good. I'm eager to get to the front as soon as possible. Where are you sending the new arrivals?"

"Whoa! Not so fast, Ben Maimon, we are in desperate need of weapons. Franco's troops are being equipped by the Italians, but so far, we have hardly any arms. We ship out the most experienced fighters with the few weapons we have, while we wait to acquire more."

Jacob felt deflated. "What now? Anything for me to do?"

"Plenty," the young man said. "For now, we need people with languages to process the volunteers and to organize the paperwork. Can you do that?" he asked.

"Of course, I can," Jacob said. At least he'd put his Spanish, French and Arabic to work. But that wasn't what he had in mind. He thought of himself as an idealist, always on the side of righting wrongs. That's why he'd smuggled arms in Palestine to Jews trying to reclaim a land that had

214

historically been theirs. When his mission ended—and he blamed himself for carelessness—he decided to use the anger he harbored toward himself to help the Republican Spaniards. That they weren't Jews, didn't matter. The work in Palestine was a result of deep commitment to his people, and the struggle was complex, with truths on both sides. Here in Spain, it was a simpler question of right and wrong—a democratically elected government was being usurped.

"Wait, wait..." The young man stared at Jacob's application. "You know a thing or two about guns! You can help us source weapons."

Jacob brightened. This was more like it. He said, "I can help you right away." He lifted his canvas bag carefully and handed it to the man. "They'll be of more use to the men at the front than to a desk man."

The man opened it and stood momentarily with his mouth agape. "Golly! What priceless beauties!" Then he inspected the contents cautiously: three bolt action Mausers, a Winchester 1895, and an Erma-Vollmer submachine gun. "You've done well, Ben Maimon! Let me get them under lock and key right away." He stood up, shook Jacob's hand vigorously and told him to report to the Dombrowski battalion for orientation.

Jacob felt a roiling mix of emotions. The priceless weapons would allow others to fight while he sat out the war. This wasn't what he wanted. Having failed his mission in Palestine, at least partly, he desperately wanted to prove to himself that he was capable, manly and not a loser. But he was also glad not to have given into his baser instincts. Surrendering his cache for a worthy cause made him feel less like an egotistical fool.

When his processing was finished, Jacob sat in the cavernous lobby waiting for Raquela. It struck him that among the din of voices bouncing off the marble walls, the only voice he wanted to hear was hers. He thought of this mysteriously sad woman's determination to do things her own way. She could be annoying in her pig-headedness, but he was glad she'd decided to come with him. He didn't pressure her; he wanted it to be her choice.

Since their arrival, her depression had begun to lift, but he knew it wouldn't last unless she could do something productive, other than fighting. He tried to sort his own feelings toward her. Raquela's exotic and exquisitely sensitive persona had occupied a large part of his brain lately. His feelings toward her had grown, but she was so mercurial, it was impossible to tell what exactly she felt toward him. He heard her calling from the other end of the hall. "I'm registered in the Dombrowski battalion. Where are you?"

"Same," he smiled.

She looked at him with surprise. "Why? I thought it was for Polish-speaking volunteers."

"True, but there will be plenty of Spanish troops in it as well," Jacob replied.

"Did you hear the news?" she asked.

"What news?"

"Tomorrow, after orientation, we are all going to an event at the orphanage on the outskirts of Albacete," she announced.

Jacob raised his eyebrows. "What for?"

"I don't know exactly." She shrugged her shoulders. "We will see soon enough."

They mingled with new recruits for a while before going home. On the way back they stopped at a panaderia to buy bread and at a tiny corner store on their block to pick up rice, beans, eggs and canned anchovies. Jacob saw Raquela looking at the food cases: octopus, shrimp, hams, an assortment of chorizos. "It's not kosher, but you'll have to get used to it."

"That's the last thing on my mind," she said.

At their new apartment Jacob remembered the awkwardness of their first night at the Carmel Guesthouse and decided to take charge. She didn't have to be his lover; he would never pressure a woman for that, but she was here with him, she chose to come, and there wasn't a point in anyone sleeping on the hard floor. "No pussy-footing about where we sleep. There's one matrimonial bed here, and we will both sleep in it."

"Who are you to order me around?" Raquela said.

Had he been too harsh? He wanted to let her know they were comrades; that he wasn't a rapist (but neither was he a gentleman). Jacob attempted to strike a better tone. "The landlady thinks we are a couple."

"We are not! Sleeping is one thing, sex, quite another," she said, turning away. "Make sure to keep to your side of the bed," she added with emphasis.

Well, yeah, Jacob thought. I could have just said that. He watched her walking toward the kitchen and heard her rummaging in the cupboard putting away their shopping.

"I'll make some coffee. Do you want some?" she called to him.

"You don't want caffeine keeping me up," Jacob replied, though at this moment he very much wanted to be wide awake, take her into his arms and kiss her graceful neck. Keep to the bargain, he told himself. Give her time.

On their second day in Albacete, they piled into trucks with other International Brigade volunteers, a disparate group of enthusiastic young people. The vehicles climbed the rutted hillside road to the Monastery of the Incarnation with great difficulty. Raquela felt a pang seeing the huge cross greet them on the horizon. She'd strayed so far from her own faith.

It was a massive stone edifice staffed by a small number of Republican nuns. Most of their sisters, having been on the opposing Nationalist side, were long gone. On this occasion, the children would be presented with candies sent via the Canadian contingent. Such was the importance of the event that even the mayor and town officials attended. After the speeches and distribution of the unexpected gift, the Franciscan nuns gave the children a signal to begin. As if by miracle, three dozen soprano voices filled the space.

Raquela couldn't take her eyes off the children's chorus. Their thin, angelic voices rose and reverberated in the high arched ceilings, loosening a flood of her tears. The little girls in gray pinafores stood stiffly like small nuns, though their cherubic faces looked out of place in the long marble hall still ringing with old prayers of monks. Yes, she was determined to find work there. She'd do far more good helping these orphans than participating in combat.

As much as her fascination with the children's voices, something else struck Raquela—the nuns themselves. Stiff coifs framed their tired faces, and wimples covering every inch of their necks right up to the chin, pressed on their well-concealed breasts. There was an air of otherworldliness to these women, though it was hard to discern their sex, and the rope belts dangling rosaries seemed inadequate compensation for the bleakness of their garb.

They had devoted their lives to their faith. And to what had she given her life? It bothered Raquela that she was at a loss to answer such a simple question. Was she here to fight fascism, or was Spain just a flimsy excuse, an escape from the disaster that had turned her life upside down? What would it take for her to give meaning to her self-imposed exile?

When the program ended, brigade members began exiting, piling back into the trucks. Raquela remained glued to the pew.

"Let's go." Jacob touched her shoulder. "You're daydreaming."

"I'm not leaving. I must speak with Commander Ułanowski."

"He is not about to linger and chat. He has a mission to attend to," Jacob rebuked her.

"You can go. I'll find my way back. I'll wait for him," she said, advancing toward the exit.

"And there he is." Jacob pointed to a wiry man with thick eyebrows reaching for a cigarette from the pocket of his navy pea coat. He lit it, took an urgent drag, and moved on.

The commander was about to walk past them, but on impulse, Raquela grabbed his arm. He turned to her, no doubt appalled by her familiar, aggressive gesture, then addressed her in Polish, the language of the majority of Dombrowski battalion volunteers. "What are you doing?" His eyebrows raised; he spoke more in surprise than anger.

Raquela felt her insides quiver. This encounter would determine her future. She gathered all her strength, and spoke passionately, from the heart. "I'd like to work at this orphanage. I know I can help the war effort here more than in the field. Our fallen will rest easier knowing their children are cared for... with love."

Commander Ułanowski looked at her, nodded and looked up toward the sky. He put the cigarette in his mouth and inhaled deeply. "I'd certainly rest in peace knowing you cared for my little boy," he said earnestly, then chuckled.

Raquela wondered if he felt embarrassed by his show of tenderness.

"Soon casualties from the front will arrive at the infirmary. I certainly wouldn't mind if you bandaged me and brought me succor," Ułanowski winked, then gave her a gentle slap on the shoulder. "So be it," he said and saluted smartly. "Now go find Mother Maria Josepha. She will give the final verdict."

Jacob, who'd been waiting nearby, nodded with approval. "Do you always get what you ask for, Raquela?" Then, "Let's hurry before the trucks leave."

25 MANUEL

Reverend Mother Maria Josepha motioned Raquela to walk with her down the long monastery hallway. Mother's rope sandals shuffled with each step as if she were intent on polishing the marble floor, like one of the many objects she must have ordered the other nuns and children to polish. She'll work me to the bone, Raquela thought, but it'll be good penance.

Raquela's pumps sounded distinctly too noisy as she walked behind the sister. She stared at the back of the nun's long black habit.

They entered Maria Josepha's austere office: a plain black wooden table without the ornate carvings typical of the region, a hard-backed chair behind the table, another in front of it, and a huge crucifix on the wall, high windows shaded by dark, faded velvet curtains. Raquela was struck by the room's sparseness. They had ventured so far away from the room where the children had performed that nothing but distant bird sounds disturbed the funereal atmosphere. Raquela thought of the black vultures she'd seen flying over the mountains behind the monastery.

Sweeping her habit aside gracefully, Mother sat down in her chair. She did not invite Raquela to sit. For a long, uncomfortable minute, Mother said nothing, just stared at Raquela, who stood there, waiting politely, eyeing the walls. Raquela noticed a portrait of King Alfonso XIII, recognized his image from her gymnasium history class. He was the deposed king, replaced by a democratic government.

Mother Maria's eyes—mean, ice-blue pools set deep below a prominent brow ridge—watched Raquela. Sister's nose was hawk sharp. She threw out her first question, "*Polaca?*"

Raquela understood. "*Judea*," a word Jacob had taught her.

Having established that the young woman standing before her was of Polish-Jewish origin, Mother Maria Josepha addressed Raquela in a rough, guttural German.

Raquela understood it well.

Mother Superior looked at Raquela intently. "Are your people observant?"

"Yes. I come from Orthodox Jews."

The reverend mother harrumphed. "I know about you people. And you? Do you go to your church weekly... at least?"

Raquela swallowed hard. An image of herself following Momma up the stairs to the balcony of the synagogue came before her. She remembered her anger at the separation of male and female worshippers.

Sister tapped her bony fingers on the table, waiting for a response.

Nothing came forth. Raquela's lips set in a determined fashion.

"Never mind. At least I hope you aren't one of those crazy anarchists like..." With that, the reverend mother stopped, changed course. "Been around children much?"

Raquela's heart lurched. "I come from a family of ten, so yes."

Mother's tone softened a tad. "Well, then... Your responsibilities will include meal preparation, cleaning, and laundry. Except for meals, the children spend their time being educated, alternating between sessions of prayer and religious instruction. They have lessons on scripture, sacraments and the church, doctrine, and morality."

Raquela found the children's schedule most distressing. She'd seen them at the choral performance; many of them were of school age. No mention of mathematics, history, geography, biology? How would they get along in life?

Mother Maria Josepha must have noted Raquela's widened eyes. She responded with a narrow-lipped look of disdain. Raquela decided not to comment, at least not to the mother superior. And the word 'mother' irked her; it stuck in her throat like a bone. Not my mother, and from the look on the faces of the two younger nuns introduced at the children's chorus—Eulalia and Candida—not theirs either. Mother

Maria Josepha had scolded them for letting the children take too many candies. An image of her own mother watching with a smile as Grandmother distributed candies flashed before her eyes. Her heart lurched; she missed Momma and Grandmother so badly.

Raquela returned from the interview at the monastery in the late afternoon. Jacob's volunteer training with the Brigades hadn't yet begun. She found him stretching on the small living room sofa, just getting up from his siesta. She said a quick hello and marched straight into the kitchen to prepare a modest meal for the two of them. An apron hung on a hook near the stove. She slipped it on. They hadn't discussed their living arrangements, and only after tying the apron on did it hit her: she'd assumed the domestic role as second nature. She frowned.

"How did your meeting with the mother superior go?" Jacob called out as she filled the teapot in the kitchen.

"Fine," Raquela clipped, wanting to hide her disappointment. Didn't want to say she'd only do grunt work, instead of working directly with the orphans. Some aid to the war effort!

"How did you communicate with her?"

"German," Raquela said returning from the kitchen with a tray of bread, an opened tin of anchovies, utensils, and plates.

"You know," Jacob said, "I should be teaching you Spanish. You won't get far with your Polish and French here, or your German." He reached for the loaf of bread and tore off a chunk.

"I'd like that," Raquela obliged, glad for a change in topic. "Go ahead, teach me something," she said.

Jacob put the bread down, sat looking at her intently, his elbows on the table, his hands on his face. "*Creo que eres hermosa,*" he said. After a moment, "Did you figure out what I said?"

"No, my languages are useless. What was it?"

"I think you are beautiful."

Raquela felt her cheeks redden. "Are these just words you are teaching me, or are you paying me a compliment?"

"You have to figure it out yourself," he said, then forked the pungent, oily fish onto his plate.

"Teach me words I can actually use," she said.

"Alright. How about, *buenos dias, niños?*"

"I think I figured out this one," she smiled.

She filled the teacups and they sat quietly looking at one another, but something sprang to Raquela's mind. "Jacob, I didn't see you bring that canvas bag back from the headquarters, the one you had with you since the tramp steamer."

"Well..." He hesitated. "I made a donation to the war effort."

Raquela sucked in her breath. "You gave up the weapons? What will you use?"

"So, you knew," Jacob said.

Raquela saw a flicker of fire dancing in his eyes. "I'm not an imbecile," she said. "I assumed the captain paid you with them."

Jacob nodded. "The volunteers heading out toward Madrid need them now. I'll try my contacts for more, but it won't be easy." Then he said, "Before each of us becomes wrapped up in our jobs, let me take the rest of the evening to teach you some Spanish."

She agreed readily. "Let me first clear the table," she said unable to tolerate the smell of the fish.

Jacob made a list of essential words and they practiced pronunciation. Time flew.

"This is fun. I like learning new languages," Raquela said. "Make me a new list. I think I've memorized this one already."

"Tomorrow, on my way to the headquarters, I'll look for a Spanish primer and dictionary for you." He looked up at the clock. It was nearly ten. "But now, I'm going to bed. *Buenas noches.*"

Raquela felt a wave of anxiety. It always happened at bedtime ever since she and Jacob had to share the cot in the Carmel guesthouse in Palestine. He was a gentleman; never made sexual advances. She tried to maintain her self-respect though she saw a hunger in his eyes. She trusted him not to do anything untoward. In bed they observed an unspoken rule: always leaving as much space between them as possible. In the darkness, Aleksander filled the space.

In her first week at the monastery, Raquela became acquainted with the fresh-faced Sister Eulalia and the reserved Sister Candida, whose hooded eyes seemed perpetually closed. They were much younger than

Mother Superior, especially Eulalia, who seemed to be nineteen or twenty—about Raquela's age. She was the one who showed Raquela what needed to be done, where the supplies were stored, and explained how the daily schedule worked. Raquela appreciated her cheerful manner and the way she used hand gestures and smiles because Raquela's Spanish was still poor. Both of these nuns seemed more relaxed and willing to speak with Raquela when the stern Mother Maria Josepha was away on church business.

Each morning, as soon as she met the children, Raquela's day brightened despite the depressing atmosphere of the monastery. "*Buenos dias niños*," she greeted the children. They responded with those sweet voices, "*Buenos dias Señora Raquela*." They generated such cheerful sounds of chatter and laughter even as they peeled potatoes, shelled peas, or washed the huge cooking cauldrons. There were a few babies and toddlers, but the majority were of early elementary school age; nearly equally split between boys and girls.

One dark-haired boy, perhaps eight or nine, reminded Raquela of her brother Saul. She'd often thought of Saul as a most annoying sibling, but now felt a gush of love, even longing for his antics. The orphan stood to the side in his raggedy knickers, barefoot, his torso lost in a shirt that must have belonged to a grown man. He followed Raquela's every step with his eyes but did not reply when she called his name. Those eyes! Pools of blackness. His eyelids drooped, and his chin quivered when she offered him an extra helping of rice.

The way this child jumped with every loud noise! It didn't matter if it was a pot, or a knife that fell off the kitchen counter, an ambulance, or a rumbling truck making its way up the hillside—it all made him shudder and crouch, his eyes filled with terror. He must have experienced something traumatic. She'd have to learn about him from Sister Eulalia when the chance came.

For now, Eulalia struggled to keep the toddlers out of trouble and alternated her instructions to the older children with cooing to the baby she nursed with a bottle. Raquela glanced at the baby's cherubic little face, and her heart sank. Such sweetness, such innocence, such trust. Just like Maya. Please God, let her not be assigned to work with the baby. Luckily, someone was tugging at her skirt. She turned and saw the dark-haired boy with the soulful eyes.

She followed where he led, a table at the far corner of the dining area. He pointed to a small, whittled figure on the table. It was a little horse. "You made it?" she asked.

The boy nodded.

At the end of the day, she asked Sister Eulalia if any time could be carved out of the schedule for teaching the children, deciding to defer the question about the mystery boy. Eulalia seemed surprised. "But we do teach them catechism and all the prayers. Didn't the reverend mother tell you this already?"

"She did, but I am thinking of more basic lessons, like reading, and math, geography, and science," Raquela said hesitantly. Science might be the last subject considered appropriate here.

Shuffling steps in the hallway became audible in the kitchen where both women stood. Eulalia put her finger to her lips.

Raquela switched the subject quickly. "By the way, can you tell me this boy's name?" She pointed to the black-haired boy who had shown her his whittled figure.

"Oh, he is Manuel, long story," Sister Eulalia answered with her eyes fixed on the door.

"Will you tell it to me one day?"

"Maybe," was all Eulalia said. She opened a notebook listing ingredients for the kettle of soup they'd cook the following day. "Here's what you need to prepare with the girls after our *Liturgia Horarum*."

Raquela was glad her Latin studies came in handy; Eulalia was referring to morning prayers, Liturgy of the Hours. She sighed. Maybe her plan to inject something secular in this place was unrealistic. Still... she'd try.

Raquela stood at the bus stop at the base of the hill, below the monastery. It had been an exhausting day. Caring for all those orphans wasn't so different from Momma's tending to her brood, though of course at the monastery there were many more. She remembered Momma saying to a young neighbor despairing of her third pregnancy. "Don't worry, after three children, it doesn't matter. Five, seven, ten—it's all the same." At the time Raquela hadn't understood it, but now it became a bit clearer. She thought of the orphans scrambling for their share of bread and marmalade at breakfast. The sounds of squabble and laughter were much like those of her siblings at home. Thinking of home made her sad. She did her best to avoid such thoughts. They always flooded her with a deep sense of shame over her absence from Warsaw.

She pushed the thought aside as she had done many times and got on the bus that had just arrived. But she hadn't succeeded. Images of home hovered in her mind with uncanny persistence: Sabbath meals at home, the smell of Momma's cholent, the way Leya looked up to her, even Poppa's unruffled look as he sipped his schnapps.

As soon as she got home, Jacob noticed she was out of sorts. "What happened today? You look so glum," he said and walked over to take her jacket, then hung it on one of the coat hooks in the entryway. His ability to detect her moods impressed her.

"Nothing happened, just another day," she said.

Jacob hurried to the kitchen. "Ugh, my soup is boiling over," he said. She heard the cover clattering. "I got home early today after we shipped out a contingent to the front. Thought I'd surprise you with a meal. Come to the table, we'll talk," he called out.

Raquela stood in the entryway for a moment, trying to choke back tears, then she washed her hands and came into the kitchen, sitting heavily. Jacob put a steaming bowl of soup before her and sat opposite. "Taste it," he said. "I am not a bad cook."

After she let the soup cool for a few minutes, Raquela put a spoonful in her mouth in slow motion. "Mm... good," she said, but she put her spoon down and stopped eating.

"What's wrong, Raquela? You've been miserable since we met, but this seems different. Tell me, maybe I can help." Jacob's tone was gentle, as if he were addressing a frightened child. His soothing words broke a dam.

Raquela began to weep, at first silently, trying to wipe away the tears with the edge of her sleeve. But her resolve to choke back her grief over everything that had happened since Maya's death had shattered when she saw the baby in the monastery. And not just the baby, but that forlorn boy. The pain of parents bereft of their children and the children's loss of those who loved them illuminated the tragedy she'd been a part of so pitilessly, she could no longer bear it alone. Deep sobs shook her chest.

Jacob walked over to where she sat and put his hands on her shoulders, "Look at me, Raquela. Whatever it is, we can work it out," he said.

"No, no, it's not... it's not resolvable," she said, trying to slow the tears. Short gasps broke from her chest.

"You'll feel better if you share it with me. Let me take a part of your burden."

She looked at his earnest face, his glistening, large eyes, and cried harder.

He handed her his handkerchief, took her arm, walked her over to the living room sofa and sat next to her. "It can't be all that bad," he said.

She began calming but remained silent. He stroked her hand. The room was so quiet, the kitchen wall clock was audible, its hands separating minutes with too much time between them. Time suffused with unbearable memory.

"I killed a baby," she said suddenly.

Startled, Jacob dropped her hand and faced her directly. "What?"

As if to prove her misdeed was as awful as she'd intimated, Raquela verbalized her crime. "Maya, my infant niece died in my care."

"Oh, that's terrible," Jacob said. "Was she sick?"

"No! That's just it. We both fell asleep—she, after a lot of crying— and when I woke up, she was dead! Dead! Did you ever see a lifeless infant? Oh, Jacob, it was so horrible."

"So where is your fault? I don't get it," Jacob said. "Did you do something to harm her?"

"No!" a wounded yelp came from Raquela.

"I've heard of babies dying this way, suddenly, for no reason. Life is fragile, and there's a lot we don't understand. Why are you blaming yourself?"

His words made an immediate impact, either because there was truth in them, or because she desperately needed someone to liberate her from the unceasing pangs of guilt. Now, she felt badly for making such a scene. She snuffled and tried to compose herself.

"I'm sorry I let the soup get cold," she said and stood up rubbing her eyes. "Let's warm it up."

"Alright, but never let me hear such nonsense. It's obvious you couldn't kill a fly."

He took her hand, and they headed toward the kitchen.

26   JACOB'S DILEMMAS

A new recruit summoned Jacob urgently to Brigade Commander Ułanowski's office. Jacob pushed away the pile of folders in front of him, stood up and walked directly to see his boss.

Ułanowski sat with his legs propped on the desk, smoking, jaw thrust forward, eyes narrowed. "Comrade Jacob, your search for weapons is failing. You've disappointed me badly. I had such high hopes for you," Ułanowski said.

Jacob closed the door behind him to mute the din in the outer office where a contingent of newly arrived volunteers milled about and chatted. "I am sorry you feel this way, but it is not due to a lack of effort on my part," Jacob said. "None of my contacts in the south are responding. I've sent multiple messages, but so far nothing. I am as frustrated as you are."

"In that case, you must try harder, Comrade, much harder and be sure your messages won't get them executed."

Jacob gritted his teeth. To calm himself, he stared at the yellow anti-fascist poster on the wall behind the Commander: an upward thrust fist on a black background with *¡No Pasaran!* above it. After a pause, Jacob said, "We communicate in code. My messages won't get them killed, but what might, is not sending enough trained volunteers to the front fast enough. You, Comrade, can do something about that by sending me instead of having me push paper all day."

Ułanowski's face turned red. "Some arms dealer you are Ben Maimon," he thundered. "You'll do paperwork until you come through with a decent weapons stash! Understand? Only then will you go fight Franco's vermin. Dismissed."

The insult stung. Jacob had been blaming himself for some time about not having been more aggressive in his weapons search, but he wanted to be careful—maybe too careful—not to get himself or his contacts killed. He hurried to his desk and studied the railroad maps to see if there was a safe way for him to slip into Seville or Malaga to see his contacts in person. They had been quite reliable in supplying him with the weapons he'd smuggled into Palestine. But the south was already mostly in the hands of the Nationalists. In his heart of hearts, Jacob suspected his contacts had been arrested or were dead.

It struck him he'd been intemperate in donating all his weapons. Why hadn't he kept at least one for himself? He dragged home dispirited. Along the way, he passed a fruit vendor and though he was extremely careful with money, he stopped in to get an orange for Raquela. He thought about her extraordinary confession. Poor girl, she'd been carrying a millstone for months. What a little fool she'd been to blame herself! Now that that she'd opened up to him, maybe there'd be less artifice in their relationship. He knew he was falling for her despite his initial ambivalence about bringing her with him. There was something so arresting about the intensity of her emerald eyes, her pouty lips, her cat-like independence, and a perverse, child-like innocence. He'd been a fool for equivocating back in Haifa.

Could they manage to make a life together? Certainly not here amid all the killing, but perhaps in his beloved blue city. The image of his mother sprang to mind. How happy she'd be to know he'd finally settled, maybe started a family. Isn't that what human survival dictated? If Raquela had a baby of her own, surely its vibrant life would erase the terrible image of lifeless Maya from her mind. She'd be a strict and protective mother. Fiercely loving. She'd be a difficult wife, but worth it. Jacob smiled at the thought: she'd not be the kind of partner to meekly acquiesce to a husband. The woman had a mind of her own... and a good one too.

He passed the little park where boys and girls chased one another as they tossed a ball. It was dusk, but no one had called them for dinner yet. How would it be to have a son or a daughter? Jacob didn't know anything about girls, having come from a family of four boys, but he could teach a son how to hunt for partridge or hares, could show him how to pursue and kill a wild boar, the way his grandfather had shown him.

He'd never forget how, on his thirteenth birthday, his grandfather said, "You are now ready, Jacob," and brought out his old Winchester 94 rifle. How excited and frightened he'd felt holding the weapon in his skinny arms. His grandfather insisted he assemble and reassemble it over and over for practice. It had never occurred to him consciously that this was the beginning of his fascination with weapons and their power. One didn't have to be Samson-like if one had a good gun at his side. The thought made him even more angry with himself for impulsively giving up all his weapons.

At home, he found Raquela sitting on the threadbare sofa scanning the newspaper headlines, their usual evening activity after his Spanish lessons. After he greeted her, Jacob glanced over the paper in her hands: "*Que tu familia no viva el drama de la guerra: Evacuar Madrid es ayudar a la victoria final.*"

"Did you understand this headline?" he asked.

"Mostly. It's exhorting families to evacuate Madrid. I suppose they'd be wise to spare themselves wartime drama," she said.

Jacob was impressed. "Your Spanish is much better," he said. "The Nationalists are armed to the teeth, but our brigades are in the area... It'll be bloody," Jacob said, then he glanced at his watch. "Wait a minute, we've missed your language lesson on account of my lateness. Can't have that."

"Alright, it's not a chore. You are a very good teacher, and I like how you speak Spanish with a musical cadence. Nothing like Señora Fuentes' rapid-fire speech," Raquela said.

Jacob felt a rush of pleasure at her words and began the lesson. "Do you know the word '*lo siento*'?"

She laughed.

"What's so funny?"

"Girls at the monastery giggle whenever they hear my lame attempts to speak their language. '*Lo siento*, Señora Raquela,' they say. I know they are sorry and mean no ill."

After the lesson Jacob said, "I'm turning in. Except for the pleasure of teaching you, this has been a miserable day."

"Why?"

"Never mind, I need to sleep."

"Who is keeping secrets now?" Raquela said, but Jacob walked into the bedroom and closed the door.

He brushed his teeth and stared at the mirror. Already, fresh growth darkened his tawny skin though he shaved carefully every morning. What did she see in him to have stuck to him all these months? He did have a good strong jawline, but that ugly scar on his temple reaching the upper cheek and the shadows beneath his eyes—no doubt from sleepless nights worrying about his contacts—well, he looked old for his thirty-seven years. God, he was almost old enough to be her father.

He finished brushing and rinsed off the sink, so no toothpaste streaks showed, then undressed, showered, and slipped into bed. He moved to the edge so as to maintain that unspoken border between them, though he didn't know how much longer he could go on with the charade.

He was in that half-sleep state when Raquela crept into bed. He didn't move, but despite the space between them, he could feel her warmth. Somehow, her foot touched his, sending a jolt of electricity through his entire body. He bit his lip, waited. She slid closer. "Why won't you tell me what made your day so miserable?" she whispered.

Jacob remained silent, turned toward the window. Though it was well past midnight, the streetlamp cast just enough light for him to see the outlines and shadows of the sparse bedroom.

"I know you are awake," she said. "I entrusted my dreadful secret to you. Can't you trust me?" she pleaded.

After a while she put her hand on his naked shoulder sending another shudder all the way down producing exactly the result he tried to avoid. "Come on, Jacob, you'll feel better," she cooed.

That did it. He sat up, grabbed his pillow, and punched it with unexpected ferocity. "I can't do this anymore, Raquela. Don't torture me!" he said. "I am a man; I have manly urges."

"But I wanted to help you," she said gently.

Jacob flung the pillow onto the floor, grabbed her in his arms. She trembled. "I have tried so hard to be considerate," he said.

"It's alright," she said and pulled him closer.

He felt her muscles slacken. He thought he actually heard her heart thumping against his chest. Gently, he brushed off the curls that had fallen over her eyes and said, "My lost bird, you are so beautiful." Even

230

in the dark he could see the delicate outline of her small nose and high cheekbones. He traced them with his index finger.

He moved closer, so close he felt her breath, inhaled her minty toothpaste. Her mouth tasted of golden Moroccan mint tea with a dash of gunpowder, poured sweet and slow in a narrow stream into an exquisite pink glass festooned with golden scrollwork.

"You have made me feel completely safe for the first time in my life," she whispered as he sought her mouth again and again.

Jacob had an epiphany: this tenacious tumbleweed had blown in from the west to be his partner in life. He'd take her to his beloved blue city as soon as this war was over.

When the lovemaking was over, an awareness dawned on Jacob: she hadn't submitted to him out of pity; he felt her quiet hunger. This could work, he thought and reached for her hand. "I think we have a future ahead of us... as a couple. I'll make it the best I can," he said.

She didn't respond, remained still at his side, and ran her fingers over the scar at his temple. What was there to say? It happened, the way life just happens, unplanned, unexpected.

Jacob reached down to the floor, picked up the pillow, and soon fell asleep.

27 SMALL VICTORIES

It had taken several sessions of furtive chats with Sister Eulalia, always interrupted by Mother Maria Josepha who prowled the corridors like a ghost, to carve out a half hour here and there to teach the children secular subjects. Raquela was willing to grab any scrap of time: after or between prayers, after chores, and even just before bedtime. It was her own little triumph in the battle against ignorance.

Raquela had just finished helping Sister Candida plant the last of the spring vegetables: cabbage, cauliflower, and broccoli. Her back was stiff; she wasn't used to this kind of work. But she liked the smell of wet earth and the chorus of rock sparrows that always appeared as they worked the garden. Today, they competed with the ambulance sirens that carried the wounded to the infirmary in the far-off wing of the monastery.

February had been unusually rainy; her boots were covered in mud. She walked into the stone entry vestibule, pulled them off and put on her shoes. Then she went to the kitchen slop sink to wash up. The children greeted her excitedly, and she saw they had just finished scooping out pumpkins for the evening's soup. The youngest ones crawled around the floor picking up errant seeds and sneaking them into their mouths.

"She is gone now," the quiet boy approached her and tapped Raquela's arm. "We can start." He'd figured out that the instruction could be done only when Mother Superior had left the monastery on errands.

Pleased to see this withdrawn child so engaged in her lessons, Raquela said, "Alright, let's gather the children in the refectory." And suddenly an idea bubbled up: she'd make him her assistant. Perhaps that would draw him out, put a smile on his sad little face.

When the children had settled in a circle on the floor, Raquela said, "I want to introduce you to my new assistant. He will help me with preparation for the lessons."

All eyes turned toward the door expectantly, but Raquela smiled and said, "He is right here!" And she approached Manuel, asking him to stand up.

"¿Yo?" Manuel's eyes widened and he looked up at her with his mouth open. The pride on the child's face was unmistakable.

Raquela decided to begin the lesson using old math puzzles she recalled from her school days. She asked Manuel if he knew how dominoes looked. He nodded. "Well, we don't have any, but you'll make them for us," she said.

"¿Yo?" His astonishment grew.

She handed him a few sheets of graph paper, a ruler, a pencil and scissors, then asked him to cut out twenty-eight equal size rectangles. The children's eyes followed Manuel's small hand as he drew the lines deftly and cut, balancing the large scissors.

"Now, Manuel, draw a line in the middle of each rectangle and put dots on each square as best you remember," she instructed.

As if Manuel were performing a magic trick, the children's eyes remained glued to him. And faster than ten Mary's Full of Grace, Manuel delivered a nearly perfect set of paper dominoes.

"Now we can have fun with addition and multiplication," Raquela announced. "Great job, Manuel!"

The corners of Manuel's mouth turned up ever so slightly, but his eyes stayed fixed on his shoes.

And the game began. With Jacob's lessons and daily usage, Raquela's Spanish had become better, enabling her to make up funny mathematical puzzles, albeit with some laugh-inducing linguistic mistakes.

"Tomorrow, Manuel will help me with a lesson on faraway lands,"

Raquela said just as Sister Candida came to take the children for prayers. A chorus of 'One more game, please' filled the refectory.

Sister Candida passed Raquela on her laundry rounds. Raquela balanced a stack of sheets and blankets in her arms.

"I hear you have made the children very happy," Candida said in a low, husky voice, looking around to see they were alone. "But dominoes are the devil's temptation. Try other aids."

Raquela couldn't tell if Candida was truly perturbed, or if she had simply offered a piece of friendly advice. She said, "I'm only glad I managed to get Manuel involved. He is the saddest child here."

"Oh dear, they all have sadness, but some are just too young to remember why," Candida said. "I've noticed he seems to respond to you more than to any of us. Why don't you try speaking with him?"

"I'll try when an opportunity comes up," Raquela said.

"I could use your help stacking the boxes of bandages, alcohol and other medical supplies," Sister said. "Please come to the infirmary when you get the chance."

"I will, soon," Raquela replied, though she dreaded seeing the wounded and had been avoiding passing anywhere near the infirmary. She rounded the corner toward the floor-to-ceiling linen storage cabinets, placed her load on the shelves, and closed the heavy oak doors. She heard shallow breathing nearby, turned around and noticed Manuel pressed against the wall, hidden by a shadow.

"What are you doing here? You should be helping serve dinner," she said gently, not wanting to frighten him.

With his eyes downcast, Manuel managed to utter in a low, tremulous voice, "Can I come with you to help Sister Candida?"

"Oh, but it's not work suited for children," Raquela said, not wanting to chide him for sneaking around, eavesdropping.

The boy's eyes turned toward her face. Tears glistened in them. "Please," he said, and his chin trembled.

"Hmm... let me speak with one of the sisters. I wouldn't want to break any rules." Raquela patted his head. "Now run along to the kitchen before Sister Eulalia sends out a search party."

Later that week, when Mother Maria Josepha had gone out of town,

Raquela decided to risk speaking to Manuel. She went into the boy's dormitory soon after the evening prayers. Most of the boys appeared to be asleep. Softly, she tapped Manuel's shoulder. He turned to face her immediately.

"I am not sleeping," he whispered.

"Come," she said.

He pulled on his clothes hurriedly.

Raquela took the best roundabout way through the series of corridors to lead Manuel to the medical supply storage room so as to avoid any areas where the boy would see the wounded or hear their moans.

Six huge cartons sat stacked in a corner of the room that was lined with metal shelving.

"We've got our work cut out for us. I can't keep you out too late," Raquela said. "Why don't we each open a carton and begin sorting the supplies."

Manuel offered a pallid smile and began. As he did in the kitchen where he was always the fastest potato peeler, the most dedicated floor scrubber, and the most eager assistant teacher—anything to please Señora Raquela—Manuel worked, but hardly spoke. Raquela had yet to learn what inscrutable secrets lay in this child's eyes, his deep black pools of pain.

Having filled the lower shelves, Manuel kicked off his shoes and climbed to the highest shelf to place a box of bandages.

"Careful!" Raquela had just noticed his monkey-like acrobatics.

"It's easy... I used to climb an olive tree in my yard," he said.

Raquela swallowed hard at this first mention of Manuel's life outside the orphanage. "Do you want to tell me more?" she treaded carefully.

"I wish I had a big box of bandages like these in my home..." Manuel began, then stopped.

She held her breath and waited.

He resumed after a while, "Maybe I could have used them on my mother."

Raquela felt a stab in her chest. That poor child!

Unprompted, he went on. "They came, three men with guns, pushed her on the floor and did things to her."

A small moan came from his chest. He chewed his lips between the

235

words. "Then bang! Bang! Bang! Each of them took a shot." His words shot out sharp and swift as bullets. His face seemed a shade lighter.

"I am so sorry," Raquela said. She walked over to him, and he threw his skinny arms around her waist, pressing his head on her chest. What she'd have given to find the right words to console him.

"She'll always be in your heart," Raquela said, but those words unleashed a torrent of tears he'd been holding back.

"I am already forgetting her face," he stuttered out.

When he calmed, Raquela described what he'd need to do the next day to get the geography game going. "You'll rake the soil on the outside yard, then smooth it and I'll draw the continents."

He smiled wanly and said, "She had a smile like yours."

The day had been long. After Manuel was back in bed, burrowing into his pillow, Raquela trudged to the bus stop. It struck her that her depression had begun to lift as she became closer to the children and had managed a breakthrough with Manuel. Was this redemption? What would it mean to Golda? Nothing could make up for her loss. Or Manuel's, she told herself. Loss is everywhere. She was immersed in thoughts and chilled through and through when a truck pulled close.

A Brigade volunteer whose face was familiar from the headquarters opened the window. "Want a ride?" he asked.

She hesitated. "Are you going toward the headquarters? I live nearby."

"Yes. I'd be happy to drop you off," he said, and she realized that his Spanish was poor and that he spoke with a Polish accent.

"Dombrowski Brigade?" she asked as she scrambled into the vehicle.

"Yes," he said and ran his fingers through his blond mop. "Jacek," he introduced himself.

"What brought you to the monastery?" Raquela asked.

"The infirmary supply run. Italy and Nazi Germany are giving so much support to the Nationalists we can hardly keep up. Soon the area stretching toward here will be central in the fight, but our boys gave them quite a licking in Madrid," Jacek said.

Raquela shook her head, didn't know what to say. After a while, she said, "I deplore violence."

"Then why are you here?" Jacek snickered.

"The orphans of this war need help." She heard defensiveness in her tone. Weren't there orphans needing help everywhere? What about her own mother, struggling with so many kids? No, Manuel made her know she was in the right place.

When he dropped her off, Jacek said, "I hope you'll reconsider and join the fighting units, our volunteer supply is dwindling."

She said, "Thank you for the ride. Goodnight." Disembarking on the silent street, Raquela turned the corner to Calle Rosario. She didn't feel defensive anymore, she felt good about her choice to work at the orphanage.

It was nearly eleven at night when Raquela climbed the three stories to their apartment. "Jacob, I'm home," she called out in the vestibule.

No response.

She was bone-tired, but so keyed up by her encounter with Manuel, she knew she'd not be able to sleep. Instead, she collected a few pieces of dirty laundry, including Jacob's socks strewn in the bedroom, and did a small wash in the kitchen sink, then sat down with a cup of tea to look at the paper.

Jacob had told her that one could not trust the papers, which were filled with propaganda of whichever faction issued them. It seemed—at least on the surface—they were all on the socialist government's side, but in fact, trade union groups, anarchists of different stripes, socialists and communists fought one another bitterly and had no common language except that of propaganda and guns.

The headline claimed that Republican fighters, aided by exhausted international volunteers battling with few working weapons, had stopped Franco's forces from taking Madrid. This was excellent news. Maybe the war would be won soon. If Madrid, the capital, was free, then the rest would surely follow. She chose to believe it. It secretly thrilled her that Jacob was still stuck in an office, organizing volunteers, instead of rotting in a muddy trench with grenades exploding just feet away. She had grown not only dependent, but increasingly fond of him. He was good to her and for her. He kept her grounded in the present and kept her from dwelling on the past. In the bleak mood of wartime she felt uplifted by his optimism and occasional flights of fancy. He was a dreamer and dreams were what she needed because right now, she had none of her own.

She heard the door open, and Jacob walked in with an odd expression. "Good evening," he greeted her and hung up his jacket on the coat rack near the entrance. "Sorry I'm so late. I had a drink with our new commander, Major Tadeusz."

It was unusual for Jacob to stay out late to socialize. Surprised, Raquela asked, "Was it about something urgent?"

"Yes," he said without elaborating and walked quickly toward the bedroom.

Raquela followed him, sensing something. "What is it?" she said.

"I have a bit of packing to do," Jacob said, standing in front of the open wardrobe.

"So, you are finally going."

He didn't respond. He stood with his back to her, shuffling through the drawers in the wardrobe.

Raquela came around and pulled out a pair of his warmest socks. "Here, you might need these. Take them with you."

Jacob's eyes misted over as he stuffed the socks into his bag. He embraced her. She stiffened initially but then wrapped her arms around him. They stood silent for a few long moments.

"I'll be back, don't worry," Jacob whispered over and over.

She pulled away from him. "I saw in Jaffa how good you are at evading bullets. You'll be fine."

"I do wish we had been better equipped. We expect to face massive fire power in the Guadalajara region. The Italians and Germans are sending huge amounts of munitions and men."

When he was done packing his bag, Jacob walked into the kitchen and rummaged through a drawer filled with a variety of tools and assorted kitchenware left by the previous renters. Raquela sat at the table watching him. "What are you looking for?" she asked.

"A knife, a good one with a sharp blade," he responded in a distracted kind of way.

"A knife?" Raquela's eyebrows moved up.

"If I hadn't been such an idiot, I'd have kept at least one of the guns from the *Pharaoh* stash," Jacob said. "A knife will have to do."

A shudder shook Raquela. "Don't be fatalistic, Jacob. Maybe they'll supply weapons once you get to the battlefront. Cheer up. You can't fight when you are so dispirited," she said.

"Cheer me up," he said.

"Alright, come," Raquela took his hand and pulled him into the bedroom. She could see the astonishment on his face, the confusion in his eyes. Even she hadn't expected such a brazen advance. She'd rendered him speechless. He kissed every inch of her body as if she were a Torah and as if each kiss transported him to the light at the foot of Mount Sinai.

It wasn't until afterwards that a chilling realization hit her: she could get pregnant! It didn't even occur to her the first time with Jacob... and with Uri... well, she was half-comatose then. In her home traditions, it was a mitzvah to have a child. She knew nothing about birth control. Women bore babies. Period. Yet she neither wanted nor was capable of dealing with an infant. Not now, probably never. No, surely never. Not after Maya.

"You will be back. I just know it," she whispered, but his even, raspy breaths meant he'd already fallen asleep. She got out of bed to make some tea.

28 THE INFIRMARY

After Jacob's departure, the small rooms of their flat echoed with emptiness. Raquela felt more alone than ever before. Did she love him? She couldn't say—at least not in the way Aleksander had made her feel where every fiber of her being quivered with joy at the sight of him—but the sense of commitment grew in her daily. She worried about him being injured at the front. And she felt more grateful than ever for time spent at the orphanage. The children distracted her grim thoughts. And ever so slowly, Manuel began to emerge from his shell.

One evening after the children were in their beds, Sister Candida was in an unusually talkative mood. Sister Eulalia wasn't well, this being her time of the month, so Sister Candida presided over the day's activities. She was older than Eulalia and more reserved. When the two of them worked in the kitchen, getting things ready for the next morning, Raquela told her what she'd learned of Manuel's history.

Candida set aside the tray of cups she was about to place on a shelf. She took Raquela's hand and held it for a moment, "This is hard to hear, child. There are many more stories like Manuel Laredo's."

Candida's gentle demeanor made it easier to pursue a question on Raquela's mind. "Sister, do you know what happened to Manuel's father?"

Candida's distorted shadow on the rough stone wall made her look taller and the moment ominous. After a long pause she said, "His father, the editor of an anarchist newspaper, was dragged out of bed and shot before Manuel's eyes. You already know what happened after that."

Raquela clasped her chest, felt a stab in it. "What monsters would do such things?"

"In this war, men on both sides have become monsters...and some women too," Sister Candida said quietly. She put the tray on the shelf, then began fingering the rosary and praying with her eyes half-closed.

Raquela finished laying out the last of the breakfast churro ingredients. "I'll be going now, good night," she said.

"Wait," Candida lifted her hooded eyes. "There are too many wounded coming in daily. I need you to spare extra time in the evenings to help us."

"I'd like to," Raquela hesitated, "but I have no training, none whatsoever. I wouldn't know what to do."

"No one is ever prepared for war. I'll teach you. It doesn't take much to empty bedpans or to bandage wounds." A hint of a smile appeared on Candida's tired face. "Don't worry, I won't ask you to operate."

Raquela's first evening at the emergency wing shook her to the core. She'd been successful in bypassing that section of the cavernous building for weeks. Now she'd be forced to face it. She had seen dead men in the Palestine shootout at Ra'anana, but this was different, personal.

She entered a huge, dimly lit hall, lined with metal cots standing a few feet apart. The wide space was mostly silent, except for the echoes of moans and whispered prayers of those still alive. The stench of blood, pus, and vomit, mixed with chlorine and alcohol, assaulted her nostrils. Many lay so still she thought they were already in the other world.

Sister Candida moved like a silent shadow among the beds, giving some patients sips of water, dabbing with moistened gauze the dry, blood-stained lips of those too wounded to drink. Crutches stood next to many beds. In some of these beds, Raquela could see the flattened area of blanket where the men's legs should have been. Yellowish, iodine-stained bandages, some colored brown by oxidizing blood, covered arms, heads and the feet sticking out from under gray blankets.

As her initial horror faded, Raquela noticed two uniformed nurses and a white-coated man, sporting a neat goatee. They stood conferring at the far end of the ward. When she approached them, Sister Candida introduced the man. "Meet Dr. Gomez. We are very lucky he comes to work here at night after his daytime shift at the hospital."

Dr. Gomez extended his hand and nodded.

"Why aren't these wounded treated at the hospital?" Raquela inquired.

Dr. Gomez replied politely, "This *is* a hospital now. These are overflow patients. All nearby medical facilities that haven't yet been reduced to rubble have run out of space. These are our people; we can't let them die."

His comment made it clear to Raquela just how dire the situation of the Republican fighters had become. "Thank you Doctor, for everything you are doing to help," she said.

Raquela went home dispirited. It had been a lonely three months. The small flat seemed too large, the coat hooks too empty without his green field jacket. She missed Jacob's quiet calm and positivity. As she got up off the sofa to make something to eat, Jacob filled her mind. She thought of the simple Moroccan egg tagine he'd made when they still had the ingredients. He liked to tease her palate, she'd joked with him, unaccustomed to Middle Eastern spices: coriander, cumin and paprika. She wished she could sit with him now and watch him dip bread into the yolks. Then she realized she wasn't hungry anymore; she felt nauseated.

When she awoke the next morning, the nausea hadn't lessened, and her back ached miserably. It occurred to her the lumpy mattress was responsible. She tried stretching, hoping to lessen the pain, but it only got worse. She could not imagine facing the day. She'd not felt well for weeks, she reminded herself, but somehow, she'd managed. She forced herself to get dressed.

When she was more or less ready, she glanced at the clock. It was already six in the morning. She had to get to the orphanage before seven to prepare breakfast for the children. She stood at the mirror and looked at her face. Who was the woman staring back? These days, she hardly recognized herself. Her sallow face, drawn and thin, purple shadows in the rings under her eyes—that was the look of a woman who had lost her way. And it wasn't only her physical state. It went deeper, to her having lost the sense of who she was or the why of her very existence. The only antidote for this feeling was to engage with her charges at the orphanage.

Before leaving home, Raquela realized that the challah she'd baked absentmindedly two nights before, but couldn't eat because of the nausea, would be a nice treat for the children. It was the first time she'd baked since... well, no use to dwell on it. She didn't know what moved her to make it but braiding the strands of dough gave her comfort. Like everyone else, she'd been short on ingredients. She skipped the eggs altogether and halved the sugar, so it wasn't a proper challah, but it would do.

En route to the monastery, she decided that after morning prayers she'd serve thin toasted slices of her braided loaf for breakfast and then take the children outside to teach them her favorite outdoor games. It was still cold, but the sky was a crisp blue, and jumping would warm the children. The flat area behind the monastery was perfect for this.

Like a flock of hungry birds, the children congregated around the challah—made chewier for the absence of eggs—while Raquela explained how she braided the dough. She illustrated it on the hair of a small girl who glowed with pride that she'd been chosen. Manuel did the honors of distributing the slices. "One day soon, I will bake one here with you," she told the children. "Who wants to help?" All the hands shot up in the air at once. Manuel's hand stood above all others.

Outside, the children acted as if they'd been released from prison, yelling, running, laughing. It took her a while to get them to settle down and listen to instructions. Raquela reached into her bag for the rope and a ball of string she had brought. Manuel eyed them suspiciously and asked shyly, "Señora Raquela, what are these for?"

"You'll see soon," she said and ruffled his thick black mane. A flicker of light danced in Manuel's eyes. He seemed more anxious to begin than the others.

The children loved best taking turns skipping rope and playing blind man's bluff. When they needed a rest, Raquela gathered them around her, unspooled the string and showed them how to play cat's cradle. Her mood now lifted, but something was happening to her body.

Her cramps became unbearably painful, to the point she could no longer ignore them. Manuel's knitted brow told her he'd noticed. She felt embarrassed. She didn't want to leave the children unattended—

there'd be hell to pay if the mother superior ever found out—but she got up off the dry grass and in a flash called out, "Manuel..." Unable to continue, she ran as fast as her legs could carry her toward the lavatory in the monastery's basement.

She felt excruciating pain followed by a gush, then a sticky trickle down her legs. She knew it was blood, and it kept flowing. She felt faint, desperately trying to reach the toilet. When she finally sat, thick, dark clots filled the bowl. It would never stop; she'd die right there. Everything went black and she passed out.

Outside, Manuel yelled to the children, "*¡Quédate dónde estás y no te muevas!*" They obeyed and stayed still. He ran to find Sister Eulalia.

Raquela came to on the tile floor, hearing Sister Eulalia calling, "*Despertarse,*" and shaking her repeatedly. Raquela was vaguely aware of a commotion around her, but her eyes seemed glued shut. At first, she wanted to remain in the pleasant haze, but she became conscious of the sister saying something about Dr. Gomez. Who was she speaking to, Manuel? She couldn't be sure because she didn't remember how she got there.

Dr. Gomez arrived quickly. He put smelling salts to Raquela's nose. She opened her eyes, confused. "What happened to me?" she asked. Her words came out slowly from somewhere deep inside as if pulled from a tangled skein.

"Looks like you've had a miscarriage, Señora," Dr. Gomez pronounced confidently. Then he turned to Sister Eulalia, "You'll need to contact her husband."

Raquela closed her eyes and did not respond. Sister Eulalia, kneeling near Raquela holding her hand, looked up at Dr. Gomez. Her look explained the situation.

In a perfectly gentlemanly manner, Dr. Gomez instructed Sister Eulalia on what needed to be done. "Too much blood lost; she may need a transfusion, and take her outside, she needs some air." Raquela heard his words, then more commotion, and people speaking over her. But she didn't care. She never wanted to move again.

As they lifted her onto a stretcher, Raquela opened her eyes and saw Manuel out of the corner of her eye. He stood behind Sister Eulalia with fright in his eyes, the boy-man who'd saved her.

In the monastery's makeshift emergency ward, Raquela's ears pricked up at the sounds of brisk evening activity: ambulances coming and going, nurses directing drivers where to place new arrivals, and moans, so many moans. Now she was one of the infirmary's unlikely patients. She could hardly move; her head pounded, and she felt absurdly weak. She could barely lift her arms to adjust the pillow. She hadn't given much thought to the few missed periods over the last dozen weeks. Her intake of food had been so reduced—much like everyone else's—she didn't doubt it affected her ovulation. A pregnancy had never entered her mind. After what had happened with Maya, there couldn't be any worse punishment.

The next morning Raquela awoke disoriented. Momentarily, she wondered what she was doing here among the fighters. She still felt weak as if she'd actually been exhausted by a fight, but soon realized her body had battled an invader from within. Her arms felt leaden, her belly ached, and the moist wads of cotton between her legs chafed.

She looked around and noticed the bed to her left was now empty. She vaguely remembered seeing a man in it when Sister Eulalia brought her in the day before. His head and face had been bandaged; he lay uttering no sound. Perhaps he'd died overnight after she had fallen asleep. The nurses chatted quietly as they changed the sheets on his bed for a fresh victim. She overheard them speaking of injuries wrought by gas. Weren't guns lethal enough? Her disgust with warfare grew.

Trying to pull herself out of despair, Raquela visualized Jacob holding a newborn. He was gentle; he'd make a good father, she reflected, then immediately pushed the thought away. She had no intention of telling him what had happened. Better to think of how Manuel had saved her from bleeding to death. How frightened the boy must have felt at the sight of her blood. She'd have to make it up to him somehow. Tired of these random thoughts, she closed her eyes and didn't hear Sister Candida asking her how she was feeling.

29 SPOILS OF WAR

After weeks of rain and mud, the temperature became balmy toward the beginning of April. Spring had arrived suddenly. Grass carpeted the hillsides that had been a sea of brown just days before. If she could just overlook the bloodshed, the whitewashed windmills and poppies wobbling in the spring breeze could convince Raquela that all was well with the world.

On this chilly Saturday morning, she sat in the kitchen, a blanket wrapped around her shoulders, and sipped a brew of hot barley coffee. It was an unpleasantly acidic drink, but it warmed her. Her thoughts wandered to Jacob. Was he freezing in a trench somewhere, dodging bullets? Would he have to resort to slitting someone's throat if he had no other weapon? She didn't want to think of him as cold-blooded. It wasn't his nature. He was passionate about the cause, and the cause meant killing Franco's soldiers. She couldn't deny that. They were raping democracy. But she was glad not to take part in the killings.

She opened her notebook and began jotting notes for new geography lessons when she heard a noise at the door. She'd become so accustomed to the silence, it made her jump, but the knock at the door was gentle. Raquela tiptoed to the door and opened it a crack.

Jacob stood before her, bedraggled, with a beard she'd never seen on his face. She flung her arms around his neck. "You are alive! You are alive!"

"Wait, let me put my loot down so I can hug you properly," Jacob said and strode into the flat.

That's when she noticed the black boots he hadn't had when he left for the front and the rifle he leaned on the sofa. "Well, well, I thought you had no weapons. I was so worried about you." Raquela smiled, relieved.

Jacob placed a box on the table, then plopped into the sofa with a creak of the springs. He looked exhausted.

"What's in the box?" she asked.

"Ammunition."

She stood eyeing the box.

"I'll only tell you I wasn't given any of this," he motioned to the rifle and boots.

Raquela stood at the table, rubbing her chin, then she turned toward Jacob. "Tell me about the action you saw and about your comrades."

"I don't feel like talking now," Jacob said. "I haven't bathed in days. Let me shave and wash, so I can give you a proper greeting, Raquela. Better yet, we can get reacquainted after I wash and sleep."

"Shall I make you something to eat first? I can do it quickly."

"Not now, Raquela, but I see you haven't been eating much. You look like a stick."

She took offense and pouted.

Jacob realized his mistake. "But you are still beautiful, like a willow in springtime," he said and began walking away toward the bathroom.

He turned back abruptly. "Yes, I took his boots and this," Joseph pointed toward the rifle. "A good Italian weapon. They provisioned every Italian soldier with these; we had hardly any firearms." He yawned broadly and closed the door with a snap.

Raquela sat down, trying to absorb Jacob's comment. Did he slit the Italian's throat? She heard the shower water running for a long time. Was he scrubbing his body clean or his conscience? She shuddered at how the war brutalized good men. Weren't there any models for peaceful resolution of conflicts thought up by people smarter than she?

After the water stopped running, she heard him walk into the bedroom. She waited a while, then stood at the bedroom door listening to his snores. She opened the door quietly, tiptoed in, and reached for an extra blanket piled on a chair. He didn't stir. She covered him and listened to his noisy breath, then lay down and spooned against his back.

His return from the front was a good omen. She got up before he awoke to rustle up ingredients for soup.

When he awoke, hours later, Jacob came into the kitchen looking more refreshed. "I have been keeping your soup hot for hours," Raquela smiled. "There, eat." She placed a steaming bowl in front of him. A lonely carrot and a piece of turnip floated above some noodles.

"I am sorry it's so watery. We are almost out of everything."

"Tastes like a gift from heaven after what I've been eating," Jacob slurped the soup noisily. "Tell me what you've been up to while I was away. Any news?"

"What news? More killings every day; more hunger. That's it."

His question made her anxious, and the slurping sounds he made grated on her nerves. She would not mention the miscarriage; she could not do this to him.

When Jacob finished the soup, he walked over to his rucksack and reached into it. "I brought you a special gift, Raquela."

"Wartime is no time for gifts," she said, wiping the tabletop.

Jacob extended his arm with a small object in his palm.

It took her a minute to respond. The shock of it! "Why did you bring me this?" she asked, her voice rising.

"For protection, isn't it obvious? I can't afford to worry about you when I'm at the front."

"There's still no fighting here and I'd not use it anyway. Don't try to make me into something I'm not."

Jacob looked puzzled. "What do you mean?"

Raquela felt increasingly aggravated by his obtuseness. "I hate violence in all its forms. I'll never be a fighter."

"Stop it," Jacob said. Then, more mildly, "Come sit here, next to me and let me explain."

He looked so crestfallen with her staunch refusal, she decided to humor him. She put down the dishes she'd been clearing and sat next to him.

Jacob draped his arm on her shoulder and pulled her close. He held the small fearsome object in his hand. "Look, this is the best small handgun in the world—a Beretta—perfect to hide in your bag... even if you never use it."

Raquela stared at the gun, biting her lip. "So small and so lethal," she said. "Like a scorpion."

"It may save your life one day. Take it and promise me you'll never be without it."

"I can't... I just can't," she said, shaking her head.

"Yes, you can, and you will." Now Jacob sounded more like a battalion commander than the man she'd come to know.

Could she still trust him, knowing he had killed for it? She shook her head at her own foolishness; she knew he did what a soldier had to do.

As if he'd accomplished his mission, Jacob stood up, put the revolver back on the table, and said, "I rested somewhat, but I could sleep for a week. I'm going back to bed. Guadalajara stories tomorrow. Today we celebrate."

She understood exactly what he meant. Since there wasn't any wine with which to toast, he'd revel in her body, but she'd not give herself as unselfconsciously as before. She'd insist on precautions. She took a long bath and brushed her hair. Her cheeks looked sunken, and her face still carried the pallor of miscarriage. Would he discern what had happened?

She slipped into bed beside him. He waited for her, took her in his arms like a starved man who'd been presented with a lavish repast. "Oh, Raquela, how I hungered for your touch. I hallucinated you were with me in the trenches. Your image gave me courage when I was most afraid," he said.

She liked that he'd voiced his fear. "I missed you too," she said, and traced his scar with her index finger. "Lucky you didn't get another," she joked. Then she hesitated, unsure how to verbalize her need, her own fear. "Jacob?"

"What is it? Am I hurting you?"

"No, nothing like that, but do you have... a precaution?" Raquela blurted out.

"Afraid of becoming pregnant by a stud like me?" Jacob chuckled. "Don't worry. War is no time to make babies." He reached for his pant pocket on the nearby chair and pulled out a Durex, held it up. "Some womanizer in my unit gave it to me; the guy never could keep his pants on too long."

Raquela breathed a sigh of relief and ran her fingers along his cheek. "Maybe you shouldn't have shaved off the beard. It made you look fierce."

"You like the warrior in me," he laughed.

"No, I like that you are a gentle giant," she said and gave herself to him fully. What else but her body did she have to offer this kind, generous man? For what it lacked in exhilaration, the lovemaking gave her a pleasurable sense of warmth and comfort, like drinking cocoa on a snowy day. Jacob's adoration was a gift she should not underestimate.

Raquela stepped out of the apartment to get some bread. She wanted to get in the queue early before it sold out. Food was becoming scarcer daily, but late April's balmy weather soothed her. The sun shone so brilliantly she squinted.

"*Disculpa, lo siento,*" the landlady bumped into Raquela, almost knocking her over as she emerged from the building's entry vestibule.

"*No importa.* Thank goodness for such a beautiful day," Raquela said.

"Oh, nothing to be thankful for today," Señora Fuentes said. Her expression was grim, the rims of her eyes red.

"What happened?" Raquela hoped it was nothing more serious than a problem with trash collection, but Señora's eyes told another story. "*Nazi bastardos!* Their planes rained a hundred thousand bombs on a busy Monday market. Crushed the town to dust! *¡La matanza de civiles!*"

Slaughtering civilians! Raquela's chest tightened. "Where?"

"Guernica," Señora Fuentes pointed north. "If we don't stop them, they'll be at our doorstep next," she said, shaking her head. "They'll even find your infirmary soon."

An attack on the children? Unthinkable! The possibility curdled her brain. Unable to find words of reassurance, Raquela said, "I am so sorry to hear this." Images of dead babies and desperate mothers searching for them filled her head. And this escalation of violence meant that Jacob would be returning to the front very soon.

She hurried to the panaderia, but by the time she arrived, the shelves stood bare. "Get here earlier next time," the salesgirl said.

By late June, Jacob deployed to the front once more. Raquela forced herself to avoid grim war accounts in the papers and, instead, to focus all

250

her attention on the children and on creating new lessons. But one headline screamed; she felt its impact in her gut: "The Bishops of Spain have collectively endorsed Franco as the legitimate ruler of the country!" She could not put it out of her mind.

The day the announcement appeared, Mother Maria Josepha greeted Raquela with a rare smile, one that distorted her bland, doughy face. It made her loyalties clear. Wanting to avoid a conversation with her, Raquela said, "Excuse me, Mother. I have work in the kitchen."

Sisters Eulalia and Candida looked glum and stopped whispering when Raquela passed them in the hallway. Were they allied with the anarchists? Was Maria Josepha capable of denouncing them now that she had the church behind her? Raquela shuddered.

In the kitchen, she worked briskly, as if washing down the countertops would wash away her disturbing thoughts. It was lucky Albacete was still mostly outside the strike zone of the bombings; they hadn't suffered the ravages of this war as much as the north and Madrid. But hunger was the one constant they shared with everyone.

Raquela reached deep into the bin to get usable potatoes for the next meal. There weren't many and some had already rotted. She was so sick of potatoes and beans, but now even those were in short supply.

Sister Eulalia walked into the kitchen and straight to the larder. She came out looking very upset. Her usually bright eyes were dull. Downcast, they swept the floor, searching for something. She paced back and forth in the kitchen.

"Sister, is there a problem?" Raquela asked.

"We have to make the portions smaller still. Our lentils won't last till next week. The bacalao has been gone for weeks," Eulalia stated the obvious.

The meager servings begun to show on the children's bodies. Their little faces looked sallow; bluish shadows crept in below their eyes. Cooking had become a daily challenge that called for incredible ingenuity and sometimes even risk. Of late, they had even begun using the ancient tomato sauce cans with rusty bottoms. Uncertain of their safety, they boiled them for hours.

After a long silence, Sister Eulalia stopped pacing and said, "I'd give anything for a few strands of saffron to season our rice."

"Saffron?" Raquela looked at Eulalia with confusion. "I've never even seen it in the cupboards here."

Sister Eulalia smiled, a wan, ironic smile. "Albacete is known for our saffron, but it has been gone since before you arrived." Pulled in by a memory, she closed her eyes and said, "Oh, if you could taste it... It is mellow and honeyed and musky—hypnotic."

"In Madrid, people substitute cats for rabbit stew. I prefer our meatless cocido leavened with a few old, dry parsnips and wilted turnips even if we don't have saffron," Raquela said.

The scarcity of food was constantly on Raquela's mind. She no longer studied her sunken cheeks in the mirror. She was preoccupied with the children's health and schemed about how to find food for them. She spoke to Señora Fuentes about it and though she, like most Albacete residents, had mostly emptied her larder, she donated a bag of rice and a bottle of olive oil.

Handing Raquela the bag, Señora Fuentes said, "Soon you will have to join the Brigades, like your Jacob. I hear volunteers have become scarcer than hen's teeth. If I were younger, I'd join myself."

The suggestion, uttered with deep sincerity, disturbed Raquela. "Thank you, Señora. I'm needed with the children."

When Jacob got a pass for a brief leave from the front in August 1937, Raquela tried to persuade him to travel with her to Barcelona. She'd hoped that in a big city, they might find more food so she could help resupply the monastery kitchen. She still had a tiny sum left from Aleksander's gift, stashed away for emergencies. She couldn't stand to see the children hungry. It was pitiful the way they pounced on every morsel of food, their eyes scanning the kitchen and dining room floors for any dropped tidbit. But Jacob informed her that the shelling in Barcelona was far worse and the queues for bread endless. "They have a much harder time finding food there. And the black market is very dangerous."

"Isn't there any place we can try?" Raquela pleaded.

"We can trek to some of the distant villages in the country. I've heard that city people go there, trying to raid farms and steal chickens."

"We won't do that," Raquela said.

"And don't forget, Raquela, this damn plain is so rocky and dry, not much grows here."

"Well, maybe we can nab a sheep," she teased.

Jacob said, "I will go on one condition. You'll have to carry the gun I gave you and use it if the need arises. It's not safe anywhere."

Raquela bristled at Jacob's demand, but knew if she protested, she'd miss a chance to do something good for the children. She could not undertake this project alone. Though she was sure her expression registered unhappiness, she nodded.

Jacob, a little surprised, said, "Well then, you are ready. Good woman."

Next day, they set out on a foot trek along dusty roads toward the surrounding villages. The heat was brutal. Their faces burned from sun and sweat. The air was so dense that shimmering waves appeared ahead of them, making the heat visible.

Along the road, they found an abandoned two-wheeled cart. Its body was rusty, dotted with holes, and one of its wheels was on the verge of falling off, but it would have to do.

It was Raquela's job to knock on farm doors and attempt to persuade the peasants to contribute anything they could spare. Few denied her request when she told them it was for starving orphans. They couldn't give much, but she gratefully accepted anything: a kilo of flour, some carrots, a bag of potatoes, a bottle of oil, a few cans of beans. One even offered two scrawny chickens that pecked and squawked as Jacob placed them in the cart.

It was Jacob's job to find their way and to pull the increasingly burdensome cart that nearly tipped over on the rock-strewn roads each time they hit a pothole. In the mornings when it was a bit cooler, and they less tired, Raquela and Jacob chatted as they trudged along.

"I'm glad you convinced me to come with you on this mission," Jacob said. "It reminds me of when my mother and I walked in the countryside gathering chunks of red clay she used for her pottery making. We'd go out just at sunrise and the mountains glowed pink and scarlet."

"And I remembered something from my childhood," Raquela said. "We used to knock on our neighbors' doors to deliver *shalach manot*, gifts of food for the Purim holiday. It was a mitzvah and we had to do it even when we didn't have much. My mother made baskets with her blueberry jam and butter cookies. Oh, I can smell them right now. It took all this time for me to realize what a beautiful tradition it was."

On two nights, farmers allowed them to sleep on straw in their barns. Raquela's feet were so blistered from all the walking, she wanted to thank the farmers, but the men were gruff and didn't want to engage in any conversation.

She lay on the creaky barn floor, inhaling the pungent odor of her body mixed with the sweet smell of hay. Though the relative coolness of the barn soothed her, she desperately wished for a shower. Jacob had fallen asleep the minute he hit the floor, but she heard worrisome noises outside: dog barks, distant voices, scratching sounds. He didn't wake up. She touched the Beretta, praying she'd not have to use it.

When the noises receded, Raquela stayed awake thinking of how instead of decompressing from combat, Jacob had accompanied her willingly on this trek. He kept up her spirits when she tired, urging her to take a few more steps. "See that barn over the rise? You can make it." He pulled her up with his wiry arm. After a while she heard a distant noise, like the rumbling of a thunderstorm. Maybe it was her exhaustion, but she could have sworn she felt the earth shake. Strange, she thought, August is so dry.

The second night, Jacob lay right on a bare barn floor and snored in minutes. Raquela couldn't sleep because hunger pangs made her stomach ache. She thought of her classmates from the gymnasium: Pessy, Evgeniya and Anita, girls from wealthy homes, accustomed to the good life. They'd never make it here. Bronka would though. She was much like her, brought up not to expect much, but always striving for more.

After three days, Jacob's leave came to an end and their pathetic cart was full enough. "Let me pull this up the hill," he said when they had reached the road snaking up to the monastery.

Raquela glanced at her watch. To make his train, Jacob needed to leave now. She feigned ample energy. "It's nothing. I can do it easily."

"Are you sure?" Jacob looked dubious.

"Yes," Raquela flexed her arm. "Look at my muscles."

Jacob smiled, and crinkles formed at the corners of his eyes. He pulled her close, her small frame swallowed up in his. She felt his scratchy beard—a thick, three-day growth—and smelled his musky sweat. They kissed a long wet kiss as if they were trying to quench their thirst, and just for an instant, their tongues battled as if preparing for war.

Raquela disengaged from his embrace and said, "You've got to go." He turned around quickly and walked away.

"Just come back in one piece," she called after him, but he didn't turn around.

She grasped the handle of the cart and yanked it harder than necessary. Then Raquela trudged up the hill, dragging the heavy cart of supplies Jacob had helped her "liberate."

An aura of disquiet—maybe it was premonition—tugged at her chest. The silence, punctuated by the crows' harsh squawks, wasn't entirely unusual here, but something besides them—sounds of farm machinery—should have been audible. Early morning fog rose from the hillsides, compounding her apprehension.

As Raquela came closer to the summit, she stopped and looked around, confused. The church steeple was gone! She rubbed her eyes. It had greeted her daily from this very spot. She'd often reflected how odd it was for a girl from an Orthodox Jewish home to be coming here. The horizon seemed naked except for vultures circling above.

She left the cart at the side of the road and rushed toward the summit, fearing what she might find. When she reached it, Raquela faced a horrific scene of devastation. The infirmary wing on the western side of the monastery was gone. The eastern portion of the refectory stood in charred ruins. The front portico and cloister walls had collapsed completely. The contents of dormitory rooms lay strewn about in eerie silence. Beds and chairs upside down, mattresses languishing in the dirt, and sheets like white shrouds hanging on bushes and tree branches. Where were the children?

Tears welled in her eyes. Her hands shook uncontrollably, and her legs stood glued to the ground. She was unable to move or process the scene before her. She knew the Nationalists had been barbarous with the civilian population. Everyone in their path was an anarchist or communist, vying with Franco for power. But it was inconceivable to think that nuns and children fell into enemy ranks.

A gust of wind brought her to awareness. Now she inhaled an odor that made her retch. It was the stink of death. She needed to get away from here, but she was powerless to move. As she stood weeping, trying to avert her gaze from the scene, yet unable to, her eyes caught a movement. "Have ghosts come to haunt this place already?" she asked out loud. Then she saw it, a small figure in the distance, huddled in the rubble.

In a daze, she compelled her legs to move and walked toward it. There she saw him, swaddled in a dirty gray blanket. Above it, his black hair stuck up at odd angles. "Manuel, Manuel, what happened here? Where is everyone? Why are you here alone?" Raquela called out.

He stood up slowly, like an old man. In a single action he dropped the blanket, ran toward her, and threw his arms around her. "Señora Raquela, I have been waiting for you," he managed to say through heart-wrenching sobs.

She swept gray flakes of ash off a boulder, sat down and held Manuel on her lap for a long time. She cradled him as if he were a baby and for the first time since she'd met him, he allowed himself to be mothered. When the sobbing subsided a little, she tried again, "Where is everyone?"

He shuddered. Tears mixed with soot made long streaks on his face. His lip quivered as he spoke. It took a while for her to understand that the mother superior had moved the children out just before the bombs rained. That gave her some relief, but immediately, a terrible thought came to mind. Could Maria Josepha have informed on the Republican sisters and the soldiers in the infirmary? Ever since the Bishops' declaration, Raquela knew the mother superior's sympathies lay with Franco. No, no! No human being would do such a thing, especially not a woman of the church.

"Where are Sisters Eulalia and Candida?" she asked Manuel.

His sobbing resumed. His thin body shook violently. "Estan muertas," he whispered.

Raquela hugged him tightly. She didn't know what to say to console him. The child had witnessed so much violence in his young life. There were not enough words in any language to soften such blows.

After what seemed like hours, Manuel fell asleep in her arms. She sat rocking him, trying to figure out what to do. He had nowhere to go; she'd have to take him home. Something inside resisted sending him back into the care of Mother Maria Josepha.

When Manuel opened his black eyes, she said, "Come with me."

He stood up and took her hand, not asking where they were headed. They walked toward the spot where she'd left the cart.

"Déjame sacarlo," he said in his small, hoarse voice, grasped the

256

handle and pulled. The cart tipped over a stone. The chickens squawked and flapped their wings furiously, but Manuel hardly noticed. Little stuttering breaths sprang from his chest.

Without a word, he righted the cart and picked up the fallen contents. Raquela neither said anything nor helped. She didn't feel she had the right deprive him of the one thing he had to offer.

They walked down the hill in silence. All the while, Raquela fought with herself: should she let him calm down, then take him back to Maria Josepha this evening, or should she let him stay with her? She didn't have any right to this boy, she told herself over and over, but her heart curdled when she imagined exiling him to Maria Josepha's care. More likely than not, she'd mete out cruel punishment for his running away. With Sisters Eulalia and Candida gone, there would be no one to take his side. Raquela feared she couldn't work with the mother superior while harboring such feelings about her.

Without Raquela, Manuel would be truly alone in this world.

30 NO PASARAN

Manuel looked like a frightened rabbit when Raquela arrived with him at Calle Rosario.

Señora Fuentes sat outside the building, fanning herself to no avail. When she saw them, she asked, "And who is this?"

Caught off guard, Raquela couldn't think of a response, so she spit out the first thing that came to her mind, "Jacob's little cousin."

Manuel nodded as if he'd belonged to the Ben Maimon family since birth.

"How will you take all this upstairs?" Señora Fuentes asked.

"He is strong; he will help me."

"Wait here," the landlady said and walked into her office bringing out two burlap bags. "Use these." She handed them to Manuel.

"We collected these foodstuffs in the countryside for the orphanage," Raquela explained, then reached into the cart and offered Señora a bag of flour.

"Can't take it from the mouths of orphans." Señora Fuentes declined.

Upstairs, Manuel looked around the flat with amazement. "You live here?" he said.

His question forced Raquela to decide on the spot. "Yes, and now you will too."

A flicker in his eyes told her this was the answer he'd prayed for all those months in the monastery. Despite the poor nutrition, a growth spurt had elongated him to a frail pole bean. "The only place I have for you to sleep is here," Raquela pointed to the small living room sofa.

"I will sleep in your home?" Manuel's eyes widened as if he hadn't understood Raquela's offer.

"Yes, right here. Go ahead; try it out," she said.

Worn down by terror of the bombing, he lay down, curled his knees close to his chin and fell asleep before she could show him the bathroom and kitchen. Raquela covered him with her shawl and watched him sleep. Even asleep, the child continued to make the little stuttering breaths as if he still cowered in the ruins of the monastery.

In the morning he repeated time and again, "*No quiero molestarte.*"

"You are not bothering me, Manuel. You can help me," Raquela said cheerfully and set before him a plate of toast and a fried egg laid by one of the liberated chickens. He devoured the breakfast and licked the yolk remnants off the plate. She did not have the heart to scold him for his manners.

After several days, Manuel seemed to have adjusted to life with Señora Raquela. Raquela realized that her suspicions about Maria Josepha were not sufficient cause to abandon the other orphans. She thought about them every day and about how much they must miss the games she played with them. In any case, she had to deliver the foodstuffs she'd collected with Jacob.

Señora Fuentes, informed by the town's scuttlebutt, said the orphanage had been moved to much smaller quarters in a farmhouse adjacent to a church in a nearby village. Luckily, the village was located at the terminus of their bus line.

When she first walked into the farmhouse, Raquela noticed that Maria Josepha would not look her in the eye. All she said was, "Grab an apron. You can see we are shorthanded."

Raquela managed a barely audible, "I am sorry about what happened."

Maria Josepha grimaced. "It's because of you people."

Though Raquela couldn't tell if she was blaming Jews, anarchists, or socialists, or if in her mind they were all the same, she was furious.

Given that the majority of the damage was to the infirmary that served the Republican fighters, it seemed reasonable to assume the attack had been perpetrated by Franco's army.

Since the orphanage remained under Mother Maria Josepha's supervision, Raquela did not reveal that Manuel was with her. She knew she'd be in deep trouble with the village police for harboring a child who wasn't hers. She needn't have worried: Maria Josepha didn't bother to inquire about Manuel's whereabouts, nor did she ask where all the foodstuffs Raquela brought came from. She just pointed to the pantry and said, "Put them there."

The children cheered when Raquela returned, but none asked about Manuel or Candida or Eulalia. A young peasant woman had been recruited to cook and care for the orphans in place of the murdered Sisters. The children seemed to like her. Raquela thought, with an ache in her heart, how like children to blot out losses so quickly. But, really, what did she know? Perhaps they felt far more than they showed. Perhaps they didn't ask because they were afraid or because they'd overheard or been told things they couldn't bear to think about.

As the weeks went by, Manuel became Raquela's steadfast companion and helper at home. On her evening homecoming, Manuel often greeted her with warm beans and potatoes he'd taught himself how to cook. The kitchen was always immaculate on her return: no spills, no grease, no crumbs, no sign that Manuel had cooked.

In the evenings, they played checkers, and he helped her prepare lessons, which Raquela still taught, though it had become much more difficult to carve out time without Eulalia's help. Now lessons took place only on days Maria Josepha was away from the village.

While Raquela was at work, besides cooking, Manuel spent hours scrounging for firewood to light the stove. She worried about leaving him alone, but she had no choice. It was fortunate that when a widowed neighbor in the building had passed away, the landlady had offered her his old books: musty volumes of *Enciclopedia Universal Illustrada Europeo-Americana*. Who'd ever have time to read them? Raquela certainly didn't, but Manuel had discovered them now and spent hours reading and rereading them, marking his favorite entries with pieces of torn newspaper.

Raquela felt that Manuel's presence carved a deep change within her, though she wouldn't know how to define it for years to come. She had become keenly attuned to his moods, constantly worried for his safety and felt prepared to do anything to put a smile on his face. It was easier that Jacob was away. She didn't need to get into any discussions or explanations. She could focus on the boy, her attention never divided.

Throughout late summer and early fall, the Republican forces held their own in some skirmishes, but not in others. In effect, the two sides were locked in a stalemate. The planned winter offensive at Teruel promised to be more challenging than any before it because much of the International Brigades had been decimated. Few if any new volunteers arrived and the unavailability of weapons was a constant.

The winter had been harsh. Raquela had very little money left for food and hardly any to heat the apartment. She had stuffed rags into cracks around the windowframes to stop the wind from whistling; scoured the fleamarket for moth-eaten warm clothing. With Jacob at the front northeast of Albacete, she might not have had the determination to stay, were it not for Manuel.

Raquela hardly recognized Jacob when he returned from Teruel that first week in March '38. His beard had grown long and unkempt after the three-month battle. He walked into the flat gingerly, like an old man.

Raquela ran to greet him. When she touched him, he winced. "What happened to you?" she asked.

"Frostbite on my toes. These shoes are killing me," Jacob said, sitting on the closest chair to pull them off. "No one can keep their toes safe in below zero temperatures, standing on watch in wet shoes." He hobbled over to Raquela. "I haven't greeted you properly," he said.

She noticed the blisters and dark purple blotches on his toes and hugged him gently. How much thinner he was! "So good to see you," she said, at once overwhelmed by how much she'd missed him. If it weren't for Manuel, she'd have felt the pain of Jacob's absence more keenly.

Just then, Manuel walked into the room.

"And who do we have here?" Jacob asked, sitting down, wincing.

"This is Manuel, the boy from the orphanage I had mentioned," Raquela said.

Manuel approached Jacob and shook his hand solemnly with all the deference due a warrior, then walked down the long hallway into the kitchen and made himself scarce.

"What's he doing here?" Jacob asked.

"Shh..." Raquela put her finger to her lips. "Let's not make him uncomfortable," she whispered.

"How long...?"

Raquela cut him off. "I am keeping him," she whispered in a way that precluded any argument.

"What do you mean 'keeping'? He is not a stray puppy you picked up somewhere."

"Shh..." Raquela's eyes turned toward the kitchen. "Let's talk about it later. Now let me take care of those toes."

She returned from the kitchen with a basin of lukewarm water. "Here, put your feet in," she instructed Jacob. She brought bandages and cotton balls from the bathroom.

Manuel walked in from the kitchen carrying a pot of barley coffee. He smiled shyly and put it on a black metal trivet. "Maybe you'd like some later," he said to Jacob.

"Come over here, kid. You might as well see what war can do. It's not just bullets." Manuel approached and stood silently watching. Raquela dabbed Jacob's feet dry with a soft towel, carefully placed cotton between his toes, then wrapped the foot with a bandage.

"Well, let's have some of that coffee now," Jacob said.

Manuel poured a cup and brought it over to him.

"Ahh... First pleasure in months." Jacob inhaled the steam. "Thank you, Manuel."

The boy nodded and made himself scarce.

After discarding the water in the basin, Raquela settled herself next to Jacob on the sofa. He took her hand and held it. "Our side lost; all our resources are exhausted. At least 50,000 killed at Teruel. Can you picture that kind of carnage, Raquela? Can you?"

"No, I can't picture it," Raquela shook her head. She felt great relief and a tickle of guilt that she hadn't gone to the front. But now she was responsible for Manuel. It was her duty to live so she could care for him.

Jacob said, "I'm just happy to be alive. With some rest, I'll fight another day." There was resignation in his voice. Just then, Manuel returned with a small plate of bread he'd toasted on the stove. "Love the smell of bread," Jacob said and hobbled toward the table. Raquela

262

followed him. The three of them sat and ate in silence like a small, unlikely family.

That night, after they had gone to bed, Raquela told Jacob what had happened to the monastery and shared her suspicion of Mother Maria Josepha's role.

"You know I'm no fan of the church," Jacob said, "but don't be so sure. Did you forget the butchery of priests by the anarchists?"

"I suppose in this war, all sides have become bloody beasts," Raquela said, stroking his shoulder. But she still suspected the woman.

Jacob turned toward her and played with her curls, twisting them around his fingers. Raquela thought of it as simple relief that he wasn't a corpse on the windswept mountain ridge. His body was too exhausted to respond to her touch.

They lay in silence for a long time before Raquela blurted out, "I want to adopt Manuel."

"Adopt? Are you mad? We are not exactly legal here. Besides, I had the impression you didn't want children."

She couldn't blame him for his reaction. It was true. She didn't want children, but there was something about Manuel, so needy and vulnerable. She seemed the perfect person to... what? Save him? She knew it made no sense now that Jacob had spelled it out. "I'm not giving up on him," she said.

"The boy is agreeable enough, but he'll bring trouble," Jacob said. Promptly, his snores filled the room.

Next morning, Jacob awoke in somewhat better spirits, a survival high, Raquela thought. But the battle he'd just been through was very much on his mind.

"How passionate we were going to battle with *¡No Pasaran!* on our lips," Jacob said. "We had planned the attack and, in all seriousness, believed the slogan—we shall not let them pass. Initially, we were actually winning." A small sardonic smile appeared on Jacob's lips.

They sat in silence for a time.

"Oh, another thing. I've been transferred to the Jewish Brigade," Jacob said.

"Jewish Brigade?" Raquela thought she'd misunderstood.

"Yes, there are so many of us, they formed the Botwin Brigade," Jacob said proudly. He explained that many were Polish and French Jews and some Spaniards too. "We even have a very interesting Polish-speaking Frenchman, Antoni Zak, who is a close associate of our political Commissar."

"A Polish-speaking Frenchman? I knew one a long, long time ago," she said. Then added, "I wouldn't mind meeting some of your buddies."

"You very well might, Raquela. We are planning a reunion soon of those who survived in our brigade."

It didn't take long after Teruel for Jacob to fall into a deep depression. Raquela had been expecting it. Having gotten over his shock that he, in fact, had survived when thousands of his comrades had been reduced to bloody corpses, Jacob spoke of how he could no longer imagine himself in battle. And the pain of his frostbitten feet didn't help.

Raquela saw the fear in Jacob's eyes, in the flat tone of his voice. Was he thinking of deserting the Botwin brigade? She couldn't imagine him doing that, given the depth of his conviction when he joined. And if he did report for the next call-up, what would motivate him? How could she help him avoid fatalistic thinking? There must be something she could do.

After Franco's forces cut off Catalonia in the north, the Second Spanish Republic, so promising at its formation, stood on the brink of catastrophe. The untold losses on the Republican side and the retreat from Teruel made the future bleak. "I can't take any more bloodshed," Jacob said every time they sat together. Raquela understood that all too well. She began to run out of encouraging words. His depression pained her because she remembered her own black mood after Maya's death and how she still barely kept it at bay.

When, in late April, the French had reopened their southern border, rumors spread quickly that they would pour in arms for the badly undersupplied Republican fighters, who had only 150 artillery pieces left in all. The beleaguered government called up more troops because the supply of international volunteers had dwindled dramatically. The fact that the new recruits would be as young as sixteen pained Raquela. Children! Only a few years older than Manuel. No wonder the Spaniards named it *Quinta del Biberon*, the call-up of the baby bottles.

Raquela did her best to help Jacob climb out of his hopelessness.

"Take Manuel on a long walk. Get some fresh air; it'll clear your head," she suggested on a beautiful May day.

"Can't you smell death everywhere?" Jacob replied.

Raquela's gaze turned toward Manuel and Jacob looked contrite.

"Alright. Come." He motioned to Manuel who stood at the ready to join him.

When they returned from the walk, Raquela wanted to ask what they had seen and what they talked about, but neither seemed in the mood to chat. Jacob sat on the sofa, pulled off his shoes with a groan and massaged his toes. Manuel ran downstairs to help Señora Fuentes.

Seeing Jacob so downhearted reminded Raquela of herself back in the Carmel boarding house and how he struggled to cheer her up. She tried again. "You've just been to the headquarters. What have you heard?"

Jacob looked at her. "You don't really want to know."

"Yes, I do," she said.

"Well, you asked for it. Our remaining strongholds around Barcelona, Valencia and east of Madrid are connected only by a narrow piece of land stretching northwest from Castellon de La Plana. It will be a snap for the Nationalists to cut the two areas and devour the remnants of our opposition to Franco."

Raquela grimaced. "That's awful."

Now Jacob had worked himself up. "As I said, you asked for it. And Hitler and Mussolini keep providing massive military support to the other side."

At least he's more animated, Raquela thought.

"The only choice we have is to cross the Ebro and push the Nationalist bastards back," Jacob said.

"It'll be an unequal fight at best. Señora Fuentes heard Franco has recruited the best-trained Moorish soldiers in Morocco. And what are we? A bunch of untrained, ill-equipped volunteers, unenthusiastic prisoners of war... and... kids," she said, aware too late that her attempt to encourage Jacob had gone awry.

"Tell me our cause isn't doomed," Jacob said. He stood up and retreated to the bedroom.

She didn't know what to say but pondered his statement all night. Was this the crucial point at which she had to put aside her long-held conviction against participating in the machinery of war? She'd been turning this over in her mind while Jacob served at the front. All wars weren't equal. In some, like this one, the ideals decent people held dear were at stake. Jacob fought for them. Thousands were dying for them. She was running out of arguments to keep herself insulated. Her pacifist ideas had been shaken.

In July, Jacob was recalled to the front, but this time, unlike in the battles of Guadalajara and Teruel, he couldn't muster the enthusiasm. The conviction that the fight for democracy was his solemn duty now began to fail him. The emotional pain wrought by the loss of his comrades and the constant physical pain in his feet had changed him. Raquela could see it in his eyes, in his slumped posture, in the way he shrank from her touch in bed.

"In two days, I'll be at the front," Jacob said. "Why don't we have one last meal together tonight? It doesn't matter if it's just some boiled potatoes."

His words felt like a stab. Raquela put down the paper filled with exhortations for the coming battle and walked toward the kitchen. "I'll rustle up something in no time, but don't talk like that, Jacob."

Manuel joined them for fried eggs and potatoes, and Raquela brought out a small flask of *orujo*, a fiery brandy Señora Fuentes had given her to celebrate the victory at Guadalajara.

The alcohol must have loosened Jacob's tongue because he finally found the courage to express what had been on his mind. "Raquela, will you join me at the front? We will have a better chance to win if every last democracy-loving person pitches in."

She looked at him soberly. "But I thought I was already pitching in. The children..."

"Look, I need you with me. Our company has been so decimated; we need every warm body."

"Am I just a warm body to you?"

"No, it's not what I meant, and you know it. I need you with me," Jacob pressed.

Manuel, whose sudden absence from the room went unnoticed, now walked into the room. Raquela realized he must have heard their exchange. It was obvious Manuel did his utmost to stand straighter and

266

taller than usual. "Jacob, please take *me* along!" he said, and his voice broke. "I know kids my age are joining in."

Alarmed, Raquela said, "You are making no sense, Manuel. I need you here with me."

"But I am almost thirteen," he pleaded.

"I thought you are almost twelve."

"You are not going, but I will," he said defiantly. His lower lip quivered. And then he shocked both adults. "I have this, and I am going to fight!" He pulled the Beretta out of his pocket and displayed it in the palm of his small hand.

Raquela gasped. He must have rummaged in her bureau to find it. She should have taken greater care to conceal it.

Jacob, who had been silent, stood up and approached the boy, then gently took the revolver from his hand. "Manuel, we need you to stay alive so you can help run this country after we win..."

Manuel's eyes filled with tears. He ran out of the room, slamming the kitchen door. It was the first time he had displayed any anger in their home.

For a long while they sat in silence.

"You know, Raquela, Manuel told me he'd been studying the weaponry entries in those musty old encyclopedias you inherited from our neighbor."

"What? How do you know?"

"It's what we talk about on our walks. He's quite the expert," Jacob chuckled.

"I wish you had found a subject to cheer him, not one focused on aggression."

"Calm down; boys like to talk about guns."

They remained silent, reaching a kind of truce. Despite the subject, it was good Manuel had found a man to bond with, Raquela reflected. Then she said on impulse, "It would be a crime to let him come with us."

Taken aback, Jacob said, "Come where? And who is *us*?"

Spontaneously, Raquela spoke out loud the thought that had been brewing in her brain for quite some time. "I'll join you at the front, Jacob."

She'd not allow herself to shrink from the reality of life, to hang back married to a theoretical concept. She felt like her old self. "Yes, us, you and me, comrades in arms," she said.

Jacob's whole face lit up. "I hope you are not teasing me."

"I am quite serious."

He walked over to her chair. He stood behind her, bent down, wrapped his arms around her and kissed the top of her head. "I always knew you had it in you, but now I'll fear for your safety. Are you absolutely sure you want to do this?"

"Yes. How could I not, after the attack on the monastery? Manuel's bravery puts me to shame. Only now I have to figure out who'll keep an eye on Manuel while we are away."

"He's quite self-sufficient," Jacob said. "But you need to learn how to handle something more serious than a Beretta."

She knew the time would come to prove her solidarity to fight alongside Jacob was real. The moment had come. Jacob brought his rifle out of the locked closet. "Go ahead, pick it up," he said. "We will go slow."

She stared at the weapon as if it were a poisonous snake.

"Here." He handed it to her. "Always treat it as if it's loaded and keep your finger off the trigger."

She accepted it hesitantly, felt the coolness of the barrel, then the relative warmth of the wooden body.

"Position the butt in the crevice of your shoulder and for now, don't point it at anyone."

She felt the rifle's heft, hating its fearsome power. It felt like a ton, though it wasn't much more than her tattered volume of *War and Peace*.

"Now kneel, lift one knee up and rest your elbow on your thigh. You'll be more stable in this position. Shooting while standing is hardest." Jacob's voice was authoritative.

It calmed her a little.

He watched her. "That's a good start, but you won't be firing now. I just wanted you to get confident handling it. Remember, it's just a tool."

Relief! No shooting for now. Raquela knew there would be more lessons, but no matter how many, she'd never be comfortable with a weapon.

Next morning, Raquela knocked on Señora Fuentes' door.

"Is everything alright?" the old woman asked.

"Maybe, if you can help," Raquela said and explained. "I will be joining Jacob at the Ebro campaign, but I can't leave Manuel entirely alone. Would you be willing to have him work for you? He can do practically anything, he's such a capable kid, strong and smart."

"Hmm..." Señora hesitated. "Food is scarce." Señora looked down, then looked up with a sly expression on her wrinkled face. "My grandson is fourteen and he's joining up. Why don't you take Manuel along?"

Raquela's face darkened. "The call-up is for kids sixteen and older. And even that's too young."

"That's where you, a foreigner—*Dios, perdoname*, I don't mean to offend you—are wrong. Age doesn't matter when you want to protect your country, when you see your fathers and uncles and brothers dying for a cause. Youthful passion is worth more than an old geezer with a gun." Señora Fuentes' cheeks reddened as if she herself was about to go into battle.

Raquela, taken aback, nodded. "I see... Those are potent words. Let me think on it."

She went back upstairs, made a cup of coffee and sat to contemplate the weighty decision. Even before her neighbor's words, Raquela had struggled mightily to overcome her conviction that killing was wrong. She thought of it every time she read the paper, every time Jacob went to the front. Her youthful, idealistic notion of pacifism seemed to be crumbling before her very eyes. How could a rational being fail to respond to indiscriminate slaughter of innocent civilians? Maybe old Fuentes was right.

31 LIFE IN LA RODA

They had arrived in Spain in December '36. Bronka watched Antoni anxiously awaiting his orders to the front; he couldn't wait to join his comrades. He'd recruited so many of them. Now he wanted to be within their ranks even though he was an officer. He was restless, his previously easygoing demeanor evaporated.

By February, Antoni joined the Battle of Jarama, just east of Madrid. Afterwards, despite heavy Republican losses, Antoni was eager to return to the battlefield.

"Aren't you afraid after seeing so much carnage?" Bronka had asked him.

"No, no one lives forever. It's nobler to die for a cause."

A noble man through and through, even at war, Bronka thought.

The engagement at Guadalajara followed.

Bronka was in her seventh month when Antoni returned from the Battle of Guadalajara. He spent a month in the field hospital gravely injured, then transferred to a monastery infirmary near Albacete. She'd picked him up on a bright May day. Along the way home, orchids, snapdragons, and swallowtails whispered a spring refrain that all would be well. With bandages on his face and eyes, Antoni could not see them, but Bronka provided detailed descriptions, ending with the tiny blue heart of the mirror orchid.

She cared for him day and night. Antoni wept when the bandages finally came off his face. "Look at me. I've become a monster," he said.

"Give it time; it'll heal. Your appearance won't change my feelings," she said. "Don't waste your time looking at the mirror. Look at the sky and flowers instead."

She felt a surge of emotion: regret at his disfigurement, love mixed with awe that he had chosen her from the ranks of strong women who signed up for the Brigades, that he wanted her. And that love, that awe was as true that day as the day she'd met him. He was the achievement of an ultimate dream, even if she suspected he could be unfaithful, perhaps even cruel. She'd seen tiny glimpses of it but chose to put them out of her mind. There was no way for her to know for sure if the woman he spoke of from his train encounter was really Rifka. So, what if it was? She had no doubt that now he was hers.

In July, on a blazing hot day, an old Spanish midwife had delivered Stefan on the bed in their La Roda apartment. Bronka would never forget concentrating on the elaborately carved footboard with each contraction. The heat in the room was oppressive. It seemed as if Bronka's huffing and puffing, compounded by the midwife's anxious to and fro movements, raised the ambient temperature.

Antoni paced the living room, horrified by Bronka's screams. He poked his head in only to bring the water and towels the midwife had requested. Bronka couldn't understand any of the midwife's mutterings and found out the sex of the baby only when she saw him lying on her belly, purplish, wet and slippery as a fish.

When Bronka's ordeal was over, Antoni walked into the room and stood at the bedside, staring at his son. Bronka, teary-eyed and exhausted, said, "Isn't he beautiful?"

Antoni nodded and studied the infant with intense focus. She read on his face a disbelief that their liaison had resulted in a whole other human being.

Antoni counted the boy's toes, then opened his tiny fist to count the fingers. In an instant the baby gripped his father's finger. The planes of Antoni's angular face softened. "I'm going to war, son, so maybe you won't have to," he said.

Then Antoni placed a miserly peck on Bronka's sweaty forehead and said, "I'm going down the block to celebrate. The midwife will stay with you."

Bronka knew he might not be back till dawn. She swallowed the lump in her throat and fell asleep thinking, a man like Antoni needs his space. He'll come around when Stefan turns into a boy he can mold.

A year later, Bronka sat in the small stuffy apartment rocking little Stefan, looking out the window onto the still quiet street. Her gaze fell on the bell tower of the 16th-century Salvador church, the only building of interest in La Roda. The chimes rang seven times. Soon the old man, a morning fixture in front of the church, would call out for alms. She could never pass his outstretched arm with contorted fingers without giving him a coin.

The rocking motion made her sleepy, but it helped Stefan. His digestive system, a major problem for the first six months, had flared up at dawn. He fussed and screamed until he fell asleep from exhaustion. It was good that Antoni wasn't home. He was a man's man. If he hadn't been at the front much of Stefan's young life, he might have run away to who knows where just to get some peace.

Bronka never tired of staring at Stefan's plump cheeks and rosebud mouth. He had Antoni's oval face, light complexion and piercing blue eyes. Now that he was quiet, she finally had a chance to wash up and drink a cup of black coffee. She moved Stefan's wicker baby cradle to the far side of the room and settled at the sewing machine. Her job was to repair jackets, trousers, and coats for the brigade fighters. Most often the fabric was coarse, nothing like the damask and lace she'd been used to. The needle constantly failed to cooperate and pull up the thread. She cursed and adjusted the stitch length.

Ever since her arrival in Madrid three months pregnant, she had been given the task of sewing uniforms. It was hard to believe that nearly two years had gone by since then and she was still sewing uniforms. They had not been easy years. She'd never forget the utter shock on Antoni's face when she first told him he'd be a father. "What? How's this possible?" She remembered how she said that he must have never learned his biology and he replied, "See what dancing leads to?"

She had to admit, it wasn't exactly convenient to arrive in Madrid as a volunteer for the Brigades in her condition. She didn't let the relentless nausea of the early months stop her from working, but the question of what would happen to her in this unfamiliar place if Antoni were killed never left her mind.

Bronka was lonely with Antoni at the front. She often thought of herself as a lone tree on the farthest outskirts of a forest. In her imagination, she had always seen herself sharing the joys and tribulations of pregnancy with Rifka. She'd resolved to banish her from her thoughts, but every now and then—she couldn't help herself—she did wonder what Rifka would think of her situation. Would she be proud that Bronka had joined the Brigades? And what if it had turned out that Antoni was the man Rifka had fallen for on her trip? That surely would put a permanent rift in the relationship already tattered by Rifka's disappearance. It pained Bronka to think that such a strong childhood bond between them could be broken.

Between the demands of caring for a baby, daily queues for food and completing her quota of sewing, Bronka felt perpetually exhausted. The busyness dampened her loneliness and the discomfort of finding herself without family or friends in an alien country. Here, the language bedeviled her. The food was scarce and the people dour, worn out from evading the bombs or worrying about their men at the front. This was Bronka's life now in war-torn Spain. She'd signed up for it because any hardship with Antoni at her side was worth it.

Once Antoni had returned to the front and Bronka had been on her own, she had been terrified by the relentless bombing campaigns. Justifiably as it turned out. Antoni had been seriously injured. Stefan was her only consolation. He was her lovechild; the best gift Antoni could have given her. Whenever she looked into the boy's trusting eyes, she saw Antoni.

Lately, Antoni's injuries at the front coupled with Republican losses had turned him into a brooding, melancholy man, nothing like the upbeat, confident ladies' man she'd met in Warsaw two years before. Now, he was trying to steel himself for the Ebro campaign. He sat brooding over his morning coffee and glanced at Bronka. "I have such a bad feeling about what awaits at Ebro."

"You might feel more upbeat after you meet your friends this evening," she said distractedly, folding diapers.

"The Nationalists have already made great advances. How can we win with these ragtag ranks of underequipped soldiers and dispirited volunteers?"

She didn't want to encourage his defeatist thinking. And it wasn't easy for her to think she might lose him. Alone with a child, but no language or money she'd be totally lost. She believed in the cause, but she had a child to raise; she'd happily sit out the rest of the war with Antoni, away from the battlefield, but she knew he wouldn't. "The train ride might relax you and then a bite with your buddies will be good for you."

After putting away the laundry, Bronka sat at the sewing machine, ready to work on the pile of jackets that never seemed to diminish.

Antoni picked up the pot to pour himself another cup of coffee.

"It must be cold by now, wait. I'll make you a fresh pot," Bronka said.

He seemed to ignore her offer. "I'm taking the bus; it's cheaper. I don't want to leave you without cash when I move out to the front in a day."

"Money has never been a problem for you," she said.

Since she'd met Antoni, he'd been a big spender, like no one she knew. She enjoyed his lavish ways, hardly gave it any thought, simply reveled in his generosity.

"In case you haven't noticed, we are fighting a war. Can't exactly stop by my bank in Paris."

Bronka heard Stefan fussing; the nap was clearly over. She stood up from the sewing machine, lifting her corpulent body with effort, and went into the bedroom to change him. It seemed ironic that in a time of scarcity, her baby weight hadn't come off. Her breasts, still heavy with milk, hung sloppily beneath her robe. Surely, Rifka would have sewn her a supportive brassiere with a nursing flap. She could have done it herself, too, if she had the time or aspiration to improve her appearance.

She changed Stefan, put him down in his cradle, and sat close by in the rocking chair, humming an old children's tune. He fell asleep. She took pleasure in listening to his shallow breaths.

Suddenly, a wave of nausea roiled her stomach. "Antoni, please, I am going to vomit. Can you bring me a pail?" she called out hearing him nearby, in the bathroom.

"Coming!" Antoni yelled.

Bronka was sure he had been standing at the mirror looking for the striking face he'd lost. Before his disfiguring injury he preened longer than she ever did. War or no war, a man of his breeding had to maintain his grooming habits. Now all that was left of his routine was meticulous care for his fingernails and mindless brushing of his thick mop.

Antoni ran in, a bucket by his side. He handed it to her just in the nick of time.

Unfortunately, Antoni's voice woke up Stefan who now sounded inconsolable. Antoni picked him up and bounced him in the air a few times. The rare sight of it surprised Bronka, but instead of Stefan's usual bubbly laughter, he fussed and spit up on Aleksander's good jacket.

"Damn it! I have to see people."

Bronka didn't reply. She wiped her mouth and took the boy from Antoni's arms.

"Let me clean up this mess," he said and rushed back to the bathroom. When he emerged, she could still see the tell-tell stain on his lapel.

"Did you eat something bad?" Antoni said.

"It's not an illness," she said with a wry smile.

"Pregnant again! Are you?" Antoni exclaimed. His eyes shot darts at her. "I don't understand. I've been using rubbers," he said and banged his fist on the dresser making a stack of clean diapers topple to the floor.

"They don't always work," she said matter-of-factly.

He shook his head. "Jumping into a hopeless battle saddled with a toddler and a pregnant woman. Can a man be more cursed?"

Tears sprang into Bronka's eyes. She felt the bitter remnants of vomit in her throat. "Don't worry, we'll manage."

Antoni left the room. She bit her lip, heard the front door close, then his heavy footsteps descending. He'd made her cry, but she'd get over it. He was anxious about leaving her, crouching in a trench somewhere thinking of her and his babies. Silently, she recited her mantra: You forgive and move on. That's how love works.

———

Bronka was asleep by the time Antoni returned from the Albacete bar where he had met his cronies. Next morning, she noticed right away that his mood had lightened.

"How was it seeing your old buddies? Who came?" she asked.

He looked at her strangely. "What difference does it make? You don't know them."

"Did you tell them you're expecting another child?"

"That's not what guys talk about," Antoni said.

Bronka decided not to pursue it, but she noticed a subtle change in him she could not define. He evaded her gaze, got up and went to polish his brown lace-up field boots. He fiddled with the laces absentmindedly then caught her staring at him.

"Aren't you glad your mother gifted these to you?" she asked. "You were so annoyed carrying them on the train from Warsaw. Remember?"

He squinted at her trying to recall. "It was your overstuffed bag that exasperated me. You had packed for a vacation, not war. That's how I remember it," he said. "And you bawled all the way to Madrid, so offended were you by my comment."

"Let's not fight now," she said. "There's plenty of fighting ahead."

He changed the subject. "Where would I have found such a fine pair of boots in this hardscrabble town?" He smiled. "Mother gave me this wool jacket too. Didn't mind my going to the front like some other mothers."

Bronka felt a stab remembering how her mother had wailed and begged her not to go.

A knock at the door. One of Antoni's chums, a sturdy Pole, came in with his backpack, leaned it and his rifle against a wall. "Sorry to intrude," he said to Bronka. "It's time to go."

Antoni nodded and pulled on his boots.

Bronka acknowledged the man briefly and stood up to tend to Stefan.

Antoni said, "Wait." He walked over to her, pulled the billfold out of his jacket, emptied it and handed her a small pile of bills. "You'll need this," he said, then fished out a piece of paper from his pocket. "My mother's address in Paris, just in case..." He moved closer to Bronka, brushed his lips past her forehead trying to plant a requisite kiss, but she pulled away quickly. She didn't want to humiliate Antoni with a wrenching parting scene.

"Stefan needs me." She choked her tears back and turned away.

32 LA BODEGA DE SERAPIO

Raquela gathered a few of Manuel's garments, a thick, moth-eaten sweater, warm socks, and a wool cap and stuffed them in her bag. Just in case... He's a kid, she thought.

Jacob packed his bag with renewed energy. He could hardly contain his elation at Raquela's sudden decision to join him at the front. "Tomorrow evening you'll meet our comrades. Good people. I think you'll like them."

She felt a flutter of anticipation. "I can hardly believe I'll be one of them," she said.

Jacob made no comment about Manuel and she, feeling uneasy about having been influenced so readily by the landlady's passionate speech, did not discuss it either. She chose to focus on meeting the comrades.

The air hadn't cooled much. People sat outside near the fountain on the square, fanning themselves; children chased one another, and the man selling *granizado* on the corner called out the flavors—the usual summer evening scene—yet to Raquela everything seemed different, more meaningful, as if she had to memorize these hours. It was the evening before their departure from Albacete toward the Ebro encampments.

As Raquela and Jacob made their way to La Bodega de Serapio, the bar in the center of town, Jacob spoke enthusiastically about members of the Botwin brigade. It seemed as if he were trying to put Raquela at ease with her decision to join. He told her most Jews in the brigade were Polish communists. "Folks, just like you," he said.

"Not me, I am not a communist," she replied, a bit miffed.

"It occurs to me we've never discussed your politics, at least not to a degree which helps me understand your reversal on pacifism," Jacob said.

"It's hard to say. I don't like being boxed in and my ideas have changed over time," she said. "I used to be fascinated by the anarchists and abhorred violence. I've grown up. Now I see a more complex picture. Some things are worth fighting for."

"That's what I love about you, your ability to change," he said and squeezed her hand. "Here it is."

They had reached the wine cellar. Inside, they'd pretend for one night that each of them would go fearless and fierce into the battle ahead. The coolness of the dimly lit place felt refreshing. Goosebumps erupted on Raquela's bare arms. Even at the door, she could hear the group chatting noisily. They occupied a long table in the center of the room and appeared to be the only guests.

Jacob led her in and introduced her to the group of men. Each, in turn, said his name, then they toasted the new member. As they clinked the glasses. *Le Chaim!* Raquela felt instantly at home. Unbid tears moistened her eyes. She wiped them quickly.

She looked at the assembled faces and recognized the types. They resembled the young men with fire in their eyes and workmen's caps she'd seen at the free lectures in Warsaw.

Though originally the brigade numbered around 100, it had shrunk due to the extreme losses at the Extremadura battle. The twenty survivors at the table had drawn lucky cards.

Wine flowed and fueled jovial conversation: jokes, war stories from previous battles, and quips about wives and girlfriends.

"Where is Antoni?" Jacob asked the group. "I wanted Raquela to meet him too."

"Don't worry, he never misses a chance for a drink," one of the men said laughing.

"I thought he'd have been here already," Jacob looked disappointed.

"It's that woman of his. She wears the pants in the family," quipped another.

The brigade mates pooled their meager resources and ordered several small tortillas de patatas to share, then kept drinking and chatting till it got late. Observing their breezy banter, no one would have guessed all of them would soon face the test of their lives. The only hint of the emotions roiling within was the excessive enthusiasm with which they called out *Le Chaim!* with each toast. Raquela envied their closeness.

Jacob kept glancing at his watch. He looked relieved when the thick wooden entrance door squeaked open. He exclaimed, "Here he is at last! Come, Raquela, meet Antoni."

She got up and followed Jacob toward the entrance.

The newly arrived comrade stood at the bar ordering a drink. From the angle at which he stood, only the side of his face was visible. Raquela noticed the man's disfigured cheek and neck, a pitted, angry red mess, skin lumpy in spots, stretched taut in others. His beard did a poor job of concealing the damage. She cringed inwardly—poor man.

"Glad you finally made it." Jacob slapped Antoni's shoulder in a playful gesture. He turned around, facing them.

"Better late than never," Antoni said, then knitted his eyebrows and focused his gaze on Raquela, pinning her in place. He stared at her intently. She stared back with a shock of recognition. Those eyes! She'd know them anywhere.

"Raquela? It's you. Here?" he uttered, flabbergasted.

Amazed, Jacob jumped in. "You know Raquela?"

Raquela felt as if she'd collapse. She placed her hand on the bar for support and tried to regain her composure. Her heart flopped like a fish on land.

"Aleksander? What are you doing here?" she managed to stutter after a long pause.

Jacob, visibly confused, said, "Raquela, you are mistaken. This man is Antoni. Does he remind you of someone else?"

Aleksander just stood there, shaking his head. "She is not mistaken," he said, and moved toward Raquela, but, instinctively, she stepped back.

"Explain this, please!" Jacob called out, now visibly disconcerted.

Neither of them offered a response.

After a long, uncomfortable moment, Antoni spoke. He said they had met briefly on her stopover in Paris en route to Palestine. "In another century, really," he added with a nervous laugh.

"Why didn't you tell me, Raquela?"

"How could I have known he'd show up here? There's nothing to tell." She shrugged her shoulders.

"Let's join the group," Jacob broke the uncomfortable standoff, and they rejoined their comrades.

Jacob, still sounding somewhat agitated by the coincidence, addressed his mates. "What do you know? Here I'm introducing them, and they already know one another."

The look on Jacob's face made Raquela wonder if he felt jealous, if it had occurred to him that Aleksander was the cause of her cool demeanor in bed when they had first arrived in Albacete.

"It's a small world," Aleksander interjected.

That seemed to close the matter, and the men got on with their conversation. Raquela had not uttered a single word. She followed the men's exchanges as she stole glances at Aleksander's face. Every now and then she caught Aleksander's gaze sweep over her, ever so briefly. He eyed her as a jewel thief would, cautiously calculating the risk. She wondered if he still desired her.

"What happened to you?" she dared to engage him after a while, gaining courage after downing several glasses of wine.

"Gas and shrapnel. War is hell on the complexion." He laughed, a hoarse laughter that bordered on hysteria. "They put me back together at the monastery infirmary, the one on the hill. Maybe you've seen it."

"No, I haven't seen it," she said absentmindedly. Her heart pounded as fast as it had a lifetime ago, in Paris. How he must have suffered. Even with the facial injuries his eyes still exuded a magnetic pull. It stunned her that after two years and all that had happened, he still had her in his grip. But one of the men had mentioned Antoni's woman. The thought slashed her like a knife. It was too late. Her mistake was irrevocable.

Raquela remembered the bandaged man in the bed next to hers after her miscarriage. Was it Aleksander? Could fate have been so cruel as to bring them together, wounded and miserable? She'd have liked to ask, but his comrades peppered Aleksander with questions about the political commissar. They were going into battle soon; what did the past matter? Yet inside her, agitation persisted. The encounter had stirred something that was supposed to remain submerged.

When the last of the wine had been drained, and only crumbs of tortillas remained, the conversation died down. The comrades parted without the usual exhortations. 'See you soon' or something along these lines would not have been appropriate this time. All knew of the brutal battle that lay ahead on the shores of the Ebro.

33 TO THE EBRO

Getting aboard a train heading north from Albacete to Amposta, near the Ebro River where the Republican offensive would begin, was only a minor challenge compared to what lay ahead. Raquela and Jacob joined thousands who had answered Lieutenant Colonel Juan Modesto's call to join the newly formed Army of the Ebro.

Manuel disappeared the day of their departure, nowhere to be found. And though Raquela was extremely apprehensive about taking Manuel along, she searched for him until the last moment.

"He'll turn up, don't worry," Señora Fuentes assured them as they bid her goodbye. The old woman blessed them and comforted Raquela she'd look after Manuel if he returned.

Raquela and Jacob, like thousands of would-be soldiers, were willing to take any conveyance to get them closer to the front. They caught a packed train and squeezed into seats at the opposite ends of the car. There was little conversation. People, immersed in private reflections, sat so close to one another, Raquela thought she heard her neighbor's heartbeat, smelled his breath. Soon they'd share trenches; might as well become comrades now.

They arrived by nightfall and crept up a steep wooded hillside in groups to the main camp. Hundreds of motley troops gathered in a huge tent for instructions on reconnaissance and plans to surprise Franco's troops. Raquela stood next to Jacob amid a crush of volunteers awaiting the commander's speech.

Jacob squeezed her hand. She saw his head and eyes turn to the furthest corner of the dim space.

There, amid a flock of bigger boys, stood Manuel wearing a serious expression, stretching himself to the height of a warrior. Jacob waved to him; Raquela felt a mixture of relief and fear for his safety. Instinctively, she wanted to go over to hug him, but Jacob glanced at her and squeezed her hand. "It's alright. Stay here. Let him be a man."

"They should have called it 'The Diaper' call-up," Raquela said quietly. "Can't you see he is the youngest of the Baby Bottle soldiers?"

"He will be fine. They can use him as help in the field kitchen or as a courier. He won't be at the frontline," Jacob calmed her.

Shortly after the Colonel addressed the troops, unit commanders began the distribution of arms. The handful of available weapons went to the younger, more aggressive men who claimed to have experience with them. Jacob managed to obtain a rifle for Raquela only when one of the commanders recognized him. "You earned it," the young man winked at him. It was the very man who had accepted Jacob's weapons donation on his first day in Albacete.

Jacob came close to Raquela and whispered in her ear, "You will have to catch every spare minute to practice. There won't be many."

The truth was the imminent use of the weapon upset her greatly. How could one prepare to take a life? She'd made an uncomfortable peace with her decision to join the Brigade, but the actual, physical act of killing... well... She'd probably never be comfortable with it. "Of course," she replied, thinking I'll never be good at killing. Never.

Jacob squeezed her hand. "You can do this."

By nightfall, Jacob had helped Raquela set up her tiny wedge tent between the trees on the hillside. "I'll set up mine as close as I can... just in case," he said and handed her a waxed canvas tarp. "Put this on the ground; it'll keep you dry."

"What about you? You only have one," Raquela said, her voice heavy with exhaustion.

"I'll be fine. I have plenty of experience," Jacob said and disappeared behind a grove of scruffy trees.

She'd wanted to ask about Manuel, but it had become obvious the boy would figure out how to fend for himself. Her sleep was restless.

Every crack of a twig, every owl hoot woke her. She wondered if Aleksander had arrived at this encampment and where he might be.

Raquela awoke at dawn to a volley of shots. Her heart pounded with terror, but it seemed the explosions came from some distance. When the shooting subsided, she heard the rush of the river below and it calmed her enough to begin the day. Members of the brigade scurried around moving large rocks to build and reinforce the defensive line. The only luck, if you could call it that, was that the area was replete with stones of all sizes, broken boulders that along with logs and bags of soil formed the trenches. Moving rocks into position was backbreaking but it gave her a sense of purpose. When she sat to rest, Raquela practiced, under Jacob's watchful gaze, disassembling and reassembling the rifle, as well as loading and unloading its magazine.

After that, the daily rat-tat-a-tat of machine guns blended with screams of the injured, shouts of the medics, and gusts of wind blowing off the Tortosa-Beseit mountain range. Raquela even became inured to the roar of the Savoia-Marchetti bombers and the booms of distant artillery. Life at the front required forgetting the sounds of normal life. Hunger was a constant, even worse than what they'd experienced in Albacete. Everyone around her looked haggard. Raquela knew she'd lost more weight. She had to tie a rope to keep her beat-up cotton denim pants from falling down. She wished she had a needle and thread to move the side buttons.

The days were not always filled with action. Instead, bored, the soldiers debated how best to defend their positions, how to climb the terraced slopes to advance, which homes might house combatants and who had cigarettes. Raquela found that the experience she'd gained at the infirmary was invaluable at the front. Most days, she tended to the injured as best she could with limited supplies.

Manuel had become a runner, carrying messages from unit to unit when he wasn't assisting with meal preparation and distribution. Raquela and Jacob saw him infrequently, but when they did, he flashed them satisfied grins, yet she worried about his safety with every assault. Every stretcher that passed near her, produced a surge of adrenaline driven by anxiety that one of her men had become a casualty. Her hands shook, her heart beat wildly, yet she could not avert her eyes: she had to look. And each time it was neither Manuel, nor Jacob or Aleksander she felt guilt at her relief.

Slowly, their unit crossed the Ebro moving forward some days, retreating on others. Each small repulsion of Nationalist units ended in too many dead on both sides, but survivors hugged, joyous to be alive; rivulets of tears carved maps of sorrow on their dirt-covered faces while the dead stared, unmoved. In their maneuvers, more than once, Raquela's company had passed areas that reeked of death. Embers of burnt bodies delivered their last messages on wisps of smoke.

By late October, the weather took a turn for the worse. The nights became too cold for Raquela's inadequate clothing. She slept in every garment she had and shivered through the night, as much because of what she expected lay ahead as for the weather.

In November, on the evening before the major push to counter Franco's troops at the Ebro, Colonel Modesto gathered the fighters. "We must cross the river at record speed; there will be no stopping until we make it across. We must surprise the Nationalists. We have no more than forty-eight hours to accomplish the impossible." After more speeches and exhortations for success in battle, the colonel announced, "Now, go get some rest. There will be no resting tomorrow."

Most of the gathering broke up, but small groups of fighters milled around, wishing one another well. Raquela noticed Jacob's mood appeared more cheerful than the situation called for.

"Antoni is here somewhere. Have you seen him?" he asked Raquela.

"I haven't seen him since Bodega La Serapio. He disappeared completely."

"That's because he was seconded to the photographic unit of the fifteenth brigade," Jacob said.

"Oh, you didn't mention it," Raquela said, hoping her disappointment didn't show on her face.

But Jacob saw it. He responded with surprise. "I thought you said he was just a casual acquaintance. Didn't realize it mattered to you."

Raquela remained silent; embers of old passion stirred. She remembered the firmness of his lips the first time he had kissed her. It confused her. Jacob now occupied a large part of her heart, but the emotion toward him was subdued—something akin to the surface of a tranquil pond—unlike the avalanche of excitement Aleksander created within her.

The sun hung low on the horizon. Groups scattered along the hillside began to break up slowly. Everyone, it seemed, was so charged up no one wanted to turn in for the night. Raquela was about to take the trail downhill toward her tent when Jacob exclaimed, "Look! Here they come."

Aleksander and Manuel walked toward them. When they approached, Aleksander immediately began joking with Jacob. "Did you bring this pipsqueak to fight?" He pointed at Manuel, avoiding Raquela's gaze.

"You'd be surprised what he knows about weapons," Jacob replied.

Aleksander shook his head. "I was only joking. Young fighters like him have no fear."

This seemed more like the lighthearted Aleksander she knew, not the tense war casualty she'd seen at the bodega. Raquela stood to the side, looking at the Punta Alta peak rising out of the austere Serra de Pàndols limestone mountains. She pointed out the purplish shadows on the mountains. "Aren't they majestic?"

"They look bruised," Aleksander said.

She looked at his eyes. Despite the spark, she saw there had been sadness in them moments earlier. It was he who was bruised. Maybe after what he'd been through, he was unable to notice beauty. She thought about their day at the museum in Paris. It seemed like another life. He changed the subject and pulled out a small object from his tan field vest. They surrounded him.

"What is it?" Manuel asked.

"It's a special little camera," Aleksander said, easing it out of its brown leather case. "A Houghton Ensign Selfix."

As if any of them would know.

"Wouldn't you rather have a weapon?" Manuel asked.

"Photographs can sometimes be weapons," Aleksander replied. "One day, you'll understand. My commander asked my unit to document whatever we could when the bullets weren't flying. But this is my personal camera. My men use bigger ones."

Manuel whistled.

Encouraged, Aleksander continued, "Look, it unfolds."

"Why don't we get a photo with those mountains in the back, before it gets darker?" Raquela suggested.

"It's probably too dark already." Aleksander wasn't enthusiastic.

"Please! Please let's do it." Manuel was excited and fumbled with the camera that Aleksander had allowed him to hold.

"Alright, you three stand over there." Aleksander relented. He pointed in the direction of the distant mountains. "I'll take the picture."

"No, let me," Raquela said. "I think all three soldiers should be together in this photo."

She tussled Manuel's hair and smiled at him, but he said, "Aren't you a soldier too?"

"Right now, just let me be the photographer," she said.

With that, Aleksander looked at her. She remembered that look that said he'd do anything for her if she only asked. He took the camera from Manuel and handed it to her, brushing by her hand, setting off long-dormant sensations. "Here is where you click," he instructed.

And she positioned the three so she could get Aleksander's good side in the snapshot. As she clicked the shutter, Raquela felt a rush of emotion: regret mixed with grief but also a weird exhilaration. The improbability of their meeting, the curiosity of what had happened to him in the intervening two years and her own transformation put her in a state of utter disorientation.

The evening air had cooled considerably. It was already dark when they headed for the encampment. The three adults walked in silence, and even Manuel had a sense of the moment, because he, too, walked quietly until he slipped away toward the field kitchen.

Then Jacob said, "I'm more than ready to get a couple of hours of sleep, but a few of us are meeting to reconnoiter and check the pontoon bridge below the mountainside." He turned onto a side path as if he knew to give Raquela and Aleksander some privacy.

They walked in silence. She felt his physical presence, remembered his scent. He smelled of musk, coffee, and earth. Her heart beat faster. Ever since she'd recognized Aleksander at the bar, her feelings for him had reawakened. She thought she was done obsessing about what might have been with him. She thought Jacob had replaced him, but now that struck her as another instance of her self-delusion. Aleksander's mere proximity flustered her like a stupid schoolgirl. It was most disconcerting, but she felt powerless to control the rush of emotion.

She was desperate to pour out her heart, to tell him all that had happened, but there was too much to say, too much to explain. She decided to say nothing. Before they parted, Aleksander reached for Raquela's hand. She hesitated momentarily before withdrawing it. His hand was so warm it felt as if he were on fire.

"Raquela... Raquela," he began, but the words stuck in his throat. He cleared it and began again, "I am so sorry. You'll never understand just how deeply sorry I am."

She stepped back in the dark, stumbling on a tree root. He tried reaching for her, but she righted herself and said, "We all have guilt over something. No use apologizing for the past. It's behind us."

"I wish we could stay here for a while," he said, but she sensed ambivalence.

A distant owl hooted.

"We have to be focused firmly on the future. Who knows what will happen tomorrow?" Raquela said. "Let's get some sleep."

With that, Aleksander handed Raquela the camera. "Take it," he said.

"Isn't it for your photographic assignment?" she asked, nonplussed.

"No. I want you to have it because it's special to me. It was a gift from my mother."

Even in the dim light, she could see the softness in his eyes, sunken in the drawn face. She didn't protest. So that was his way of apologizing for that ugly performance in Paris on what could have been their last night of joy. Or perhaps it was for something else...

She felt the camera's heft, ran her fingers over the smooth surface of the case. "Thank you. Maybe it'll come in handy one day... when this is all over," she said quietly.

A few more minutes together and... What? What might happen? She didn't know but felt it could be another huge mistake. She needed to get away from him. She turned abruptly and walked off.

Afterward, she sat shivering in her tent in pitch dark, wrapped in a scratchy wool blanket, going over every detail of the commander's instructions, but all the while, Aleksander's sorrowful face stood before her. She could not tell if fear of the coming battle caused her trembling, or if the minutes she spent with Aleksander were a kindling for the growing blaze within.

Later, with hundreds asleep around her, she could not quiet her mind. As things stood, all she'd ever have of him would be that damn camera.

Next day, at nightfall, their unit crept single file to the positions in the trenches: the leader and several men up front, then Aleksander and Manuel behind him, followed by Jacob and Raquela. In the pitch dark, Raquela stumbled several times on rocky limestone outcroppings. The rifle weighed her down; she struggled to keep it from slipping off her shoulder. Its length, nearly her height, would be awkward for a five-foot two woman under any circumstances. And she had not much experience climbing with a heavy backpack.

Jacob caught her by the hand near the ridge and whispered, "You are getting the hang of it. Stay strong."

When they retreated toward the trenches, Aleksander motioned to Jacob. "I am going to borrow Manuel. He'll be better off with me. I'll look out for him while you look out for Raquela."

"Good idea, thanks," Jacob said quickly, pulling Raquela toward the trench.

Aleksander and Manuel disappeared into their section of the trench before Raquela had a chance to protest. All others, too, shortly disappeared into the trenches. In the darkness Raquela couldn't be sure who went where.

Jacob set himself up in the trench, inspected Raquela's Russian Mosin rifle, and positioned it between the sandbags on the parapet. Then on the spur of the moment he handed Raquela his six-round Carcano and reassured her she'd have no trouble with it. "I trained you. Remember?"

"But why are you giving me your weapon?"

"It has better safety."

This was no time to argue. She accepted it. Except for a distant howl, it was totally quiet. For a while it seemed to Raquela she was playing at war. Nothing was happening. She was tired from the climb, the sleepless night, and the tense preparations of the day. She yawned.

Jacob squatted down and lit a cigarette. The tranquility around them seemed ridiculously incongruous with the situation. But just as she began to get literally bored, she heard whizzing sounds.

"Get down, get down!" Jacob yanked her down. "These are bullets, not bats."

Despite his warning, she popped up for a minute to look toward Aleksander's trench. Was it Manuel's head peering out? Quickly, it disappeared. She assumed Aleksander pulled the boy down to safety; it soothed her. Then, all at once, bombs exploded from all directions for what seemed like eternity. Now terror, cold as ice, seized her. A mad dogcatcher had released a thousand rabid beasts to attack them.

She couldn't say how long into the shooting, her body—though not her mind—registered a thud, a scarcely perceptible movement of the boards beneath her feet, as if a sack of flour had tipped over, but it was no time to investigate. She kept firing. Keeping her eyes glued in the direction of the incoming fire, she didn't realize immediately that Jacob had fallen.

When she turned during a brief pause in the shooting, she saw him lying soundless, wounded, she assumed. "Hang on, Jacob," she called out, but bullets whizzed overhead. She acted without consulting her brain. In a split moment, she dropped her empty rifle, grabbed his, hoisted it over her shoulder, and like a wild woman continued shooting at anything and everything beyond the trench. She had no idea if she'd actually hit anyone.

The shooting on all sides stopped. Was it minutes? Hours? An eerie silence ensued. Her mind couldn't absorb what had happened. Initially, the silence around her felt like the quiet of a tomb, but soon she became aware of piteous moans and a terrible gurgle. She looked down and realized it was coming from Jacob. He lay on his back on the rotting planking of the trench with his eyes open as if the fusillade of bullets had surprised him.

The dark curtain that had enveloped the battlefield became a shade darker as clouds covered the sliver of moon that had provided scant illumination to the gruesome scene. She lit a match and bent over Jacob. He lay perfectly still; the narrow trickle of blood at the side of his head and mouth the only signs of the dreadful truth. Her fingers brushed by the stickiness on his forehead, the blood congealing quickly in the cold.

She sank to the floor and cradled his head in her lap. "Jacob, Jacob," she whispered, but even as she uttered the words, she knew he was gone.

At that moment, with adrenaline still coursing through her veins, she had no instinct to cry out. How could she get him out of there? She couldn't bear the thought of leaving him behind. But even as the imperative to bury him dawned on her, she knew it would be impossible. She sat with him for some time—couldn't say how long—saying her silent goodbyes, her head spinning like a broken carousel, her heart cracked. Had the cigarette he lit made him a perfect target? What was the use thinking of that now? Now it seemed plain that in the war for which none of them were prepared there was no end of mistakes, blunders, and miscalculations to be made. All she knew was that she'd undergone a transformation. Her understanding of life and death would never be the same.

Later, at twilight, she moved through the field of corpses like an apparition, looking for Aleksander and Manuel. She tripped over lines of barbed wires, frozen lumps of mud and fallen bodies. At last, she made it to their trench. It was empty. Shock, then a flicker of hope. Had they somehow managed to escape? She could not bring herself to sit with another corpse. From now on, finding Manuel would keep her from losing her mind.

The urgency to look for the boy pushed her ahead. She tripped over an obstacle and saw that it was the corpse of an Italian soldier. He was tall, and up close, she saw he was young. Two bars on his collar, perhaps an officer. Maybe it was he who had shot Jacob. She wanted to spit on him but stopped herself; survival instinct kicked in. She grabbed his wool cap and put it on her head. She had to get away, but emboldened, she bent down to remove his knee-high leather boots. It was more difficult than she thought, but she was determined. Fueled by adrenaline and fear, she twisted and pulled. The corpse gave them up. She thrust her ruined suede oxfords aside and ran in the liberated boots with every last ounce of energy. The victors would soon be here.

PART 4

SOUTHERN FRANCE

34 INTERNMENT CAMPS, FRANCE: ARGELÈS-SUR-MER, FEBRUARY 1939. GURS, APRIL-NOVEMBER 1939

Grief-stricken over losing Jacob and drained of every ounce of energy, Raquela followed throngs of refugees: men, women and children, all trudging north. Tarragona's fall in January '39, just fifty miles to the east of the Ebro encampments, unleashed a mass exodus of civilians sympathetic to the Republican cause. Driven by fear of retaliation by Franco, people commandeered everything that moved: wagons, carts, trucks, buses and rushed to reach the French border before Barcelona, too, fell. Those without wheels, trudged on foot. But crossing the border meant scaling 10,000 feet up the towering eastern Pyrenees.

Now Raquela stood at the foothills of the majestic mountains whose peaks she'd admired from a distance. She looked up, gripped by a wave of dizziness: she'd have to climb these forbidding walls in the cold, in the freezing rain, in snow. How would she find the strength?

Ahead, she spotted a line of children walking in pairs, holding hands. Behind them, a group of nuns with blankets on their shoulders, thrown over their habits. She caught up to them, chatted a moment with one nun and discovered they had rescued orphans whose anarchist parents had been shot early in the war. She looked for Manuel, but he was not with them.

"Come with us, don't do this alone," the young nun told her.

"How will you find your way across these mountains?" Raquela asked.

"We are supposed to meet a *mugalari* right near this barn." The nun pointed several hundred feet ahead to a dark gray structure with a sagging roof. "He will guide us. Our priest has paid him."

Gripped by fear of going it alone, Raquela stood with them for a while, considering if she'd be too much of a burden. She waited, watching the children jumping from one foot to another, slapping their hands to warm up. They reminded her of her charges at the monastery— sweet, trusting faces, still unsullied.

When the sky darkened, an older nun said, "We can't wait. He may not show up. Let's go now. Join us," she motioned to Raquela.

"It'll be hard enough for you to get these children across," Raquela said.

"We can share," the nun said and unceremoniously handed Raquela a burlap sack. "Help me carry some of our supplies." Her hands free now, the nun picked up the youngest child, a pale girl of about four. "She's not well. I'll carry her for a while."

And so commenced a punishing, nerve-racking three-week trek through the harshest terrain imaginable. Sheer stone cliffs, slick with moisture, falling rocks and howling wind were the least of it. Nationalist planes flew overhead, raining bombs. People fell, injured or dead. Some managed to hide in rock crevices and caves, stood up and walked, tripping on the newly killed and the frozen bodies of those that came before them, until a new barrage of fire.

Raquela couldn't fathom why the Nationalists were so intent on wiping out those escaping. They had already won; the Republican fighters having surrendered back in November. But apparently victory was insufficient. Franco lusted for the blood of his opponents.

As grateful as Raquela felt for the boots she had taken from the Ebro killing fields, they were so ill-fitting that each day new blisters formed, making the day's progress tougher. Protection from frostbite was paramount, but so was a place to stow her only valuables: the Beretta and Aleksander's camera. She vowed not to lose these mementos of her men. She slipped the gun into one boot; the other one held her camera. Her skinny legs swam in the boots, but she laced them tight and adjusted the buckles. The hard, ice-cold objects wrapped in an extra pair of socks abraded her calves, compounding the pain of fatigued muscles.

By day, they marched ahead, trying to outrun the bombs, the

weather, and the numbing cold. At first the children, enchanted by snow, picked up handfuls and ate it, but after days of the trek, they lost interest. They no longer asked "¿Y cuándo llegamos?"

By night, they huddled around small fires to warm up and fed the children thin gruel made of canned beans. Raquela told them stories she'd made up to take her mind off the pain in every muscle, but the little ones were so tired she couldn't tell if they heard her.

On lucky days, at higher elevations, they sheltered in rock cabins left by shepherds who had moved to lower terrain for the winter. In a few places they came across a lone shabby house where the shepherds had left some cans of supplies and they used them, praying for forgiveness.

Once they came across a group of escaping Republican soldiers who'd face execution in Spain. The men shared with them a roasted bucardo, an Iberian wild goat they had hunted down. The children gnawed on chunks of meat like small savages, but it was the skull with magnificent horns that got most of their attention.

When they descended to lower elevations, many with twisted ankles, sprains, frostbitten toes and fingers, gypsies besieged them, offering to change pesetas for centimes to use on arrival in France. They'd lose on the exchange, but who had money to spare anyway?

Just before the final push to the border, a twenty-inch snowstorm blanketed everything and everyone. Three of the children froze to death overnight. In the morning, Raquela and two nuns placed their slight bodies in a nearby cave. The nun's tears made frozen tracks on their faces as they prayed, but Raquela couldn't weep; she was numb. In a Sisyphean gesture, she tried to cover the children's corpses with handfuls of snow, but one nun pulled her away. "They are in a better place," she said.

———

By January 29, 1939, completely depleted, they arrived at the border where hundreds of others had been waiting to cross to safety. In Cerbère, they finally stepped on French soil. Here the refugees waited to be assigned to temporary migrant camps. Raquela craned her neck, hoping to find Manuel and Aleksander among the crowd, but all she saw were the unshaven faces of strangers. All she smelled was sweat and fear of what lay ahead.

When French police accompanied by Moorish colonial troops arrived to take the nuns and children to a separate area, the older nun said, "She's with us," pointing at Raquela. The policeman inspected Raquela's documents and nodded his consent.

They finally entered the camp at dusk. Before the haggard survivors, rows of hastily pitched tents stretched on the beach as far as the eye could see. All Raquela cared about, as soon as tents were assigned, was to get the children something to eat, anything, even a crust of bread would do. They sat starved, silent, and wide-eyed, no longer expecting anything. Weeks of trekking had worn them down to little old men and women.

Raquela immediately volunteered to walk the long distance to the kitchen tent to bring back buckets of rapidly cooling, watery soup. It was a wonder the fierce winds hadn't frozen them solid by the time she delivered them.

Raquela sat on damp straw that had been her camp bed for several nights now. She lifted her bedraggled long skirt and brushed the sand off her legs. Now she regretted discarding her denims that had been stained with Jacob's blood. The grit seemed to have invaded all the crevices of her body. She wanted to rub her painful feet so badly but winced every time she tried to brush the sand from in between her toes. The pain shot through her mottled, purple skin like needles. The nurse in her tent said it was frostnip, almost frostbite but luckily not quite. Despite making huge, weeping blisters on her heels, the boots taken from the corpse had saved her.

Snatches of the Ebro battles flashed before her mind's eye: the rat-tat-a-tat of Jacob's rifle as he fired furiously at the Italian troops across the trench. Flashbacks of the mountain crossing— three little girls left in a cave like forgotten luggage—caught her in their relentless net at any time of the day, snuck up on her like thieves and robbed her of a chance to process the unimaginable.

The slightest noise startled her. She was constantly on edge, ready to scream or cry. It almost didn't matter. This was her life now, Raquela kept reminding herself, but as hard as she wished to get accustomed to being alone, with all of them gone, she couldn't. She had almost forgotten how to live, but the children had not. Even the smallest children had a knack for digging themselves into the beach sand to gain a bit of warmth. They scraped out fistfuls of wet sand and maneuvered their skinny behinds in. Though it was damp, somehow it seemed warmer than the bitter winds sweeping through the tented camp.

Rumor had it they'd be transferred to another internment camp soon. If they survived to live another day things might improve. Daily, the nuns and Raquela harassed the camp guards to get bread and warm soup for the children. And when they succeeded, they knew this was what defined happiness now.

By the time they were transferred to Gurs, the newly constructed internment camp in the southwestern corner of France, just below the Pyrenees, it was April, and the rains made every path a grotesque mudslide. It was nearly impossible to move one foot in front of the other as the deep ruts sucked in shoes. The paths were littered with them, firmly and permanently planted in the mud. Raquela and the nuns had to carry the little ones in their arms, though the mud was often the cause of the children's amusement. Between rains, they'd sit in front of the huts and play with it, making odd-looking towers until mud covered their hands, faces and clothes.

The living conditions here were a bit better than in the flimsy tents of the beachside camp, but still extremely primitive. Now they shared space with fifty to sixty other internees in cabins made of thin plywood covered with tar fabric that leaked with every rain. Inside, there were no windows and no lights. Several hundred of these flimsy structures packed within inches of one another, separated by wire fences, stood in orderly rows, trying to contain the miserable inhabitants whose lives had been shattered by the Spanish Civil War.

As much as she hated the constant cold, hunger, lice, rats, and the soggy straw mattress she curled up on each night, the thing that was the greatest insult to Raquela's sense of being human were the toilets. Rudimentary troughs in open fields in which she had to relieve herself robbed her of dignity. Below the troughs, huge buckets collected excrement, which had to be carted away by inmates.

Thousands of dispirited souls thronged the camp, but Raquela wished to find just one, one frightened boy who she prayed had survived the slaughter. When she had last seen him at Ebro, it was just the top of his head poking out from an adjacent trench. Now she traversed the muddy expanse of the camp looking for Manuel. Her heart leaped every time she saw a boy Manuel's height and slight build, especially if he had dark curly hair. But the faces were always those of other children suffering the aftereffects of war. She desperately wished to develop the photo she'd taken the night before the battle. It would have helped in the search, but it was far too risky. The camera and undeveloped film remained securely stowed in her boots, making ever-larger abrasions on her ankles, no matter how she wrapped them in underwear or socks.

After several weeks at the internment camp, a fellow internee, an older Spanish woman, ran into the barrack excited. She kicked off her muddy shoes and pulled Raquela over. "I have news!" she said. Her eyes glowed with excitement.

Raquela knew that all sorts of rumors flew through the grapevine on a regular basis, so she wasn't as inclined to be enthusiastic. Feigning interest, she asked, "So what did you hear today?"

"Some of us can get permission to work outside. Outside!"

"Who can and who cannot? Did you hear that too?"

"Well, of that I'm not sure... The circumstances for approval are rather opaque," the woman said mysteriously.

Raquela didn't know if the woman truly didn't know or didn't want any competition. She'd have to look into it herself.

With the exception of snores from all directions, the barrack was quiet that night. But Raquela heard a murmuring. She sat up and scanned the dark space. Several spots away, she noticed movement as if two people were trying to squeeze onto one "mattress," trying to get comfortable. It was the mattress of the same woman who'd passed on the rumor in the morning. The figures shifted, pulling the blanket over their heads, but one of them spotted Raquela looking in their direction. She waved her over.

Barefoot, Raquela tiptoed carefully on the filthy floor, trying to avoid her sleeping neighbors and the known wet areas caused by the leaky roof. She approached the women, crouched down, and saw the fright in their eyes. They whispered to her the latest news the younger woman, a girl really, had picked up on the radio as she cleaned the administrator's office: Hitler was saber-rattling; all-out war was all but imminent. The

Sudetenland had already been annexed. A chill shot through Raquela's body: would Poland be next?

Concerned that three voices would wake up more women and create a ruckus, Raquela touched the girl's shoulder for reassurance. "Your secret is safe," she whispered, put her finger to her lips and slinked back to her spot. Lucky that in their section of the camp security was fairly lax, she thought.

News from the most recent broadcast churned in Raquela's mind. She had to get work, make money, find a way to return to Poland before it was too late. Her forged birth document showed her born on February 15, 1916, in the town of Muret, near Toulouse, France. Although her British passport showed her to be a Palestinian national, her birth in France made her a natural-born citizen here. That should count for something.

For several days Raquela tried to make an appointment with the camp's administrator to see about permission to work outside the camp but dealing with internee problems was not a priority for him. Months went by, time filled with humiliation, depression and a constant search for Manuel. Still no appointment, but she'd not give up.

By September 1939, rumors became facts: Hitler had invaded Poland. Fears about those she had left behind tortured Raquela. Their fate and the need to look for Manuel never left her mind. Even before she'd left home, she knew Hitler's hateful policies toward her people. How would his minions behave now that Germany was openly at war?

On a warm October day, she decided to scour a section of Gurs that housed a new group of detainees. There had been a massive influx since the war began: mostly German and Eastern European Jews, but some transfers from other camps too. Maybe Manuel was among them, and if not he, maybe Aleksander. She'd already checked her area many times to no avail. The women she questioned recognized her desperate look; many searched for their own loved ones. Mostly, they looked away as she approached, tired of saying, "No, I haven't seen such a boy."

This day she'd go past the children's area because the late fall heat drove most of the camp's girls and boys outside, but she wasn't hopeful.

The burgeoning crowds of dirty, malnourished children all began to look alike to her—hollow eyes and unending pleas for food.

As she approached a long barrack, she noticed a strange scene from a distance: a huddle of small girls stood off to one side while two larger figures spun a jump rope. She could just make out the jingle they sang as they skipped.

"Una, dos, el lobo feroz,
Caperucita con su abuelita,
Fueron a la plaza..."

She stopped when she came closer. One of the taller rope spinners resembled Manuel, but she wasn't sure it was him. She'd been mistaken before; didn't want to be disappointed for the thousandth time. She held her breath. Not wanting to distract the young man, she stood off to the side, her heart pounding, but he, too, noticed her, dropped the rope and ran toward her. All the children stood agape, watching.

"Raquela! Raquela, you are alive!" he exclaimed. Then he threw his arms around her neck and said, "I can't find Jacob or your friend, the one who took me to help in the trench."

Tears clouded her eyes. She squeezed him tight. Without any words, he understood.

"You will be with me now. We will be alright together, Manuel." She smiled through her pain.

"*No quiero perderte de nuevo,*" Manuel said. He didn't want to lose her again. She could see that some of his shyness had evaporated. He had grown; he'd have not said it out loud before. She could tell from his lanky body and the blemishes erupting on his forehead that puberty was changing him already. It was impossible to say how. A man without a childhood; she was saddened by the thought.

Despite the malaise that had plagued her, Raquela awoke with a jolt of energy the next morning. She felt lighter, comforted, knowing Manuel was in her life now.

35 WHITE TERROR, MARCH 1939

"We will have no mercy!" the headline screamed. Anyone who had supported the Republican cause would be prosecuted by a military tribunal, incarcerated, or shot on sight. Bronka's eyes grew wide with terror as she read it. Not only had she been living with one of the leaders within the Brigades, she'd worked for them sewing uniforms!

Bronka's awareness of the danger did not prevent her from wishing fervently Antoni would return to her. She wanted to see him playing with Stefan, but most of all, she wanted him to take her in his arms. How she'd missed him! She wouldn't care if his beard was unkempt, if he was more disfigured or if his mood was foul. His very presence would be reward enough for the misery she'd suffered in the four months he'd fought in the calamitous Ebro campaign.

Of course, she wasn't entirely alone, she had Stefan. The boy had his charming moments, but he wasn't an easy toddler. He had no toys; except the pots she gave him to bang on with a big wooden spoon. The racket he made grated on her nerves, but the happy babble and his Antoni-like smile won her over every time.

Stefan balked at almost every food she prepared for him. There wasn't much to choose from. She tried nursing him longer, but her milk had dried up. She couldn't understand why it was happening during her second pregnancy. The constant anxiety and hunger must have had a bad impact on all her systems. Her hair had thinned, and she no longer took pride in her appearance. Stefan's teething was difficult. He wailed for hours making her feel despondent. She felt bad for him and tried rubbing his gums with the bits of leftover liquor in Antoni's stash at the back of the cupboard. Sometimes it helped, sometimes it only made Stefan cry harder.

Bronka's only interaction with one neighbor in the building, Señora Vargas, a sixtyish widow who lived on the floor above her, filled Bronka with unease. She feared that Señora Vargas might press with questions about her husband or simply denounce her for a reward. Franco's government did not tolerate unmarried couples. A pregnant unmarried woman was considered a whore of abominable morals and usually shot on sight. Was Señora Vargas a friend or a foe? Would she betray her?

Yet, Señora Vargas was the only one who didn't give Bronka strange looks or ask what had happened to her husband. Though Bronka didn't much like the señora's habit of non-stop smoking, at least she was willing to tolerate Bronka's abysmal Spanish. They'd exchange pleasantries whenever the two met in front of the overflowing trash cans. It was better than talking to the wall.

Señora Vargas looked longingly at Stefan wriggling in Bronka's arms. "Children don't seem to run in our family."

"What do you mean?"

"We never had any. My dear departed Santiago desperately wanted a son. And my brother..." Never mind, Vargas waved her hand.

"Go ahead, you can tell me," Bronka saw the woman was upset.

"Well... his wife, such a shrew, she left him for another man before they could have any babies; made him miserable with her demands, the greedy *puta*."

The focus on children and babies made Bronka uncomfortable. In her situation it was best not to encourage it. "My son is restless. I have got to give him some lunch. See you around." Bronka made a hasty exit from the courtyard.

As her pregnancy became more evident, Bronka tried to avoid Señora Vargas assiduously to forestall questions, but her tactic did not succeed.

Señora Vargas appeared at her door with a pot of mint tea. "I grew it on my windowsill. Drink, it'll help you and the *bebé*."

"*Gracias*, Señora Vargas," Bronka managed to stutter.

"We have known each other long enough; you can call me Carmen."

Carmen walked into the apartment and made herself comfortable on the settee, then lit up a cigarette. "You seem lonely. On Sunday, my brother, Javier, is coming to visit. I'll introduce you." A satisfied puff of smoke curled into the air from her cigarette.

Bronka stared at her uninvited guest. Fortunately, Stefan began fussing giving Bronka an excuse to extricate herself.

For the rest of the week, Bronka couldn't stop thinking about how to evade Carmen and Javier should the supposed visit materialize. She remembered one of her first conversations she'd had with Carmen in which she'd spoken approvingly of a male relative in the Guardia Civil. Could Javier be that man?

Still, it haunted her when she went to sleep on Friday. On Saturday, she awoke with a throbbing toothache. She rinsed with salt water, rubbed alcohol on her gum; nothing helped. By the end of the day, she was exhausted from the pain. When she woke up on Sunday the pain was worse.

In the afternoon, just as she picked up Stefan to try and put him down for a nap so she could rest herself there was a knock on the door. Carmen stood there in her Sunday best, a red dress with flounces. A stocky, silver-haired man with a pencil mustache, wearing a well-tailored navy suit, accompanied her.

"As I promised." Carmen flashed a wide smile and introduced the man. "My brother, Colonel Javier Martins, of our local regiment of the Guardia Civil. And this is Bronka, the neighbor I've been talking about."

"*Mucho gusto. Bienvenidos.*" Bronka moved aside meekly to let the guest in. Her heart thumped furiously. A paramilitary man in her home; this will bring nothing but trouble!

The man held a large package wrapped in crinkly blue cellophane. Stefan reached for it. Javier's face lit up in a smile. "*Regalo por bebé,*" he said.

Bronka looked at the man in utter confusion. This was definitely not something she'd expected.

After they sat around the table, Javier unwrapped the gift and presented a yellow truck to Stefan who immediately grabbed it and spun the wheels, amazed he could make them move.

Javier chuckled, then said, "*Muchachito inteligente. Cuántos años?*"

"Twenty-one months. He'll be two soon." Bronka spoke dully, preoccupied by the pain.

Carmen asked, "What's wrong?"

"*Mal dolor de muelas.*"

"*Pobresita,*" Carmen said. "You need a dentist."

Bronka was in too much pain to think of refreshments, but she filled a kettle with water.

"Leave that to me," Carmen popped up from her seat. "I have some biscuits upstairs. I'll fetch them and make some coffee, so you can just relax." With that Carmen left Bronka and Javier alone.

Maybe that was her plan all along, Bronka thought. She looked fearfully at Javier, wondering if the toy had been some kind of ploy.

But he moved his chair closer to hers and took her hand as if he had a right to it. His touch was gentle, confusing her. "I've come to help you. I don't support the Caudillo's policy of shooting pregnant women who'd been associated with the Brigades. It disgusts me."

Bronka tensed up but didn't pull her hand away not wanting to offend him. Could she trust his kind words? Maybe Carmen had already blabbed about Antoni having gone to battle and not returned. Bronka blurted out, "You are a real gentleman."

Javier smiled broadly. "My Guardia men would get a good laugh out of that."

Carmen arrived bearing a tray of biscuits and figs. Bronka was relieved not having to carry on a conversation in her inadequate Spanish. She surmised Carmen must have gotten the treats due to Javier's connections. After Carmen prepared the coffee, the conversation paused. Both she and Javier lit up cigarettes. Javier offered one to Bronka, but she refused politely.

"Smart women don't smoke during pregnancy. Good for you and your baby," he said.

"I told you this lady is special." Carmen took pride in the introduction.

"Ah... but you didn't tell me how beautiful she is," Javier said.

If her toothache weren't killing her, Bronka may have smiled just to be polite, but she didn't bother. The man's overfriendly behavior made her uncomfortable. She watched him observing Stefan.

Not too much later, Stefan tired of the truck, pushed it away and began crying. "I have to put him for a nap now," Bronka said, signaling the end of the visit.

Javier stood up first, took Bronka's hand kissed it, and said, "I'm coming tomorrow to take you to a good dentist I know. Don't worry. You'll be safe."

After they left, Bronka questioned everything Javier said and did. He seemed too nice and yet too bold in assuming she'd acquiesce. Was he grooming her for something? What did he mean about his men laughing at her statement he was a gentleman? Did they know him to be a brute? Why would an officer in Franco's regime look kindly on someone like her, someone considered a traitor? And what were Carmen's motives in all of this? Was she trying to find a safe whore for her brother, one that would not have a leg to stand on if she were to reject his advances? She'd been alone so long, and the pain made it difficult to puzzle it all out. What would the decisive, fearless, Rifka do in this situation?

Bronka had barely gotten Stefan washed and fed when she heard an assertive knock on her door. It was Javier in full uniform: black knee-high boots, dark green uniform with a gold sash across his chest and the *tricornio,* a three-cornered shiny black leather hat; he looked fearsome.

"*Buenos dias, he venido por ti,*" he said.

At first, she tried to object, but he took her arm gently and said, "No talking. Come with me. Carmen will take care of your little man." Bronka hadn't noticed Carmen standing right behind Javier. The intense pain made it difficult to resist. She heard Stefan's screams as she and Javier descended the stairs.

Javier ushered her into a black Mercedes and sat with her in the back. A uniformed driver took them to Albacete, about an hour away. When they stopped and exited the car, Javier gripped her arm and whispered, "Just walk close to me. I'll pretend to have arrested you." Then he instructed the driver to wait.

They walked through a quiet passage with only a few pedestrians. It looked as if one café was getting ready to open. At intervals, civil guards stood on watch, each saluted Javier smartly.

As soon as they entered a building Javier loosened his grip on her arm. They walked up one flight of stairs, neither of them speaking. Javier rang the bell and a heavy, ruddy-faced, balding man opened the door. "*Comandante,* good to see you."

"Let's get this young lady taken care of, *Doctor*.

Through the entire car ride, Bronka had been so upset to have left her little guy with someone he barely knew, she hardly thought of her tooth. Now she snapped out of her overwhelmed state when the dentist asked, "Show me where it hurts."

She thought she'd jump out of her skin when he poked at the tooth with an instrument. He shook his head and repeated twice, "*Es mui malo. Solo una opción.*" He reached into the instrument tray near the dental chair and came very close to her face rubbing something foul on her gum. He wanted her to brave, the one characteristic she did not have.

He grasped her molar with his pliers and pulled, then pulled and twisted. She moaned and saw sweat running down his forehead, struggling with the tooth as if it were a vicious enemy. When he finished, he held it up, "*El chico malo. Lo siento.*" He apologized.

She walked out with a mouthful of bloody gauze. Javier spoke with the dentist in a nearby office for a few moments. She heard some raised voices but couldn't make them out. As instructed, Bronka bit down on the gauze throughout the drive back to La Roda. She could neither speak, nor wanted to.

About halfway home, Javier asked the driver to stop at a roadside bodega to get him cigarettes. When they were alone, he said, "I hope in a few days your pain will subside, then we will need to have a private talk."

What could he possibly mean by that? Bronka dreaded it, but now felt somewhat beholden to him for having gone to so much trouble. She had to keep in mind who he was: a powerful member of the paramilitary. After he dropped her off at home, he went up one extra flight to bring back Stefan while she ran into the bathroom to spit out a mouthful of blood.

Javier returned with Stefan fast asleep in his arms. She pointed toward her bed, and he put him down gently. "Please thank your doctor friend for me. I didn't get a chance. And thank you," she said.

Javier lowered his head and glanced down. When he looked up, his dark eyes held a hint of bad news. "What?" Bronka said.

"Well, I'm not so sure you'd want to thank the doctor. I must leave now. We will talk in a few days. I'll see myself out." And he was gone.

Bronka stood in the middle of the room dumbfounded and felt chills creeping down her back. What did Javier mean? Why did she get tangled up with him? Damn it, Antoni. Where are you? She picked up Stefan, still asleep, and cuddled him in her lap. He was all she had in the world now. Him and the little person squirming inside her. She covered his head in kisses, but he didn't wake up.

By morning, Bronka's cheek swelled. She looked like a chipmunk. Even Stefan noticed because he poked at it with his little finger. She didn't care. All she wanted to know was what Javier wanted to say in the private conversation he'd mentioned. She didn't need to agonize long. Next afternoon, Carmen appeared at her door with an ointment to help the swelling and she told her Javier would be coming in the evening.

Thankfully, Javier arrived after Stefan was asleep with the truck at his side. Javier sat on the settee. She offered him a cup of coffee. It was the least she could do to be polite.

"You look beautiful even with your swollen cheek," Javier said and the expression in his eyes softened. He lit up a cigarette and said, "Sit here with me for a few minutes. You don't really know me, but I'm not one to beat around the bush. The doctor did me and you a favor, but he expects payment."

She was ready to pop up to look in her bag to check how much money she'd left, but Javier took her hand and pulled her back down. "It's not a cash payment."

What can I possibly give him? She thought he wanted her body and a wave of anger flooded her. Bile rose in her throat.

"It's not what you want to give him. It's what he wants to take," Javier said in a low voice.

She was livid, yet tried to keep her mouth in check, "Say it already!" The words shot out fast, like bullets.

"He wants your child."

"What? How does he know about my boy?" She felt faint. Her heart pounded.

"Not the boy, this baby," he pointed at her abdomen.

She began to weep unconsolably, unable to catch her breath; couldn't find the words to fight him.

Javier put his arm around her shoulder and spoke quietly. "You won't appreciate it now, but it'll save your life. You have to live for your boy. Women in your situation are shot on sight—two for the price of one. Carmen has feared for your life ever since she noticed your condition and asked for my help. The doctor's daughter is wealthy, married to *General de División* (a major general) but she's childless. Your baby will have a good home. This is the best I could negotiate for you. I am so sorry."

She began to calm down, knowing she had to compose herself in front of this cruel man. She asked him to leave. "Please, please go."

"I understand," he said and held her hand. "I am an honorable man. Honor is my badge. It's supposed to be the badge of the Guardia, but most have lost it. I just want to save your life. Please, believe me."

She saw moisture in his eyes. He left quietly without another word. She estimated she had about two more months to go before giving birth to her second child. How would she manage with two when she had practically no money left? If she ate even less maybe she could scrape out enough money for one more month's rent. Then what? Sell her body? She sat at the table thinking until dawn. Maybe Javier's solution was best. Her heart ached even to think it.

The labor pains came in April, a month earlier than she'd expected them. As she was forced to agree, the doctor had paid her rent and supplied nourishing food for her and Stefan. Now with one call to Javier she'd be taken to a private clinic to give birth while Carmen cared for Stefan.

Compared to her previous birthing experience, this one was comparatively easy. Two uniformed nurses and a doctor delivered the child in a spotless birthing room only a couple of hours after she arrived. She heard the cry of the child, but before she could ask to see it, one of the nurses carried it out. "Please, please let me see my baby!"

The nurse sponged the sweat off her face, "It's better this way."

"Was it a girl or a boy?" Bronka wept so hard she wasn't sure the words had come out.

The doctor patted her hand, "It doesn't make any difference. All I can tell you is the baby is healthy."

After they cleaned her up, the nurses took her to a bright recovery room, painted in lustrous white. One of them brought a pitcher of orange juice and left it with a glass on the nearby enameled table. Bronka was exhausted and fell asleep almost immediately as if she'd been drugged. When she awoke all she could think of was I have to get back to Stefan. She called out and a nurse came in. "Please, ask *Comandante* Martins to take me home."

"Yes, Señorita, we will call right away."

As distraught as Bronka was, she could see from the moment Javier stepped into the room, something was wrong. He had a grim look on his face and circles under his eyes she hadn't noticed before, but he hugged her and said, "I am sorry. There aren't enough words to express how distressed I am."

"You are distressed?" she said with no small dose of irony.

"Sit down. I'm afraid I have more bad news."

She couldn't picture anything worse than what had happened already. Did they find Antoni and execute him? Yes, that would be worse. No, Brigade fighters were too smart to return. He'd not do it even for her.

"What bad news?"

"It's Stefan."

She screamed out, a visceral scream like a wounded tigress, "What happened to him?" She grabbed Javier's jacket lapels and pulled. "Tell me! Now!"

Javier bit his lip. "My general wants to take him."

"Take? Take? What does that mean? Where is he? Take me to my boy!"

"He is with Carmen. She's hidden him. I will bring him to you. Then we will get out of this hell."

Javier wrapped his arms around her and held her tight. "Some of us have become beasts. Caudillo allows his men to do anything they like when it comes to dealing with children of undesirables. My general wants to raise Stefan as a Christian, give him the best education... remake him in his own image. I won't let that happen. I promise."

"No! No!" she cried to no avail and pounded on his chest with her fists, then threw herself back on the bed, face down, and sobbed until there were no tears left in her. Javier sat in the chair nearby. When she was all spent, drained of all emotion, she got up and poured some juice into the glass. "Javier, what will become of me?" she asked, her voice hoarse and harsh.

"That is all I have been thinking about since the day I met you. I've

311

fallen in love with your innocence, your sweetness, your courage... And I have a plan."

"What plan?"

He opened his briefcase and took out something. "Here is a Spanish passport for you. I am taking you and Stefan with me to Argentina. I will love him as if he were my own child. We must get away from this godforsaken place."

At first, she didn't understand, but he went on telling her how he'd take care of them expecting nothing in return, stressing that her life would always be in danger here. It was true, with her baby gone and Stefan in danger she couldn't remain here any longer.

He looked at her with softness in his eyes. "I know it may sound absurd that I've fallen in love so quickly, but I thought about you a long time before we met, based on what Carmen told me... and then when I saw you..." He held both her hands. "There is no reason you should feel the same, but give us a chance," he pleaded. "You may even come to like me one day." A faint smile rose on his lips. His expression almost like Kazio's when he first kissed Bronka: a blend of shyness and triumph.

"But what about you? This is your country, after all."

"I cannot stay in a country that commits such atrocities. Besides, they know I'm protecting you. It wouldn't surprise me if I am already on the enemies list. Come with me. We will make a new life."

"But your sister is here... alone."

"She wants to come too. I wouldn't leave her behind."

The nurse came into the room. "Everything alright *Comandante*? Does Señorita need anything?"

He glared at her. "This is Señora Martins."

The nurse mumbled an apology and made herself scarce.

36 BERLIN, GERMANY. EARLY SPRING 1939

When he first came to, all Aleksander could think about was that he could remain lying there forever. It was peaceful, tomb-like: no sound of artillery, no whizzing bullets, not even the sound of wind howling. And all he saw was white, though he was vaguely aware it wasn't snow because whatever had covered his eyes wasn't cold. In fact, it was rather warm. Had he found himself in the white tunnel people traversed when they died?

He touched his face and felt a stickiness. What had happened? Where was he? He lay quite indifferent to his situation. He couldn't say for how long he'd been out of it; nor did he care. Then, slowly, he attempted to move his body and an awareness dawned: the boy! His name escaped him. Where was he? He called out, but the sound of his own voice was not audible, nor was there any response. Wasn't there a boy with him before... but before what? He couldn't think and realized that his head hurt as if all his brains had been shaken. His scalp burned.

Slowly he managed to get on his knees and to stand up, grasping a nearby shrub, but still, all he saw was white. The pain and his inability to see came into focus. He must have been shot and blinded! He began walking haltingly, wishing he had a long white stick with a red tip like the blind man who'd lived in his building. Hearing absolutely nothing, Aleksander decided he had lost not only his sight but his hearing as well.

He made ridiculously small, wobbly steps, trying not to stumble, but after several paces, he tripped on something and fell. The object was soft in places, stiff in others. Feeling around, he realized it was a body. Terror gripped him. Was it the boy? As he tried to stand up, the whiteness before his eyes began to dissipate. He saw blood on his hands and his jacket, long wavy bands of red as if he had taken a shower in blood. He touched the side of his head from which the pain radiated and felt the warm oozing blood. A realization dawned: a bullet had grazed his head. Soon he might go into shock from loss of blood. His body shivered; his hands trembled. He saw himself standing by a fallen man, a young boy, really, on whose body he'd toppled.

It was dawn. Thin light illuminated a field of death, bodies scattered everywhere. He forced himself to walk, thinking that perhaps he could make it toward the caves where a first aid station had been set up. The field of battle was still silent though he heard distant sounds like firecrackers. Seeing no signs of life, he kept staggering forward, faltering, then moving on. After a time, he realized he must have reached the positions occupied by the Nationalists. There, he saw almost as many of their fallen. A single thought flitted by briefly: the machinery of war.

And right there, in front of him, a corpse of what must have been a commanding officer by the look of his uniform showing from inside his open long coat. That coat! It beckoned to Aleksander. With enormous difficulty, he stripped it off the stiff body and noticed the hated red and black insignia with yellow leaves: Divisione d'Assalto LITTORIO, a member of the despised Italian 4th Infantry Division. He put the coat on. It was tight, but anything to stop the shivering. It would do. A few steps forward and everything went black. He felt himself falling.

Aleksander awoke, feeling as if he were airborne. The up-and-down movements made him retch. In a haze, he saw a man with a white mask over his mouth tending to him. He was saying something. Aleksander had a hard time making it out. Disembodied words floated in the air, *"Keine Sorge, wir werden Sie sehr bald im Krankenhaus haben."*

Krankenhaus—hospital! Why was the man speaking German? Aleksander closed his eyes. His mind swirled. The burning sensation on his scalp had intensified, a hot knife slicing his skin. After a while, he began to make out the shape of what must have happened. The insignia on the coat he'd lifted from the corpse! German medics thought he was one of theirs, picked him up and now carried him to one of their military hospitals. In many battles, he'd seen Junker air ambulances swarming the skies picking up the Nationalist's fallen, rushing them to Germany. How would he get out of this mess?

A monumental headache funneled mixed-up images to his mind's eye. Like pages ripped from a book, then thrown together at random, they flickered: the boy he took to his trench looking over the parapet, him yanking the boy down; Stefan screaming his name though he couldn't yet say more than "Dada;" Bronka puking her brains out; his mother saying, "come back alive;" Raquela and that Moroccan whose name he couldn't recall and who thought she was his. Aleksander wanted to open his eyes, but they seemed to be glued together.

Suddenly he felt his stretcher lurch, some commotion and a voice saying, *"Der Chirurg wird Sie jetzt sehen."*

A surgeon? Why? Gowned hospital nurses rolled Aleksander's stretcher into the operating theater.

The Empress Augusta hospital in Berlin's Mitte section was a sprawling complex in which top military neurologists applied innovative treatments for brain-injured soldiers. In this respect, Aleksander was lucky. It was also fortunate that he'd learned enough German from his art dealer friends that he could attempt to fake his way out of this dangerous situation.

On the one hand, his noble title might impress the Germans and earn him favor. On the other, his mother's Jewishness would probably get him arrested, if not worse. Aleksander wasn't aware that in the month of his brain injury, the Nazi persecution of Jews had taken a brutal turn: 1,400 synagogues in Germany and Austria had been torched and Jewish men forced to add a typically Jewish name. He'd no longer be either Antoni or Aleksander. He'd be Israel.

Professor Doctor Otto Schneider took a keen interest in Aleksander's case. He'd been studying traumatic amnesia for some years now and this patient presented with interesting symptoms. Though he could neither state his name, nor date, or place of birth, he spoke haltingly in both German and French. The professor concluded, based on the soldier's well-groomed appearance, languages, and sophisticated vocabulary that he was the son of a good family, not one of the low-class males who sometimes chose combat to indulge their inborn aggressions.

The professor had been studying Aleksander for weeks: tests, X-rays, different drugs, observations and still couldn't come to a conclusion as to his prognosis. For his part, when his scalp wound began to heal and the full extent of his predicament became clear, Aleksander had decided to feign amnesia for as long as possible or until a solution became clear.

Several weeks later, on one of their long-scheduled visits, the professor said, "So who shall I say you are, mystery man? I need to write something on all these forms. Can you now remember something... anything?"

Aleksander leaned back in his chair, looked up at the ceiling, then nodded slowly. "It is coming back. How could I have forgotten it?" He stated his surname quickly, lest it trigger unwelcome connotations.

"Aha! A good noble name, I thought so. The German Zabielskis had built that fine castle in Bavaria. Have you seen it?"

Aleksander nodded. It occurred to him that some of the medical staff must have seen him naked. But for his father's prescient decision not to circumcise him, he would not be here chatting with the professor.

On this spring Sunday, he sat on a bench in the hospital's garden, watching a splendid row of cherry blossoms and struggling to figure out how to contact his mother in Paris. Professor Schneider strolled by and sat next to him. "Sunday rotation," he said and pointed at the spring flowers. "But at least these *Frühling Blumen* are my reward."

Aleksander made a comment about the sculpture of a mermaid on the nearby fountain, and the professor said, "My goodness, this kind of assessment makes you sound more like a sculptor than a soldier."

"But can't one be both?" Aleksander couldn't resist.

This was how his "amnesia" slowly unraveled. They spoke for a long time: fauvism, Cubism and Dadaism. The professor was very taken with Aleksander's comments and understanding of art. "We are kindred spirits, you and I," he said. A sense of excitement emanated from his face and eyes.

As a feeling that he could trust this learned man grew, Aleksander blurted out, "I need to get to Paris now that I am beginning to feel more myself. Can you help me?"

The professor adjusted his spectacles and looked at him closely. "I should say you seem definitely better, young man." He smiled. "The magnetic pull of Parisian exhibitions. Isn't it?"

"Yes! But I lost all my papers in that horrific war, full of ugliness, diametrically opposed to art and beauty. Without them I'm just a cipher."

The professor stroked his goatee. "Hmm... well, as it happens, I'm having dinner tonight with members of a French physicians' association. I believe they'll be accompanied by the French consular attaché. Let me see what I can do."

Aleksander's ten-hour train journey from Berlin's Stadt Bahn railway station was turning out to be far more exhausting than he anticipated. Though the doctor had judged him well enough to travel, the truth was he'd put on the most positive spin on his health so he could get out, the sooner, the better. A sore area on his scalp felt mushy, even though he had been told the surgery removed all the dead tissue. He felt more than a little dizzy. The awful headache that had plagued him since his injury returned with incredible force.

Aleksander struggled to distract himself from the pain, trying to think of anything but his throbbing head. He recalled Professor Schneider's enthusiastic parting words: "When you return, my friend, I shall take you to my club. We'll enjoy a dinner with Sauerbraten, some good wine, and you'll tell me all about the exhibitions you saw."

Thanks to the professor's connections, Aleksander received a gift he never expected: a round trip ticket to Paris and a temporary passport. The two had parted warmly, more like friends than patient and physician. The professor's prolonged handshake came to Aleksander's mind.

Until this moment, it hadn't occurred to him that the professor may be of a different sexual persuasion, yet now the possibility seemed entirely logical. He should have been more observant: the intensity with which the professor studied him as he conducted the interviews— running his gaze along Aleksander's body as if it were a physical caress— only now did it look like lust. The way the professor always found time to stop by his room even when no specific test or appointment was on the calendar, that could have been a clue. Well... no matter. He was on his way home.

In normal times, there would be nothing more beautiful in the world than Paris in springtime, but as Aleksander's health continued to deteriorate, he could not venture outside to see his beloved city. And it was just as well; the spring of 1939 had been ominous. Talk of war with Germany was on everyone's lips. Signs directed Parisians toward trenches dug for shelters right in the city's squares and parks. Civilians received gas masks.

Relentless headaches plagued Aleksander. They made him so nauseous he vomited repeatedly. Just like a woman! He thought of Bronka and was equally disgusted with her and himself. He began to lose considerable weight. He faltered when he walked from one room to another in his mother's apartment, so much so that he began to rely on a cane. And how he hated that cane! An old man at thirty-three. He had become a disgrace: no longer grooming his hair or nails as he used to, and letting his beard grow.

Countess Zabielska, at first overjoyed by her only son's return, was now in a state of terror over his health. He refused to go to any more doctors, to endure more medical procedures and tests. He was morose, practically refused to speak with her when she herself, not the maid, brought meals on a tray to his bedroom.

On this Monday, having made an appointment with a highly recommended surgeon for Aleksander, she resolved to get through to her son. She walked into his bedroom, carefully balancing a tray with a pot of tea and his favorite BN Strawberry Biscuits. "I see you are up, son. That's good."

Aleksander sat on his bed looking dazed and very pale. She placed the tray on his nightstand, approached him, and put her hand on his shoulder. "We used to be close, you and me. Why won't you let me help? Why won't you tell me what had happened to you over the last two years?"

He began slowly. "*Maman*... I have seen so much... done so much." His head hung down as if he were looking for his slippers.

Gently, she lifted his chin and cradled it in her hand. "What have you done?"

Softly, he said, "I have a son."

At first, her eyes lit up, but soon her mouth drooped in disappointment. "You married, had a baby, and didn't tell your own mother?"

"It wasn't like that, *Maman*, nothing like that at all."

"What do you mean?" She looked at him, perplexed. Then after a moment of silence, "I see..." Her head bobbed up and down. "You and women. You could never get enough."

He knew she'd have questions, but the exchange had exhausted him. He'd say no more.

She moved closer as if to embrace him, bent down over his head, suddenly exclaimed, "God, what is that green patch on your scalp? It looks lethal!"

"I don't know, *Maman*. I don't care," Aleksander said and collapsed onto the bed.

Frantic calls to her personal physician, followed by visits from specialists, confirmed that Aleksander had been suffering from a brain infection. Apparently, Professor Schneider's surgery had failed to remove enough compromised tissue; the infection breached the hairline fracture on his skull. They tried all available remedies: another debridement, plenty of mercurochrome, and substantial doses of morphine for the pain. But Aleksander became weaker daily and remained in his bedroom with curtains drawn to relieve an extreme light sensitivity.

Day after day, Aleksander lay awake with his eyes closed, thinking of all the mistakes he'd made in his life. On some days, everything spun out of control, and he couldn't keep track of a thought he'd had a moment before, but on this day his thinking was a bit more ordered. He knew he would not last much longer despite his mother's ministrations. The poor woman, she was trying so hard to save him, but he wasn't convinced he merited saving.

He'd disappointed too many women, left his infant son behind and not been kind to Bronka. She was another woman who'd tried too hard. He hated how she forgave all his boorish behavior. If she had ever gotten angry or screamed at him, he'd have not felt as bad, maybe respected her more.

He'd let the only woman he ever truly respected slip out of his hands. For what? A drink. And those wasted plans to scour Warsaw to find her. All for naught. How stupidly he'd allowed himself to be seduced by Bronka—sweet soul, good in bed, but... oh, what did it matter now?

He dragged himself out of bed. A chill shot through his body. He realized his nightshirt was thoroughly soaked in sweat. He barely made it to his desk and groped for paper and pen. Hesitating for a moment, he decided to first pull an envelope from the box of monogrammed stationery in the upper shelf of his rolltop desk. He almost fell reaching for it.

On it he wrote: *For Mlle Raquela Bluestone: to be opened only by her should she ever be found.*

Then he took a sheet of cream-colored paper with his embossed initials and poured out his heart. He used the blotter, dried the ink, folded the single sheet and placed it in the envelope. Now he was ready to die.

37 MME TRAVERS

When France fell to the Nazi army in the spring of 1940, the rumor mill in camp Gurs exploded. Everyone said that France had been carved up: Paris, as well as western and northern France, fell into the Occupied Zone under the direct command of the Nazis, but Gurs and the neighboring town of Pau ended up in the Free Zone, just to the east of the so-called Demarcation line. The collaborationist Vichy regime of Marshal Pétain was in charge here.

As crowded as the camp had been, truckloads of new inmates began arriving from the east. At first, Raquela was excited. Maybe her family members would be among them. Soon she was disillusioned to discover they were German and Belgian Jews. No one was saying anything about the fate of the Polish Jews. What she wouldn't give to see her parents, any of her siblings or Bronka.

Food shortages in the camp grew, fights broke out over anything: spilled soup, a wet straw mattress, a stolen shoe, an inch less of space. The new arrivals were designated as enemy aliens. Raquela bristled at the label. She was one of them.

Some newspapers made it into the camps, albeit torn, crumpled, or used as wrapping for supplies. From them and the new arrivals from the Occupied Zone in the north, Raquela gleaned the mood on the outside. The French, who had been victorious over Germany in The Great War, felt offended and horrified. General de Gaulle exhorted his countrymen to resist.

A pretty, young woman, a recent arrival at camp, told Raquela how internally displaced people heading toward the Free Zone clogged the roads and overstuffed train compartments.

"But," she said, "Jewish foreigners, like me, were dragged off the trains, arrested and brought here because Marshal Pétain wants to out-German the Germans."

"People say he is a big fan of Herr Hitler," Raquela said.

"Isn't it ironic Gurs is in the 'Free Zone?'" the woman said. A sardonic look marred her expressive face.

Raquela nodded in agreement. "Come with me. I'll show you the ropes, things you'll need to know to survive here."

Despite the new reality, Raquela continued her efforts to get permission to look for a job outside the camp. The war would end, and she'd go home to Poland, but she wouldn't do it without a franc in her pocket. Her request to see the camp administrator took months to process and it took a volunteer from the Nîmes Commission, a burly blonde American who assisted her, to make it happen. By the time she was called in to see the administrator, it was early December. The weather had turned much colder. She walked the muddy paths to the makeshift office careful not to splash her skirt.

As soon as she greeted the thin, bespectacled man behind a rickety desk, he didn't appear as formidable as she'd expected. She handed him her papers and took a gamble. "I understand that French-born individuals, like me, might be released for work."

He nodded slowly, looking at her documents. "First you'll need to find work. You think that's easy in wartime?"

Raquela's heart quickened. There was hope. "No, I don't think it's easy at all, but I have skills."

When she revealed she could sew, the camp administrator mentioned she should inquire about jobs with tailors or dry cleaners who did alterations of women's garments. A wave of anticipation surged through Raquela. How she'd love to get away from here, sit at a sewing machine, but a memory of her abandoned shop swiftly dampened her enthusiasm.

The administrator shuffled in a desk drawer and handed her a paper.

"This is a list of potential employers. Try your luck in Pau, a grand old resort city swarming with rich international tourists. It should hold the best chance of employment but be very careful. Things are different now."

"I've heard," she said.

"Stuck here, you don't know the half of it. Even if you manage to find something outside, you'll find Monsieur Pétain has done everything to crush our spirit, even canceled public dancing in hotels, dance halls and weddings!"

"I suppose he wants France to remain in mourning until victory," she replied, seeing the administrator bristled at the occupation.

"Give me back the paper I just gave you," he said.

She put it back on the desk. He ran his pencil down the short list and made some marks. "Try the one with the checkmark first."

"Thank you very much," she said quickly and stood up to leave lest he change his mind.

"Good luck and keep in touch... if not, the police will track you down."

This morning Raquela felt nervous. After all, the Germans were just beyond the Demarcation Zone, near the coast, but she felt excited too. Manuel was alive and if she were to land a job, life might begin to normalize.

She took extra care grooming for her job interview, which under the circumstances meant putting on her only clean blouse. An older barrack mate loaned her a long navy skirt and a moth-eaten jacket to make her more presentable, and another gave her two tortoiseshell combs to fasten her upswept hairdo.

Luckily it wasn't raining. A cloudless sky matched her mood, though the air already had a strong hint of winter. The breeze off the Atlantic lessened the usual humidity, making for a more pleasant day than would be expected in December.

She tried to borrow a bicycle from one of the guards who had been kind to the inmates, but it had a flat, so she decided to try hitchhiking the twenty-five miles to Pau. She walked out on the road that ran near the camp and stopped to wave her arm every time some form of conveyance heading toward Pau passed. The list of employers on the yellowed sheet of paper in her pocket looked old; she hoped one of them would still be looking for a seamstress.

After she'd walked for about forty minutes at a brisk pace, a farmer pulled his horse and wagon to the side of the road and stopped. The thin, silver-haired man leaned toward her. His watery blue eyes, beneath bushy eyebrows, gazed at her. At first, he spoke in a strange language that only later she'd learn was Gascon. Soon he realized she did not comprehend him and addressed her in French. "You are from the Gurs camp, aren't you?"

"*Oui, Monsieur.*"

"But where are you going?"

"Looking for a job, trying to get to Pau."

The farmer arched his brows and gave her a narrow-eyed look. "You are Jewish."

It wasn't so much a question as an observation. He shook his head. "*C'est dangereux pour vous ces jours-ci. Fascistes partout.*" After a somber warning, he asked, "Where exactly are you going to look for work?"

She handed him the list. He reached down from his high seat to take it from her, then squinting, looked it over. His finger ran up and down the paper, then he pointed at one establishment, the Hotel Continental. "This is the only place. Don't go to the others. Trust me; it's for the best."

She noticed it was the one the administrator of the camp had marked with a check. "Thank you," Raquela was grateful for any advice. "What is your name, sir?"

"I am Maurice Bonheur," he leaned down again, extending his papery hand to shake hers. "Climb in," he said. Awkwardly, because of the long skirt, she made it onto the platform, her legs dangling. She sat very straight, trying not to lean on the bales of hay so that the jacket would not pick up pieces of dry grass or dust.

They rode in silence. The steady clip-clopping of the horse calmed her. When they came to a crossroad, Monsieur Bonheur had to turn. He bid her a very gentlemanly adieu but followed it with a dire warning, "Don't get yourself killed."

Raquela stood on the side of the road, brushing off stray pieces of hay. Her mind churned. How would she know who was out to hurt her? Were her looks so Jewish that anyone would know? And what if they did? She tried to shake off the warning, to convince herself she wasn't terrified, but the queasy feeling in her stomach said otherwise. Thanks to the lax camp security, she did have the Beretta from Jacob in her boot, but only because it was a solemn promise she'd made to him. She'd never break it, but she didn't plan to fire it either. Still, it made her a tiny bit more at ease.

She knew things would improve from here on in when a beautifully polished red and beige roadster pulled to a screeching halt. It was the fanciest car she'd ever seen. To her great surprise, a good-looking, blond motorist—she guessed he was twentyish—addressed her in German, "*Allein reisend, junge Fräulein? Wohin gehen Sie?*"

She replied in German, slyly with a broad smile, "Now don't make assumptions about me. I am on the way to the Hotel Continental in Pau."

He whistled, "*Schöne Stadt* lovely city" then opened the passenger door and motioned her to join him.

Throughout the ride, she reminded herself to stay calm whenever he spoke admiringly of Herr Hitler and his sweeping reforms. But the uglier his words became—"We will rid the world of the Jewish vermin" —the more courage she gained. She must have been quite convincing because he heaped on the compliments. "We need more bright women like you here, not these pushy Jewesses flooding in from Germany."

She screwed up more courage to engage him. "Where are you from?"

"I am from Munich, but I'll be deployed soon; France— great assignment." He winked. "My friends and I love to vacation here. And you?"

Her mind scurried to the first Spanish city captured by the fascists: "I am from Seville, but I was born near here."

"*Ja, ja,*" he said. "*Sie haben den dunklen Look einer spanishen Königin.*"

Hmm... He thought she looked like a Spanish queen. What a fool. She'd have to get out of this car before digging herself in deeper.

Soon they reached the outskirts of Pau. She saw churches and increasingly nicer buildings, wide boulevards and elegant couples strolling. They passed an old castle with the Pyrenees looming as backdrop. About fifteen minutes later, they arrived in front of a grand edifice with a mansard roof atop its circular corner facade. Large, gilded letters spelled out: Hotel Continental.

She thanked her driver and made a hasty exit.

He leaned out the window and called after her, "*Bis bald!* See you soon!" Then he gunned the engine and sped off.

Not if I can help it, she thought.

Located on the chic Rue du Maréchal Foch in the center of Pau, the hotel facade made Raquela feel she'd stepped back into Paris. The elegance! Coming from the abysmal camps, she'd nearly forgotten what civilization looked like. She stood for a while taking it in, then walked briskly into the ornate lobby with a polished marble floor and inquired about the woman whose name was written on her list.

"She's the wife of the hotel director, and does all the hiring," the doorman said, giving Raquela a look that she interpreted as: make a good impression; it won't be easy.

She followed the doorman's instructions up three carpeted flights to the office and knocked on the door. She took a deep breath to steady her nerves.

"*Entrez, s'il vous plait.*"

Mme Travers, a thin, elegantly coiffed fiftyish woman in a stylish gray suit, sat in a salon outfitted with brocaded settees and marble-topped coffee tables. She looked at Raquela, inspecting her with a keen, inquiring gaze. Her thin lips pressed together gave no indication of her temperament. "You may sit," she motioned to the settee across from her desk.

Raquela sat down, smoothed her skirt, and waited, trying to interpret the woman's coolness. Might Madame Travers be of the same opinions as the not-so-charming German driver who left her here with a promise to return soon? No, it couldn't be. Monsieur Bonheur seemed trustworthy, and he specifically instructed her to inquire for work here, not in any of the other places.

"You've come from the camp," Mme Travers finally spoke.

It would not do to lie; Raquela took a chance. "Yes, I have."

Mme Travers' poker face revealed nothing. She leaned toward Raquela, extended her hand. "I hear you are a talented seamstress."

How had she heard? But Raquela put all mistrust aside, said, "I have sewn all my life."

"In that case, you should have no trouble making alterations to the gowns we clean for our guests."

Raquela breathed a sigh of relief. "No, no problem at all."

"Did you bring any documents with you?"

Raquela handed Mme Travers the British-Palestinian passport and the birth certificate. Mme Travers put on her spectacles and inspected the papers closely. The lenses magnified her eyes. Raquela watched with trepidation.

"Alright," Mme Travers said with no discernible expression on her face. "They will do... for now."

For now? Did she spot a problem? No one before had taken such a close look at her papers. Would Madame report her to the police? Raquela sat in nervous silence.

"From your passport, I assume you are quite familiar with the Holy Land." Mme Travers pinned Raquela to her seat, like a butterfly in a display case. Raquela hadn't expected this line of questioning. "A fascinating mix of people," she said.

The telephone on Madame's desk rang, a loud, jarring sound. She picked up the receiver, listened, snapped, "Not now," annoyed at the disturbance and turned back to Raquela. "Let's just make this short. We lost our dressmaker recently. A backlog of dresses awaits alterations. They'll keep you very busy."

"So... am I hired?"

"Yes, didn't I just say so?"

"Oh, Madame Travers, I feel so fortunate. Now I'll have to find a place to live in Pau."

"No need. I will assign you a room on the top floor of the hotel. It will be a part of your compensation."

Raquela stood up, relieved. This was too easy; she extended her hand toward Mme Travers.

Mme Travers returned a firm handshake. "In time, we shall discover all your talents, Mademoiselle Bluestone." She rummaged in her desk drawer and took out a key. "Here," she gave it to Raquela. "Paydays are on Friday."

"You'll never regret hiring me. Thank you for your kindness."

Was there a slight smile on Mme's upturned lips? Breathless, Raquela ran up to the fifth floor and opened the door.

It took no time for Raquela to settle into her small spartan room. Besides the bed, covered with a cotton duvet, the furnishings included only a chest of drawers, a tiny desk, an upholstered chair, and a standing lamp with a large, fringed shade. Here she'd have her own sink in the corner of the room. Best of all, she had a window.

Initially, Raquela felt better than she had in a long time. Then she thought of the facile promise she'd made to Manuel as they parted: I will bring you to live with me as soon as I find employment. Without a realistic plan, it was a hollow gesture. She had no idea how to deliver on it. Her satisfaction in landing a job was mixed with guilt.

Later that day, while padding down to the toilet, at the end of a long corridor, she glanced through a partly open door. Seeing the room had the same layout and simple décor as hers, she surmised there were other employees lodged here. And as soon as the thought came to her mind, she saw two dark-haired women, one about her age, the other older, come from around the corner speaking in hushed tones. The younger one carried a bucket, the older, a broom and dustpan. They stopped speaking when Raquela passed them and gave her a long glance. She could have sworn they spoke Yiddish. She was puzzled. Maybe it was her imagination.

But now, convinced that at least some employees were lodged here, she hoped she could get Manuel a job here too. He was strong, adaptable, hardworking. The idea took root. She had to find a way.

The sewing machine stood at the back of the dry-cleaning shop in the basement, at the back of the hotel. Initially, Raquela had a hard time getting used to the odor of solvents and spotting agents used in cleaning different types of fabrics. Carbon tetrachloride and perchloroethylene, especially, had a noxious, sharp, sweet ether-like odor that made her nauseous, but after a while, she hardly noticed them.

Monsieur Lavalle, her boss in the shop, was a nice man in his sixties whose colorful ties, a protruding belly and two-tone wingtips were his most distinctive features. He was a man of few words, but he liked her and often commended her performance. "You are twice as fast as our last seamstress," he said often.

Raquela spent her days working and scheming how to bring Manuel. She worried that with his growth spurt and approaching maturity, he might be transferred to the men's camp soon, making it less likely she could intercede on his behalf.

She rarely ventured out after work. Monsieur Lavalle cautioned repeatedly: it isn't safe. And she'd gotten some taste of it from remarks made by chambermaids and bellboys. In their day-to-day encounters with guests, they witnessed endless negative comments about Jews, Gypsies, and anyone who wasn't native to Pau. Most of the invectives came from the Germans who favored this hotel and were known as much for their rudeness toward the help as their vile language.

The few times she'd been out, to purchase sewing notions, Raquela felt alarmed. The store owner called her a greedy Jewess when she pointed out that he'd given her the wrong change. She preferred to get her fresh air sitting in the little yard behind the dry-cleaning shop.

Raquela took her meals at a long communal staff table in a room adjacent to the kitchen. The employees ate leftovers from the guest menu. Compared to the slop they ate at Gurs, here food was more than adequate, though the chef thundered, "This is barely fit for human consumption. The markets are empty. Soon we shall serve cats!"

Meals did more than nourish Raquela and her coworkers. Here in the relative privacy, buffeted by the clattering of pots, chambermaids and doormen exchanged tidbits of information and gossip: "The Nazis have forbidden Jews to travel by trains," "Finland and Denmark surrendered to Russia." It was impossible to know what was true and what wasn't. But when one day, the wine steward said, "Warsaw has been bombed flat," Raquela felt so sick she rushed out to the toilet and vomited. Later, she tried to console herself: the old wino probably had too much to drink. She'd heard other waiters say he liked to embellish his stories. Her mind refused to accept an image of her city flattened. The idea was preposterous.

The work kept her grounded. Sewing hems on gowns or making size adjustments for the well-to-do European tourists and German officers' wives wasn't all that different from fitting the undergarments she used to make back in Warsaw. Sometimes the work required superhuman patience, as on the day Frau Becker came in to pick up her dry-cleaned dress.

She inspected it for spots and though there were none, exclaimed, "You've ruined my best gown, shrunken it to half the size!"

Monsieur Lavalle rejected the accusation patiently, explaining it was impossible because of the nature of the process.

The heavy, imperious woman became outraged. "You... you people can't do anything right!"

Lavalle directed her toward Raquela. "Don't worry, our seamstress works miracles. She'll fix it if it needs a fix."

Frau Becker turned to Raquela and instructed her to let out the side seams; apparently, she knew she'd grown far too fat for the gown when she brought it for cleaning.

"Let me see what we can do," Raquela smiled, marshaling her stamina and directing Frau Becker to the fitting room. "Please put the dress on," she said and watched as the woman struggled to shimmy into it.

Frau Becker fumed. "There's plenty of material in the seams. Just let it out and don't make such a big fuss. A child should be able to do it."

Raquela measured and pinned every which way, but there wasn't enough to widen the bust. "I am sorry to say, there just isn't enough material. It's impossible."

"*Ach Scheisse!*" Tears stood in Frau Becker's eyes. "My husband insists I wear this dress for his officers' function."

Raquela felt a sudden surge of sympathy. Maybe her husband was a Nazi monster. "I have an idea, Frau Becker. We have a beautiful leftover piece of contrasting silk. I could incorporate it, make it work. It would look quite nice."

Frau Becker brightened, dabbed at her eyes with a lace hankie. "*Danke*, I need it tomorrow."

Raquela was well practiced in speaking to customers in a reassuring tone, complimenting them on the fit. There was satisfaction in it, yet with every stitch, she remembered telling Bronka she'd be back in their shop. Now that she had a job and things began to stabilize, she decided to try communicating with Bronka once again. She'd written her a postcard shortly after she discovered one could post mail from the Gurs camp, but she never received a reply. In that postcard she had instructed Bronka specifically to address her reply in care of Raquela Bluestone, not Rifka Berg.

Thoughts of writing home must have been a premonition because within only a few weeks of starting her job, Mme Travers called her to the office and handed her a letter that had been forwarded from the camp by a volunteer working with one of the refugee relief organizations set up at the Nîmes conference.

Raquela accepted the envelope with trepidation. She did not know the sender, someone named Bogdan Nowak. Apparently, it had arrived in Gurs just before the war and prior to the suspension of postal delivery by the occupiers.

"I will read it in my room, after my workday. I have a client coming in for a fitting soon."

Mme Travers looked disappointed or annoyed; Raquela couldn't tell.

Raquela fingered the envelope in her skirt pocket all day. Something didn't feel right. She was not eager to open it. At the end of her work shift, Raquela ran up the stairs to her room, sat on her bed and examined the battered envelope. It had been long in reaching her: it was dirty, creased and addressed in an unfamiliar script in the care of Raquela Bluestone—exactly as Raquela had instructed Bronka. She tore it open.

Warszawa, April 5, 1939

Droga Pani Rifka Berg,

I am afraid I have some rather bad news for you. I am writing to you on behalf of your landlord because it seems you signed the lease. I am sorry to inform you that I have repossessed your shop for non-payment of rent. Your business partner, Pani Bronka Edelman, paid it for a while, but then she closed the shop; simply abandoned it.

To recover a part of the lost rent, I opened the shop on October 5, 1937 (at the direction of the landlord) and removed for sale at auction the following items:

2 sewing machines
8 bolts of fabric

1 floor-length mirror
1 round oak table
1 velvet covered easy chair
Miscellaneous notions and sewing supplies.

Initially, I had gone to your home address to see if I could get in touch with you, but the building caretaker said that Pani Berg and her children had moved to the Ukraine. I do not know where Pani Bronka E. went because I was unable to reach her at her address. My assistant spoke to the owner of a shop next door to yours who mentioned Pani Bronka met a Frenchman quite some time ago and may have left the country with him. My assistant found an old postcard from you to Pani Bronka as he swept the shop's floor in preparation for our merchandise inventory. It had the address to which I'm sending this letter.

Regrettably, I have no additional information.

Signed: Jan Nowak, Adwokat (Jan Nowak, Attorney)

No shop! No Bronka! Raquela could not believe it. A vice-like pain squeezed her temples; a wave of nausea washed over her. How had Momma been getting along without the earnings Bronka was to give her? Did Momma move to Kiev where they had a well-to-do uncle, long estranged from the family? His bakery in Kiev was part of family lore. But why no mention of Poppa?

The news was disconcerting and confusing. It made her head spin with speculations. Maybe Poppa went ahead to see his brother in Kiev, trying to repair the rift. Or maybe it wasn't the money so much. Maybe they'd become fearful when talk of impending war with Germany circulated in the synagogue. How humiliating it must have been to swallow their pride and knock on the uncle's door like beggars.

But wait, she stopped theorizing: by now, even if it wasn't flattened, Warsaw had been bombed; the war was in full swing. It didn't take much imagination to know things had to be dire back home. Maybe it was lucky her family ran east, away from the mayhem.

Raquela swallowed hard but could not clear the lump of guilt choking her. She washed her face with cold water and concluded: Bronka would never just abandon the shop. Something terrible must have happened to her. And for the first time she consciously admitted to herself it was a grave mistake not to return to Warsaw after the Palestine disaster. If she'd swallowed her pride, returned, and faced Momma and Bronka, things might have been different. She shook her head in disgust and shoved the letter into a dresser drawer.

38   A SPECIAL ASSIGNMENT

The letter from Poland was still very much on Raquela's mind, keeping her on edge, on some days making it difficult to concentrate on the work. Loneliness was eating away at her too. Perhaps if she could persuade Mme Travers to hire Manuel, she would not be as miserable. Despite her apprehension—she didn't want to be seen as pushy and had no documents for Manuel—Raquela resolved to see Mme after hours one day and simply ask. The woman seemed like an impenetrable fortress; it wouldn't be easy, but how bad could it be?

The day before had been particularly stressful at the hotel because the mayor had finally approved a dance to be held in the grand ballroom that had stood shuttered since Marshal Pétain had imposed the ban on dancing. There was much scrambling and running about to collect supplies stored in the basement. But from what she'd overheard in the morning, it went off without a hitch, and the influential patron was very satisfied. She concluded Mme Travers would probably be in a good mood. Today is the day, she decided, though she still didn't know where she stood in Mme's estimation. Careful not to be seen, Raquela navigated the back corridors to Mme's suite of rooms. She knocked gently then heard a gruff, "Come in."

Mme Travers sat behind the grand, ornate desk Raquela had admired the first time she was interviewed. The woman had such power.

Instead of a greeting, she said, "You have been upset ever since I handed you that letter."

Raquela was astonished at how observant Madame was. Her plain face still revealed nothing. Raquela didn't feel right divulging the disturbing news she'd received and didn't want to encourage questioning as to the hows and whys of her life. She remained silent.

The two women sat across from one another. Mme Travers sucked on her cigarette, sending tendrils of smoke into the air.

Haltingly at first, Raquela began, hoping she'd not be interrogated about the letter. "I have come to ask you for a kindness."

"Speak up, please, I can barely hear you," Mme Travers said calmly.

"I overheard the doorman saying the hotel was short on bellhops. Is there any chance you could hire my brother?"

"You have a brother? You didn't mention him when you first came here." Mme Travers' face registered alarm.

"I... I didn't want to abuse your generosity and you didn't ask me," Raquela stumbled over her words.

Mme Travers pursed her lips and looked at Raquela with enough intensity to examine the contents of her brain. A barrage of questions about the brother followed. Raquela made up the answers on the spot: they shared a mother, but not a father; he was born in Spain, he was fourteen, and so on. The more questions she answered, the calmer she became. Lying was too easy.

"Last question. Can you vouch for his trustworthiness? It's what I care about most," Mme Travers said.

"He is young, but I'd trust him with my life."

"I'll see what I can do." Mme Travers flicked her cigarette ashes into the ashtray. "The manager at the Gurs camp is one of us; maybe we can make it work. But now it is my turn to ask you for something," she said.

Raquela was mystified. What did 'one of us' mean?

"I believe I have come to know you well enough to trust you. You'll have to keep everything I tell you to yourself. Strict confidence. Understand?" Mme looked very stern as she spoke.

Raquela sat up straighter. This wasn't the conversation she expected. "Please, I'll do anything for you, Mme Travers," Raquela's tone turned reverential. She had nothing to offer as a sign of gratitude.

"Don't get so excited. The job I will ask you to take on will be dangerous and may seem odd, but I won't be able to explain much."

Mme Travers' brow wrinkled. She lit another cigarette. Her eyes drilled into Raquela's. Awed that something important was happening, Raquela remained silent, but nodded in solemn agreement.

"So here is what I need you to do: first, collect as many empty glass bottles as you can, then come speak to me."

"That's it? Bottles? Where is the danger in that?"

"You will see. For now, it's what you do, but no one must see you collecting them."

Clearly, there was more to this woman than her crusty exterior. As she thought about Mme's assignment, Raquela realized this seemingly simple request wouldn't be as easy as she thought initially. Where to find these bottles and what kind? In the kitchen? The wastebaskets chambermaids removed from guest rooms? She expressed her gratitude and hurried to her room.

A week later, the doorman came by her sewing machine. "Come upstairs. You've got to see something."

Raquela was nonplussed; she'd hardly ever spoken to the man. In the grand lobby, she found Manuel standing shyly in the doorway. Mme Travers had kept her promise!

She hardly recognized him in his spiffy uniform with gold braid at the lapels of a well-fitted jacket, black slacks with a red stripe and a charming red cap that might have fallen off if not for the chinstrap. It teetered on his mop of curls. The uniform and a grown man's black wingtips made him look taller, older.

He saluted, then gave her a hug right in front of hotel onlookers. She felt his scrawny frame. Someone will have to fatten him one day, when this war ends.

"Are you sure you can haul heavy valises?"

Manuel's eyes darkened; he frowned. "Why do you ask? You know I can."

"I was just teasing. Come to my room after dinner."

Manuel's arrival lifted a burden off Raquela's shoulders. Mme Travers had kept her word and she would keep hers as well. The knowledge that from now on, Manuel would be safe and living at the hotel relaxed Raquela. Her risky assignment would now be easier. She continued gathering the glass bottles with added zest.

It took her almost two weeks to gather a dozen bottles because workers hung around the kitchen late, even after the manager left, and the room cleaning crews took their time. Raquela found a basket in a back storage room and carefully placed in it the assortment of found glass bottles— liquor and perfume flasks, hair tonic and apothecary bottles discarded by the guests. She used discarded fabric remnants to muffle the clinking. Now she was ready to head back to Mme Travers' salon late at night, as instructed. This time, she walked more confidently but with far greater care, stopping to check the corridors at the slightest noise.

She found Mme Travers sitting on a silk-upholstered gold settee. Madame pointed to a matching chair nearby. Raquela set the basket on the floor before sitting down. "I don't know how I can thank you for hiring my brother," she said.

Mme Travers ignored her thanks. She motioned toward the basket, "Well, now that the bottles are ready, you can help by taking the next step." As before, Mme Travers' face was inscrutable.

Raquela knew full well that the bottle-gathering must have had a purpose. She was anxious to do something more challenging.

Mme Travers looked at Raquela closely, as if assessing her readiness for something big. "Let's talk about the project," she began. "You must remember to keep everything in total confidence. If it is discovered, many lives, including yours, could be lost. And as a Jewess, you are at more risk than most."

Ever since the Vichy government had begun treating Jews as enemies, Raquela felt more Jewish than ever before. Throughout her life, her Jewishness was as much a part of Raquela as her organs, something essential yet unobserved, something that didn't require scrutiny. Even the antisemitic attack on her shop hadn't produced any deep introspection about her Jewishness. But the atmosphere in Pau— government-sanctioned derogatory comments she'd overheard in shops and from some hotel guests— always kept her on edge. Jewishness became a finger poked in her eye, questioning her very right to live. It scared her to hear that she could lose her life by engaging with Mme

Travers' project, but Madame wasn't Jewish herself and she was putting her life on the line. Raquela could do no less. "Don't worry, Mme Travers, I will never do anything to compromise the project."

"So here is what you'll do."

Raquela listened with her entire being; she couldn't forget the tiniest detail. Such an honor to be considered trustworthy for a clandestine operation.

First, she was to wash the bottles, then fill them with every kind of chemical the dry-cleaning operation utilized. Tongue twisting liquids in brown, gallon-size jugs would require careful handling because they were flammable and, if spilled, could be smelled by passersby outside the dry-cleaning shop. She'd have to decant the noxious chemicals only after every single worker left.

"The next step will be even more dangerous," Mme Travers continued.

Raquela sat wide-eyed and super attentive, like an animal preparing for the hunt.

"Next, you'll take these filled bottles to our forger, a member of our Resistance cell, so he can produce the documents we need. I'll give you his address and the code if you think you are up to it."

Raquela gulped hard. "Of course, I am up to it," she said earnestly.

"The first documents our man will need to work on are yours and Manuel's," Mme Travers said.

"But I already have documents," Raquela reminded Mme Travers politely.

Mme Travers laughed, the deep tobacco-infused snigger of an experienced, older woman. "No, no dear, they aren't good at all. Your anglicized name screams 'Jew.' It's too dangerous now. Pick a good French name."

The smirk of the British soldier at the checkpoint in Palestine stood clearly before Raquela's eyes. Did he choose to overlook her poor imitation of a passport? "Is it alright if I ask for papers in the name of Simone Bonheur?"

It was the first French surname that came to her mind and Monsieur Bonheur was a kind man. She'd honor him by taking his name. As for the given name, Raquela had a vague recollection of a French actress—Simone Mareuil—who'd starred in a film *The French Jew*. She hadn't seen it, but they had discussed the play in her French class at the gymnasium.

"I like that; you are quick on your feet. Now let's get on with the business at hand." Mme Travers' tone turned cooler. Do you know where the Saint Martin church is?"

Raquela crinkled her eyebrows, trying to recall the town's layout. "Yes, I believe I've passed it on the way to the sewing supply shop. Isn't it the one near the funicular and the river?"

"Yes, exactly. Good. Now listen to me carefully: you'll have to use this code at the forger's door." Mme Travers rapped her knuckles on the coffee table, tapping out a specific sequence of taps. "You'll have to do it exactly like this, or he won't let you in."

Raquela nodded. "I'll be careful," she said, realizing the gravity and danger of the assignment.

"Well then, here is the address. Memorize it, tear it into tiny pieces and flush it down the toilet before you leave the hotel." Mme Travers handed her a slip of paper and dismissed her.

39 FATHER CHAPELLE

Late at night, Raquela's heart raced as if she were running when she set out the glass bottles on the counter of the shop. Her ears pricked up for sounds of footsteps in the corridor outside; her heart pounded. She waited, and when she heard nothing, steadied her hands, and slowly poured the chemicals, using a funnel she snagged from a friendly cook in the kitchen. Not a drop could spill on the counter to leave a tell-tale mark. She'd collected from the trash as many discarded wine corks as she could, then shaped them to fit the bottles and flasks missing stoppers. Her best finds were two 50 ml alcohol sample bottles that must have been left by the liquor salesmen.

She fastened the tops as tight as she could, wrapping paper and strips of fabric around them in case of leaks, and carefully tying string around them. She listened for noises outside. Silence. Gingerly, she nestled the bottles in the basket among additional fabric scraps, covered them with a folded piece of burlap, lifted the precious cargo, holding it steady, and locked the shop.

To avoid the elevator, she walked up the five flights of stairs to her room and opened the door as silently as she could. After placing the basket on the dresser, she sat on the bed, awestruck at what she'd just managed to pull off. Her heart still pounded so fast she thought she'd pass out, but she couldn't quite tell if it was excitement or fear. She looked at the address to which she'd take the contraband and reviewed the city map in her head; the streets she'd take, and which alleys she'd avoid.

And then an idea came to her. The camera! She'd taken it from Aleksander only because it was a token of something unfinished between them. The darn thing was nothing but trouble to safeguard. She'd give it to the forger. He could use it to make passport photos and who knew what else.

The city was completely silent and dark when Raquela stepped out of the Hotel Continental. In the distance, the distinctive snow-covered double peaks of the Pic du Midi d'Ossau loomed like monstrous hooded figures. Her footsteps sounded much too loud even to her own ears. She'd have to find rubber-soled shoes next time. The large basket of bottles held tightly against her hip dug into her ribs; she couldn't risk jostling it. She'd have to make it down a steep staircase, all the way to a narrow alley behind the Saint Martin church. She took each step cautiously, trying to stay in the shadows.

When she arrived at the unremarkable gray-green door, she knocked in the pattern Mme had shown her: three quick taps, a moment of silence, then four more quick taps, pause and one more tap. For a few moments, she heard nothing, then shuffling sounds and a small, gray-haired man cracked the door open. "I have something for you from Mme Travers," she said.

"*Viens vite,*" he opened the door, scanning the alley.

It took a few minutes for her eyes to adjust to the light. She placed the basket on the table near the entrance and took in the narrow, crowded room, which appeared even smaller and dimmer due to the bare rafters of the low ceiling, while the man stood sizing her up with his hands in the pocket of a brown apron. The room was musty, but a pungent scent competed for dominance. It bothered her throat. She noticed stacks of papers on the desk in the corner. Near the pale-yellow back wall stood a long worktable with a jumble of bottles, inks, stamps, colored pens, sponges, and glass jars filled with dirty water of different hues. A large goose-necked lamp illuminated the table.

"I am Father Chapelle," the man introduced himself.

A man of the church! She certainly didn't expect that. He looked like a common laborer.

"Mme Travers says good things about you," he said in a gravelly voice.

"I brought you the chemicals, but can you tell me how you use them?"

He chuckled. "Exactly as your shop does, some dry-cleaning."

Raquela knitted her brows. "I don't understand."

"La curiosité est un vilain défaut."

"But tell me."

"I use them to wipe out useless information on old passports and other documents, so I can write in what will help people survive."

Raquela nodded, picking up her bag. She had many questions about the process but knew not to ask them. "If there's anything else I can do, just tell me, Father."

His blue eyes smiled solicitously. He did look like a priest. "You want to be one of us? It's very risky."

"Well, I guess I'm in already," Raquela said softly. "I don't know anything about your organization, but I'd do anything to help people survive. I have seen too much death." Her voice trailed off. This was not the time to speak of the Spanish Civil War; there was a newer war to fight.

Father Chapelle turned away and fiddled with some papers on his desk. "Well... as I said, our work is dangerous; we have to keep information flow to a minimum to protect our people."

Raquela nodded. "I understand."

"But there is something you can do. Mme Travers told me you used to do some design work in your country."

The very reference to her old life made Raquela nervous. "Yes, some, but that was a long time ago."

The priest opened a desk drawer and pulled out a sheaf of crinkly tracing paper. "If you can wield a pencil, you can do this, and I know you can do more." He showed her old document stamps, on formerly official papers. "You'd trace them, then ink copies in on the passports. You see, like here, where I've removed old, incriminating information."

"I see," she said. "I promise to do my very best." Her heart pounded.

"Mme Travers can get you a supply of pens and nibs, colored inks. I will provide blank baptismal certificates from the church, of course. And other required forms will come from one of us who may or may not work at the town hall."

"I almost forgot," she said near the door, opening her bag and pulling out the small object.

She handed the camera case to Father Chapelle. He held it in his palm, then pulled the camera out, turned it on all sides, nodding approvingly. "An Ensign Selfix! A very good model."

"For passport photos, perhaps."

"Surely." He gave her a long look. "And many other uses."

Raquela acknowledged him with a nod, but felt ill at ease to make more conversation: what other uses? Perhaps she ought to have asked Mme Travers if her gifting the camera was appropriate.

She plunged out into the night and gulped the moisture-laden air. She'd be one of them. Already was! It was thrilling to know that for once, she could do something noble for which she'd not have to repent for the rest of her life.

She hurried along the cobblestones.

Raquela returned to the hotel with a renewed sense of mission. She worked hard on the garments of rich Germans during the day, but after hours she transformed into a forger's assistant, working zealously into the night. It didn't take her long to get the hang of tracing and copying the stamps. She had never thought about the variety of shapes and colors that could determine a person's fate. Keen attention to detail was the key. Some stamps hadn't been inked fully, so she had to leave parts of the circles, squares, and triangles unfinished and looking faded. The ink wasn't applied in the same intensity, so she had to vary the pressure of the pens to match the originals.

She glanced at the clock: almost five in the morning. She lay down, glad to have an hour of sleep.

40 RAQUELA REINVENTED

By November 1942, the main buzz in the staff dining room was about how the German military had assumed control over the entire country, including the south of France. The older chambermaid from Simone's floor could not contain her anger. "We were in the 'free zone' until last month! What a damn farce!"

The chef, who rarely minced words, said, "If you'd had your ears open, you'd know that already back in 1940, the Vichy goons issued the Statue on the Jews requiring your people to register with the police."

"I knew that," she mumbled.

Raquela thought of him as a decent sort, always making sure the skinniest among them got enough to eat. He probably meant no harm. She'd also read that quotas on Jews in the professions caused the dismissal of thousands of Jewish professionals from their jobs and internment in detention camps of anyone who had two Jewish grandparents. Jewish property was confiscated. It left the same taste in her mouth as when her shop had been vandalized.

The kitchen staff who went outside regularly to get supplies reported with disgust how German officers strutted the streets of Pau. "The bastards clearly enjoy our balmy weather, while we suffer curfews and rationing of almost everything," the bald cook ranted. "Queues everywhere! German officers billeted in the nicest Pau villas."

Even Raquela, who tried to stay in as much as possible when she was not on a mission, sensed the air of suspicion that permeated the fabric of the city. The Vichy goons encouraged neighbor to suspect neighbor: to sniff out who was a collaborator and who aided the Resistance. The wrong conclusion could cost a life. She feared the situation might be very similar in Poland, and dread about the fate of everyone she knew back home was a constant, assuaged only by the covert work she was doing for Madame Travers and Father Chapelle.

Raquela's daytime and evening workload occupied her mind and pushed painful thoughts aside. But it also lessened the time she could spend with Manuel playing games and chatting. She'd taught him strategies for winning at gin rummy. Sometimes they played checkers. She liked studying the intensity in his face when he concentrated. It saddened her the boy had grown up without a childhood. But she could see that he had grown into a very thoughtful, sensitive, and perceptive young man, someone who'd have made his family proud. He hadn't shown any of the insolence or dismissive attitudes that she'd noticed back home in boys his age.

Lately, the work on the forgeries was intense, taking all of her spare time. After she declined to play with him for the third or fourth time, he ignored her and came up to her room one night. She could not refuse him entry.

He walked in, looked around the room, saw the paperwork and her supplies spread out on every surface. "What's this?"

"Uh. I... am working on a project for Mme Travers."

Manuel looked perplexed. "Does it have anything to do with all those whispers I've been hearing?"

"What are you talking about?"

"I think the doorman on my shift is a Jew. People say Mme Travers hires Jews to hide them from the Germans."

Raquela pressed her lips together and began picking up the paperwork strewn around the room. Those worried looks on the faces of the whispering chambermaids she'd run into along the corridors began to make sense. She chastised herself for being obtuse, then turned and faced Manuel. "Promise me you won't breathe a word about this to anyone. I mean anyone."

"I'm not a fool. I know about being scared."

"Of course, you do. I shouldn't have said it."

"Tell me about this work you are doing, Raquela. I can help you... whatever it is."

It was the beseeching look in his eyes, melting her resolve not to divulge, that did it. "Look, Manuel, there are good people who are risking their lives to protect others. They don't care what religion these people practice; they only focus on our common humanity." She paused, looked at him intently. "And you must realize that I'm Jewish."

Manuel sat on the edge of her bed, cracking his knuckles, but his gaze was fixed on Raquela's face as if she were an icon.

"I want to be a part of it, Raquela," he said quietly. "If I'm to be your brother, I am a Jew too."

She nodded. "Here's something you'll have to know first: I'll no longer be Raquela to you. From now on, I'll be Simone Bonheur. Memorize it and don't ever slip."

"Simone Bonheur," he said, sounded unsure of himself, then repeated in a more assertive tone, "Simone Bonheur."

"Good," she said.

Manuel's eyes opened wide. "But who will I be?"

"You'll still be Manuel... but your last name may change to Bonheur... I'm not sure yet."

She'd have to tell Mme Travers she'd enlisted Manuel and hoped Mme would not be angry. But at least he'd have a new set of documents soon, as Mme Travers had promised. It would be good if his papers were in a good French name too. The Vichy government considered Spanish refugees as undesirable as Jews, communists, criminals, and homosexuals.

After Manuel learned of the forger and how dry-cleaning chemicals and documents needed to be smuggled back and forth, he pleaded with her to participate.

"Not yet," she said. "I have already told you more than I should have."

Raquela—soon to be Simone, she had to keep reminding herself—bid him goodnight and watched him leave with disappointment etched on his face.

The general air of disquiet in town grew into palpable tension among the citizenry. All the long queues for basic staples made the town's inhabitants cross. Raquela saw hungry children beg for food whenever she went outside. Even for the average French person who wasn't likely to be under threat of death—unless one was found to be a part of the organized Resistance—life was difficult. Raquela felt all of this, but she also knew that despite her expected French papers, she'd have to be more careful: a Resistance member and a Jewess, lethal combination.

When she'd journeyed to Palestine as a Jew and even when she ran away from it to hide from reality, it had been her choice. Here in Pau, she had to remain hidden not because of something she'd done, but for who she was. Here the invaders wanted to erase her personhood.

Raquela felt apprehensive the day a bellboy ran all the way down to the hotel's dry-cleaning shop and breathless, called out, "Mme Travers wants to see you. Now!" Just a day before, Raquela had finished a complicated alteration of a gown for the wife of a German official.

Could she have complained? Raquela thought the dress looked good, but the stout matron refused to wear a corset and some of her bulges couldn't be concealed. Raquela set aside the garment she was sewing and headed up to Mme Travers' salon. Facing the woman who ruled this vast hotel as if it were an empire always filled Raquela with anxiety. By now the two had established trust, but a complaint from a German could bring scrutiny and trouble.

When Raquela arrived in Mme Travers' office, there was no hint of a problem. So far, so good.

"Look, they are ready," Mme Travers waved the new documents.

Raquela took them and inspected them closely. Incredible how authentic they looked and how different from the Nudelman version.

She looked up at Mme Travers. "Meet Simone Bonheur," Raquela said with as much assurance as she could muster.

But Mme Travers looked very serious. "From now on, Simone Bonheur will have to slide off your tongue like honey. Practice saying it. And remember that as a foreign Jew, you are subject to deportation if your true origin were ever uncovered."

"Simone Bonheur," Raquela repeated more assertively.

It seemed deceptively simple to become someone else. She had done it successfully before. Would her newest identity bring about a forgetting of who she had been? Never. In every cell of her body, she'd always remain Rifka. Simone Bonheur was simply a new security blanket. Yet, she wouldn't mind being a blank slate: a new woman with fresh memories.

Mme Travers began using the new name immediately. "Simone, tonight, when you take the next batch of chemicals to Father Chapelle, he will give you the list of names and addresses."

"List?" Something new before she'd quite digested her new name.

"Yes, this is the next step. All those passports and baptismal certificates, we put them to good use."

"Yes, of course."

She'd been so immersed in collecting the bottles, tracing the document stamps and delivering them, that she hadn't given much thought to whose hands would hold the prized French documents.

"I believe your first assignment at this stage will be to accompany Ida Rubinstein and take her to Tarbes, a town about an hour southeast of here."

"Who is this woman?"

A rare smile showed on Mme Travers' face. "We hope she'll grow up to be a woman, but now she's only four and a half. The deacon at the Tarbes cathedral will make sure to get her to Sainte Marguerite, a Catholic boarding school under the auspices of Bishop Gabriel Pignet in Montauban."

"Deacon, bishop?" Simone looked puzzled.

"We have a variety of people in the Resistance," Mme Travers clarified, but Simone was still stuck on her previous statement.

"This young child will travel without her parents?"

Mme Travers nodded. "We can't save everyone; we focus on the children."

Simone felt a nearly physical stab in her chest. Another child torn away from her mother and she, Simone, would be the instrument. It was too agonizing to contemplate. Dormant pain shot through her being. It pulsed in her veins, stung her nerve endings.

Mme Travers noticed Simone's changed demeanor. "You look pale. Are you alright?"

"Give me a moment; I will be fine. It's just that... Never mind. I am up to it." Simone sat up straighter and regained her composure. She could not crumble, not now when she had such a chance to save the life of a child.

"There will be many more after Ida, but some will be boys. You might consider taking Manuel along; he might make it easier to calm the children. Most are very distraught." With that, Mme Travers handed Simone Manuel's documents. "For your brother," she winked.

"Thank you," Simone managed a wan smile.

As she left the salon, Simone thought about the bereft mothers of the children she'd be rescuing. She imagined the look on the mothers' faces at the moment of parting. It would be the same as on Golda's when she'd learned what had happened to Maya. She had to protect these children at any cost.

41 R IS FOR RESISTANCE

Simone sat on her bed for a long time while trying to calm her nerves. Looking at the clock, she realized she would have to leave soon to take the contraband to Father Chapelle and pick up that wretched list of addresses. The Germans had increased the patrols in their neighborhood recently. Every sound on the street past the curfew hour was suspect. She'd have to be extra careful; couldn't afford to be off her game and she still hadn't found any rubber-soled shoes. Let me just get through this evening, she thought, then stood up, took the Beretta out from the dresser drawer, and put it in her bag. As much as she resisted carrying it with her, now that she was in the thick of resistance, Jacob's voice echoed in her mind. "Promise you'll always have it with you."

As nervous as she felt making her way to Father Chapelle, a quiet stream of excitement propelled her forward. She was doing something important.

Father Chapelle looked pale and tired when he opened the door. "Hello, Simone," he said.

So, he knew she'd become more French.

"Are you feeling ill, Father? I can ask Mme Travers for some medicine and bring it to you tomorrow."

"It has been a difficult week. Three of our colleagues have been arrested."

"Oh, no!" she exclaimed.

"This shouldn't shock you, Simone. There are probably as many Nazi collaborators as there are members of the Resistance. Our men haven't been shot yet, so there's hope our boys can liberate them."

Simone stood for a moment, unsure what to say. Then said, "Mme Travers told me I'd be picking up little Ida Rubenstein next week, but she didn't say how I'll get her to Tarbes."

"Don't worry; our driver will meet you at the appointed time, but he needs to find petrol. You know how hard it is to get any. Just remember to soothe the girl. Loud crying will call attention to her... and you. No need to call the wolf out of the woods."

Father Chapelle fumbled in a desk drawer. "We have already placed fifty Jewish children in homes, schools and churches throughout our area. With help like yours, we can save more."

Finding what he was looking for, Father Chapelle pulled out a narrow piece of paper, folded accordion-style. "This is the list of children and their addresses." He straightened it out and handed it to her.

She glanced at the names. "So many..." she said.

"Not enough," Father Chapelle said. "It's a question of finding decent French people who'll take the risk. After you memorize the list, destroy it. It isn't safe to keep anything even remotely incriminating."

She thanked him and put the list in her pocket. All she could think of was how to get the list safely back to the hotel and memorize it.

Simone picked up her bag. "Father, I wish you—no, us—" she corrected herself, "luck in liberating those three colleagues. She felt good acknowledging she was part of them.

Father Chapelle smiled and patted her shoulder.

Simone walked out into the alley and looked around, ensuring the shadows were not human figures. Now that she had the list, she felt a special obligation to make her way back to the Hotel Continental as quickly and unobtrusively as possible. When she heard the distant rumble of an automobile, she ducked into the shadow beneath a balcony, folded the list into a small square and tucked it into her brassiere for safety.

Beyond Boulevard des Pyrenees, the mountains stood in sharp relief against the clear navy sky illuminated by a sliver of moon. As she approached Rue Barthou, Simone heard voices.

It was impossible to tell if men were arguing, but as she got closer, she made out shouting, cursing and laughter. They sounded drunk. She remembered a bar in the area and regretted taking this street. She decided to turn at the corner and take a different route, but it was too late. She was spotted.

A man shouted after her, *"Mademoiselle, Mademoiselle, venez ici!"*

With her heart in her throat, Simone began to run, but he ran after her. She heard his footsteps hitting the pavement, getting closer and closer. When he grabbed her shoulder, she turned around and blanched. She recognized him! It was the blond German who'd picked her up in his roadster and dropped her off at the Hotel Continental.

It seemed that even in his drunken state, he, too, recognized her. *"Ich kann nicht glauben, mein Glück, die spanische Königin! Oberstgruppenführer zu Ihren Diensten."* He saluted her, clicking the heels of his black, knee-high boots.

So, he remembered calling her the Spanish queen all those months ago. She stood there in disbelief with her guts churning but put on a brave front and said, "It's late, I have to get home."

She saw him now for who he was: a Nazi officer in full gray-green regalia, not the carefree vacationing motorist from Munich she'd met on the way to Pau.

He bent his face very close to hers, overwhelming her with the stink of alcohol and garlic on his breath. "Let's go dancing," he said, and pushed her against a building easily, as if she were weightless.

She heard the laughter of his companions receding.

"Not here," she said, her heart flapping wildly. She offered a frightened smile. She'd walk with him for a little bit while she planned how to extricate herself.

He held her arm in a vise grip and began whistling the tune to the Nazi song, *Die Fahne hoch*. They'd walked a block, maybe two, and she was trembling, alternately pulling away and ahead, when he stopped whistling abruptly and said, *"Lass uns nicht warten.* Let's not wait." He pulled her into a nearby dark alley, pinning her to the wall.

She struggled to push him off, but he laughed a cackling, demented laughter, and dragged her, like a rag doll, deeper into the alley. Terror and bile rose to her throat when he began tearing at her blouse, grabbing the edge of the brassiere with clumsy fingers. The list! She had to save it and herself. He continued clawing at her and slobbering on her neck. She shoved her knee into his groin as hard as she could, but she must have kneed his thigh instead because he didn't react. Maybe he was too drunk. Then, she leaned into his face as if to kiss him and bit his lip hard as if it were a chunk of tough meat.

He howled in pain. It gave her a momentary advantage. She fumbled in her bag blindly, felt the Beretta's hardness, slipped it out of her bag, stuck it in his belly and pulled the trigger.

Instantly he fell, gasping; his hands clasped over his abdomen. Horrified, she tapped her chest to see if the list was still there. The officer's eyes remained opened, shocked at her audacity more than anything. Not sure if she had killed him, she pumped three more shots into his chest and ran.

Terrified she might be spotted by the hotel's night watchman stationed at the entrance, Simone ran around the building and slipped in through the dry-cleaning shop's back entrance. She saw herself in the long mirror: blouse torn and a wild look in her eyes. Unnerving thoughts shot through her mind. His cronies must have heard the shots. They'd be here any minute. She would be executed.

She had to tell Mme Travers what had happened. Simone raced up to Mme Travers' suite—she'd heard there was a bedroom behind the office. She looked in both directions along the hallway and seeing no one, knocked gently using the signal Mme had instructed her to use at Father Chapelle's door.

By now the rush of adrenaline had waned, and Simone began to tremble uncontrollably. Awareness dawned that she had likely unleashed the dogs. Killing a Nazi officer would bring dire consequences. She prayed fervently that Mme would understand.

It took a few moments, but Mme Travers opened the door. She stood there in a long flannel nightgown; her face creased from sleep and her normally well-coiffed hair disheveled. In this state, she looked old and frail. "Come in quickly," she said calmly. "Just tell me what happened."

Simone sat in the chair, trying to pull her blouse closed though the missing buttons made it impossible.

"Go ahead, it's been a bad week, but you are here, not arrested, so we will deal with it," Mme Travers said.

"I've been attacked."

353

"That's obvious. Who was it?"

Simone stammered, "A Nazi officer. He tried to rape me, pulled me into a dark alley. But I have the list... he didn't get it."

Mme Travers' eyes opened wider; her eyebrows arched. "How did you manage that?"

Simone eyed the patterns on the rug. "I shot him. He's dead."

"Where is he?"

"Let me think... Rue Mal-Joffre and Rue Gassion? No, not that corner."

Simone cracked her knuckles, looked up at Mme Travers. "Rue Maréchal Joffre and Rue Sully."

Mme Travers yawned. "Go to your room, wash up and compose yourself," she said calmly, as if she were dealing with nothing more serious than an unusually difficult hotel vendor. "*Merde*. Our people will clean it up. Never speak of it. Ever."

Next morning, Simone awoke with a massive headache. The sick feeling she'd experienced since the night before worsened. Hoping for relief, she opened the window to breathe some fresh air. She looked down. Below, a large cluster of Nazi soldiers: skull and crossbones on a sea of black caps, black boots hitting the pavement. She felt paralyzed with fear.

The clamminess of her body made it hard to dress for work, but she went down to the shop as usual.

When she opened the door, Monsieur Lavalle took one look at her. "Simone, I've never seen you looking like this. You look sick, take the day off."

"No, thank you. I'll be fine. Frau Weber is coming in for a fitting." Let me just stop by the kitchen to get some tea."

In the kitchen, she discovered that the entire hotel buzzed with news: a Nazi officer from a nearby regiment was missing and foul play was suspected. On her way back to the shop, she noticed them: placards posted at elevators, on restaurant doors and hallways.

Achtung/Attention

All guests and staff at the Continental and all neighboring hotels will be interrogated in connection with the disappearance of our officer, Oberstgruppenführer Krause. Make yourself available immediately. For each day no one comes forward with information, one of yours will be shot as an example. We will stop at nothing to find the perpetrator!

Simone's blood froze. The bloodhounds were on her trail.

Back at the shop, Frau Weber, a stout German matron, went on and on about the ungrateful, murderous French. *Hosenscheisser* a coward, she called the perpetrator. Her cheeks reddened with hatred. "I'd throttle him with my bare hands myself," she spat out dramatically.

Simone spiraled deeper into dread. The resolution to the disaster she'd created couldn't wait. She had to see Mme Travers—the woman who seemed able to make Solomonic decisions with total equanimity—to tell her of what she'd decided: she'd turn herself in. There was no other choice. Simone felt a pain squeeze her heart. What would become of Manuel with her gone? No, no pondering! She excused herself and cautiously climbed to the office, checking she wasn't seen. Her heart fluttered wildly as she ascended the stairs. A film of tears made everything look hazy.

Simone sat in the chair facing Mme Travers, trying to compose herself. She chewed her lip. Then she blurted out, "I am going to turn myself in. I wanted you to know first. I expect to be arrested and shot. I have only one request. Would you please take care of Manuel?"

Mme Travers listened, then pronounced, "We must never lose sight of our goal. Never. We do not allow the invaders to distract us. It was most fortunate you protected the list. Well done."

She then coughed and motioned for Simone to move closer. Simone leaned forward.

Mme Travers whispered, "It's been taken care of."

Simone's eyes widened, "How?"

"We have a connection to the German security head. We gave him a collaborator as the perpetrator of the killing, a real snake responsible for deaths of two Jewish children en route to a sanctuary."

Simone was speechless.

A hint of a smile lit up Mme Travers' face. "When we say Resistance, we mean it."

It was at this moment that Simone grasped the depth of commitment and solidarity of her fellow maquisards. She'd never betray any of them.

Now Mme Travers sat up straighter and reached for her silver cigarette case. She pulled out a cigarette, inserted it into an ivory holder, lit it and took a deep drag.

"Ready to pick up Ida Rubenstein, or has the incident frightened you out of your wits?"

Simone's head was still full of wonderment at being spared. "Oh, I am ready," she said with fervor.

"Remember, delivering the children is a danger both to them and yourself."

"You can count on me," Simone said, her heart still heavy with the shame of putting so many in danger. She stood up. There was important work to do, and she was ready.

Two weeks had passed since she'd killed the Nazi, yet Simone's distress over her act of violence continued to haunt her. It was so personal, so different from killing enemies at a distance at Ebro. She remembered riding in his car when he turned from a chivalrous man to a bigot. She had the instinct to get away from him. But killing him? Never. She still saw his eyes open wide in surprise, the blood oozing from his contorted mouth. She'd never get over it. She turned over in her mind for the thousandth time the reason she killed him. Panic, fear? No doubt. But was there something deeper, like his hatred of Jews or that he might take the list of children and doom them. There was that, but also her horror of being raped. It shocked her to consciously realize there were reasons to kill, that she could resort to violence when circumstances warranted. She tried to stay calm, to remind herself that with all the Nazi guests at the hotel, she'd be safer if she didn't show her roiling insides.

A knock at the door. "May I come in?"

Manuel's voice was a welcome salve for her jangled nerves. They'd play some games and she'd try, at least for a time, to forget. Manuel strode in, took off his hat, said wearily, "Just finished my shift."

Simone looked at the clock: 10 pm. "I don't remember you working this late before. Have your hours changed?"

"Well... sort of."

She didn't know what he meant but noticed his deepening voice and the faint fuzz on his lip. He was growing older. She should not be interrogating him. "Want to learn some new strategies for winning at poker?"

Manuel smiled, "Sure," he said.

They began to play.

"You are watching me," he said.

"Yes, I was. You look sad. What is it?"

He put his cards down, hesitated. "I miss Jacob."

"I miss him too," she said, surprised by his admission.

"What happened to the photo you took at Ebro of me, Jacob and the other man? I'd like to see it."

"The photo?" Simone slapped her forehead, momentarily stunned into silence. "I can't believe it. I have to confess, Manuel, I've done something very, very stupid."

Manuel looked at her, puzzled. "What?"

"I donated the camera to... let's say a good cause. It's no longer in my possession. In my haste, I forgot there was some undeveloped film in it."

"Can't you get it back?"

"Well... not the camera, but I'll ask about the photo. I promise." Now, reminded of it, she thirsted for that photo as much as the boy. Next time she'd ask Father Chapelle if perchance he'd found it when he developed the first roll of film from the Selfix.

They played for a while longer, but she noticed there was more than sadness in Manuel's face.

"Manuel, are you alright?"

His body tensed. "Yes, I'm fine. Stop watching me."

"You are keeping something from me."

Manuel looked up. Now he was observing her, assessing. After a long pause, he said, "I have a special job after my regular shift."

"Another job? Who gave it to you?" Simone felt a twinge of alarm.

"The head concierge."

She scanned Manuel's face for an explanation.

"Oh, I don't want to keep secrets from you, Simone. I'm a courier for the..." He paused, "Well, you know..." He leaned toward her, whispered, "The concierge is one of us."

Simone's eyes widened. "It's dangerous."

Manuel's face turned more serious. "Boys like me slip through unnoticed. Don't worry. I'll be fine, but for your safety I can't tell you more."

"I understand," she said, stood up and paced the room. "It's late. You need to sleep. So do I."

Manuel stacked the cards and reached for his hat. Before he made his exit, she hugged him. "Goodnight," he said.

Simone noticed he looked self-conscious. Maybe he was getting too grown up for hugs. Manuel slipped out of the room quietly and Simone felt a mixture of sadness and pride in his bravery.

42   IDA RUBINSTEIN

All afternoon Simone had been waiting for the driver: the child had to be delivered to Tarbes before the 10 p.m. Friday curfew. She grew more anxious by the minute.

He showed up at seven thirty in the evening, an expressionless young man—not much older than Manuel—sporting a leather jacket, a tweed cap and a cigarette dangling off his lip. He seemed nonchalant, but his nerves were betrayed by his concentration; he had little interest in conversation. "Let's go," he said brusquely as if she were late.

They drove in silence across the darkening streets. Remembering Father Chapelle's and Mme Travers' mentions of traitors, she wondered about the driver's loyalty. His detached manner compounded her disquiet.

Pedestrians scurried in and out of shops to complete their errands before the shops closed in observance of the curfew. If she hadn't known better, the boulevard might have given an impression of normalcy. But the sense that residents gritted their teeth at the brutal enemy simmered silently under the surface calm. To Simone, the tension in the air was palpable.

After many twists and turns, the driver stopped in front of an elegant edifice: same decorative stonework around the windows, same filigreed ironwork on the balconies and small windows on a mansard roof as she'd seen in Paris. She checked the number; the Rubinstein girl lived here.

Grumpily, the driver agreed to park nearby and wait for her and the child. No use frightening her with yet another unfamiliar face. Simone scanned the names on the directory and buzzed the apartment. A lively ring, incongruous with the occasion, greeted her. She entered the lobby and cracked her knuckles waiting for the elevator, glad for the brief reprieve. When it came, she slid closed the scissor gate. Filled with a sense of unease, she went up to the third floor.

A short black-haired woman opened the door a crack after Simone rang the bell. "Mme Travers sent me."

The woman's eyes darted around nervously. She opened the chain, let Simone into a vestibule and shook her hand more vigorously than the situation required.

"Mme Rubinstein, is Ida ready?"

Tears sprang out of the women's eyes, but she wiped them quickly, and said, "Come in, please."

She led Simone down a long corridor to a dining room, apparently ready for the Sabbath meal. A small girl with curious black eyes and black braids ending in red bows sat playing with a napkin ring, ignoring the visitor.

The table was set with care. China plates rimmed in gold, silver place settings, crystal glasses, silver candlesticks, an ornate Kiddush cup and a large challah made it look as if important company were expected.

"Who are you expecting for dinner, Mme Rubinstein?"

The woman's face crumpled. "It's just me and Ida."

"And your husband?"

Abruptly, the woman pulled Simone over to the side, put her finger to her lips and whispered, "Moshe was arrested on Monday. I don't know where they took him, but I wanted Ida to have a nice Shabbat before..."

A lump, the size of an orange, stood in Simone's throat. She glanced at her watch. So many barricaded streets. There was less than an hour to the curfew, and the trip could take as long. There was no time for dinner; they had to leave now.

Simone cleared her throat several times and began, "Mme Rubinstein..." then hesitated and tried again. "I am so sorry; we need to go now. I can't take a chance on being on the streets past the curfew."

Mme Rubinstein choked back tears. "Can I just give her a bowl of chicken soup before you go?"

Simone heard a horn honking. She didn't know if it was her driver. "Yes, but let's do this quickly."

While the mother went into the kitchen, Ida's fascination with the napkin ring waned. Her lip quivered. "I want Momma."

"Hello, I am Simone. Do you want to play a game with me?"

"Where is Momma?"

"She'll be right back; she's getting you some delicious soup."

"I am not hungry." Ida pounded her little fists on the table, making the glasses tinkle. "Where's Papa?"

"Listen, Ida, I will say some magic words. See if you can repeat them with me. It'll be fun, I promise."

Ida pouted and looked at Simone suspiciously. Simone began in a sing-song cadence: "*Notre Père qui es aux cieux...* Our father who art in heaven..."

It was the prayer children had recited at the monastery. Simone thought that if she could introduce it to Ida, it would be a useful step toward her new life. Even if she didn't memorize it now, she'd have to very soon.

Ida sat spellbound for a few moments; her eyes wide at the chanted strange words. When her mother walked in with the steaming bowl and set it in front of the girl, Ida exclaimed, "Papa is in heaven!"

Mme Rubinstein stood thunderstruck, choking back her tears. "No, silly goose; he will be home soon."

"I want to see him now!" the girl screamed and pounded the table, knocking over the bowl of soup onto her lap.

Her mother sprang into action, awakened from her agonized state, wiping the child's knees and belly with a towel and napkins. Then she picked Ida up and ran to change her dress and tights. Ida continued her gut-wrenching howls. It was hard to tell if it was the pain of a burn or the pain of loss. Simone understood the child's emotions viscerally; she'd experienced that ache and disorientation herself. She gasped at the memories—Maya's death, Jacob's. She had to be strong. It was lucky that mother and child had left the dining room. Simone needed to compose herself. She hadn't anticipated how wrenching this would be. For a moment, her fury at the Nazis was so powerful she could hardly breathe. But this was not the time for that. She had a job to do.

Repeated glancing at her watch didn't help. Simone tiptoed down the corridor until she saw an open door. It was a child's bedroom: a bed festooned in a pink gauze canopy and decals of elephants riding along the mid-section of the wall. Mme Rubenstein sat on the bed, cradling and rocking the girl whose chest still let out little gasps. Her crying had abated, but now she was firmly attached to her mother.

"I am so sorry, Mme Rubinstein, we have to leave now. We cannot delay any longer... It'll be too dark soon."

Mme Rubinstein nodded and stood up, still holding Ida. "We'll get your coat and bag now," she said softly to the girl and left the room.

To give mother and child privacy, Simone slipped out to wait in the foyer. Very quickly, mother and child reappeared. Ida wore a red cape.

"What do we have here? A Little Red Riding Hood," Simone exclaimed as cheerfully as she could muster, and extended her hand to the child. "Come, I will tell you a story," she said, but Ida stood in one spot, much too subdued for what had just taken place. Her unexpected stillness added to the women's anxiety.

Simone picked her up. The girl lay her head on Simone's shoulder as if she'd given up.

Mme Rubinstein handed Simone a small bag of Ida's belongings and a rag doll.

"You will have a lot of fun on this trip," the mother called out to Ida with forced cheer as Simone put her hand on the doorknob.

At that instant, the hysterical shrieking resumed full force. Ida flailed and screamed, "Momma! Momma!"

Simone struggled to keep her from falling and hurting herself. "We will take good care of her," she called out, then immediately walked out and shut the door behind her with more force than she intended.

The slam shocked the girl into calming a little, but she made hiccuping, gulping sounds. When Simone slid the elevator's scissor gate closed, the mother's wailing was clearly audible. Ripped from her mother's chest, Ida turned and grabbed at the gate, clawing, and screaming as if she knew it would be the last time she'd hear the sound of her mother's voice.

The elevator arrived at the ground floor after an agonizing, endless ride. Simone held on to Ida and her belongings and made a quick exit to the street. She kept repeating to the child, "We will have a nice trip. You'll see..."

Ida quieted momentarily.

Simone entered the waiting car, settling the bereft child on her lap to cuddle her. She gave her the rag doll, but Ida was disconsolate. She threw the doll on the floor and resumed shrieking.

The driver turned around, gave her a disgusted look and spat out, "Make her shut up! Now!"

His voice frightened Ida. She clutched Simone's jacket and went quiet as a frightened puppy. Simone's heart ached. This was just the first time. How would she bear the pain time and again?

When she next saw Father Chapelle, after several weeks and five nerve-racking rescues of other children, Simone asked him about the undeveloped film she'd left in the donated camera.

"Ah, yes... I've been meaning to give you these." Father Chapelle pulled out an envelope from deep in his desk drawer. "With the increasing arrests, I've so much on my mind, I almost forgot about this."

"Thank you, Father. I understand. I've been preoccupied with the children and their grieving parents. I shan't ever forget the mothers' sorrowful expressions. It was good Manuel was with me when I took little Avram Katz; he was a handful."

"They'll survive and maybe forget..." He paused. "The youngest ones, I mean."

"But their parents never will. It'll pain them for the rest of their lives." Neither will I, she thought. The visceral pain of pulling the children away from their parents haunted her. They came to her in dreams. Once she dreamed Maya hadn't died, that she'd rescued her and took her to a convent in Haifa. Each mission became harder, not easier.

After picking up some new baptismal certificates to work on, Simone left, anxious to see the contents of the envelope. She hurried to the hotel.

She ran upstairs, tossed her jacket on the chair, and sat on her bed to examine the photos. She opened the envelope hastily, spilling its contents. Several fell on her lap; others landed on the bed and a few on the floor. She grabbed the nearest photo. In it, a group of men stood in a wooded clearing, some with rifles slung on their shoulders, others making a victory sign. She did not recognize them. Perhaps an encampment at another battle. Teruel?

She realized she didn't know when Aleksander had arrived in Spain, and in which battles he had fought. A vague memory that his commander had assigned him to lead a photographic unit scratched at her head. In the next few photos, she did recognize the men: smiling faces, hunger-sunken cheeks. They were members of her Botwin company. She closed her eyes. How many of them had survived? She pushed the thought away. She wanted to find the photo Manuel had asked about.

Turning the next photo over, the memory of the moment rushed back in with the force of a hurricane. How could she have forgotten it? It was the photo she herself had taken of her three men: Aleksander, Jacob, and Manuel on the fateful night before the big battle. It was near sunset, the light making shadows on the men's faces. She remembered how Aleksander wanted her to be in the photo, but she'd insisted she'd take it. Perhaps this was why he had persuaded her to take the camera. He wanted her to have this memory of him. She felt aggravated with herself for having swept it to the back of her mind. She stood up and leaned the photo on the dresser mirror, making a mental note to get a frame when things calmed. She stepped back and looked at the image. Her heart ached seeing Jacob's unshaven face staring at her. How tenderly he'd handed her the rifle with better safety. And what had happened to Aleksander? Where was he? The pained look in his eyes when he'd left her on the hillside was still fresh in her mind. She bent down and picked up the last photo that had slipped to the floor.

She gasped. Were her eyes fooling her? The image she saw shocked and confused her. Staring at her were two familiar faces. No! It couldn't be true. But there, in front of her very eyes, stood Bronka nestled close to Aleksander, looking up at him with a victorious smile, her braids encircling her head like a crown. Aleksander held one arm somewhat stiffly on her shoulder, his gaze toward the photographer.

How? Where? Simone squinted into the photo and recognized the building behind them: the storied Polonia Palace hotel in Warsaw with its unmistakable arched windows and mansard roof. How could she? Simone felt weak; her mind swirled, making ridiculous speculations. None made any sense.

She kept blinking, hoping the image in her trembling hand was a hallucination. But Bronka remained in place, looking angelic, as if she had finally achieved her highest aspiration—romantic love materializing in Aleksander's flesh.

Such betrayal by both of them! Simone felt nauseated and paced the room, unable to sort out her feelings. She struggled to remember. What exactly had she written in that letter she'd posted to Bronka from Palestine? What had she said to Aleksander about her business partner? She didn't remember saying much. She considered a thousand scenarios and discarded each. Then, slowly, recognition dawned. Maybe it was just dumb fate that threw them together. An unfortunate coincidence. Would this discovery tarnish her feelings toward them?

She sat numbly on the bed with a searing headache and picked up the photo again. Tears clouded her vision as she sifted images in her mind, trying to bring up the good memories of each of them: Bronka's beaming face on the first day in their shop; the Parisian breakfast with Aleksander, how proudly he'd introduced her to the café owner.

After staring at the photo for a long while, she tore it exactly down the middle, separating them.

43   IN PARIS ONCE AGAIN

In August 1944, Parisians could finally breathe. Though General Eisenhower had not accepted Germany's unconditional surrender until May 1945, Paris had already been liberated, and its traumatized citizens threw off the yoke of a four-year occupation. Simone managed to arrive in the fall on a train overcrowded with internally displaced people trying to restart their lives. But the city's mood was hardly receptive. Fierce winds blew leaves across neglected streets, reminding Simone of humanity scattered by war, wondering if they could ever be reconstituted into families.

On her very first walk through Paris after liberation, Simone passed the Madeleine church, not expecting to be surprised by ghosts. She had worked hard to banish much of what had transpired over the eight years since she'd left her Warsaw home, and though it didn't come naturally, she practiced looking forward lest she become a prisoner of the past. She knew finding a place to live in the devastated city would not be easy; the streets, still gray with the pallor of war, mirrored her inner self. Yet she walked toward a rental agency filled with anticipation. How would it be, living here in his beloved city?

As she turned the corner, she could have sworn she saw his shadow —Aleksander's tall figure with wild, wind-blown hair. Surely, he'd take her in his arms, press his body against hers and plant a warm kiss on her mouth with his full lips. She could almost taste his salty-sweet saliva. A shudder of intense yearning traveled through her body. Some memories could be terrifyingly vivid, yet false. She hastened her pace. It was no time to linger or to admit she'd once been someone else. The naive girl who had first met Aleksander was now all too well-schooled in life. There was little doubt in her mind that the wars, and especially all the Resistance missions, had changed her. She had become hardened, more confident in her ability to summon up courage when it was needed most and as much as she regretted admitting it to herself, she was prepared to use the Beretta if children's lives were threatened by the Nazis or collaborators, and she felt less guilt about it.

She recalled how she had shot at a collaborator who stepped out of the shadows when she followed Manuel on a mission to lay grenades. After that, Manuel begged her not to do it. Now it's my job to protect you, not the other way around, he had said.

On her way to the rental office, she passed Place de la Concorde. Her eyes misted, seeing the majestic fountains Aleksander had explained in vivid detail. The city whispered of longing; she felt its magnetic pull. What if he had survived? She discarded the thought promptly, remembering the betrayal. He'd not find her anyway. She was now Simone Bonheur and planned to remain so. That name had saved her life and helped her save others. She was keeping it. It was her badge of courage.

If not visions of Aleksander, Simone was accosted by dramatic street scenes. One in particular stayed with her, a stubborn memory that lodged in her brain. A crowd of men, women, and children most sallow-faced, thin and bedraggled, stood around a small square cheering. Simone approached the carnival-like scene to see what was going on.

A middle-aged woman sat tied to a chair. Her eyes were large with terror, her nylon slip inadequate coverage for her shame. One man shaved her head calmly as if this were an ordinary day at the barber shop. The other held her shoulder steady with a tattooed muscled arm. Her hair fell around her shoulders, then gathered at her bare feet in brown, compost-like piles. Some stuck to her face wet with tears and sweat. Half her head shaved with furrows like a freshly plowed field. An odd image that seemed to entertain the crowd and elicit a fresh wave of jeers. Summary executions of collaborators and public head-shavings of women who had slept with the enemy were not uncommon. The scene caused an eruption of cold sweat on Simone's forehead. The scene shook her deeply, yet she was glad that her recent history of taking part in violence had not killed her ability to empathize, to feel.

The visit to the real estate office turned out well; Simone quickly accepted the first apartment she saw. Not many had money for rentals, but she was lucky; Mme Travers had given her a modest sum to make a start in Paris. Montparnasse, like the rest of the arrondissements, had been drained of vitality. Many buildings stood in a dilapidated condition, resembling Parisian women who'd been reduced to prostituting themselves so they could feed their children. Yet Simone had faith that the artistic energy that had resided there between the world wars would return. If she had no hope for the future, not only she, but Manuel would be lost. She'd issued this stern warning to herself more than once.

Of all the city's privations, hunger was the worst. Simone and Manuel stood in endless queues daily. Her calves cramped with exhaustion. A new rationing system attempted to correct the Vichy failures, but there just wasn't enough food. Her first successful purchase of food after three hours in a queue was shocking in its meagerness. She scored three ounces of meat for the week and a single small egg. If she had a child under three, she could get three ounces of butter a month and milk, but all she had was a hungry teenager. He'd have to buy his own ration. She rushed home madly to cook the meat before the electricity was cut as it was limited to a few erratic hours a day. If she didn't make it in time, her hard-won bit of protein would spoil without refrigeration.

The fact that life was difficult didn't trouble Simone. Now nearing thirty, she was determined to live, really live. It was high time. Manuel had survived the Resistance missions physically unscathed, but she was unequipped to tally the emotional damage of all he'd lived through. No matter, he was with her. That was enough; they'd get through the lean times together. And just walking the streets where she'd had her first taste of love, or perhaps something she mistook for love, was enough to convince Simone she'd made the right decision to return.

An apartment of her own helped ground her. Whenever she could manage to silence the rush of thoughts about her family's fate, she felt fortunate to be here, in Paris, with Manuel, who gave her life purpose. The third-floor walk-up on Rue Boisonnade, a side street off Boulevard Raspail, was plain but adequate because she could subdivide the living room to make a private, if tiny, bedroom for Manuel. He was a young man of seventeen who needed his privacy. She installed a shelf in the bathroom to segregate her few toiletries, so they'd not get in the way of Manuel's hair combs, brushes, and pomade for his ducktail pompadour. There was also a razor, blades, and his shaving mug; he was becoming a man.

When she instructed him to rinse the sink clean of facial hair and soap scum after his morning routine, he glared at her with his jaw clenched and uttered a barely audible, "Sorry."

"It's fine, you'll learn," she said.

Sometimes Simone wondered if mothers felt, as she did, a small bit of regret that a child who could once be cuddled had grown into a gangly, slightly bent, pimply teenager who could no more be embraced than a porcupine.

The best feature of the apartment was the light let in through the tall, narrow windows. Nowadays they needed the light not only to lift their spirits, but because when electricity was cut, they could read *Le Monde* by the windows.

The specter of her family's uncertain fate was never far from Simone's mind, but news of Warsaw's devastation discouraged her from thinking of returning. With the war over, many agencies had established lists of survivors: the International Red Cross, Joint Distribution Committee and Refugee Aid, the Camps Commission, Central Commission of Jewish Assistance Organizations, the Polish Red Cross, Jewish Agency for Palestine, DP registers. Simone visited every one of them, placed and read dozens of personal ads in "Looking for Relatives" columns. Nothing. Each negative result was a new jolt to her guts, but she still held out hope they might be found. There were so many of them; someone must have survived.

Sometimes she calmed herself, knowing Momma had taken the children to Kiev. Surely, things there must have been better than the rumors circulating about the Warsaw ghetto and the death camps. She had refused to believe tales of inhuman atrocities. But when news of what the American soldiers had discovered in Nazi concentration camps all over Poland was reported by respectable news sources, Simone vowed never to return.

The first time she'd come across an account of General Eisenhower's visit to a German internment camp expressing his anger at the bestial treatment of humans, she crumpled the paper into a ball and hurled it across the room, knocking over and shattering her favorite faience bud vase. Soon, more such news flooded the papers and airwaves; there was no escaping it. With each new piece of news, images of her mother, or sisters in the striped garb of concentration camp inmates came to her. She saw their terrified faces clawing at electrified fences or skeletal figures picking out scraps of food from garbage cans. She struggled to push away the unfathomable horror of these images. They had to have survived in Kiev.

Her brain played tricks. Each day she woke up determined to find at least some of them on the survivor lists she scoured daily—even one would be thrilling. Sometimes she imagined running into Leya or Bayla on the street and them falling into each other's arms, holding on for dear life till tears of joy threatened to drown them. For now, all she had in this world was Manuel.

———

After she'd found a place to live, Simone struggled to figure out how to get a job before her money ran out and before something disastrous happened to Manuel. Manuel, she suspected, had begun stopping in a particular bar on Champs Élysées. It was said to be a hangout for unsavory types, including some US Army deserters, who worked on recruiting middlemen to fence black market goods. She was terrified of Manuel getting lured into that world, a universe unto its own where mob bosses ruled, and men and their molls were completely dispensable.

One day she thought she'd seen him going in there after they came away from a queue empty-handed and she turned to return home. That evening she waited up to confront him.

"You walked into that bar? Everyone knows it's a dive for mob types." Simone couldn't contain her anger. "Why, why on earth?" she shouted. She had always been calm with him, but fear for his safety got the better of her.

"So what? I want us to be able to eat," he said defiantly.

"We do eat. No princely portions, but you aren't dead yet," Simone fumed.

Manuel stood there truculent, running his fingers through his thick mane and a surprised look in his eyes. He'd never seen that side of Simone. Suddenly, he raised his shirt. "Here, look at this. Do I look like a man or a scrawny rat?"

It was true; his ribs stuck out and his belly was concave.

"The black market is full of thugs, common criminals. I don't want it to be your introduction to life," she said quietly.

"You've cared for me all these years, Simone. It's my turn to help."

"Not this way, it isn't." She wanted to hug him but didn't dare offend his effort at being a man.

"You tell me how," he yelled and walked out of the room, slamming the door.

Manuel had been her faithful companion during the worst years of her life and quite possibly among the youngest members of the Resistance. She remembered all too well the nights she'd spent consumed with worry about him when he began going out to help on jobs—blowing up bridges and trains—with men of the Resistance. He'd already shown exceptional bravery in his young life, but now he was at a vulnerable juncture, neither child nor man, when everything could go to hell.

Simone vowed to steer him in a better direction. It was true, he wasn't her child. It even seemed ridiculous now, she at twenty-eight and Manuel almost eighteen, living together they could be mistaken for lovers. But she'd assumed responsibility for him and would do anything, even give her life for him.

It had been a long day, and Manuel's outburst disconcerted her. She went into the bathroom to wash her face, brush her teeth, and get some sleep. Maybe things would seem brighter in the morning. She stared at the mirror and noticed for the first time a silver hair among her curls. Life had moved at such breakneck speed since she left Warsaw, she hardly noticed getting older.

Her eyes remained on her image, but her mind moved on. Sometimes one had to look at the mirror and see behind its surface.

There were days when all the pain she'd caused her mother, Golda, Eli and Bronka ate at her. This was one of these days. And not just them. She'd not loved Jacob enough. She had pulled children away from their parents. And though it ultimately saved them, she'd become the agent of torment, inured so she could do the job. And she'd killed. Yes, evil men, but they had once been someone's child. Had she become hard like the heavy, cold slug of the iron she'd used as a girl in her Warsaw home?

Simone sat on her bed, dressing. She picked up her shoe and looked with concern at the deteriorating sole: no money to have the pumps repaired. The miles of streets she hoofed daily looking for work recorded on the soles. She was prepared to take any job, nothing would be too demeaning, but work was as difficult to get as food and electricity. She was tired of hearing, "Sorry, we don't need anyone."

One day she passed a photo shoot on a dilapidated street. She stopped to look. It was amazing how they managed to mount huge floodlights on trucks to illuminate the young model in a dazzling dress against the bleakness of the street. A mob had gathered to ogle. Such display of extravagance was new in postwar Paris. The amazed faces of the women and catcalls of workmen made it clear just how desperately the city needed something dramatic to shed the wartime gloom.

Simone stood in the crowd, unable to take her eyes off the waif-like model. The poor girl was so thin she looked ready to pass out at any moment, but the flared, calf-length organza dress shimmered. Simone speculated it must have been supported by layers of stiffened muslin underskirts and padding on the hips. The girl's torso sported a wasp-like waist and pert, uplifted breasts.

And suddenly, Simone was struck by a thunderbolt. No woman could look like this without properly engineered undergarments. Perhaps her skill as a corsetiere and brassiere designer would come in handy to the creators of such dresses. Simone knew she could design brassieres and corsets that would not only be as beautiful as the dresses, but *also* perform well undergirding the dresses, skirts, and cinched-waist jackets. This could be a ticket to survival!

44 LE PETIT THÉÂTRE DE LA MODE

Simone stood in yet another queue, but this one excited her. Though it was a freezing March day in 1945, she hardly noticed the cold. A glamorous show had opened its doors to the public at the Louvre. On her first try, Simone couldn't get in because the crowd was so thick. Smartly attired men and women disembarked black, chauffeur-driven cars. The crowd parted to let them in. Must be foreign diplomats or tourists, Simone observed; few Parisian women had anything fresh to wear. Day after day, Simone attempted to get in and finally succeeded a day before the exhibition closed.

The grand Le Petit Théâtre de la Mode show dazzled Simone. Fashion critics and journalists crowed about its extravagance. For Simone, the glamour was a sign the world was finally emerging from the dark days of war. It felt like an intravenous shot of optimism.

One hundred and seventy female figures, one-third normal size, populated the exhibition, exuding beauty and refinement. With rationing still in effect, the designers had used audacious amounts of material for each lavish outfit. At this rate, a dress for a full-size model might use twenty yards of fabric! Defying wartime scarcity, the tiny mannequins sported jewelry to scale designed by Cartier! Milliners made dramatic hats and beneath them, top coiffeurs created elaborate hairdos. Huge teams of craftspeople employed extraordinary imagination to secure materials that were scarce, or made substitutions for those simply unavailable: leather, felt, fur and even straw.

Simone ran straight home, excited; her head buzzed with ideas. Sitting down with a cup of tea, she contemplated a strategy to get into the haute couture field. Papers brimmed with articles about how fashion designers like Nina Ricci, Jean Patou, Christian Dior and others would restore the city. Simone thirsted to be a part of the burgeoning haute couture field that was bringing life back to Paris. No, more than thirsted: she resolved to be a part of it, one way or another. The tea cooled. She hadn't taken a sip; she was still immersed in thought.

She remembered the tiny dresses she had sewn all those years before for the daughter of one of Momma's wealthy clients. I do have an eye for design, she reassured herself. Since paper was scarce, like everything else, she pulled out the old, yellowed sheets of paper that lined the bureau drawers, and began drawing furiously. In that instant, she no longer felt like a refugee, a woman who'd lost her way. She felt like an artist, feverishly pulling concepts from her brain as they bubbled directly to her hand.

The work she'd done for Father Chapelle—the precision, the imagination and finesse—had prepared her for this. Now it was fanciful designs for brassieres with feather boning to support breasts, covered with exotic flower-patterned lace. She had no idea if such fabric really existed, yet she was sure that if one of those renowned couturiers liked her design, they'd find a way to realize it. She drew sketches for corsets with built-in hip padding, and boning extending above the waist so it could be cinched in. She felt like a sculptor, not one working with marble or stone, but one who would sculpt a living, breathing woman.

The work excited her. It made her feel in control of her fate, the way she did back in Warsaw when she commanded her own shop and customers clamored for appointments. Now she only needed to find an outlet for all her undergarment sketches. She was convinced that someone in the couture trade would be interested but didn't know who, or how to get to such an individual.

The next morning, in a rush of energy, Simone rummaged through her purse, coat pockets and dresser drawers for her rapidly dwindling change. She ran to the central post office to place a call to Mme Travers. The call was expensive, but she came away from the post office elated. Now she had the name of a woman—Cécile Duval—and an address of a café where former members of the Resistance liked to gather and reminisce over a strong cup and a good smoke.

"You'll like her," Mme Travers had said. "She was a member of the Polish intelligence unit based in Paris during the war, a brave woman, just like you."

She ran home, picked up a folder of her sketches and ran out again. It was already late afternoon. Any later and the woman might be home trying to scrape up dinner. She borrowed a rusty bicycle from a neighbor and pedaled as fast as she could through the empty streets.

At the café, a few men of various ages sat playing chess and smoking, but most tables stood unoccupied. Simone spotted Cécile immediately, as she was the only woman at the café. The woman wore a stylish hat with a long red feather and sat one knee over the other, smoking a Gauloise. A thin ribbon of smoke curled above her, but the newspaper lay on the table folded and apparently unread, with a pair of gloves on top. She looked as if she were just waiting for Simone.

Simone couldn't tell how well the woman knew Mme Travers because there was hardly a sign of recognition when Simone uttered her name. Cécile assessed Simone, then launched directly into the matter at hand in a businesslike manner. "Let me see what you've brought."

Simone opened the folder and moved it closer.

Cécile stared intensely at the first drawing of a brassiere, nodding, and absentmindedly flicking the ashes on the floor. "C'est merveilleux!" she exclaimed.

They chatted briefly. Simone told her about her experience in the business in Warsaw and at the dress alteration job at the hotel in Pau. Cécile didn't say much but put her cigarette out in the ashtray and shuffled through the drawings, inspecting each one carefully, holding them at different angles. Simone didn't take her eyes off Cécile. There was something arresting about her dark eyes with their abundant crinkles radiating toward her temples, and her determined full-lipped mouth. She'd been beautiful once.

At the end of the meeting, Cécile pulled out a sheaf of crisp bills from her purse and handed them to Simone discreetly. "I hope this will cover this group," she said. "I'd like to see more."

She liked them! Simone's heart leaped. Not wanting to appear greedy or desperate, Simone didn't count the money, just slipped it into her jacket pocket.

Cécile stood up and handed her a business card for an address on Avenue Montaigne, Paris. "Go there tomorrow morning if you want to get involved in this line of work. Don't let it frighten you," she said with a crooked smile.

"Frighten? Why?"

"It's cutthroat." With that, Cécile stood up, picked up her gloves and bid Simone goodbye.

Next morning, Simone styled her hair and dressed in her only decent dress—navy with white polka dots that Mme Travers had gifted her before she left Pau—then headed out to the address Cécile had given her. The possibility of a job thrilled her. Even if it didn't work out, Cécile was interested in buying more of her sketches. And Simone had so many new ideas!

"Excuse me, can you direct me to this address?"

Simone stopped a well-dressed woman and showed her the business card. The woman looked her over. "You are going to visit the *Maison De La Mode* dressed like this?"

Simone blanched. Her heart pounded. "Why? What's wrong with my dress?"

"Everyone knows it's a fashion Mecca. Where have you been?"

The woman gave her a puzzled look and pointed to the right. "Make a turn there, you won't miss it. It's near the corner."

The woman's words bothered Simone. Did she look too dowdy for this atelier? Her confidence now somewhat bruised, Simone stood in front of the five-story façade, gathering her courage. A uniformed doorman noticed her. She showed him Cécile's business card and he directed her to the second floor.

Filled with trepidation, she walked upstairs and down a long, wide corridor painted a stark white, reaching a huge room humming with activity. She stood at its threshold, trying to make herself inconspicuous, surveying the scene. Women of all ages, most in simple white smocks, stood around giant tables handling yards of white fabrics with gloved hands. Many wore little pouches around their necks from which they pulled pins and small scissors. Behind them hung boards festooned with patterns made of delicate tissue paper. Simone could see herself among these women.

A bald man approached her with a quizzical look. She stated her name and explained why she'd come. "Yes! I've already seen your drawings, Cécile brought them by last night," he said.

His warm handshake and smile gave Simone an extra measure of self-assurance.

"I am Pierre Durand, manager of the dress atelier."

"My skills are in undergarments, not dresses."

"I admire your honesty, but Mme Cécile, the owner's sister, and I already discussed your abilities." Durand smiled and patted Simone's shoulder.

She felt herself blushing.

"Don't look so surprised; skills like yours are valuable to us. We depend on properly designed corsets and brassieres to make our *Style de Guêpe* fashions work."

It was clear now the wasp-waisted look on the model she'd seen was not accidental. Simone noticed some of the women casting glances in her direction and made a sudden decision to speak up. "When can I start?" The words sprang out so quickly she worried M. Durand would think her overly aggressive, but this was a once-in-a-lifetime chance. She had to grab it.

"Today, if you like." Durand smiled and shook her hand.

"I'd like that very much."

She spent the day being introduced to other staff, securing her sewing machine and tools of the trade. Much of what she was shown was thrillingly familiar: super-sharpened scissors, pincushions, chalk markers and thimbles almost the same as she'd used back home. To her, the whirring of the sewing machines filling the space was the sound of a happy Mozart sonata.

By the day's end, Simone wasn't tired. Energized, she ran home, only stopping at the black market for a baguette at five times normal price; it was worth it! At home, there was still some leftover cheese a neighbor had brought from the country. She'd celebrate with Manuel.

45 JEAN PETIT

Simone's career as a master corsetiere took her into a long series of haute couture ateliers. Her artistry surpassed that of her peers in the business, and she received promotions and raises that surprised even her. She was headhunted time and again by the best of the fashion houses, all of which engaged in vicious competition. One atelier's loss was another's gain. It pleased Simone that her brassiere designs weren't simply prosaic containers for women's breasts: they were more like bejeweled crowns for the most iconic parts of the female anatomy. They allowed women to luxuriate in their bodies.

The first time she'd accepted a new position, she felt a tiny bit of regret leaving dear M. Durand who had given her a chance in this ruthless business, but the offer was too good to pass up. It meant a better life for Manuel and her. She felt acknowledged and grateful that her training by Momma proved to be their lifesaver. Sometimes she thought of opening her own atelier, but the notion of undertaking it without the kind of collaborator Bronka had been sent her mind into a tailspin. The last thing she needed was a disloyal partner. And she liked the freedom her status in the field gave her. She didn't need to worry about business aspects; she could focus on the artistry.

Now that her financial life had been secured, Simone turned with renewed vigor to the one mission that consumed her: finding her family.

She'd exhausted nearly every avenue, but every now and then a crumb of new information trickled out.

One day, after work, Simone relaxed on the sofa, perusing the daily paper. She'd gotten into the habit of kicking her slippers off and curling up on the sofa with a cup of strong tea nearby. She saw a headline that caught her attention. She tried to read the article but at first all she could see was the word "Kiev," "Kiev," "Kiev," on every line, like a procession of black ants in her visual field. It was as if she had been afflicted with a strange eye disease. She shook her head. No! Then her breath froze in her chest. All of them gone? Impossible! Yet here it was in black and white just like the news of Auschwitz she'd heard before: an account of the Jews of Kiev, detailing how in just two days in 1941, all them had been shot in Babi Yar, a forest ravine near the city.

Kiev! Where Momma had gone for safety with all the children. Simone could not fit this idea in her brain. Cold sweat flowed down her neck and back, then everything went black.

"Simone! Simone, what happened?" Manuel had come home a few minutes before. He stepped into the living room after hearing a thud and lifted her head.

She opened her eyes wide. "Have I fallen?"

"It looks like you fainted. Are you ill? Shall I call the doctor?"

"No, Manuel, the world is ill," she said slowly, her voice thick and weary. A remembrance of Tisha B'Av flashed before her. She could almost hear the prayers and heart-rending lamentations in the Warsaw synagogue. The saddest day on the Jewish calendar commemorated the destruction of the temple in Jerusalem and other calamities that befell the Jewish people. When she was young, she hadn't quite understood the depth of her father's sorrow. Now, she felt it in her gut. *This* would be her personal Tisha B'Av. She promised herself to fast and stop at the synagogue on every Tisha B'Av to share her mourning with nameless others.

Manuel helped her to the sofa.

She handed him the paper, pointing to the article.

"It's horrible, but what does this have to do with you?" he asked after scanning it.

She told him and for the first time could not hold back her tears. A dam that had been holding her pain in check for years finally gave way.

Something that could never be repaired broke inside her. She felt completely naked; her weakness exposed for him to see.

This time it was he who held her, then patted her hand awkwardly. "But we are here. We made it."

It wasn't until much later that she reconsidered. The world wasn't entirely devoid of her family. She had a sister in Israel. She allowed herself to say it out loud for the first time since that fateful day set her life on such an unexpected course. The thought gave her little relief. Golda would be far more problematic to contact. That disgraceful ending. Could she ever face her?

The discovery that her family had almost certainly been slaughtered had a devastating effect on Simone's creativity. Ever since she'd read the article, it was a chore to get herself up in the morning and go to work. It was as if the spigot of ideas had been turned off. She'd chastise herself for sketches she'd made. Crumple them into balls and hurl them into the wastebasket. It took months for her to regain a sense of balance and self, to restart her previous love affair with design.

By 1950, Simone's savings had grown enough to buy her own apartment in Saint-Germain-des-Prés. What attracted Simone to the neighborhood was the intellectual energy emanating from literary cafés, jazz clubs, bookstores, and the nearby university. Though Simone had not had the chance to get a higher education, she still wanted to learn. Perhaps her former intense desire to 'swallow the world,' as Bronka had called it, had diminished now that she'd seen its ugly underbelly, but she still maintained the desire to taste everything new: music, literature, anything, and everything in the arts. She also noticed that unlike other parts of the city, the races mingled here easily, adding to the vitality of the neighborhood.

The new apartment was larger and had indoor plumbing, unlike many of the dwellings in Saint-Germain-des-Prés. She luxuriated in having her own toilet and a deep soaking tub. Manuel finally had a proper bedroom and bath of his own. Now in his early twenties, he wasn't earning enough to live apart from her. He had had a succession of temporary jobs and was spending more time outside the home.

Simone had introduced him to a fashion photographer, Jean Petit, a handsome, somewhat reserved man whom she got to know well. He was sought by many of the best fashion houses in the same way they courted her for her design talent. Jean took Manuel under his wing, inviting him to photo shoots all over Paris and to his darkroom, introducing him to his unique film-developing techniques. Eventually this led to a job in a photo studio, making Manuel happy that he could finally help Simone by paying a part of her mortgage.

There was nothing petite about Jean Petit. He was much taller than typical Frenchmen and had large hands, perfectly suited to juggling his Rolleiflex cameras. She'd observed him sometimes in his photo shoots. He had a mop of straight brown hair that often fell over his right eye and flopped back down as soon as he brushed it away. His hazel gaze was intense as if he were pinning the subject down for inspection.

Contrary to the charming persona he showed her, he was a tyrant with the models, directing them on how to move, where to stand, how long to hold a provocative pose, when to smile and when to look inscrutable.

At first, she thought him unapproachable. When he'd finished his photo shoot the day, she'd first met him, he threw her a warm, toothy smile and said, "In the mood for an aperitif? I know a great place."

Then, before she had a chance to reply, he took her arm. "Come, it will relax you."

And she decided not to resist.

She hadn't quite realized how the absence of male companionship impacted her outlook on the world until she'd met Jean. Like her, he was lonely, and they began spending more time together. Being with Jean lifted her spirits. Despite her professional success, a sense of failure as a woman had cleaved to her since Palestine and became like skin, a part of her anatomy.

It didn't take long for Simone and Jean to become lovers. At first, they snatched solitary moments when Manuel was out, but after a while Jean stayed overnight and Manuel never so much as raised his eyebrows seeing Jean at breakfast.

As if her eyes were windows with years of grime cleaned off, the world began to look brighter, despite all its imperfections. Simone luxuriated in making love after so long. She liked Jean's musky smell and the sleepy look of his eyelids in the morning before they shared their first cup of coffee. Almost as soon as they became involved, Simone realized that now she actually enjoyed sex and that she had buried this need of hers for far too long. Like discovering that her design talent could bring satisfaction, her sexuality gave her new energy, a kind of zest for life she had never experienced.

Jean was neither as romantic as Aleksander nor as sensitive as Jacob. The best thing about him was that he knew how to make her laugh; she'd forgotten the sound of her own laughter. In the evenings, he liked to make her tea, and they'd sit snuggled on the couch with Jean telling her funny stories about growing up on a farm in Normandy. Simone was careful not to disclose much about herself, and Jean didn't insist. He liked talking about himself so much that sometimes she thought him incredibly self-centered.

Often, they'd promenade along the Seine. Most of the time the walks were companionable and pleased her. It was better than roaming the streets alone as she'd done many times, but the walks also brought back memories of Paris with Aleksander and occasionally reduced her to silence. Then Jean would be alarmed and ask, "Have I said something to offend you?"

"No, not at all," she'd say.

"What is it? Are you carrying some deep dark secret?"

"Maybe," she'd say.

Jean, whose family had suffered their share of wartime losses, must have understood. She did not want to talk about Palestine, Spain, or her Resistance missions. She was glad to have participated, but the killings— though necessary—she'd never feel proud of those. On this day she regaled Jean with stories about her school days and the teachers whose ideas had opened her eyes. "Mrs. Janina made me fall in love with Paris and French fashion. She's at least one reason why I'm still here."

"What's the other reason?"

"Never mind. I am here, aren't I?" And she went on to talk about Mr. Gutkind. "Can you believe, way back when... he dangled the notion that women could be what they wanted to be. It was quite the revelation. And Mrs. Mayer, the history teacher, introduced me to pacifism," she said and laughed.

"What's so funny?"

"The one idea that didn't exactly stick."

46 ADINA

On a sunny Sunday, Jean and Simone strolled by the Seine. She could never get enough of watching the artists at work on the riverbank.

Jean was unusually quiet this day. All of a sudden, he said, "I want to tell you something, but promise you won't tell you heard it from me."

Simone's eyes widened. "I had no idea you were harboring a secret."

"Your son, Manuel, has a lover."

She didn't know what surprised her more: that he thought Manuel was her son, or that he'd matured so quickly. She decided not to correct Jean. Maybe that's what he'd told Jean. "I am not surprised. Manuel has become a charming and confident young man. He used to be so shy," she said.

Jean grinned. "He certainly has no difficulty engaging the models at photo shoots in conversation and taking them at the end of a day to smoky jazz clubs."

Simone thought of Manuel's habit of coming home very late and if she was still up, coming into her bedroom to regale her with stories of Duke Ellington and the many African American servicemen he'd met in the jazz clubs, but he'd not mentioned the girl. She turned to Jean, "So who is this girl? Have you met her?"

"A beautiful model, Adina Carlsbach. Remember the young woman I pointed out one day in a restaurant?"

"Oh, her? She's stunning, hard to forget." Simone remembered the black-haired girl, who stood in a group of other models, looking younger and more willowy than the rest. Her face appeared nearly translucent, delicate as Sèvres porcelain.

"What a frightened rabbit she is," Jean said.

At first, Simone was surprised at Jean's characterization but soon reflected and said, "Who hasn't experienced trauma in the last years? Everyone has a dark story lurking beneath the new tender shoots of life."

Jean nodded. "Adina is a reflection of Manuel. He's super sensitive to suffering. I think he feels a real connection to her."

After Simone brought up Adina's name, Manuel spoke of her, but infrequently; he appeared reluctant to divulge too much. This signaled to Simone that he was falling in love with the girl. Now, she wanted to meet Adina more than ever, but Manuel found any number of excuses to decline Simone's invitations for a meal at their home. "Manuel, what is it you are afraid I'll find out?" Simone asked him at last.

"Adina is very nervous and self-conscious. I'm just trying to protect her from stirring up bad memories if you ask her questions."

"I'm not Tomas de Torquemada. I promise not to pry."

Manuel smiled and agreed he and Adina would come for a Friday night dinner soon.

Since her professional success now allowed Simone to do more than think about survival, she'd begun to make Friday night meals special. She'd found a lovely pair of silver candlesticks and a beautiful old goblet at the Montreuil flea market. When rationing ended, she resumed her challah baking. On Fridays, she'd dress the table in a starched white tablecloth, light candles at sundown and always have wine on hand to fill the goblet and make the blessing. The words tumbled out of her mouth so easily. She hadn't forgotten.

It struck her that when she was growing up, she had been indifferent to the fact of her Jewishness. It was a part of her, neither a burden nor something prized. It was paradoxical that just when it was least convenient to identify as a Jew, during the Nazi occupation, she felt more Jewish than ever, more prepared to die because of her Jewishness.

When Manuel had first taken notice of her Shabbat preparations, he'd asked, surprised, "So now you are going back to religion?"

"No, no, nothing like that. It's tradition; it reminds me of my family."

She remembered how Manuel's eyes had misted over. "Look, Manuel, I am not religious. I can't believe in God after what I've have seen."

"Without tradition, you are just tumbleweed," Manuel had said, his eyes downcast.

The longing in his voice, even a lump of tears in his throat were still clear in her mind. She could tell how much he wished he'd been able to have customs of his own.

All day that Friday, Simone felt nervous as if she were the mother of a groom about to meet his betrothed. She took the day off work and buzzed about the kitchen, preparing the Sabbath dishes. She didn't want to do anything to inadvertently distress the girl, or Manuel. He was happy now and fully entitled to his happiness. She reminded herself that there had been no talk of marriage; the girl was just a model who interested Manuel. It was ridiculous for Simone to feel so nervous. She reprimanded herself for ascribing much too much to this relationship and this dinner. In her tizzy to make the best chicken soup she could, she cut her finger while preparing the handmade noodles that Manuel loved.

The two 'kids' arrived just before sundown. They stood in the entryway, removing their coats. Simone could feel their youthful energy filling the space. After he hung up the garments, Manuel made the formal introduction between the women. "Madame Bonheur," he said with a flourish, "Meet Mademoiselle Carlsbach."

"I hadn't realized Manuel's mother was so young," the girl said with a broad smile on her pink cheeks.

"Oh, but she's not my mother!" Manuel exclaimed.

Simone could see how perturbed he was at having to explain.

"I'm his sister," Simone jumped in.

"So sorry," Adina retreated into her reserved self.

"Don't worry. I hope we will be friends by the end of this evening," Simone assured her warmly.

They sat at the table set with a steaming tureen of soup. "Let's light the candles first." Simone struck a match and began reciting the prayer.

As she spoke the Hebrew words, Simone glanced at the girl. Adina mouthed the words and stared into the lights with a faraway look; her eyes glistened. Before the prayer was over, tears ran down the girl's face.

Alarmed, Simone asked, "Adina, are you alright?"

"I'm fine. It just reminds me of..." Her voice trailed off.

Manuel stood up from his chair, walked behind her and put his hands on Adina's shoulders, massaging them gently. He threw Simone a hurt look.

Simone was mortified, had no idea what provoked the tears. "We have all experienced unspeakable things in the war. You can tell us your story; you are with friends."

"More than friends," Manuel jumped in, and the girl smiled through her tears, dabbing her eyes with a handkerchief.

Simone ladled spoonfuls of broth and matzo balls into Adina's and Manuel's soup bowls.

Adina bent over her bowl and inhaled. "It smells like home," she said. "Thank you."

"Where is... or was home?" Simone asked. For a moment, the question hung in the air.

Manuel threw Simone a withering look.

"We came to Paris in 1935 from Berlin after my father lost his job as a professor of mathematics at the university. I was only three years old."

"But during the war, what happened?" Adina's response pulled Manuel into the conversation. "How did your family stay safe?" he asked.

"A man took me away to study in a special school, so I stayed safe. But after the war, I found out from our old neighbors that the Nazis arrested both my parents. I never heard from them after a man took me from our home."

Manuel had a pained expression on his face. "You must have been only ten at the time. Were you frightened?"

"I didn't know I'd not see my parents again, so not really. My mother had said I'd be studying right here in Paris and my student name would be Marie. She gave me a baptismal certificate with Marie's name and told me never to lose it. It was just a piece of paper. I didn't think much about it."

"Where did the man take you?" Simone asked.

"To Monsignor Pezeril's residence. I learned only recently he was an important man of the Catholic church."

Simone and Manuel looked at one another and nodded knowingly.

"How about a short break? I'd like to serve the next course."

"I'm starving," Manuel said.

Shortly, Simone presented a fragrant platter of roast duck and vegetables. It wasn't until after the crème brûlée that Adina told them she'd reclaimed her real name in memory of her murdered parents.

"It's important you've honored them this way," Simone said. And just as the words escaped her lips, a stinging sense of disquiet, like a dark cloud on a sunny day, brushed her mind. She'd made a different decision.

Ever since Manuel brought Adina for the Sabbath dinner, he seemed calmer. The girl had a decidedly positive influence on him. Simone felt increasingly confident that with the photography training Manuel received from Jean and a good young woman by his side, Manuel was on the right track. It was a load off her mind. But the positive feeling did not last.

One day Manuel came home earlier than usual. Simone was glad she had some stew left over from dinner to offer him. But Manuel barely greeted her; his expression was grim.

"Are you alright?" she asked.

"No!"

He walked into his bedroom and shut the door. Simone was very disturbed. It wasn't like him. Soon sounds of nose blowing and sniffling emanated from the room. Crying? She wasn't sure. Alarmed, Simone knocked on his door. "Manuel, what happened? Come out and tell me."

He didn't respond.

He's not a child. I should probably leave him alone, she thought, but the sounds from his room made her anxious. She waited a few minutes and knocked again. "Haven't we always helped one another, Manuel? Let me see if I can help."

He came out looking as forlorn as he had been after the monastery bombing. This time she resisted hugging him.

"I'll warm up a bowl of stew for you, then we can talk," she said.

He nodded and plopped at the table. "She's leaving," he said in a barely audible voice.

"Who?"

"Adina." His crumpled expression told her tears may soon follow.

"Have you two broken up?"

"No, she's going to Israel; she's decided to make *aliyah*."

Simone's eyes widened. It was true, the new state of Israel was now open to anyone claiming to be Jewish. The country was young; it needed youth to build it into a nation. Simone's memory of Kfar Vitkin stood before her mind's eye. The notion that this young woman wanted to make her future there excited Simone. The girl had spunk! She reminded Simone of herself way, way back. Working the land would suit her better than being a mere hanger for pretty dresses.

After a long silence, Simone said, "No need to despair, Manuel. I have the perfect solution."

He looked up at her with a wretched expression.

"Tell me first if you really love her. And I mean love like you've never loved anything in this world."

"Yes, I do. I really do."

"So, it's easy. Go with her to Israel."

He dropped his soup spoon and looked at her, "But I am not a Jew."

"It doesn't matter; you have a Jewish soul. Besides, there were plenty of crypto-Jews in Spain after the Inquisition. You never know. They'll take your word for it; they need brave young men like you."

Manuel looked dubious, but his eyes brightened. "I will speak to Adina. See if she wants me to come along."

"Promise me that if you end up going, you'll stop by a village called Kfar Vitkin. You'll like it. I'm sure."

"You've never been there. How do you know?"

Simone knew it was time to come clean with Manuel and told him a little more about her history, her family, her birth name, and her visit to Palestine, including only the initial impressions.

Manuel listened, spellbound. "I had no idea. Why don't you come too?"

"No, my life is here. I have an unhealthy attachment to Paris. I am staying here for good, but you've found someone special. In Israel, you'll make your own traditions."

Manuel smiled as if he really wanted to believe it.

Though she wasn't entirely sure why, the idea that these two young people who had been through so much would end up building a country for Jews appealed to Simone. She couldn't fall asleep. When sleep finally came, she dreamed, but when she awoke the next morning, all she could remember was the impossibly blue color of the Mediterranean and the frothy white caps on the waves.

PART 5

THE PAST IS NEVER DEAD

47   PARIS, FALL 1973

Once Simone became financially comfortable, she took great pleasure spending her Sunday afternoons reading the op-ed and art sections in *Le Monde,* writing and doodling in her sketchbook at Café de Flore. Despite the November chill, Simone opted for an outside table, hoping the heaters would provide sufficient warmth under the shelter of the awning. The red and white checkered tablecloth added a note of cheer as did the glass of gentian-infused Suze she ordered even before sitting down. Today, she needed it more than her usual coffee.

She pulled out her sketchbook and began to make notes of her ideas for a new line of spring undergarments. Each season Simone refreshed her designs, always aspiring to make her corsets and brassieres a form of women's expression. These days her styles—sensuous and less structured—emphasized women's empowerment rather than serving as symbols of female suppression. It made her feel good to contribute something so seemingly innocuous as lingerie to women's struggle.

Her hand moved swiftly over the pages, broad strokes arcing into unabashed bralettes, teddies, basques, underbust corsets, torsolettes and bustiers. She paused to take a sip of the Suze and smiled. These daring designs would have made her blush back in Warsaw and scandalize her clientele. Even her distinctly French habit of sipping Suze, almost nonsensical for a person of her upbringing, underscored how much she'd changed. As for the drink, she liked its melody of bittersweet citrusy flavors, so reminiscent of her own life. But her designs...? Times had changed, as had her conception of female sexuality. Simone stirred the single ice cube absentmindedly, watching the smattering of pedestrians on their Sunday stroll, scanning the street for Pierre.

They had arranged to meet this Sunday when they ran into one another at a meeting of old Resistance members a few weeks before. She attended these meetings infrequently and with a dose of disquiet, but now and then she had an urge to refresh her links to the past. One shouldn't forget the past; one must remember and learn from it. Over time, unfortunately, it had become painfully obvious to her people weren't learning.

What a brutal century this has been! Simone shook her head at the sheer number of violent events she'd witnessed in her life: antisemitic attacks in Warsaw, the bitter strife among Jews and Arabs in Palestine, the Guardia Civil in Spain and Franco's nationalist thugs, the Nazi atrocities and then—even more frightening—her own participation in the fighting, the killings of Nazis and their French collaborators. Even now, terrorist, and anti-terrorist clashes dominated the headlines. Could a person experience so much violence and hatred and still retain their humanity?

The violence and devastation of past wars seemed to have been forgotten as quickly as the pain of labor. Not that Simone had any personal knowledge of labor; it was what her friends who were mothers had said. Yes, she decided, the ability to forget, to push unwelcome memories to the farthest corners of one's brain was an adaptation that allowed humans to move forward. It had certainly allowed her to function. But Pierre was so anxious to recount his experience of being ratted out by collaborators and arrested by the Nazis that she couldn't refuse him. Learning from the past; yes, of course, she'd meet him, she'd said.

Shortly, she spotted him. Pierre's open jacket flapped, and the breeze almost swept the beret off his head. His ruddy plump cheeks and full lips formed a charming smile when he noticed her. After planting kisses on both her cheeks Parisian-style, he hugged Simone in a way that suggested he wanted more than a collegial relationship. She had met someone after Jean moved to London and wasn't looking for another lover. She wasn't attracted to Pierre anyway. He was squat and balding.

"A Suze for you?" she asked when he sat down and caught his breath.

"Sure, I need something to warm up." Pierre made himself comfortable in the wicker chair.

"You can have coffee or tea instead. Alcohol is not required."

"I see you have become a true Parisian," Pierre said. "I'm just a novice from Marseille."

Simone knew Pierre was one of a small minority of city administrators in Marseille who put his life on the line helping Jews evade deportation orders.

"All it took was simple, common human decency," he told her when he launched into his long-winded tale. He shook his head vigorously. "If I live another lifetime, I'll never know how people didn't see the cruelty of the Germans, how they looked away and didn't step up to save their neighbors."

Simone nodded and chewed her lip. "The human heart is complicated. People have a curious way of distancing themselves from unpleasantness."

Simone waved the waiter over. "Let's order another round and talk about something else." She remembered the shock upon turning on the television, just several weeks before, on October 6. The jolt of it had just barely worn off. The Arabs attacked on Yom Kippur, the holiest Jewish holiday. She sighed and decided to ask Pierre, to get a Frenchman's perspective. "What are your thoughts on the Yom Kippur war? We are not a month past it, and it's off the front pages."

"The Israeli military handed the Syrians and Egyptians their asses wrapped up with a bow," Pierre laughed out loud, his mood brightening. "You've got to be proud of your people, brave warriors."

"Still... War is ugly, no matter who wins. It debases fighters on both sides," she said after a long pause.

"Come on, Simone! Aren't you glad your side won?"

Pierre's question highlighted her perpetual struggle to reconcile non-violence with the need for self-preservation or standing up for treasured values like democracy and human rights. She'd once come down on the side of violence and was not ashamed of it, but it still pricked her conscience at times. It added nothing to her self-esteem. Two opposing ideas in a single brain, still fighting.

She'd always noted the word 'soul' appearing five times in the Yom Kippur Torah portion. Her soul, *dusza*, was pure back when she'd followed her parents to the synagogue; then she had nothing to atone for, but now...?

"You've fallen silent, Simone. What's wrong?" Pierre asked, interrupting her musing.

"Hmm... My side? I suppose," she said and reached into her bag for a cigarette, extending the package to Pierre.

He took one out, "I shouldn't but..."

She lit hers and admitted she was glad Israel had prevailed. After all, Manuel and his children were there. That had been her first thought when she heard the news. She had called Adina right away. Still, notwithstanding her experiences and the Beretta in her purse, she'd never endorse violence, except to save innocent life, and even then, only with the conscious realization that another human was being deprived of life. Violence was barbaric. Despite all evidence to the contrary, she desperately wanted to believe humans had evolved.

The waiter approached and refilled their glasses. They toasted the victory.

48 PARIS, SPRING 1981

Soon after her retirement Simone enrolled in the École de Beaux-Arts, an art school she'd admired ever since her first trip to Paris four and a half decades before. She threw herself into painting, first studying and later renting a studio where she spent many hours each week. She never took her artwork as seriously as her sculptural creations with undergarments. For her, painting created no pressure and no expectations. She only had to please herself. And the canvases of extravagant flowers did just that. They were as enjoyable to her as tending a garden, giving her extra pleasure in winter without the effort of pruning and weeding.

Simone returned from the studio to attend to some unfinished chores, like reviewing her accounts, investments and, very reluctantly, a draft of her will that M. Vogelman, her lawyer, had sent for her review. She sat at her desk but couldn't concentrate. A melancholy mood struck her unexpectedly—it happened sometimes—invariably bringing her inchoate thoughts to the past. She stood up and walked around the apartment, stopping at the refrigerator for a drink of juice, but failed in pushing Warsaw out of her mind.

Bronka's image at the sewing machine the day Rifka had promised to return quickly, haunted her. Though Simone had many friends, none could ever replace what she had had with Bronka. She applied the term 'friends' to her Parisian acquaintances with caution. None struck her as individuals who'd risk everything for Simone or for one of her ideas, the way Bronka had. Bronka had known Rifka with all her faults and still liked her, more than liked, she'd worshipped her. It was an innocent, youthful bond, unsullied by life. She regretted losing it and acknowledged her own role in that.

By now Simone had mostly overcome her anger at the shocking photo long ago. Having torn it back in Pau, it sometimes taunted her to look at it again. Having all that distance, she could look into Bronka's and Aleksander's eyes and try to imagine the truth. The image of them side by side had taken on a patina of age, like a painting, outside of reality; today she saw the figures simply as artists' models.

Through all the years, Bronka's fate remained undecipherable to Simone. She wondered if Bronka had joined the Brigades but discarded the notion. Bronka did not have a political bone in her body. Did she have a romantic attachment to Aleksander? What woman wouldn't? The photo hinted at it, but abandoning her family and the shop too? Simone shook her head and lit up a cigarette. Were the two of them the same, after all, both behaving irresponsibly, abandoning their families? She'd never know for sure. She grew aggravated just thinking about it. Bronka's name never turned up on the survivor lists. Simone closed her eyes, trying to imagine a reunion with Bronka, but choked by old embers of resentment, no image materialized.

She felt too out of sorts to check the accounts and contemplate the will. Instead, Simone stood up to put up a pot of tea and pick out an outfit for the gala dinner she'd been invited by Cécile to join that evening. Cécile Duval, the doyenne of Parisian haute couture, was not someone to be refused. After all, it was her recognition of Simone's designing talent that had launched her on a path of success. Cécile was getting on in years, but still impressive in her engagement with social causes and her extraordinary style. Her friends were also old. Today's event was a birthday celebration for Cécile's nonagenarian friend. Simone was persuaded to attend not only because no one refused Cécile, but because the guest of honor was said to have been an important figure in La Resistance. Simone would always honor such people.

Attired in a dark blue velvet gown with long puff sleeves, Simone checked the mirror one last time. She didn't care much for the large bow at the small of her back held in place by a rhinestone clasp, but it was too late to change. She added a string of pearls and matching earrings, brushed her silver hair styled in a neat bob, and made her way to a waiting taxi.

Cécile met her at the entrance to the venue. "Ooh, la, la! You still have the figure for that pencil silhouette."

Simone acknowledged her with a smile. It was true, she'd never allowed her body to acquire the softness of age.

"Let me introduce you to the honoree," Cécile pulled Simone's hand and led her across a large marble lobby illuminated by a huge crystal chandelier. Arriving guests milled about, jockeying for access to the guest of honor.

When they made their way, Simone saw an elderly woman of regal demeanor exchanging pleasantries with a couple. Though her face looked world-weary, the wrinkles seemed to be carved in just the right places, enhancing rather than detracting from her fading beauty. She wore no obvious makeup save for pale pink lipstick. Her swollen, arthritic knuckles were the only major marks of her age.

When the couple stepped aside, Cécile hugged the woman and said, "Let me introduce you to Simone Bonheur. You might know her from the stories written of her in *Modes & Travaux* and *Elle*."

Simone stared at the old woman and a flame of recognition licked at her brain. Those penetrating blue eyes! She'd seen them somewhere. Simone extended her hand just as Cécile said, "You must have heard of Countess Zabielska."

The countess crinkled her brow. "Why do I feel as though we had met somewhere in the distant past? Oh dear, I am too old to remember." A youthful giggle made her look decades younger.

Temporarily overcome by an avalanche of memories—Paris with Aleksander when life was still full of possibilities—Simone felt faint, as though she might fall. "I hear birthday congratulations are in order. I hope this will be a wonderful celebration," she said, her voice thick with emotion.

Soon guests assembled in the dining room where toasts, accolades and anecdotes about the honoree were delivered with flair by tuxedoed men. It was clear that the assembled had enormous respect and affection for Countess Zabielska. Throughout the evening, Simone's mind raced. Could this, indeed, be Aleksander's mother? Perhaps there were other women in the Zabielski clan, and Simone had gotten herself stirred into a tizzy for nothing.

"Are you alright, Simone? You look very distracted," Cécile remarked.

"How well do you know the countess?" Simone asked discreetly, leaning toward Cécile so as to avoid being overheard by others at their table.

"Very well. Why do you ask?"

"Does she have a son named Aleksander?"

"You mean, had?"

Simone's face fell. She shouldn't have poked the past like a space where a pulled tooth had been.

"Sorry if I've been too blunt. Aleksander died ages ago, victim of Franco's thugs in Spain. I've read in your interview in the *Modes & Travaux* that you know a bit of that history," Cécile said quickly as if to ameliorate her faux pas.

The toasts and chatter in the room drowned out conversation. Simone willed herself to remain in command though the thought of him gone from the earth made the world seem suddenly shrunken to the size of a walnut. She coughed, trying to hold the tears at bay.

"If you'd like, I'll call Countess Zabielska tomorrow to arrange a meeting," Cécile said. "She was very close to her son. If you had been a friend of his, I'm sure she'd like to speak with you."

"It was long ago. I wouldn't want to stir up sad memories," Simone said.

She was still shaken on her return home and fell into a pensive mood again, something she'd engaged in a lot lately. It seemed to her life could be studied through two opposite, equally potent engines: love and hate. Everything in between was but a mundane day-to-day necessity for existence, no more significant than yesterday's breakfast or last year's snow. But those intense emotions were the turbines of most lives. Her burning passion for Aleksander was like an illness that inflamed all her nerve endings, a condition from which she'd never fully recovered. Her obsession with him reminded her of smokers who continue to light up even when they know the downside. Later, with Jacob, it was a steady, quiet love that felt wholesome, like freshly baked bread. But it was the innocent, totally selfless love for Manuel that stood out in her mind as the purest expression of love.

A week had passed since the birthday celebration for Countess Zabielska and Simone still couldn't bring herself to ask Cécile to arrange a meeting. But the urge to know was too great. She picked up the telephone and asked Cécile to broker a meeting. "I won't take much of her time," Simone said. "I just need some closure."

"Aha! So, you had an affair with Aleksander like half the women in Paris?" Cécile had snagged another juicy tidbit for the gossip mill. She laughed, a mirthless laughter.

Simone wished she'd held her tongue. "Nothing like that, Cécile, though yes, I had met him once, briefly."

The meeting took place in Countess Zabielska's salon, a grand room filled with paintings by old masters. Simone thought she'd recognized a nude by Velazquez and a Matisse. The countess lounged on the settee with a lap blanket, though it was warm outside. A silver tea service sat on the low table in front of her. She motioned to Simone to join her. "I'm glad to meet you away from the crowd." She smiled. This time, at close range, her age was more visible. Her hand trembled slightly as she filled two tea glasses. "So, I understand you knew my son... My one and only son," she corrected herself.

"Yes, I'd met him on a train from Warsaw. Goodness! I was just barely out of my teens." Simone felt a warm flush rise on her neck and face, something that hadn't happened in decades.

The countess stared at Simone. "Why do I keep thinking we've met?"

"Your memory is exceptional. We did meet once in the shop where Aleksander took me to pick out some clothing, as I was robbed on the train."

The countess squinted as if she were trying to look into the sun. She nodded and her gnarled finger thrust into the air. "That's it! I do remember wondering why Aleksander had done it. He had never

401

brought a woman to my couture inner sanctum. I knew right then you were different. Special."

"I hate to bring up a painful subject, but I'd like to know what happened to him. We lost touch, so much had happened... to both of us, it seems."

The countess sighed. "Time... and chance... They wreak havoc in people's lives."

Simone, deeply apprehensive of how she'd respond to whatever she'd learn, sat quietly, feeling uncomfortable to have troubled this grand old lady.

"Wait!" The countess startled Simone. "Might your name ever have been different?"

Simone hesitated, responding haltingly, "In the Resistance, one couldn't be too careful. Surely you know all about that."

The countess nodded and Simone continued. "Simone Bonheur is an alias I'd assumed in Pau. Before that, I was Raquela Bluestone."

The silence in the room was disturbed only by the countess's quick shallow breaths. "Wait here. I have something for you," she blurted out suddenly, stood up, and walked out, leaving Simone in distress. Simone picked up the glass of tea, gone cold, and sipped to steady her nerves.

The countess seemed to have been energized by her errand. She returned after just a couple of minutes, handing Simone an envelope yellow with age. "You cannot imagine what pleasure it gives me to fulfill my son's last wish."

Simone took it and held it gingerly as if it would disintegrate were she to open it. "Would you mind very much if I read it in private when I get home?"

"Of course, dear, though I can imagine what it says. I believe you were the love of his life." The countess smiled, a gentle angelic smile, and patted Simone's hand. "Had I been younger, you and I could have been good friends."

For the next half hour, Simone listened to Aleksander's mother describe how she moved heaven and earth in occupied Paris to get him the best medical care, but to no avail. Before they parted, just as Simone picked up her purse to leave, the countess said, "One more thing."

Simone turned to her. "Aleksander had a son... from a liaison in Spain." She paused, closed her eyes, shook her head. "Men don't always behave honorably... It was wartime..."

Suddenly, she stood up. "Wait! I have something else that may be of interest. A letter arrived about a dozen years after Aleksander's death. At first, I thought it a mistake because it was addressed to someone named Zak, but it had my address, so the postman gave it to me. Let me show you."

Simone wasn't sure she wanted any more revelations. Her head spun. Could this be Bronka and Aleksander's child? Her heart sank. She stood frozen like a pillar of salt waiting for the countess. Countess Zabielska returned to the salon slowly. Her age showed more than at her birthday celebration. "My feet are my enemies," she said handing Simone another envelope. It bore purple, green, and reddish stamps reading Republica Argentina; all bearing an image of a stern-looking general with long sideburns. Argentina? Simone knew no one in South America. "I don't think, I can—" she said, but almost immediately paused in mid-sentence. The handwriting on the envelope looked familiar. Hesitantly, she opened the letter. It was written in Polish.

Buenos Aires, June 7, 1951

Dear Countess Zak,

You don't know me, but your son, Antoni, had given me your address when he left for the Ebro battlefield. That was the last time I saw him. Antoni, the man I met in Warsaw, was someone I loved deeply. I joined him in Spain. He left me with our son Stefan and an unborn child I carried.

I have not heard from him in the last twelve years—I can only assume he was one of the thousands that perished at Ebro—and have made peace with his death.

I am deeply saddened to tell you that I was robbed of our second child by the brutes of Franco's regime. Luckily, a decent man rescued me and Stefan, married me and spirited us to Argentina via Portugal and London.

I have told Stefan of your existence, but he is a teenager and not very interested in making connections with his father's family. He is angry Antoni abandoned us. I hope you forgive him as he is a good boy and his father's spitting image. I have had two children with my new husband, and we live a good life in the land of the tango.

Sorry for intruding, but I thought you'd want to know about your grandson's existence.

I wish you good health.

Respectfully, Bronka Martins

P.S. Enclosed you will find a photo of my family. Stefan is the tall boy on the right.

For a moment, Simone stood shaking her head in disbelief. So, it wasn't just a casual relationship. Unbidden tears sprang to her eyes.

The countess, intrigued by Simone's emotional response, asked, "Does it make sense to you?"

"Nothing makes sense."

"I am so sorry to have upset you."

"No, no apologies are necessary. The woman is someone from my past. I have wondered for years about her fate. Now I know. She's well and happy. That's all that counts. I should be thanking you. Now let me look at the photo."

Simone pulled the photo out of the envelope: a formal black and white family portrait. Bronka no longer had her signature braids, her hair cut in a stylish bob made her face rounder, but Simone saw pain in her eyes. The husband, a silver-haired man with bushy eyebrows was clearly at least a decade, maybe two, older. The young man—Stefan—stood a tad apart from the others. He had his father's arresting gaze and confident stance as if the whole world belonged to him. "You have a handsome grandson. I hope he'll find his way to you when he matures," she said all choked up.

"Oh, dear, I have burdened you with too much of the past."

"The past is always with us. We don't really forget it; we have a way of pushing it to the far corners of our brain so we can move on." Simone smiled halfheartedly and dabbed her eyes with a hankie. "I shall be going now. Thank you for your time." Two proper Parisian kisses on the cheeks and she was out.

On her way home, hoping to ease her mind, Simone stopped for a glass of Suze. It would calm her nerves and its bitter sweetness would match her discoveries. The thought that Bronka did not end up with Aleksander didn't console Simone as much as she thought it would. In fact, it saddened her greatly that Bronka lost her second child. She could feel her pain. A wave of feeling overwhelmed Simone. Her emotions, disturbed and confused, swirled in her head as though they had been caught in a hurricane.

Simone ordered a second glass of Suze and a strong coffee. She asked a man at a nearby table for a cigarette. He gladly obliged. She didn't know how long she sat there, but when she finally paid and walked out, she had a flash of recognition: the emotion she felt was forgiveness. And the mention of tango in the letter now gave Simone a mischievous chuckle. The old girl still loved to dance! How shocked she'd be to learn that her old friend missed dancing with Jean to the smoky sounds of Count Basie and Lionel Hampton at the la Huchette jazz club.

49   PARIS, WINTER 1996

The year had begun ominously. In January, President Mitterrand had died. He was eighty, born the same year as Simone, a landmark she'd achieve very soon herself. It was frigid outside. Simone decided to stay home and peruse the paper. All those articles eulogizing the President in the Sunday paper. She read many of them and set the paper aside to think.

For two people so different, they did share some characteristics, she thought. Somehow, the realization took her by surprise. He had been the leader of the Socialist party and though she never put herself in a political box, her sympathies lay on the left side of the spectrum. Both of them were former members of the Resistance. Having seen the Nazi concentration camps, Mitterrand abandoned his Catholic faith. In his dismissal of religion, he reminded Simone of herself. Mitterrand had been a conservative nationalist early on in his political career, but he had changed. Simone had been a fan of pacifism in her youth, but she decided there were causes that warranted taking up arms. That was another thing they had in common, the ability to change in the face of evidence.

Simone felt that new political winds would soon impact France, but since she no longer had much passion for politics, she decided to turn her attention to herself, something she did more frequently as she aged. She was generally satisfied with her life now, but had she found the freedom she'd longed for since girlhood, become the woman she'd wanted to be? It was hard to answer. Now that she had the luxury of thinking, she couldn't answer these questions to her complete satisfaction. As with many things in life, the truth was neither black nor white; it was as always, a muddy gray.

Yes, she was solely responsible for herself and her actions. She lived where she wanted and how she wanted. But remembering how good it had felt assuming responsibility for Manuel—now that she had none—she realized she wished for such rewarding obligations. She hadn't wanted to be encumbered by marriage, but there was something special in the common bond of hardships she had shared with Jacob, the things he had taught her. She realized too late in life that the kind of ties that bind don't form overnight. They take the better part of a lifetime to develop and bear fruit: a fruit she sorely lacked. It took her too long to appreciate Jacob, to recognize that what was initially gratitude had turned to love. As painful as it had been, she was now, all those years later, glad that she had been able to cradle his head as he lay dying. It was the least he deserved. It took her too long to gain perspective on life and love.

Simone sat in her comfortable recliner, sipping well-brewed tea and ignoring the sounds of tires outside slipping in the snow. She reflected that love was something she hadn't understood before, not completely. Now she was finally ready to admit that her initial infatuation with Aleksander was just that, an excess of emotion in a young woman whose sexuality had been squelched by religion. But she was convinced of something else too. Had fate given them a chance to be together, her feelings would have matured into love. Bronka would not have taken her place. Of this she was unshakably certain, as certain as she was that she'd never leave his city, despite the rising ill will against Jews that had begun in the 1980s with the bombing of a synagogue in Paris, then a grenade at Goldenberg's restaurant. And then, all those desecrations of Jewish cemeteries, tombs defaced with swastikas, kicked over, even bodies dug up. No rest, not even for the dead.

The remembrance of those ugly, cowardly acts disturbed her afternoon. She got up and pulled out a cigarette—she now seemed to smoke only in moments of stress—lit it and tried to restore her calm. She sat back down and picked up her tea, but it had gotten cold.

As much as she resisted brooding about the past, it kept coming back. Back then, if anyone could have read her thoughts, they'd think the monastery had turned her into a nun. She chuckled at the absurdity of the thought. She was a very sexual being indeed. When she began seeing Jean, she'd discovered the wonders of her own body and enjoyed the physical closeness without a sense of guilt or shame. She'd finally conquered the *shomer negiah* rule. Jean was a great lover, experienced, but not in a way that made her feel like his student. When he moved away, she missed him, but then met other men who had filled the hunger she had for sex, for life, for forgetting the past.

The cigarette had burned to nothing, and she had removed the ashtray in an effort to quit so she collected the bits of ash in her hand and walked to the kitchen to dispose of it. Walking back to the living room, her gaze alighted on the mantle photo. She looked at Manuel, the boy soldier. He had grown into an intelligent man, self-assured and respected by international peers in security services. She was proud of him. She smiled. He had never missed her birthday. If he was unable to travel, he called. Soon he'd be coming to see her, the thing that warmed her heart most.

Manuel always sailed through airport security, thanks to his Shin Bet credentials. Now he settled into his seat, leaned back, closed his eyes and relaxed. All that unfinished work on his desk, the hasty packing, and the rush to the airport always created a bit of anxiety. Though he traveled on business extensively, he never got used to parting with Adina, not knowing how a mission would turn out.

The plane was filled with a noisy assortment of passengers: men with long beards, black hats and *peyes*, women carrying babies and diaper bags on their shoulders while pulling overstuffed roll-on bags. A smartly dressed El Al flight attendant in a tight navy skirt tapped his shoulder and asked if he wanted a drink, but Manuel declined. He just wanted to decompress from what had been a very rough winter. Hell, the whole year had been brutal. The assassination of Prime Minister Rabin in November—by one of their own!—was a grisly culmination of months of bombings and bus attacks, plus the massacre at Beit Lid by Palestinian suicide bombers.

Manuel didn't want to dwell on any of it now, though the way his boss had been criticized for a fling in Paris while his Prime Minister was murdered seemed quite justified. Manuel didn't like the man's tactics and had gotten into a pissing match with him more than once for the way the boss had relaxed the rules on treating Palestinian detainees. The events of the day before still sat heavy in his heart.

A young Palestinian, barely a teen, had been dragged in shackled. He was said to have served as a lookout for his older brother, who had been suspected of throwing a homemade grenade at a checkpoint. The boy was terrified; a dark stain at his crotch, spreading down the leg of raggedy jeans spoke volumes. Manuel wanted him questioned and released, but his boss wanted to hold him in solitary for an undetermined period. All the years in this job, rising through the ranks, and Manuel never lost his humanity, as did too many of his coworkers. One needed to feel pain, real pain, to understand the suffering of others. And it was all thanks to Simone. She was the one who taught him to be sensitive to others—to be a *mensch*—as she had often said.

Simone, ever since he'd met her as Raquela, had been his guardian angel. Even now, as a man on the verge of retirement, he'd never forget the day he first saw her at the orphanage. It was as if his mother had risen from the dead. He still wouldn't know how to put it—they didn't look the same—but it was something about her intense gaze, her delicate hands, and the way she cocked her head when she spoke that reminded him of his mother, in a way that pierced the armor he'd worked so hard to build around himself. Without speaking, he could tell she knew how the Mother Superior singled him out for all the little indignities, how she punished him more severely than the others. If Raquela hadn't taken him from the ruins, he'd have wandered into the mountains and died of loneliness, if not starvation.

Manuel thought of how she steered him away from the postwar black market. He'd wanted to help her so badly; he'd have turned to crime if he had to. The American soldiers who hung around the bar late into the night plied him with cheap cigarettes and booze and tried to recruit him. His facility with French and Spanish and his quickness was exactly what they needed. There was no question, he was enticed. They'd have given him a gun too. But every time he'd come home and see Simone, he just couldn't. Twice he'd promised a burly sailor from Marseille, who'd been an important fence, that he'd show up for what they called 'the mission,' but he never did. He was certain that if they had found him, they'd have put a bullet through his head because he'd learned too much about their operations.

And Adina, too, had saved him, but even she was a gift from Simone. Simone had been responsible for everything good in his life. Not that living with her in his teen years had been simple. The few friends he had suspected Simone was an older lover of his. Hard as he tried, he couldn't convince them otherwise. They had laughed and called him a gigolo.

She was still very beautiful then with fire in her green eyes, always dressed nicely even though they had so little to live on. And when he was truthful with himself, he had to admit that sometimes, as his hormones raged, he was attracted to her. It usually happened on weekends when she came out of the bath with a pink glow on her face, wearing a robe and towel, turban-style, making him think of her naked in the tub while he fidgeted in bed next door.

When he left for Israel, just after its formation, so he'd not lose his beloved Adina, he was pained to leave Simone. She had sustained him and buttressed him all those years; he didn't know how he would manage without her. He couldn't have known that he would stand out in the Israeli military, recognized by his superiors for his steadiness and calm, never overeager to draw the weapon. They had recruited him for the Shin Bet when he was still very young, in fact, the youngest leader of a division.

Manuel traveled to Paris frequently on business. This week he would be meeting with his counterparts at the French Directorate of Internal Security to discuss cooperative counterterrorism measures. But Simone would be the highlight of the trip. This was the real reason he didn't send a subordinate to represent him. Instead, he'd brave the freezing temperatures to which his body was no longer accustomed. For her, he'd endure anything.

50 POINTS OF INFLECTION

It wasn't until Simone returned from her walk that she realized it was high time to prepare for meeting Manuel. The morning altercation with the anti-Muslim thugs had distracted her. She was glad to have been there at just the right moment to help old Monsieur Hamdi. He was a good man with whom she'd become friendly over the years. Indeed, he served as a kind of test for her potential lovers, way back when she still thirsted for male company. When Jean took a job in London, Simone had a succession of new male companions. If they looked askance at her positive attitude toward Hamdi, they'd be tossed out of her favor and her bed.

When the sky darkened, she walked over to her closet and rummaged for the right attire to wear this evening. Manuel was coming to take her to dinner to celebrate her eightieth birthday. By now, nothing much excited Simone, she had experienced so much in life that nothing felt new. It was as if she'd run out of fresh experiences. Perhaps she'd by now actually swallowed the world. Yet this dinner would be special. She looked forward to it.

Through the years, she hadn't seen Manuel very often, but he stayed in touch regularly. His letters and calls were always refreshing and brought with them a whiff of the sea and images of palms swaying against the sky. He and Adina had made a good couple. He was still working for the Shin Bet and Adina was a psychologist. By now, their two children, Jacob and Eulalia were adults with children of their own. Simone wondered if they would be joining, but if not, just seeing Manuel would be a treat. She relished the thought that she had had a hand in shaping him. He had grown into a successful man, widely respected in his field, and devoted to his family. This gave Simone more fulfillment and pride than anything else she'd done in her life.

She chose the Chanel white wool jacket with black hounds-tooth weave and dropped shoulders. It would go well with the white silk blouse and black pencil skirt. Luckily, she still had the figure for it. A black chiffon scarf and chunky gold earrings would complete the look. She didn't like to be overdressed and always stuck to classic couture designs. There were too many of them in her closet. She needed to thin them out soon, though she had nostalgia for some that made her put off the task.

Having decided on the outfit, Simone sat to do her periodic cleaning before she dressed up. It was the only chore she did regularly these days. First, she emptied the chamber, then disassembled the gun, laying all the parts in front of her on a clean white cloth. It was a good thing the thugs had walked away, or she might have had been forced to fire the Beretta. Maybe she looked scarier than the gun, or else they were all chickens, she thought as she fingered the parts.

Though a touch of arthritis in her hands had slowed her assembly a bit, the skill Jacob imparted all those years ago was still fresh. It gave her a measure of comfort to do this, though it really didn't need cleaning, except to prevent rusting, as the gun hadn't been fired since... Well, she didn't like to think of it. It was the only cleaning job she hadn't entrusted to Anna, her housekeeper.

The one aspect of this procedure that she wasn't terribly fond of was the smell of the cleaning solvent because it reminded her of the work with the forger and the terror she felt each time she had to walk after curfew to deliver the documents. Still, it was important not to forget.

She was about to apply gun oil to the bore cleaning brush and insert it into the barrel when a sharp sound of the doorbell startled her. She looked up at the clock; it must be Manuel. She was late! She walked to the front door and opened it. Manuel stood in the foyer with a giant bouquet of roses. She noticed the gray at his temples. He was still handsome, though his face was lined and tanned. He was lean, and his eyes still held mystery in their blackness.

"They are waiting for us in the restaurant; let's get the show on the road," he said, embracing her. He towered over her. Age had diminished her stature, and she was never tall to begin with. She took the roses and walked into the kitchen to find a vase.

"It'll take me only a few minutes to give these a drink and to dress. I promise. You can time me if you want."

He strode over to the table where she'd been assembling the Beretta. "What is this? You are still at war?"

"Not with people, just with my demons."

Simone turned to walk down the hallway to her bedroom. "Jacob told me never to be without it," she called out. "It is never out of my purse, except when I clean it."

Her voice hung in the air. Her youthful lilt was still in it.

"Hurry, please, Simone, I have a big surprise waiting for you."

When she was dressed, she walked over to the table. "Give me just a moment to finish the last of the assembly."

"Go ahead. I wouldn't want to contradict Jacob's directive."

Manuel sat at the table and watched her. She lifted the gun carefully to avoid getting oil on her clothes, completed the task, loaded it and put the safety on then slipped it into her purse. She wiped her hands in the cloth and looked them over. "Sorry, I need to wash them." She walked toward the lavatory and came out promptly. "There. Now, I'm ready," she said.

A black car waited for them at the curbside. The chauffeur began exiting the car to open the doors, but Manuel signaled he'd do it. He held the door open for Simone. She smiled. Despite all these years among sabras, he hadn't lost his chivalry with women.

"I don't know how to prepare you for this meeting," he said, as the driver maneuvered in heavy traffic, spraying melting snow.

"What do you mean? What meeting?"

"I mean, the dinner."

"Have you ordered some extraordinary dishes for me? I'm starving."

"Well... I think you'll find it extraordinary, but it may not be the food."

She adjusted her scarf and said, "Now I'm really curious."

They entered the classy restaurant and checked their coats.

"Come." Manuel took Simone's hand. His grip was firm and warm.

What has he cooked up here, she wondered as they walked deeper into the restaurant. Of all the things she could have imagined, the scene before her would have never been it.

She stopped and stared at the group seated at their table. Adina was there, still as thin, and beautiful as ever. Jacob and Eulalia, she recognized from the photos Manuel sent her periodically. She hadn't seen them since their teens. Both had Manuel's dark Spanish looks. But who was the elderly woman with them?

Something odd scratched at the back of Simone's brain. Could it be? No. She'd be eighty-seven by now, maybe not even alive. She moved closer to the woman who sat looking at her intensely.

"Rifka?" the old woman ventured, her voice tremulous with age and emotion.

The amazement on the faces of the group at the table was unmistakable. "Who is Rifka?" Eulalia asked, but no one answered.

Simone's heart thumped furiously.

They must think the old woman with them suddenly succumbed to dementia.

"Golda? Is it you?" With that, Simone, clutching her chest, collapsed onto the banquette near her sister.

"I'm asking the manager to call an ambulance," Adina said with alarm while Manuel shook Simone gently, calling out, "Simone, Simone, are you alright?"

Simone sat up slowly. "Yes, yes, of course, I am alright. It was just the shock of it. Sorry for creating a commotion." She leaned toward Golda, put her arms around her and kissed her cheeks again and again.

"Kissing is fine. Just don't hug me too tight. My bones are fragile." Golda chuckled and wiped the tears streaming down her cheeks. Her face was extremely wrinkled, but her eyes were as bright and blue as they had been when she could wrap Eli around her finger.

"I have longed to see you all these many years," Simone said. "I just didn't know how to ask for your forgiveness. There were no words for something like this."

"No need to apologize. These things happen. SIDS has taken some of our babies in Atlit. Thank God, I have three children and seven grandchildren. You'll need to meet them."

Those at the table couldn't follow the cryptic conversation, but it didn't matter.

Manuel gave the signal, and the sommelier poured the 1990 Veuve Clicquot into crystal flutes.

The conversation and laughter could have gone on, but Simone noticed how tired Golda looked and said, "I have a great idea. Why don't we go to my place and have a relaxed cup of tea to wrap up this extraordinary evening?"

Manuel glanced at his watch and said, "I need to drop Golda off at her hotel. Tomorrow is another day for catching up. After that, you'll have to come to Israel to continue."

"Let me stay with Rifka tonight," Golda said. A weary smile appeared on her lips.

"Done!" Manuel said. "I'll take both of you in the car which is still waiting for us. You, Jacob, follow us with your mom and Eulalia in a taxi."

A small commotion at the coat check, sorting out whose coat was which, then they filed out with Simone looping her arm through Golda's, holding on for dear life. They slid into the back seat, Manuel, and driver up front.

The pavement glistened in the dark; the melted snow having frozen as the temperature dropped.

"I'm curious to see your place, dear sister. I have no idea how you live," Golda spoke.

"It'll give me great pleasure to host you," Simone said, pulling Golda close. "Oh, Manuel, I just remembered, I'm almost out of tea. My favorite grocer, Monsieur Hamdi, has my favorite, Mariage Frères. Please drop me off. You remember, just across the street from my building. It'll only take a minute and I can grab some fresh halvah to go with it. Perfect." Simone's voice brimmed with excitement.

"It's late. Won't the shop be closed?"

"No, he stays open late. He had a bad day. I need to check on him anyway," Simone said.

Manuel instructed the chauffeur accordingly. They drove along Boulevard Hausmann. Manuel and Simone alternated pointing out various landmarks for Golda. They noticed groups of stragglers from the day-long demonstrations. At one corner, two niqab-wearing women, accompanied by bearded men, were being pelted by fruit from a nearby stand. The men, attired in long tunics and skullcaps, struggled to shield the women while yelling words in Arabic.

"I am so embarrassed by some of our French citizens," Simone said.

"Things aren't that much different in Israel," Golda responded, and they remained quiet.

It didn't take long for the car to arrive near Hamdi's shop. A line of parked cars prevented the driver from stopping directly in front, so he pulled over several car lengths away.

Manuel said, "Simone, let me get it, please. It's slippery out."

"No, I'm perfectly capable and I do need to ask Hamdi something." Simone was her usual stubborn self. She clambered out of the vehicle.

Manuel watched Simone taking small, careful steps toward the shop. Satisfied, he twisted back in his seat to chat with Golda. She reached out for his hand and held it. "I'll never forget what you've done for me and my sister. I never thought we'd be reunited. I was so unkind to her."

"It was another time. Don't think of it."

Simone was no more than two steps from the shop when a band of young men approached. She thought she'd recognized the thugs from the morning encounter. Still out looking for trouble, she thought, and decided to ignore them, to go straight into the shop to avoid a confrontation. Not now. All she wanted to do was to bring Golda and the rest of them upstairs.

As she put her hand on the door handle, she heard him, recognized his low growl. It was the tall, pimply one saying, *"Allez on s'la fume cette salope."*

She felt a punch on her back and half turned seeing a grimace on his face. A moment later, confused about what had happened, she collapsed, and everything went black. A searing pain overtook her body. She couldn't tell if it was on the side or back, then... nothingness.

By the time Manuel turned back from chatting with Golda and faced forward, he saw Simone lying on the sidewalk and three men running down the block in the opposite direction. What had happened? He hadn't heard anything. He jumped out of the car and raced toward Simone.

"Simone, Simone, stay with me," Manuel shouted, knelt, and cradled her head. He saw the wide band of blood gushing away from her side. He moved her body enough to press his jacket under her in a vain attempt to stanch the bleeding. He held her wrist, feeling for a pulse, then looked up scanning the sky for Mars, the God of war. Surely, it had to be there on a night like this. But his eyes only found a single bright star illuminating the sky. He swallowed the lump in his throat.

At that moment, Jacob's taxi pulled up. Jacob ran over and called for an ambulance.

Hamdi must have heard the commotion because he stepped out and stood frozen for a moment before letting out a pained scream. "Mme Bonheur! What happened to her?"

"It looks as if she'd been stabbed," Manuel said in a flat voice that sounded as if he already knew he'd lost the woman who'd been his savior.

"Rest assured, we'll get them, Jacob said as emergency workers placed Simone's inert body on the stretcher.

"She was an angel. A true angel of kindness." Hamdi sobbed. "She saved my life today."

EPILOGUE

Paris, March 1996

Manuel sat in the office of a prominent Parisian wills and estates attorney and pulled the last cigarette from the pack. He'd promised Simone and Adina he'd stop, but the night of February 15 unnerved him more than any horrific event to which he'd been a witness, and there had been too many in his life. Somehow, losing Simone pained him more than the loss of his parents. By now, he barely remembered them, but Simone had been the steady presence in his life, his guide, and his teacher.

He'd notified Simone's horrified housekeeper, Anna, the night of the stabbing. She came next morning—swollen eyes and a woeful, puffy face —with her keys to meet him and open Simone's apartment, which echoed with her absence. The old woman was disconsolate. "Mme Bonheur gone. I can't believe it. I can't!" she repeated over and over.

Before he left, taking some papers, Anna said sheepishly, "I have something of Mme Bonheur's to show you."

Now he was waiting for her to arrive to join him at this meeting as the attorney had, inexplicably, requested her presence at the reading of the will. She arrived shortly, breathing heavily, her eyes reddened and sat next to Manuel in the waiting room, dabbing her eyes. She placed a large bag on the chair next to her and kept glancing at it as if she feared it being stolen.

Shortly, M. Vogelman came out of his office and invited them to the conference room down the hall. He was overweight and spoke French with the accent of a foreigner. "Let us begin," he said, pushing his glasses up on his nose and opening a thick file folder in front of him.

"*Excusez-moi*," Anna said, "I have something you might like to see before we proceed."

M. Vogelman looked at her with a dubious expression. "Can this wait?"

"Perhaps not."

Manuel spoke up. "I think Simone would allow Anna to interrupt. She had very high regard for her."

Vogelman opened up his arms in a gesture of resignation, and Anna pulled out an overstuffed manila envelope from her bag.

At first, she spoke hesitantly, stumbling over her words. "I... I probably shouldn't have done it." The envelope shook in Anna's hands. "Mme Bonheur was gone when I'd come to clean on the morning of her birthday. When I picked up the garbage bag to take it to the trash room, I noticed it was unusually heavy, so I opened it to check. I thought this envelope may have fallen in by accident, so I took it home. I'd intended to ask Mme Bonheur about it... Here it is."

Manuel unraveled the string from around the closure. He didn't ask if she'd looked inside, but just dumped the contents on the conference table in front of Vogelman. Little by little, they examined the collection: a Fanny Pozner gymnasium identity card with young Rifka Berg looking wide-eyed, like a newborn doe; Simone's most recent passport where she looked confident, if aged, her wrinkles confirming her eventful life, and a British passport in the name of Raquela Bluestone. Manuel recognized her instantly: his dearly loved rescuer. And there were lists, many lists. Manuel picked up one, folded accordion-style with what was now a faint list of names and ages. The first name on it: Ida. Immediately, he recognized it—children Raquela had rescued as part of her Resistance work. There was another list that he could not make sense of at first: eight German surnames and five French. Six of the names had been crossed out.

When Vogelman looked at the list and pointed out one name. "I know for sure this is a well-known French collaborator."

Neither Manuel nor Anna needed further interpretation.

Anna whispered reverently, "Mme Bonheur... She was a hero."

There were many black-and-white photos and assorted yellowed letters festooned with stamps from foreign countries. One photo, now yellow with age, was notable for it had been reassembled with tape. A corner was still missing. In it, a man and a woman posed in front of a hotel somewhere. And there was another, a formal family photo: parents and three children, including a teenager. It was stamped Panorama Studios, Avenida de Mayo, Buenos Aires. He had no idea who they were or why Simone kept it with her papers.

Manuel, shaken by the envelope's contents, just wanted to move forward and leave. He said, "There's too much here to absorb now. I'd like to take it all with me, give it proper due and preserve these mementos."

"Not so fast, we aren't finished yet," Vogelman said. "This note is for you."

Manuel opened the folded piece of paper bearing his name, not even an envelope. Must have been written in haste, he surmised.

My dear Manuel,

To spare you unpleasantness, I have already arranged for my headstone. You won't see Simone Bonheur carved on it. It will read thus:

Here lies Rifka Berg who struggled to keep her soul from turning to iron.

"Let's get on with it," Manuel said, impatient to mourn in private the woman who had been his beacon of light in his darkest days.

The attorney nodded and began the formal reading of the will. Anna discovered that she'd inherit Simone's palatial apartment and its contents. She shook her head, saying, "It's a mistake. For sure. Mme must have been distressed. She could not have meant it."

"There is a notable sum in Simone's savings account and investments for you, Manuel," Vogelman said. "Plus, one other small item."

Manuel looked baffled.

"Here." Vogelman pulled out a desk drawer. "The police returned it to me after the inquest. They found it with Simone's belongings. I knew her well enough to know she'd want you to have it."

Manuel smiled, took the Beretta from Vogelman, and stared at it.

She had tamed the petite beast to do good.

ABOUT THE AUTHOR

Author, poet, educator, and scientist, Annette Libeskind Berkovits was born in Kyrgyzstan, a former Soviet Republic, near China's western border. She is the daughter of Polish Jews who survived World War II in Soviet gulags. Daniel Libeskind, the noted international architect and master planner for rebuilding Ground Zero in New York, is Annette's brother.

Annette received her primary education in Łódz, Poland and in Tel Aviv, Israel. On her arrival in New York as a teenager Annette entered the highly selective Bronx High School of Science not speaking a word of English, the only student to ever be admitted without taking the required entrance exam. She earned a BS in Biology from The City College of New York (CCNY) in its heyday and, later, a master's degree in Educational Administration and Supervision from Manhattan College.

In her three-decade career with the Wildlife Conservation Society, based at New York's Bronx Zoo, Annette became one of the Society's first female Senior Vice Presidents. During her tenure, she led the institution's nationwide and worldwide science education programs and spearheaded partnerships among school systems and conservation organizations. Berkovits negotiated the first ever agreement to bring environmental education to China's schools, long before China became an industrial power. Later her programs spread to Papua New Guinea, Bhutan, Cuba, India and elsewhere.

For several years, she served as the Chair of the International Association of Zoo Educators. Even before being elected to lead the international association, she convened the First Pan American Congress for Conservation Education in Venezuela attended by representatives from dozens of nations.

Recognized for her leadership in the field of science education by the National Science Foundation, Berkovits authored and edited numerous science education publications for children and teachers. She continues to pursue her life-long love of writing full time.

Berkovits and her husband divide their time between Manhattan and Florida.

Her poetry has been published by Silk Road: a Literary Crossroads; Persimmon Tree; American Gothic: a New Chamber Opera; Blood & Thunder: Musings on the Art of Medicine; and in The Healing Muse. Her essay appeared in Curator: The Museum Journal.

Her first memoir, **In the Unlikeliest of Places**, a story of her remarkable father's survival, was published by Wilfrid Laurier University Press in September 2014 and reissued in paperback in 2016. A Polish translation, titled *Życie Pełne Barw* was published by Biblioteka Centrum Dialogu in 2020.

Her second memoir, chock full of entertaining stories about humans and wildlife, ***Confessions of an Accidental Zoo Curator,*** chronicles her three-decade career with the Wildlife Conservation Society. It was published in April 2017 by Tenth Planet Press.

In 2020, Tenth Planet Press published her poetry collection, ***Erythra Thalassa: Brain Disrupted***, a tender look at a mother's grief.

The Corset Maker is her first historical novel.

A third memoir, ***Aftermath: Coming-of-Age on Three Continents*** will be published by Amsterdam Publishers in the fall of 2022.

For more information on the author and her books, as well as events and more, please check the website:

annetteberkovits.com

Read the excerpt from *Aftermath: Coming-of-Age on Three Continents* below:

PART I: RED

I spent the first three years of my life unaware of the disaster that had befallen my family. My most vivid recollection of that period is standing in my crib under fragrant trees whose boughs hung so low I was able to reach the peaches that hung on them and imprint each with a tiny nick of my two teeth. My fingers still remember their fuzzy skin, softer than my camel hair blanket.

The world was drenched in red; the fiery orange red of poppy fields, the blood red of the flags, the flickering red embers glowing in the center of the huge yurt where we slept. Like the Uzbeks who shared their home with us, my parents and I lay like spokes of a wheel covered by thick wool rugs, warming our feet near the central fire pit.

Long before I remade myself into the all-American image of Annette Funicello, the Disney Mouseketeer, I was Anetka, a little girl living in one of the remotest corners of the world.

The town of my birth, Kyzyl Kiya, was nestled in the fertile Fergana

Valley of Kyrgyzstan, Central Asia. In millennia past it was a welcome rest stop along the Silk Road for traders and their camel caravans laden with exotic cargo: Persian rugs, yak wool, silk, cinnabar, and the rare spices and flavors of the Orient.

By the 1940s the only remnant of those heady times, when a Babel of languages passed through, was the raggedy mix of Eastern European refugees thwarted on their southward journey by impassable mountain ranges. The snowcapped Pamir Mountains, part of the formidable Tien Shan range, towered to heights of over 24,000 feet, but the valley in their shadow seemed hospitable enough to my parents, Nachman and Dora Libeskind.

It was my most carefree time yet the bleakest of all for my parents. Living hand to mouth and counting the days until it was possible for us to return to Poland, Nachman and Dora couldn't afford much beyond the barest necessities. I had no toys to speak of but that did not mean that I went without amusements. The portraits of the Party's Central Committee luminaries that hung in my father's office, at the brick factory, were my earliest playthings. Father would point at the portraits, and I would call out their names. With each additional one I recognized, Father would clap his hands and laugh as if I were the smartest child in the world. Soon I was able to identify each and every one of them as Father pointed, sometimes in order, sometimes at random when he wanted to increase the challenge of the game. I stored them in memory under what must have been my first concept of the alphabet. The "K's": Krupskaya (Lenin's wife); Kalinin, Kaganovich, Khrushchev; the "M's": Malenkov, Mikoyan, Molotov; and Stalin, in a category all by himself. ..."

Want to read more? The book will be available in September 2022.

Dear Reader,

If you have enjoyed reading The Corset Maker
please do leave a review on Amazon or Goodreads. A few words would
be enough. This would be greatly appreciated.

Alternatively, if you have read my book as an eBook
you could leave a rating. That is just one simple click, indicating how
many stars of five you think this book deserves.
Thank you very much in advance!
Annette Libeskind Berkovits

AMSTERDAM PUBLISHERS BOOKS

The Series **Holocaust Survivor Memoirs World War II** consists of the following autobiographies of survivors:

1. Outcry - Holocaust Memoirs, by Manny Steinberg

2. Hank Brodt Holocaust Memoirs. A Candle and a Promise, by Deborah Donnelly

3. The Dead Years. Holocaust Memoirs, by Joseph Schupack

4. Rescued from the Ashes. The Diary of Leokadia Schmidt, Survivor of the Warsaw Ghetto, by Leokadia Schmidt

5. My Lvov. Holocaust Memoir of a twelve-year-old Girl, by Janina Hescheles

6. Remembering Ravensbrück. From Holocaust to Healing, by Natalie Hess

7. Wolf. A Story of Hate, by Zeev Scheinwald with Ella Scheinwald

8. Save my Children. An Astonishing Tale of Survival and its Unlikely Hero, by Leon Kleiner with Edwin Stepp

9. Holocaust Memoirs of a Bergen-Belsen Survivor & Classmate of Anne Frank, by Nanette Blitz Konig

10. Defiant German - Defiant Jew. A Holocaust Memoir from inside the Third Reich, by Walter Leopold with Les Leopold

11. In a Land of Forest and Darkness. The Holocaust Story of two Jewish Partisans, by Sara Lustigman Omelinski

12. Holocaust Memories. Annihilation and Survival in Slovakia, by Paul Davidovits

13. From Auschwitz with Love. The Inspiring Memoir of Two Sisters' Survival, Devotion and Triumph Told by Manci Grunberger Beran & Ruth Grunberger Mermelstein, by Daniel Seymour

14. Remetz. Resistance Fighter and Survivor of the Warsaw Ghetto, by Jan Yohay Remetz

---

The Series **Holocaust Survivor True Stories WWII** consists of the following biographies:

1. Among the Reeds. The true story of how a family survived the Holocaust, by Tammy Bottner

2. A Holocaust Memoir of Love & Resilience. Mama's Survival from Lithuania to America, by Ettie Zilber

3. Living among the Dead. My Grandmother's Holocaust Survival Story of Love and Strength, by Adena Bernstein Astrowsky

4. Heart Songs - A Holocaust Memoir, by Barbara Gilford

19. Creating Beauty from the Abyss. The Amazing Story of Sam Herciger, Auschwitz Survivor and Artist, by Lesley Richardson

20. Painful Joy. A Holocaust Family Memoir, by Max J. Friedman

---

The Series **Jewish Children in the Holocaust** consists of the following autobiographies of Jewish children hidden during WWII in the Netherlands:

1. Searching for Home. The Impact of WWII on a Hidden Child, by Joseph Gosler

2. See You Tonight and Promise to be a Good Boy! War memories, by Salo Muller

3. Sounds from Silence. Reflections of a Child Holocaust Survivor, Psychiatrist and Teacher, by Robert Krell

4. Sabine's Odyssey. A Hidden Child and her Dutch Rescuers, by Agnes Schipper

---

The Series **New Jewish Fiction** consists of the following novels, written by Jewish authors. All novels are set in the time during or after the Holocaust.

1. Escaping the Whale. The Holocaust is over. But is it ever over for the next generation? by Ruth Rotkowitz

2. When the Music Stopped. Willy Rosen's Holocaust, by Casey Hayes

3. Hands of Gold. One Man's Quest to Find the Silver Lining in Misfortune, by Roni Robbins

4. The Corset Maker. A Novel, by Annette Libeskind Berkovits

5. There was a garden in Nuremberg. A Novel, by Navina Michal Clemerson